THE
CHOICE

OTHER WORKS BY HENRY DENKER

NOVELS
I'll Be Right Home, Ma
My Son, The Lawyer
Salome: Princess of Galilee
The First Easter
The Director
The Kingmaker
A Place for the Mighty
The Physicians
The Experiment
The Starmaker
The Scofield Diagnosis
The Actress
Error of Judgment
Horowitz and Mrs. Washington
The Warfield Syndrome
Outrage
The Healers
Kincaid
Robert, My Son
Judge Spencer Dissents

PLAYS
Time Limit
A Far Country
A Case of Libel
What Did We Do Wrong
Venus at Large
Second Time Around
Horowitz and Mrs. Washington
The Headhunters
Outrage!

THE CHOICE

Henry Denker

William Morrow and Company, Inc.
New York

Library of Congress Cataloging-in-Publication Data

Denker, Henry.
  The choice.
  I. Title.
PS3507.E5475C46   1987   813'.54   86-32426
ISBN 0-688-06745-X

Printed in the United States of America

First Edition

1 2 3 4 5 6 7 8 9 10

BOOK DESIGN BY RHEA BRAUNSTEIN

To Edith, my wife . . .

Acknowledgments

For the scientific medical and surgical research that serves as a basis for this novel the author wishes to express his deep appreciation to Joseph M. Lane, M.D., Professor, Orthopedic Surgery, Cornell Medical School, Chief, Orthopedic Surgery, Memorial Sloan-Kettering Cancer Center, New York City; to Robert Green, M.D., Chief, Orthopedic Surgery, Good Samaritan Hospital, West Palm Beach, Florida; to Lawrence Cone, M.D., Chief, Immunology and Infectious Diseases, The Eisenhower Medical Center, Palm Desert, California; and to Susan Ramirez, Chief Technician, Chemotherapy Department, The Eisenhower Medical Center.

And to Pegeen Mularchuk, Senior Research Technician, Hospital for Special Surgery, New York City, whose experiences as a patient have made this a richer, more authentic work.

THE
CHOICE

1

I N Surgery Three, on the fifth floor of University Medical Center, Dr. Walter R. Duncan was experiencing difficulty implanting the titanium hip prosthesis designed for the sixty-eight-year-old patient under his strong, skillful hands.

Restraining his frustration, working diligently and applying his great strength, Duncan finally succeeded. Once he had tested it and was assured that the appliance would respond easily and efficiently, he was ready to withdraw and close the incision. His nimble fingers now worked with accustomed ease and sureness, so his mind was able to turn to the other events that had crowded in on his hectic day.

He glanced up at the wall clock. Already past four. He knew now that the difficulty he had encountered with this patient had made it impossible for him to appear at Simone's school for her very first performance in her class play. Emily would be there, of course. But for Simone that was no special treat; her mother was always there. But Daddy . . .

Walt Duncan could already visualize Simone's face when he went upstairs to kiss her good night. She would insist that she understood why Daddy couldn't be there. But the look in her moist eyes would belie her acceptance.

He often wondered, *Who is better at pretending, doctors or their children?*

Having closed the incision and carefully packed and splinted it to immobilize the hip, Walter Duncan pulled back from the table, removed his mask, ripped off his thin surgical gloves and tossed them into the refuse can. He hurried out of Surgery to the locker room and was changing back into his own clothes when he heard himself paged.

He picked up the wall phone, announcing briskly, "Duncan!"

"Walt?" A most familiar voice greeted him so softly it sounded like a rebuke.

He knew that voice. Knew it well. Had known it since he had been graduated from medical school. In those days, though it was more vigorous, it was always as warm. The first time Walter Duncan had heard it he was being called in for his introductory interview after he had applied for a place as resident on the Orthopedic Service at the hospital.

Ever since Walter Duncan was a young boy he had known that he was destined to study medicine. He had earned his way through college on a tennis scholarship. There, he was always held up as an example of the rare indentured athlete who was also a scholar. He had to be, to gain entrance into medical school.

But his devotion to the specialty of Orthopedics was the result of his experience in Vietnam, where as a troubled, concerned young lieutenant he often had stood alongside his wounded men when they were being treated at a forward medical unit. He had marveled at young military surgeons who possessed the skill to mend broken, torn and shattered limbs. To be able to make mangled young bodies whole again had become, to Walter Duncan, a physician's finest work. After military service, he entered medical school, determined to pursue a career in Orthopedics.

If that were to become his specialty, there was only one hospital and one man he could aspire to serve: University Medical Center. And Dr. Simon Rosen.

On that first day, during that first interview, Walter Duncan was a very surprised young man. Most surgeons as famous as Rosen had reputations for being busy, brisk, brusque men. Surgeons were not expected to have pleasing bedside manners. Their

12

special skills exempted them from such niceties.

But Rosen was soft-spoken, did not seem to be in a hurry and was most solicitous of this young surgeon's ambitions and ideas. Rosen took the time to acquaint Walter Duncan with the rigorous life of a surgeon on his Orthopedic Service. He did not demand total dedication, he expected it without demanding. He also expected a substantial measure of volunteer work for the hospital as an institution devoted to community service.

"Yes, there eventually will be money," Walter could recall Rosen saying. "Too damn much money. A devoted doctor should not have the leisure time to spend all that much money."

Walter Duncan would discover later that Sy Rosen had no close family. Never had married. Had no children. Many times Walter thought that if Rosen had had a wife and offspring, they would have felt grievously neglected.

Regardless of his own personal life, Rosen was always understanding of Walt's obligation to his own family. On the day Simone was born and became his namesake, old Rosen had sent gifts to her and to Emily. Nor had he ever failed to do so on Simone's eleven birthdays and Christmases since that day.

Sy Rosen was now past his own days of active practice and had been honored with the title of professor emeritus, which he often referred to as a living eulogy. He was considered the prime consultant on all difficult orthopedic cases in the entire Midwest. Many were the times his fingers itched to operate on cases he now had to pass on to younger men who possessed the strength and the skill he had once had in such talented abundance.

The toughest cases, the ones in which Rosen foresaw potential difficulties and complications, he referred to Walter Duncan. He looked upon Walt not only as a protégé and successor, but as the son he never had. Walter Duncan was one of the few young surgeons who came through Rosen's service and chose to remain, despite offers of much more money and the ease of life in private practice.

All that and more came to Walter Duncan's mind when he heard old Sy Rosen's voice.

"Sy, you calling me?"

"Look, I know you're busy. Simone's play today—in fact, aren't you a little late now?"

"I ran into some problems with my last case," Walt said.

"I figured as much," Sy said, "when I checked with your secretary and found you were still here. So, tell you what, I took a liberty. I hope you don't mind."

"Liberty?" Walt asked.

"When you get to your car in the parking lot, you will find a file. Take it home, glance at it tonight. Let's talk in the morning. Okay?"

"Of course, Sy."

"Good. Now get going. Maybe you can make it before Simone's play is over. And give her a kiss for me."

"How did you know about—" Walt started to say.

"My godchild is in her first big role in her school play, and I'm not supposed to know about it?" Sy demanded, then ordered. "Get the hell over to that school, Walt!"

On his drive to the school Walt realized that Emily must have called Sy, urging him to get her husband out early on this day. When he arrived at the school, the empty parking lot told him all he needed to know. He headed his car homeward. He debated about stopping to pick up a gift for Simone, to make his late arrival more welcome. But he recently had become aware that such diverting little bribes were not nearly as effective as they had been when Simone was younger.

By the time he arrived, Simone had already had her early dinner and gone up to bed. It would have done no good to explain to his wife. Her beautiful face, her soft pale-blue eyes, her silence were a more telling rebuke than any words. Words, at least, would have given him a chance to explain.

He asked only, "How was she?"

"Wonderful! For the first few minutes I didn't even know it was her. She was so into her part."

14

"She still awake?"

"Unless she fell asleep crying," Emily said softly.

That was all the spoken reprimand there was. He climbed the stairs, making himself all kinds of promises. A long vacation, the three of them together, when school was out for Christmas. Or Easter at the latest. Scheduling his surgeries even earlier in the morning so he could be home for dinner more often. He would also work it out so his time on the Tumor Board and on the Morbidity and Mortality Committee at the hospital would be curtailed.

He was full of righteous resolutions by the time he arrived at Simone's door. Emily and he had always made it a point never to enter her room without knocking. The child should have a sense of privacy, a world of her own. But when he knocked, there was no answer. He knocked a second time, again softly. Still no answer. If Simone was asleep, he would not be invading her privacy. He opened the door gently.

The room was dark except for the slant of light from the hallway that fell across her bed. Little Simone was lying on her side, legs drawn up, huddled as if against the cold, her blanket drawn tight around the outline of her young body. He knew she was not asleep, not in so tense a posture. He approached her bed and knelt down beside it. He whispered, "Baby?"

She clenched her eyes even tighter. He kissed her on the cheek. She opened her eyes. Emily was right. She had been crying.

"Baby, I'm sorry." She did not react. "Mom tells me you were so terrific she didn't even recognize you at first. I wish I'd been there to see. Tomorrow at breakfast you must act out your whole part for me. Okay?"

She did not reply. He kissed her again, then buried his face in the soft warm crook of her young neck. Finally her hand stole out from under the blanket to embrace his hand.

"Next time?" She sought to exact a bargain. "Promise?"

"Next time, baby," he said.

She kissed him. "You need a shave, Daddy," she said. She turned on her other side and drifted off to sleep.

15

* * *

He had his dinner in the dinette. While he ate he caught up on reading the most recent *Orthopedic Journal*. Emily was quite aware that he was avoiding conversation. Which he usually did when he felt guilty. She did not press the issue beyond asking, "She asleep?"

"Uh-huh," he said. "We talked a little. She felt better."

Emily did not respond. No sense pursuing it. The harm had been done.

He skimmed the case history. He held up the X rays to his desk lamp. He studied the results of the scans. He was puzzled that Sy had asked him to get into the case. It was not a case in which he would have recommended surgery. Some surgeons might have, but to him the result to be obtained did not justify the time, expense and risks of surgery. Anytime you invaded the body there were hazards. Anesthesia alone was a risk. Yet, in this case, surgery already had been performed. To judge from the rest of the file, it had not been performed too well. It was a little late to seek to correct that now.

Why, then, had Sy given him this file to review? And why had the names of the patient and the surgeon been removed from the file?

He would ask Sy in the morning. By the time he looked up to pay some attention to Emily, he discovered that she had gone up to bed. If he neglected his daughter, he was even more neglectful of his wife, always assuming that she understood the demands of his career.

Walter Duncan had first laid eyes on Emily Ingraham as she was entering the library at University Medical Center, where he had begun to serve his residency in Orthopedic Surgery. She seemed a petite, attractive, but extremely serious young woman. A nurse possibly, or even a female med student. She possessed a face of small but perfectly matched features. With her dark hair and her black-framed spectacles, she appeared to be a sober,

16

dedicated young woman intent on a mission.

Standing alongside her at the librarian's desk, he heard her ask for a medical textbook that time and scientific progress had turned into a storehouse of superstitions rather than a reliable source of up-to-date medical information. She surely was no med student or nurse.

His curiosity stirred, both by such a pretty young woman and by her peculiar taste in medical literature, he volunteered, "If you're looking for information on the proper treatment of tuberculosis, I can suggest a much better book. Up to date and authentic. *Miller on Thoracic Disease.*"

She had turned to look up at him, a hulking six feet three inches tall, with shaggy hair because he was always too busy to remember to get it cut. She noticed that he had a strong face, a jutting jaw, but he had brown eyes that softened the total impression. Her first glance reflected resentment at his intrusion. Then she smiled, her face turning from merely pretty to warm and inviting.

She appeared to be amused by him, a quality he did not relish. Young, and sensitive, he did not like to be considered an object of amusement by young women. He preferred to be considered witty and entertaining, but never, never unintentionally amusing. For there is an implied condescension that any young man would consider demeaning. Above all else, young Walter Duncan insisted on being taken seriously by women. Especially attractive women.

Again he suggested, more firmly, "If you want the latest and best information on tuberculosis, ask for Miller."

"If I ever do want the latest and the best, I will," she said, turning back to the librarian to renew her request for the outdated volume.

"Boy!" Walter Duncan exclaimed in annoyance. "It takes a woman to be that stubborn!"

He watched her start off toward the stacks to which the librarian had directed her. He noticed that this particular young woman had a trim and quite feminine figure. Good legs, too. And she wore flat-heeled shoes, of which, as a budding orthopedist, he approved. *Sensible girl,* he thought, *but what the hell is she doing with an outmoded textbook on chest diseases?* He could not resist. He followed, reached her when she was straining to take down the volume she sought from the high shelf on which it rested.

She succeeded, but as she turned away she collided with him. They both apologized. That done, he proceeded to lecture her.

"Young woman, if you are interested in the treatment of tuberculosis, you will get nothing but a lot of misinformation out of that volume. The treatment of tuberculosis has changed radically since that time. They used to advise sunshine and fresh air, especially in cold climates. That's a thing of the past. Today, antibiotics. That's the new treatment. And far, far more effective. So you are wasting your time with this."

He took the volume out of her hands.

"Now, just one minute—" she started to protest.

"Look, tell you what I'll do for you. I will personally introduce you to Dr. Leonard Sanderson, Chief of Thoracic Medicine. He will tell you everything you want or need to know about diseases of the chest. But this book is a waste of time."

"I want that book," she insisted.

"I have noticed one thing about women, particularly young women—they are most stubborn when they are most wrong," he said, replacing the volume on the high shelf with ease.

"Is that your specialty, Doctor? Studying women, 'particularly young women'?" She started to reach for the volume again, standing on tiptoe.

"My specialty is going to be Orthopedics, but I can tell you now that straining to reach that way is not doing your lower back any good." He took down the volume but did not hand it to her. "I'd feel like an accessory to a crime, adding to the enormous amount of medical misinformation that circulates in the world today."

"I have noticed one thing about doctors, particularly young doctors—they are most stubborn when they are most wrong," she mimicked.

"What the hell does that mean . . . Miss . . ."

"Ingraham," she informed. "Now, Doctor, if you were less intent on telling me and more on finding out what it is I want to discover, we might get on a good deal better!"

"I assume you want to learn the best treatment for tuberculosis,'" he declared.

"In 1927," she corrected.

"Nineteen twenty-seven? Why would anybody in her right mind want to learn how to treat a modern-day disease with ancient outmoded modalities?"

"Because, my dear young Doctor, I am in the process of editing a novel that takes place in the 1920s, and I want to check on the authenticity of some of the author's facts."

"Is that what you do, edit novels?" he asked, intrigued.

"With a B.A. in English lit, what better could I do?" she asked.

"Well, that's . . . that's different," he said. "I thought, well, you know what I thought."

"I certainly do," she said, taking the book from his hands and starting toward a reading table.

He followed her. "Miss Ingraham . . . do you also happen to have a first name?"

"Most people do. Emily."

"Emily . . . Emily Ingraham. I like the sound of that. Tell me, Emily Ingraham, do you ever edit novels about orthopedic surgeons?"

"Not so far," she said.

"Too bad. I could be a great help there."

"Well, if I ever do, I'll call on you, Doctor . . . uh . . ."

"Duncan."

"Okay, Dr. Duncan." She continued toward a chair at the table.

Disappointed, he called, "Don't you even want to know my first name?"

She pretended to consider her reply, then said, "I suppose, whether I want to or not, I'm just about to learn it."

"You damn well are. Walter," he declared.

"Walter Duncan, orthopedic surgeon. I like the sound of that," she said, smiling impishly.

A bit sheepishly he admitted, "I'm not really an orthopedic surgeon yet. Not board certified yet, that is. I'm in training under Dr. Rosen. Simon Rosen."

"The way you say it, it seems I should be familiar with his name," she said.

"Yes. Because he's the best there is. I'm very lucky to be part of his group. If you'd like to meet him, I can arrange it."

"Can you?" she asked, pretending to be interested.

"He runs a Wednesday-night seminar at his home. For a small group of selected residents. A discussion group on some late development in Orthopedics. Then coffee and cake and usually some schmooze about hospital politics."

"*Schmooze?* A medical term?" she asked.

"Sy's word. For gossip. I think it's Yiddish."

"This Wednesday-night seminar—does he permit outsiders?"

"Some married men bring their wives. Others bring their girl friends. Sy welcomes them all."

"Even those who aren't wives or girl friends?" she asked.

"For someone as pretty as you, I'm sure Sy would make an exception," he said, taking the book from her once more.

She blushed a little.

"Are you free Wednesday evening?" he asked.

"If I can get done editing this novel, I will be," she said to remind him that he was holding the book she needed.

As if he had suddenly discovered he was in possession of a hot stove lid, he surrendered the book to her at once.

"Wednesday," he said. "I'll pick you up. Say, around seven?"

"Seven," she agreed.

"Where?"

She wrote out her address for him.

That Wednesday evening was the first of Sy Rosen's seminars that Emily Ingraham attended. After that she became a regular. By the time Emily and Walter married, Sy Rosen was close enough to both of them to serve as Walter's best man.

Through the early years of their marriage and until their daughter was born, Emily worked as an editor for the same publishing house. She continued through her pregnancy, working at home, and for the first year of Simone's life. Once little Simone became more active and mobile, Emily resigned her job to spend all her time with her daughter. After Simone began to attend school, Emily Duncan would take on an occasional free-lance assignment to edit a manuscript of special importance. In the last six months no such manuscript had claimed her attention.

At breakfast, Simone proudly repeated her performance in the school play. She was everything her mother said she had been. Intense, well prepared, knowing her lines, giving them the proper readings, overdoing only very few times, Simone Duncan did indeed have acting talent. Enough to make Walt silently hope that she would not pursue so risky and frustrating a career as show business.

When she had finished, Walt kissed her and held her and said, "Someday you're going to be on television. Or even on the stage!"

"If I am, will you come see me then, Daddy?" she asked quite pointedly.

That was the end of all playacting, hers and his. He avoided Emily's look and gulped down the last of his coffee and left for the hospital.

"Sy, I went over that file," Walter Duncan reported as he seated himself across the desk from the old consultant.

"And?" Sy asked, tugging gently on the narrow fringe of white beard that bordered his ruddy face. He always joked that any man with professor emeritus attached to his name should have the dignity of a beard to add to his appearance of sage wisdom.

"The dates."

"For instance?" Sy asked.

"The first examination, the initial X rays and the electromyogram all in a space of three days. Then four days later, surgery.

21

Too fast. Much too fast. I wouldn't call that prudent practice. Not in a case like this."

"Yes, it seemed a little hasty to me, too," Sy agreed.

"With these X rays in hand, and even more with the results of that EMG, I should think he'd have tried to avoid surgery. At least until more conservative measures had failed to relieve the patient's pain. It seems to have been nothing more serious than sciatic pain down to the foot accompanied by some muscle weakness. Both of which might have responded to rest, medication and other noninvasive treatment. But surgery—" Walt shook his head.

"Nothing in these findings that indicates a life-threatening emergency," Sy said. "Why would a doctor rush into surgery that way?"

"Sy, I'd hate to tell you what I suspect," Walt said.

"Smacks a little of greed, doesn't it, Walt?"

"Surgery performed for the doctor's benefit, not the patient's," Walt agreed. "And the surgery was botched. Unfortunately, as in many cases we get, beyond repair. I wouldn't know how to cure the dropped foot that resulted."

"He'll never be able to control that foot again. Have to wear a brace the rest of his life." Sy concurred.

"Sorry, Sy," Walt said, handing back the file. Intending to close off all discussion, Walt added, "Young man—seventeen, eighteen by now, I guess—to go through life with a dropped foot, never play football again. Too bad."

Sy did not reach for the file. "Keep it, Walt. Study it further. Because we have a decision to make."

"Decision? There's nothing we can do to repair the damage."

"This file was sent to me by the young man's attorney. There is a very large malpractice suit involved here."

"They want expert testimony, is that it?"

"That's why it was sent to me," Sy informed him. "But that old bastard Worthington, in Cardiology, tells me that my heart is no longer up to the strain of testifying. He's afraid a rough cross-examination might be more than I could take."

Walt was too solicitous of Sy's feelings to remind him that "that old bastard Worthington" was four years younger than Sy himself. But he was aware of the unexpressed purpose of Sy's statement. Since they both possessed the same righteous anger toward surgeons who practiced their profession as if it were a trade, Walt knew he must volunteer.

"Okay, Sy. So long as it doesn't cut too deeply into my time in Surgery. I won't have to wait around cooling my heels in some courtroom corridor before I testify, will I?"

"Aren't you going to ask any other questions?" the old man said.

"The case is quite clear."

"But the patient, and most especially the doctor. Don't you want to know who they are?"

"It wouldn't matter. The file is enough." Then, taking his cue from the grave look on Sy's face, he did ask, "Who was the surgeon?"

"Enright," old Sy said.

"Enright? Peter Enright?" Walt asked.

Sy nodded.

"Never did like his work when he was on staff here." Suddenly a thought occurred to Walt. "Say, this didn't happen here, did it?"

"At the hospital back East where he served just before he got here. Frankly, if I'd known about this, he'd never have been accepted. Thank God, he's gone. Even so, it won't do the reputation of this hospital any good if they hang this on Enright."

"I know. For the rest of his career it will say on his record, 'formerly of University Medical Center.' That can't be avoided. But there is the patient to consider, and the harm done. This is not the kind of inadvertent result that could happen in the course of well-done surgery."

Sy nodded once more.

"We can't let this hospital's reputation become a shield for unnecessary and careless surgery, no matter where it took place," Walt said. "Okay, Sy, I'll testify."

"Thanks, Walt. Believe me, if I could do it myself, I would.

I'm old enough, prestigious enough to take the flak. But unfortunately too old for the job. Too old for so many things these days," Sy said sadly.

"Call that lawyer. Tell him I'll meet him at some time that's mutually convenient," Walt stated.

The agreement to testify added to Walter Duncan's already crowded schedule. So again he was late getting home for dinner. As so many times before, Simone had already had her dinner and was up in her room doing homework. Walt found her just closing her writing pad, her math all done. He reached down, picked her up in his strong hands and swung her high up over his head as he used to when she was younger. It had been a game they played that always made her laugh.

However, this time she winced.

"Did I hurt you, Simmie?"

"No, Daddy."

He knew she was trying to spare his feelings. He insisted on examining the sensitive area of her young body. There was a bluish mark on her side, a slight hematoma.

"Now, how did we get this?" he asked as he gently palpated the blemish.

"I don't know. Maybe I banged into my desk at school," the child said.

"Well, you ought to be more careful, baby," he said.

Walt Duncan woke, lay there a moment, then became aware that he was in bed alone. Emily. Where was Emily? Why would she be up before he was? Usually he kissed her and left her half-awake and went on his way to the hospital for early surgery.

He felt remiss, derelict in his duty to be abed at this late hour. He turned on his side to look at the clock on the night table. Four minutes to eight. Late indeed! He started to move quickly and then realized . . . Sunday. Today was Sunday.

He had promised Emily that this would be a special Sunday. A whole day devoted to Simone. For Emily had warned, "She's going to forget what you look like. So this Sunday is Simone's day. Sociologists say that it isn't how much time you spend with your child, but the quality of the time."

This Sunday was to be a quality-time day with Simone.

He got out of bed, did the same routine of calisthenics to prevent bad backs that he prescribed for his patients. He insisted they do them religiously. Every day. He did his about once every seven or eight days.

He went down to breakfast to find Simone fed and awaiting him. She was dressed for some form of active sports. Tennis, he hoped. He was still fairly good at that. All through breakfast he listened to her relate the events of her week. School. The birthday of some girl he could not remember ever having met. An exam on which she had received a B plus. Also a complaint about one of her teachers who was far too strict.

When Walt had finished breakfast, Simone went to the hall closet and brought out the equipment for their game. Two curved sticks. And a hard black rubber ball. So it was to be field hockey, he realized. He had never played the game. But he was determined to do his best.

As Simone led the way, he looked back at Emily, who silently ordered him to follow his daughter.

Fortunately it was a fine, dry spring day. The grass made a soft fragrant cushion on which to fall and roll whenever they made contact. He pretended to give his daughter strong physical opposition, however, always managing to fall first at the crucial moment.

Throughout, she instructed him in the strategy of the game and the maneuvers involved. He pretended to be a slow and uncoordinated pupil so that she could become impatient with him and thereby display her superiority. In time they were both sweaty and breathing hard.

In one moment of physical contact, Simone winced and seemed to catch her breath.

"Did I hurt you, sweetheart? I'm sorry." He apologized quickly.

"No, I'm fine, Daddy," the child protested. To admit pain might mean the end of their game and her fun.

"Let me see," he said.

"It's nothing," she protested again.

"How do you know it's nothing if it just happened?" he asked. When she did not answer, he said, "Or didn't it just happen? Let me see."

She turned to him. He pulled her shirt out of her shorts and discovered a black-and-blue mark larger than a half-dollar.

"Well, how did we get this? Practicing hockey?" he asked.

"I guess," she said.

"Well, you'd better be more careful from now on," he said. "Shall we play one more? Or is it time we take Mommy out to lunch?"

"To that nice place where they have the delicious sticky buns?" Simone asked.

"Exactly what I had in mind." Walt was happy to agree.

While Simone was showering and changing clothes, he said to Emily, "You know what I was just thinking, hon?"

"No. What?"

"When I was a kid and my dad used to take time to shoot baskets in the peach-basket hoop out back of our house, we used to have a lot of fun, too. Only we never called it quality time. It was just a dad and his son having fun together. Nowadays they have a scientific term for everything, even the simplest, most natural things in the world."

"Whatever they call it," Emily replied, "a father should spend as much time with his daughter as possible."

"Agreed. Hey, another thing. Do you think hockey is too rough a game for girls?"

"I played it and grew up rather well," Emily said. "What makes you ask?"

"Simmie's got a bad bruise on her side. Like someone hit her with a hockey stick."

"Nobody hit her with a hockey stick," Emily said.

"How can you be sure?" he asked.

"Because official practice at school only starts next week."

Before he could pursue the matter, Simone appeared in the doorway dressed in a pink dress that he favored. With quiet gratification he realized that she was all dressed up especially to please her father.

"Ready, Daddy?" she called to him, smiling.

"Ready!" he called back.

Emily whispered, "Are you sure you two need me today?"

"Come along anyhow," Walt said, laughing.

On the drive out to the suburbs Simone kept up a frivolous chatter with him, asking him riddles with funny answers and playing word games with him.

All the while he kept thinking, *Watch that bruise on her side.* For some undefinable reason it troubled him.

2

THREE mornings later, very early, for his first surgery was scheduled to start at seven, Walt Duncan slipped quietly out of bed so as not to disturb Emily. He had long ago established the practice of not troubling her to wake up with him when he had early-morning hours.

It was a holdover from his boyhood. His own mother had risen at five in order to pack a lunch for his father, who was a motorman on the trolly-car line that was one of the last remaining in their state. Dad was on the early run, starting from the carbarn at six to pick up workers destined for the seven-o'clock shift at the steel mill and the wireworks. It was just after World War II, when automobiles and gasoline were still in short supply. People depended on mass transit, even outmoded kinds like trolley cars.

He would never lose that memory of his mother. In her clean but faded kimono, standing at the kitchen counter, packing two thick sandwiches in his father's battered metal lunch can. On winter mornings she added a portion of hot soup from supper the night before. His father would reheat it on the potbellied stove in the carbarn office.

By the time Mom had packed Dad off to work, it was time to wake the boys. Owen and Walter. Owen was the older, so she awakened him first. Soon as Owen was on his way to the only bathroom, Mom would wake Walter. In Walter's earlier days, his kindergarten days, she would have him half-dressed before he even opened his eyes. Later, after Owen took sick, it was Walter's place to be first. After Owen died at the age of ten, there was only Walter to be awakened. Sometimes, in very sad moments, or after days of crying, his mother would call him Owen instead of Walter. It gave him many unhappy moments because he suspected that perhaps she had loved Owen more and she would not have grieved so if he had been the one to die.

Nights when he pretended to be asleep and overheard his father and mother talking were when his ambition to become a doctor was born. His father seemed even more inconsolable than his weeping mother. In his stolid dry-eyed way he kept bemoaning, "Such a wee lad, he was. Why would a merciful God choose to inflict such trouble on so young a lad? The pain of it, the pain of it."

Walter himself had little remembrance of young Owen's being in pain, for by that stage of his disease Owen had been removed to the hospital to die.

Twice his parents had taken Walter to visit the Children's Ward. He would never forget that long dismal room that seemed to be two endless rows of beds. In each bed a young boy, sick and seemingly given up to dying, since only the sickest and the terminal were deemed worthy of hospital treatment. Later he discovered it was a matter of economics. The family savings was expended only on the most seriously ill. The rest were treated at home, with mothers and sisters for nurses.

Those two hospital visits convinced Walter Duncan of one thing: He would never serve in a hospital where they had those long, long rooms called wards. Things would change, even if he had to change them.

By the time he became an intern, things had changed.

All those thoughts passed through Walter Duncan's mind as he silently slipped through the kitchen of his fine home and opened the door to the garage before he remembered that he had not even had his coffee. But there would be fresh coffee at the hospital. His secretary, Claudia Holcomb, would make sure of that.

Claudia was a black woman whose sweet, disarming smile belied the fact that, when Walt's tight schedule demanded it, she could be a tyrant, even with him.

It was four o'clock in the afternoon. Walter Duncan had performed lengthy surgery on three cases, had been called into consultation on four other cases, had had a chance to eat half the sandwich Claudia had forced on him when he was getting ready to make rounds and look in on his morning cases in Recovery. Clad in a white coat, he was leaving his office when Claudia intercepted him. He was wanted on the phone.

"Later, Claudia!"

"It's Dr. Rosen," she said.

Walter Duncan went back to his desk to take the call.

"Walt?" the old man said, seeming even more tired and troubled than usual. "In this modern age things happen faster than they used to. We've already got some flak."

"Flak?" Walt asked, puzzled.

"Russell" was all Sy said and all he needed to say. For that name was most frequently used in the hospital in place of some other expletive. James Rowe Russell was the only trustee who had inherited his place on the Board of Trustees. His father before him had been the prime mover in building the University Medical Center, having been the largest and most generous donor. Thus the current Russell looked upon the institution as virtually his own possession. He considered anything that reflected on its reputation a slur on his dear, long-departed father.

"What's Russell want this time?" Walt asked.

"He's heard about the case against Enright."

"How?"

"Enright's lawyer figured if he could involve Russell, he'd bring pressure to bear on any doctor who was considering testifying. And, of course, he's right."

"So?"

"Russell would like to talk to you," Sy warned.

"Okay," Walt said. "I'll call him."

"Right away," Sy suggested. "Give him time to brood about it, and he'll be five times as angry by morning," Sy pointed out needlessly, since Walt and every doctor on staff knew Russell's personal peculiarities.

At the same time that Walt Duncan had Claudia place his call to James Rowe Russell, tennis practice was under way at Midvale High School under the watchful eye of Lars Olafsen, whom everyone called Swede. Swede had been physical education instructor and tennis coach at Midvale High for more than a generation. His hair, which had been the color of standing wheat when he started, was now white as snow. His face, which had been pink and unwrinkled, was now a deep, ruddy shade of weathered skin that resembled old parchment.

But his blue eyes were as sharp and discerning as ever when he paced behind the courts watching his pupils in their various stages of practice. Some were hitting with crisp strokes, following through with brisk but full sweeps so their rackets ended up above their shoulders. Others were in the early stages of warming up, their eyes fixed on the ball. Swede always said, "Until you can read the label on the ball, you're not following it. Watch that label. Watch those seams. Concentrate on that ball. Because no matter what else you do right, if you don't have your eye on the ball, you can't hit a ball correctly."

His boys' teams of the past had earned their share of citywide and statewide honors, as the trophy cases in the school gym attested. This year his team again promised to go all the way to the state finals and was even a fair bet to win the championship. However, unlike previous years, this time his players had a shot at the girls' title, too.

His ambitions for a double title rested mainly on the excellent strokes, the good eyes and the agile, graceful style of fifteen-year-old Amy Bedford. Deceptively slender for a girl who hit such powerful strokes, Amy Bedford reminded old Swede of some of the greats he had seen when he was young. There was something reminiscent of Helen Wills about Amy. Even a hint of

Maureen Connolly, who was called Little Mo when she ruled the courts in her mid-teens. Neither appeared to be large or sturdy but could generate tremendously powerful strokes. Coupled with a steadiness that reminded Swede of Chrissie Evert, Amy Bedford could not only win the state championship but might go on from there. Possibly she might one day join the professional women's tour and become one of the best in the world.

But, Swede cautioned himself, first things first. For now, the state championship.

This afternoon Amy seemed to be having an off day. She still could take on any girl on the team and defeat her handily, but Swede noticed that coming off her right foot when shifting her body weight Amy betrayed a slight hitch. It was sufficient to indicate to him that she was experiencing some difficulty. Possibly pain, or else a break from form that sometimes asserts itself when a player is overdetermined or overtrained. He would advise her to ease up.

When Amy came to the side of the court to towel her wet and pretty face, Swede suggested, "Enough for today, Amy."

"Why?" she asked, almost resentful.

"You're losing your smoothness, your ease of stroke. If it isn't fun, it isn't good practice."

"I'm trying to work it out," Amy said.

"Work what out?" Swede asked, taken by surprise.

"I've got a slight pain in my right leg," Amy admitted. "But I'll work it out before the tournament. So don't worry, Swede."

"Okay, Slugger," Swede said, smiling and resorting to the pet name he reserved only for her. "Just don't push it too hard."

He kept a cautious, furtive eye on her for the rest of the afternoon. He did not want to give her cause to feel she was the object of serious concern. But anytime a player favored one part of her body to ease a pain, it placed a burden on other muscles and tended to impair them eventually. He considered forbidding her to practice for a few days to see if that would eliminate the pain.

Later that afternoon, after his charges had deserted the court, showered, dressed and were leaving, Swede Olafsen watched as

32

Amy Bedford strode down the school corridor toward the open doors, her trim, youthful figure silhouetted against the bright afternoon sunshine. She walked with a slight hitch, too.

He must watch her closely for the next few days.

James Rowe Russell, a man in his late fifties, was generally described by the media as "the wealthy philanthropist" because he had lived all his life on the fortune his father had accumulated. His face reflected the sun-filled, wind-burned days he spent as an international yachtsman who on occasion had placed first in the Bermuda races and was once a third-place finisher in the New York to Southampton race.

Aside from his achievements in maritime circles, Russell's main activity was running the University Medical Center, which he considered his private fiefdom. He was instrumental in selecting and managing to appoint to the board only trustees who respected his views, so he could always rely on a favorable majority on any issue dear to him. Since he controlled apportioning much of the research monies, he held unusual power over even those physicians and surgeons who resented him.

One thing everyone had to concede, however, under Russell's leadership the center had become one of the best equipped in the Midwest. Only a few of the larger university medical centers could boast achievements as important. The man's knowledge of matters medical and scientific proved he was no dilettante. Resentful as they might be, the professionals had to respect that.

At this moment Walter Duncan was facing James Rowe Russell, considering how to respond to Russell's question: "Duncan, if you're so sure of your opinion about this lawsuit, wouldn't *most* surgeons feel the same way?"

"Most honest surgeons, yes," Walt granted.

"Then it shouldn't be hard to find other experts who would testify on behalf of this patient," Russell said. "Why must it be a doctor on staff at our particular hospital? In other words, why you? Unless, of course, this shyster lawyer is calling you to deliberately cast aspersions on our reputation?"

"The file was originally sent to Sy. To Dr. Rosen, that is. Why, is quite obvious. What orthopedist in this part of the country has a better reputation? Whose testimony would be respected more? When, for reasons of health, Sy was advised not to appear, he turned the matter over to me."

"And, of course, you couldn't refuse. You never refuse him anything, do you?" Russell asked.

"We generally agree" was all that Walt replied.

"The lawyer who is representing this man, he's Jewish, too, isn't he?" Russell asked suddenly.

"I don't know," Walt said. "I was concerned only with the medical facts of the case."

"Silverstein," Russell said. "His name is Silverstein."

"Frankly, I hadn't noticed," Walt said. "'I don't even recall the patient's name. It wasn't important. At least not to me."

This last was aimed at discouraging the trend of Russell's last few questions.

"Well, *frankly*"—Russell accused—"it seems to *me* that Silverstein picked Rosen for quite obvious reasons. And Rosen was collaborating with him for the same reasons."

"Whereupon," Walt suggested, "this Dr. Simon Rosen called in Presbyterian Walter Duncan to become part of this Jewish plot. Since, through the ages, Jews and Presbyterians are notorious for having conspired together."

Russell's weathered face became ruddier now that he was angry. "To put the matter directly, Duncan, it would do this institution great harm if you were to testify against a man who once had been on staff here."

"It would do this institution even greater harm if it became known that we concealed the truth out of a mistaken sense of loyalty to a former staff member whose standards are less than professional."

"It is not this hospital's job to take part in lawsuits," Russell protested. "Particularly lawsuits in which we are not involved. This happened at another hospital and to a man who is no longer our responsibility."

"Mr. Russell, I would like to point out that anytime the prac-

tice of medicine is less than it should be, it becomes the responsibility of every physician to point that out!"

Walt rose from his chair to pace as, to Russell's distress, he
continued, "I know what you're thinking, Mr. Russell. And I don't
blame you. A big verdict against any hospital raises the cost of
insurance for all hospitals. Also the cost of our malpractice insurance for this hospital already runs into the hundreds of thousands."

"More than a million!" Russell corrected.

"Millions, then." Walt conceded. "And why? Because for years
and years the medical profession tried to sweep its failures under
the rug by virtually blacklisting any doctor who dared testify on
behalf of an unfortunate and damaged patient. Until now, when
juries, giving vent to their outrage, have been handing down those
large multimillion-dollar verdicts. Well, the answer isn't to go
back to the old ways, but to practice a standard of medicine higher
than before. And, if need be, to drive out of medicine those men
and women who cannot maintain such standards."

Both men knew that the last word in this encounter had been
spoken. Walt left so angry and determined that he almost collided with a strange man in the waiting room.

Later that afternoon, on his way home from the hospital, Walter Duncan stopped by the offices of Silverstein, Brennan and
Mancuso to confer for the first time with Andrew Silverstein about
his testimony in the Enright case

A small, frail man, Silverstein was surprisingly well prepared
for Walter Duncan's visit. He displayed a level of expertise in
the surgical problem involved that would have done credit to any
physician. By the time the interview was over, Silverstein felt
confident enough of the case to suggest, "Dr. Duncan, maybe we
can settle this matter without the necessity of a long, drawn-out
trial."

Home again, late again, Walter Duncan reproached himself as
he pulled his car into the driveway. He hoped Simone was still

awake. No one answered his cheery call from the front door.

"Hi! Simone?"

He went to the kitchen. Neither Simone nor Emily was there. The dishes that indicated they had been having dinner were still on the table. Not like Emily to leave dirty dishes sitting on the table. He often accused her of having a neatness fetish. He was joking, of course, since as a surgeon he appreciated cleanliness.

He went to the foot of the stairs. "Hi! Anybody up there?"

"Daddy?" came Simone's voice. Tense, different from usual.

He bounded up the carpeted stairs, reached the door of her room and discovered Emily sitting on the bed alongside Simone, who lay on her stomach, her nightgown pulled up so that from her shoulders down her body was laid bare.

"What's wrong?" he demanded as he crossed the room to draw close to the bed.

"She had another black-and-blue bruise. On her arm this time," Emily said, pointing out Simone's left arm. High on the inner side of her daughter's left arm, almost hidden by its proximity to her chest, Walter Duncan saw an irregular blemish on her smooth young skin.

"How in the world could she get a hit from a hockey stick there?" he asked, drawing close to make a more intensive examination of the spot. He flexed her arm, which moved easily. He pressed the bruise, but Simone did not respond with any sign of pain. He finally concluded, "Let's stop hockey practice for a while. A week at least."

"But, Dad . . ."

"There are other forms of exercise at least as good and not so dangerous. Why not track, or tennis?"

"Gee, Dad . . ."

"I know"—he anticipated—"all your best friends are into hockey. But for now let's do something else."

Before the child could continue the argument, Walt kissed her and said, "Your father was a tennis player and it didn't do him any harm. Did it?"

He smiled; she finally smiled. "No, Dad, it didn't."

36

"Tell you what, you decide to take tennis lessons. I'll ask Swede Olafsen to make you his special pupil. Private lessons. With a new racket. One of those new ones that's even bigger than you are. Okay?"

"Okay." Simone finally conceded.

Emily sat across from him as he ate his late dinner. He divided his attention between his food and the latest issue of the *Orthopedic Journal,* which reported a case that gave promise of a simpler surgical technique for treating bone injuries due to severe trauma resulting from motor-vehicle crashes.

He was turning the page when Emily suggested, "It's getting cold."

"H'mm? What?"

"Your roast beef is getting cold. If I have to warm it up again, it'll be too dry."

"Oh. Yeah. Terrific beef," he said, because he felt guilty for not enjoying it more.

"How did it go today?" she asked.

"The usual," he said.

"I mean that session with the lawyer."

"Oh, that. He said they had enough of a case now to settle. He didn't want to go to court if it could be avoided."

"Then you won't have to testify? Good!"

Her relief made him put aside the journal and put down his fork. "What does that mean?"

"I ran into Millie Enright today. We were both having lunch at the club. She ignored me. But only after first glaring at me."

"I'm sorry about that," Walt said. "But it can't be helped."

"Walt, are you sure Enright handled the case that badly?"

"It's plain from the patient's history. There was no need for immediate surgery, if at all. And the condition in which Enright left the patient proves the surgery was done badly."

"I don't understand. If Enright is so inept, how come he was even accepted on staff at the medical center?" Emily asked.

"And asked to leave very soon thereafter. Don't forget that,"

37

Walt protested. "Terminated is closer to the truth."

"Still, there must have been some reason for accepting him in the first place," Emily insisted.

"Frankly, that troubled me, too. So before going to see Silverstein I went down to the records office and looked up Enright's file. With the recommendations he had, any hospital in the country would have grabbed him. Which set me to thinking. How could a surgeon so good blunder so badly with a relatively simple case like the one under suit now? So I called Dick Forester."

"What would he know about Enright?"

"Enright was on Dick's Orthopedic Service before he came to us. Dick didn't have much good to say about him."

"But you said they gave him such a great recommendation when he left," Emily argued.

"Of course. Dick admitted that he had to do it. His trustees insisted, in order to avoid being sued by Enright if Dick wrote the letter of condemnation he was itching to write. That's what hospitals do in these litigious times. Send off their failures with great recommendations and sighs in relief, saying, 'Let him become some other hospital's problem.' "

"That's how Enright originally became your problem and Sy's." Emily realized.

"That's how. It's going on all over the country. Thousands of inept doctors and surgeons go right on practicing at the expense of and danger to patients," Walt said grimly.

"Something should be done—" Emily began to protest.

"Whenever people say, 'Something should be done,' you can be damn sure nothing is, and nothing will be," he said.

His appetite failed; he pushed back his plate.

"I made some chocolate mousse," Emily said, starting for the refrigerator.

"No, thanks, hon. I've got too much reading to catch up on."

He kissed her and before starting for the den, he said, "Keep an eye on Simone. I don't like those bruises."

3

WHILE Swede Olafsen watched his charges work out, in his mind he was designating the final teams he would submit to the tournament. With such a wealth of talent, he had a tough choice to make among the boys. Who was to play number one singles, number two, and number three? And which two of his best should he team up for the doubles?

He was having an easier time with the girls. He was taking his own special inventory of speed, strokes, anticipation, court sense, when he noticed Amy Bedford, who had been about to serve, suddenly turn away from the baseline, hurry to the fence and lean against it. Her young body seemed to convulse in spasmodic, involuntary gaspings. Swede ran toward the fence. He was still some paces away when he realized the girl was vomiting.

"Amy! What is it, Amy?" he called out.

She turned away to hide from him, embarrassed by what she had done. He reached her, put his arms around her and made her face him. He pulled out his handkerchief, wiped the bitter bubbles from her lips.

She was breathing in short spasms and began to weep.

"Easy now, Amy, easy does it," he whispered. "Come with me." He shepherded her toward the door to the gym.

She was seated in his office, looking guilty, as he asked, "What did you have for lunch?"

"I . . . I didn't have any," she admitted.

"What was it, then, nerves?" the old coach asked. "You don't have any cause for nerves, Amy. I've never seen a girl better prepared for the state finals. Just do what you know how to do and you can win. But not if you're going to go without sleep, without food, and start working up a case of nerves. If you'd had some lunch, this wouldn't have happened. So no more of that from now on. Okay?"

Amy hesitated. So Swede had to insist. "Okay?"

"It—" Amy started to say, "it wasn't going without lunch."

"What, then?" Swede asked, prepared for almost any answer after his many years of dealing with teenagers.

"I think it was the aspirin," Amy finally admitted.

"Aspirin—why aspirin?" Swede asked.

"The pain in my leg. It wouldn't go away. So I started to take aspirin. It didn't help. I took more. I was up to six tablets this morning," she confessed.

"That would be it," Swede observed grimly. "Get up, Amy. Let me see you walk away from me."

The girl complied. The old coach watched as Amy walked toward the door of his long narrow office. There was no question. She still manifested that limp.

"Still hurts, doesn't it?" the coach asked.

"Uh-huh," she said, half-looking back at him.

"Worse than before?"

"Yep."

"Come back," he said.

She started toward him. The limp was less pronounced as she approached him.

"First thing," he said, "we will not take more aspirin. Or any medication. There's no sense trying to hide pain."

"But I want to be ready to play," Amy protested. "I need that title to get into some of the more important tournaments. You said that yourself."

"Amy, dear, your health is more important than any title. If you don't play this year, you've still got a year of eligibility."

40

"Not play this year?" she replied, tears welling up in her deep-blue eyes. The thought was impossible for her to accept. "But I had it all planned. I was even going to talk to my father about it."

"About what?" Swede asked.

"Turning pro. Going on the tour. Making all that money," Amy said.

"Okay. Fine. But first things first. Your health. Instead of aspirin or other drugs, let's try a few days of rest. Then we'll see."

She was about to protest, but old Swede shook his head firmly. "A few days of rest, Amy."

She relented, shrugged, turned and left the office.

The old coach sat there, staring in the direction in which she had departed. Other coaches he knew would resort to all sorts of treatments to provide temporary relief from pain for a highly prized protégé who was facing a special event. There were sprays, injections, many drugs. But Swede had never believed in such measures with athletes so young. The damage to their bodies could be long lasting. No title or trophy was worth it.

Then, as he often did when confronted by such a problem, he turned to the phone and dialed a number long familiar to him. When he received an answer, he asked, "Is Sy there for Swede Olafsen?"

In moments Sy Rosen was on the phone. "Hi, Swede, how you been?"

"Can't complain," the old coach said, his usual reply. "You, Sy?"

"I could complain. But it wouldn't help." Rosen's usual reply. That formality over, Sy Rosen asked, "What's up, Swede?" Rosen knew that when Swede called in this manner he had more in mind than a friendly chat.

"Sy, I've got a girl on my squad—Amy Bedford—"

"Amy Bedford? Didn't I hear about her?" Sy asked. "She's real good, isn't she? Sure, I read about her in the local paper. What about her?"

"She's having a little pain, Sy. And we got the state finals coming up."

41

"Pain? Where?" Sy asked.

"Right leg. You see, that's the leg she pivots off of when she comes to the net—"

"Where in her right leg?" Sy interrupted.

"Seems to be just below the knee. In the front. It must be bad because she's been overdosing with aspirin. Enough to make her throw up today."

"Swede, send her in. I'll have her X-rayed. Probably nothing. But let's make sure."

"Thanks, Sy. She's my best. With a good chance of going pro. I haven't seen the likes of her since I first saw Chrissie Evert in Florida before she went on the tour."

"Send her in, Swede. Can't hurt to have a look, can it?"

Sy hung up the phone, more curious and concerned than he would admit to Swede. But no sense stirring up fears and concerns on mere suspicion.

He had gotten more than a few such calls from Swede over the years. The veteran coach was most protective of his young charges. So Sy was always quick to respond to Swede's concern.

In earlier years they had had a regular foursome. Every Sunday morning, early, Swede, Sy Rosen, and two other men from the hospital staff, Harry Osmun and Cliff Westerveldt, had met at the tennis club and played three stiff sets. Sometimes, four. Then the doctors would go off to the hospital to make rounds. Sy always suspected that Swede threw a few points to make their matches appear to be closer than they actually were. For it was a game played for fun by a group of men who desperately needed relaxation from their overtaxing profession.

Eventually a cerebral accident eliminated Osmun from the group. A coronary at the operating table removed Westerveldt. Sy and Swede had tried to continue the tradition by playing lazy man's singles, not running for every ball, but the enjoyment had gone out of the game. So, without any special agreement, the habit had just petered out. But the two had remained good friends. Sy had become unofficial team doctor to Swede's young protégés.

His plan to X-ray Amy Bedford was no different from what he had done dozens of times for Swede's players. Most times Sy was relieved that his suspicions proved unfounded. But that never exempted him from the obligation to be diligent each time.

"X ray? Why, darling?" Marion Bedford said when Amy told her. "For a slight pain in the leg? Let me see."

She knelt beside her daughter and ran her fingers up and down the area just below Amy's knee.

"There's no swelling," Mrs. Bedford concluded. "I'd better call Dr. Corey before we do anything. What did you say that doctor's name was, the one Swede mentioned?"

"Dr. Rosen. Simon Rosen," Amy said.

Mrs. Bedford placed her call, was forced to hold on for some minutes before Corey was free to respond. During that time she brushed back the strands of her long blond hair that tended to fall loosely in times of stress. Though she had attempted to minimize the problem, instinctively she feared there was something terribly wrong. Her concern reflected her husband's attitude, expressed most often with considerable impatience: "Damn it, Marion, I work like a dog all day and part of the night. It's your job to run the house and take care of our daughter. I hope that's not too much to expect."

Thus Bedford rid himself of all responsibility for the care of his daughter, whom he loved but with whom he felt unequipped to deal. A workaholic, he was much more at ease when in control of the production facilities at the large machine-tool business he owned. There he did not have to contend with forces outside his knowledge and control. Such as the conduct and habits of teenage girls in a world in which teenagers were so free and liberated that anything was possible, meaning drugs, alcohol and unwanted pregnancies.

When Dr. Corey came on the line, Marion Bedford explained the situation and the recommendation Swede Olafsen had made. Corey asked only one question, "Who did Swede recommend Amy see?"

"A doctor at University Medical Center named Rosen."

"Sy Rosen?" Corey asked.

"Yes, I think so. Simon Rosen."

"She couldn't be in better hands," Corey said. "Just tell Rosen to call me when he gets the results."

"Relax, Amy," Dr. Rosen said. "It is Amy, isn't it?"

"Yes, sir," the girl said, playing nervously with her fingers, which rested in her lap.

To put the girl at ease, Dr. Rosen said, "Well, now, it seems you and I have some things in common, Amy. We both have the same tennis coach. Or had. I don't play much anymore. But when I did, he was my coach. And my partner in doubles. Until I got so good he thought I could beat him. . . ." Sy Rosen chuckled. "No, I never got that good. And he never got that bad. Just every so often he would throw me a game to keep me from quitting. Well, now, Swede tells me we are having a little pain in the leg."

"Yes, sir," Amy responded.

"Just where?" Dr. Rosen asked, leaning forward in his old swivel chair.

Amy drew a circular line around the area just below the knee of her right leg.

"Aha," Dr. Rosen said. "Get up, child. Walk. Just to the door and back."

Amy followed his instructions. He detected the same hitch in the way she walked, a reflection of her pain. When she was seated again, the old surgeon knelt beside her and palpated the area of pain. There was no swelling, but Rosen's sensitive fingers detected a very slight difference in surface temperature between that area and the lower part of her leg. Slight as it was, it disturbed him.

"Well," he said, pretending to be casual and amused, "let's have a go at that X ray. You've been X-rayed before, haven't you?"

"Only at the dentist," Amy said.

"Then you know there's no pain. You won't feel anything. So you can relax. Mrs. Kruzsik, my nurse, will take you down to X ray. And I'll call Dr. Corey and tell him what I find."

"You know Dr. Corey?" Amy asked.

"Of course I know Dr. Corey. Known him for years."

That made the tense teenager feel much better.

Sy Rosen watched as the girl walked out of his office, his eyes fixed on that right leg, which, though perfectly formed, was in pain and causing her to limp somewhat.

Damn it, damn it, damn it! he said to himself. *Why do I always have to look at the dark side of things? It could be nothing. Most likely is.*

Yet years of instinctive hunches, renowned in the profession as his diagnostic skills, warned him otherwise.

Walter Duncan was scrubbing for his first surgery of the morning. A long, laborious process that was never allowed to vary, it gave a man time to think of many things. The operation he was about to perform. A reminder to take one more look at the X rays and the scans before starting the procedure. What Emily had said that morning, just before he left, something about another school function and this time he absolutely must make it. When he kissed Simone, who was still asleep, did she have another black-and-blue mark on her side? Or was he beginning to imagine things? No wonder doctors were not supposed to treat members of their own families. Too subjective, never objective enough and professional.

He had just about finished scrubbing when one of the OR nurses came in to tell him that Dr. Rosen had called to ask him to drop by when he was done in Surgery.

The procedure was one calling for considerable skill but fortunately one of those cases where the surgery was corrective and promised a high percentage of success. Since it was arthroscopic surgery, which could be performed without extensive invasion of the leg, healing would be swift and the young patient would soon be able to start practice again with his college baseball team and be good as new, if not better, by the time the season started.

45

* * *

Walter Duncan's third surgery of the day was completed. He started to make his rounds of postoperative patients. Fortunately he found them all to be in satisfactory condition, with no fevers or other complications that sometimes plague surgeons. He was free to join Sy in his consultation room.

When Walt opened the door, he found the room dark. Sy sat in a corner of the room. Even in the darkness, Walt could tell the old man was grim and deeply concerned.

"Sy?" Walt asked. "You wanted me to look at a set of X rays?"

"They're mounted in the shadow box. Take a look."

Walter Duncan approached the wall of opaque glass, snapped on the backlight and studied the two X-ray films of the long leg bones of a young patient. It took no longer than a few moments. He turned to Sy.

"X rays like this aren't definitive. You know that better than anyone, Sy. Still . . ."

"Still *what?*" Sy asked.

"I might kid myself, but I can't fool you. Bone scan. CAT scan. And eventually biopsy. That's the only way to be absolutely sure."

Old Sy nodded grimly, for a Computerized Axial Tomography scan should give them a three-dimensional picture of Amy's condition.

"Who's the patient?" Walt asked.

"A fifteen-year-old girl."

"Figures. If it turns out to be osteogenic sarcoma, that's the age group. Still, it doesn't have to be bone cancer. It could still turn out to be a unicameral bone cyst or a fibrous dysplasia."

"Could," Sy said, but his tone and attitude indicated that he was not optimistic that it would be either of those less life-threatening afflictions.

"Fifteen-year-old girl," Walt Duncan said as he studied the X rays again. "H'mm, too bad."

"Girl named Amy Bedford," Sy said.

"The young tennis player I've read about? One of Swede's protégés?"

46

"That's the girl."

"Good God!" was all Walt could say. Then he asked, "Wasn't there something in the newspaper about her turning pro?"

"Swede told me she's good enough," Sy said.

"Whom do we talk to?" Walt asked.

"Chuck Corey's her pediatrician. We'd better start there."

"Of course," Walt said.

"I'll call Corey so he can inform the family," Sy said. "Will you take on the case?"

"Of course," Walt said, knowing that of all cases the ones involving young people were to him the most taxing emotionally. His sad memories of his brother Owen's death had become even more obsessive once Simone had been born. Each child he treated was as if he or she were his own. Ironically, his reputation for tenderness with children had caused more and more cases of younger patients to be referred to him.

It was early evening before Dr. Corey, a busy pediatrician, could return Sy's call. The conversation was brief and pithy.

"Chuck, I'm arranging for Walt Duncan to take over Amy Bedford's case. Meantime, would you arrange to give her another X ray right away?"

"Another X ray?" Corey asked, puzzled.

"Her chest this time."

At the word *chest,* Corey's quick mind instinctively came directly to the point. "What do you suspect, Sy? Metastases to the lungs from osteogenic sarcoma?"

"We only suspect, Chuck. We don't know for sure."

"I'll get her in for chest X rays first thing tomorrow," Corey said. "What next, Sy?"

"Radioisotope bone scan. If it is a sarcoma, it may not be primary. We have to make sure it isn't a metastasis from another part of her body. And to see, if it is primary, if it has spread. Meantime, get that chest X ray. Two plane."

"Of course," Corey agreed. Sy could hear the grimness in Corey's voice. Amy Bedford had been his patient since the first few

47

hours of her life. "Do . . . do your best for her, Sy," Corey added, for want of anything else to say.

"Chuck, about her family, how do we handle that?"

"Her mother is a good, strong woman. Has to be. Because her father is a high-strung workaholic who'd have you believe he's all business. But from my experience, I think he does it to cover up. The man can't handle personal problems. So I can't guarantee how he'll react to this. When the time comes . . ." Corey corrected himself. "*If* the time comes, I suggest we hold a joint consultation. You and Walt to answer the technical questions, of which Bedford will have plenty. And me to reassure them, as far as possible. But first I'll get those chest X rays and broach the need for the scans."

"And a possible biopsy," Sy reminded.

Sy Rosen and Walt Duncan were in the darkened room staring at a wall-sized viewing box on which were displayed the results of all the X rays, bone scans and CAT scans of Amy Bedford. As they moved from one film to another, studying shadows, bright hot spots and other indicia of her condition, there was little need for conversation. The only encouraging aspect was that the chest films Corey had sent over showed that at least the girl's lungs were clean.

"Schedule that biopsy as soon as possible, Walt."

Walt Duncan studied the films as he observed, "Blind needle biopsy won't do. Not in a case like this."

"Tumor's not readily accessible," Sy agreed. "And we don't want to risk getting too few cells. No surer way to arrive at a wrong diagnosis than having too few cells to work with. Open incisional biopsy is the way. Especially in this case."

Without having resorted to the specific words, both surgeons had confirmed their worst fears. The next step would prove to be the final confirmation before major surgery had to be decided upon.

The last thing before he left for the day, Walt Duncan had Claudia call and reserve Operating Room time and an anesthetist for Amy Bedford's biopsy. A week from Tuesday offered the first available surgical facilities for any case not deemed a life-threatening emergency.

When he arrived home, Simone had already had her dinner and was upstairs getting ready for bed. He went up quietly, hoping to catch her unawares and make a game of his late homecoming. Guilt often forced him to resort to such diversions. He found her in her bathroom, naked, standing before the door-length mirror. He was amused at his daughter discovering her developing young body.

His amusement was short-lived, for he noticed her feeling another contusion, this time on her shoulder. *Damn,* he thought, *I said she was to give up hockey.*

He surprised her when he said, "I hope you hit back this time."

Simone turned to discover her father. With the growing sensitivity of adolescence, she reached for her robe to cover up. Once she had slipped into it, she replied, "I think I banged into the door of my locker. But I can't remember."

He held out his arms to her. She came to him. He kissed her good night, at the same time pushing aside the shoulder of her robe to examine that bluish spot. He pressed it. She did not react in pain. He looked into her face.

"Something wrong, Daddy?" she asked.

"No. Nothing. Just get into bed. It's late."

With no word of protest, the child obediently went to her bed, climbed in and turned on her side ready to give way to sleep. Walt lingered only long enough to kiss her again. Then he went below to the den, where Emily had his predinner drink waiting.

"Did you know she had another one of those things on her shoulder?" he asked.

"No," Emily said. "She gave up hockey, you know."

"Did she make much of a fuss about it?"

"No. Which surprised me," Emily admitted. "I thought she'd be her usual rebellious self. But maybe she's maturing faster than we think."

"Maybe," Walt said, preoccupied. "Does she look the same to you?"

"Of course," Emily said. "Why shouldn't she?"

"Isn't she pale?"

"Light-skinned brunets always seem pale," Emily said. "They used to say that about me when I was a kid."

"I mean, paler than usual." Walt corrected.

"Not that I've noticed," Emily said. "Bring your drink to the table. Dinner's ready."

"Okay," he said, still preoccupied.

Sy did not wish to alarm the Bedfords unnecessarily before all the medical evidence was in. Especially since he had been warned of the volatile nature of Amy's father. So he broached her biopsy as a routine bit of minor surgery. Ed Bedford left the details of it to his wife, while he devoted himself to his business, as he always did, in avoidance of all things emotionally threatening.

The afternoon before the biopsy Marion Bedford brought Amy to the hospital. The girl was installed in her room and interviewed by the anesthetist, gave a blood sample for routine lab tests and was checked out for her general condition by a staff resident. Walt Duncan stopped by her room.

As he had expected, despite all her efforts to appear at ease as she thought was expected of her, the girl was tense. Her mother, a thin blond woman in whom Walt Duncan suspected a slightly neurotic strain, stood at the foot of the bed, her fingers wrapped so tightly around the steel bed frame that her knuckles were revealingly white. She tried to smile. It turned out to be a flicker that appeared and reappeared as on some animated doll.

"Now, Amy," Walt began, "what we do tomorrow is very simple. You'll be under total anesthetic so you won't feel a thing. Afterward there'll be a little wound about two inches long that may sting a little. But it'll leave practically no scar." He did not mention that it was possible that one day (and sooner than he liked to contemplate) that scar might be removed, along with her leg.

"Now, all I will do is take out some small bits of your leg

50

bone. You won't feel it. During or after. But it will help us determine how to treat your pain."

"Dr. Duncan, do you think it's possible for me to still play in the state finals? Swede thinks I have a good chance at the title."

"We'll do everything we can to see that you make it, Amy," Walt said. "I'll see you up in the OR tomorrow morning."

"Okay," the girl said, but it was obvious to both Walt and Amy's mother that she was not yet resigned to her enormous disappointment.

At 6:45 in the morning, without having had any breakfast, Amy Bedford was wheeled up to the fifth floor on a gurney. Before she was taken up, she had been given a preanesthetic sedation. She was already woozy when Walt Duncan, dressed in OR greens, came by for one last word of encouragement.

"Just remember, Amy, you won't feel a thing. So relax. And give yourself to the anesthesia. I'll see you when you wake up."

With Sy Rosen as a most interested observer, Walt Duncan had scalpel in hand. He looked to the anesthetist, who nodded his assurance that the patient was completely under. He checked with his charge nurse, who nodded. Then he made the first incision. A small straight line just short of two inches, it hardly seemed visible until the surge of blood delineated it.

With his assistant retracting the skin and tissue of the wound, Walt Duncan went in with an electric drill and used curettes to scoop out tiny samples of bone from the area indicated on the CAT scans as the focus of the trouble. He dispatched a part of the biopsy material to the lab for an immediate frozen section and tentative diagnosis. The final and definite diagnosis would depend on lab tests, which would take at least five days. Only then would he and Sy know for sure the precise tumor they were battling. That would determine all their future decisions.

Walt did not withdraw or close the tiny wound until the results of the frozen section were reported to him. Both he and Sy greeted the word from the lab with the same bit of self-deception: "A frozen section is never definitive."

But the results of the frozen section were alarming enough for Sy to order, "Just for the hell of it, why don't we do our own chest X rays? I'd hate to think we missed something."

Walt was meticulous in closing the area from which he had extracted the biopsy material. If they broke loose from the tumor, sarcoma cells had the potential to seed in soft tissue. That could make for a very dire prognosis.

When they left surgery, Walt Duncan sent the cell samples, along with Amy's X rays, scans and medical history to Dr. Alan Woodside, the chief pathologist. He would need all that material to arrive at a correct, final diagnosis.

Amy's new lung X rays were clean.

Six days later, Woodside's pathology report reached Sy Rosen's desk. The report affirmed that Patient Bedford, Amy, fifteen years old, was the victim of a full-blown case of virulent, aggressive osteogenic sarcoma.

When Walter Duncan read the report, he knew what procedures were dictated now. He must implement them without delay.

He would discuss the case at tomorrow's meeting of the Tumor Board. But treatment would have to be started at once.

4

IT took several phone calls and one meeting postponed at the last minute before Ed Bedford, his wife, Marion, and his daughter, Amy, could be assembled in Sy Rosen's consultation room along with Walter Duncan and Dr. Corey.

It devolved upon Sy to make the first explanation. Warned of Bedford's proclivity for being convinced only by what he could see, Sy relied on the X rays and the body scans. Addressing himself to the impatient father, Sy spoke in his calmest manner. "You see here, Mr. Bedford, on this X ray, this dark shadow?"

"Yes," Bedford said impatiently. "What is it?"

"Evidence of a neoplasm. An unnatural growth."

"Unnatural," Bedford repeated. "Which means what?"

"A tumor," Sy explained. "A tumor of the bone. Now, on these bone scans you can see this hot spot in the same area—"

"Hot spot," Bedford again repeated, with a disdain indicating he disapproved of such slang in a medical situation.

"That hot spot is a pretty clear indication of a *dangerous* tumor," Sy said.

Suddenly coming to the realization of what Sy was leading to, Bedford interrupted. "Are you telling me that that . . . that thing in my daughter's leg is a cancer? Impossible! Fifteen-year-old kids do not get cancer!"

"Ed, please." Marion Bedford interrupted. Though she herself was on the verge of tears, she tried to give comfort and support to her daughter by reaching for her hand. She found it to be extremely cold, betraying the fear that had overcome her.

"Look"—Bedford exploded—"I'm a man who deals with facts. Whatever you doctors know, I want to know. I'm no dummy. I can understand. Just come right out and tell me."

"Ed, just a minute. . . ." Dr. Corey tried to intercede, at the same time casting a glance at Sy that apologized, *I warned you about him.*

Bedford turned on Corey. "Damn it, how could such a thing be there and you not know about it? God knows Amy's in your office every six months, like clockwork, for a complete physical! How could you miss such a serious thing? And to think of all the money I've paid you over the years. Hell, you can't rely on anyone these days!"

Walt Duncan rose to his full six feet three inches and seized Ed Bedford by the shoulders. "Hold on, Bedford!"

Bedford glared up at him. He seemed poised to swing out to break Walt's grip. Instead, he continued to stare, seemed to shrink in size and became far less belligerent.

In a calmer voice, Walt continued, "Mr. Bedford, this is an insidious disease. It is rarely if ever picked up on a routine physical. No doctor can suspect it until there are some signs, some symptoms. That's the most common problem we have diagnosing and treating bone tumors. Failure to suspect their presence. Pain is the first symptom. When pain appeared, the doctors did the proper thing. And we did discover it.

"Now, rid yourself of another common fallacy. Cancer is not solely a disease of the aging. Fifteen-year-olds *do* get cancer. So forget all your preconceived notions and listen. Very carefully. Because a choice has to be made here today. The most important choice of your daughter's life."

Chastened by those words, a pale, sweaty Ed Bedford sank back into his chair. Walt Duncan stayed on his feet, addressing himself more to Amy than to her father. For he could see how her father's uncontrolled reaction had shaken her. If, at a crucial time like this, a child could not derive confidence from her own father, what did she have to fall back on?

"Amy, I won't minimize the seriousness of your disease. It is nasty business. And I won't lie to you. *It can be fatal.* But—and thank God that in these times we have lots of *buts*—it can be treated. In several ways. That's where you and I have to make a choice."

Out of his despair, Ed Bedford muttered, "The Kennedy boy . . . they took his leg . . . amputated it."

With a soft gasp Amy Bedford started to weep. Her mother put her arms around her. Walt Duncan dropped to one knee beside the tearful girl. He took her hand; he lifted her chin so that she had to look into his eyes.

"Amy, remember that I didn't use that word. Nor did Dr. Rosen. Nor did Dr. Corey. I said we have a *choice,* you and I. Yes, amputation is one alternative. Maybe the safest one. In a way, the easiest one. But there is another way, if you choose it."

As if she had not heard, the slim, blond-haired teenager continued to weep.

Damn it, Walt thought, *with a different father this could have been done with so much less anguish. We are going to have to be not only her doctors, but her fathers as well.*

"Now, Amy, dear, listen to me very carefully. Because when I am done we will want *you* to make your choice. Yes, we can amputate. But there is another way. And this is what it consists of: For the next six to ten weeks we will put you on a regimen of chemotherapy. That's a form of anti-cancer medication. If that succeeds and causes the tumor to shrink, it will indicate we have the sarcoma under control. Then I can perform an operation on you. Dr. Rosen will be there. Dr. Corey will be there. We'll work as a team. During that operation I will remove the part of your bone that is cancerous."

"Amputate?" Amy dared to ask.

"Not amputate, Amy. What we call *resect.* That means take out the diseased part and leave the healthy part."

55

"But if you take away part of my leg—" The girl protested.

Walt firmed his hold on her quivering chin.

"Amy . . . Amy, listen to me." Her moist eyes surrendered. "Once we perform a resection, we then insert what we call a prosthesis. A long metal device made of strong, lightweight titanium, which replaces the bone we remove. A substitute skeleton, if you wish. If we have to, we even can replace your knee."

"If it works, will I be able to walk?"

"If everything goes well, you will be able to walk."

"Will I be able to play tennis again?'" she asked.

"Not as well as before," Walt replied.

"Then that's my choice," Amy said at once.

"Not so fast, my dear," Walt said. "First, this won't be easy. Second, there are no guarantees. I must be completely honest with you. Those sarcoma cells may have already spread from your leg into your bloodstream, which could deposit them in other parts of your body. Fortunately your lungs are clean. They are the area most vulnerable to these cells. They're clean, so we may be lucky. We may have caught this in time. But I want you to know all the risks. We are going to be honest with you all the way, Amy."

Such complete disclosure of the dangerous possibilities apparently gave the girl increased confidence in Walter Duncan.

"Now, Amy, dear, about the choice. If you choose this resection and prosthesis procedure, you must be willing to undergo a year of chemotherapy, surgery, physical therapy and all the pain and suffering that goes with it. That means if you make this choice, you must be prepared to give us one year of your life. It's a gamble. But if you make this choice, we can get you well."

"A whole year?" she asked.

"A whole year. Forget tennis. Forget all other activities. Go to school only when you can. But your main job for the entire next year is to help us get Amy Bedford well and healthy again. What do you say?"

Amy hesitated, then said, "All right, Doctor, I'll do it."

As if he had gained confidence from his daughter, Ed Bedford nodded, too.

"Look, sorry about before. This whole thing is obviously going to cost money, lots of money. Don't worry about it. The money'll be there. Just help my little girl get well."

"We'll do our best," Sy said. "First step, we want Amy to arrange a meeting with Dr. Bristol, our oncologist. She'll explain all about the chemotherapy. What it is, what it's supposed to do, what the side effects are. I've already called Bristol's secretary. She's expecting you."

"Amy," Walt suggested, "why don't you and your mom go down the hall to Dr. Bristol's office and see her secretary?"

Ed Bedford realized that it was a request that he remain. Once the door was closed and only the men were closeted in the room, Bedford reached into his inner coat pocket and took out his checkbook. "All right, gentlemen, how much to start with?"

"That's not the reason I wanted you to stay on, Mr. Bedford," Walt said. "Financial matters will be handled in due course. But we want to impress something on you. Your daughter is about to undergo a long and arduous process. Chemotherapy has some very distressing and painful side effects, worse in some patients than others. She's going to need all the willpower and all the courage she can muster to see it through. She may be facing a year of hell. But we think it's going to be worth it.

"What she needs from you is not money, but guts. A show of strength from which she can take strength. If you have to shout, in anger or denial, go down to your office, or out to an empty field, and shout. If you have to cry, go into the bathroom and cry. If you have to curse fate or God because of what's happening to your daughter, do it out of her sight and hearing. What we want from you is a smile. A genuine smile that says, 'Stick with it, Amy, darling, and we'll all make it.' What we want from you are words of encouragement. The clasp of your hand to comfort her. Let her know how much you love her and that you have confidence in her that she'll beat this thing.

"Above all, don't ever give her the feeling that by getting sick she's let you down. Disappointed you. Betrayed your ambitions for her. You loved her before, love her more now. She needs it. Always remember, no one was to blame for this. No one could have prevented it. It just happened. That's all."

When Walt was finished, Ed Bedford nodded humbly. His lips moved erratically, but no sounds came forth. The man was trying to promise but could not find the words. After some moments of silence, he rose and started for the door. There he stopped.

He turned to face the three physicians. "They didn't know. Not Amy. Not her mother. But I've been putting aside bonds, tax-free bonds, for three years now. To finance her first year on the tour. Twenty-five thousand dollars' worth, to see she got started right. Now it's all yours, gentlemen."

Irked by the man's crass assumption, Walt Duncan asked, "What if we said it will take ten times that much?"

"It's there. You name it, you got it," Bedford said. "Only do something. Save her!"

His eyes welled up and he slipped out before he started to weep.

Walt looked at Sy, who said, "Poor man, if health were for sale, it would be easy for him. He'd buy it for her. I wonder what he'll do now."

Dr. Corey said simply, "I'll do what I can to keep him on track. But he's helpless in situations like this. He runs his family like he runs his business. I don't know how he'll react now that he has what he considers a damaged daughter. If she were an employee, he'd know what to do."

Once Corey had left, Sy said, "Walt, don't you think you were overreaching, being so optimistic in your promise to cure her?"

"I had to," Walt said. "It'll give her the will she needs for what she has to face in the next year."

The events of the afternoon had affected Walt Duncan even more than he realized. The face of Amy Bedford followed him as he went on rounds of his patients. It was with him when he sat in consultation with doctors who had brought patients to him for surgery, and when he was summoned to Emergency to render his opinion on the treatment of an auto-crash victim with compound fractures. It was with him so persistently that he finally asked Claudia to call off his last two appointments so he could get home in time to have dinner with Simone and Emily. He had realized that different as their vocations might be, Ed Bedford and Walter Duncan had something in common.

It was an enjoyable dinner for all three of them. Simone talked elatedly throughout the meal. More times than one, Walt had to urge, "Darling, your chicken is getting cold. We'll have plenty of time to talk later." But the child insisted, relating everything that had happened to her in school not only that day, but the day before as well. To his dismay, Walter finally realized her excitement, the sparkle in her eyes, was really a rebuke. She was taking advantage of every moment with him because the opportunity to have him to herself was so rare. He made a number of well-intentioned promises, few of which he would have time to carry out.

She started from the table, stopped in the archway. "Come up and kiss me good night later?"

"Of course, darling," Walt said, amused at her conduct. His young daughter was becoming more mature.

As soon as he had finished his coffee he started up the stairs. He found Simone's door partly open, as if in invitation. He peeked in, intending to make a game of it. But she did not respond. He went to her bedside. She was already asleep. She must have been very tired. He bent down to kiss her on the cheek. He patted her on the bottom and quietly slipped out of the room.

When he went down to the den, Emily was already waiting with the look she wore when she had some urgent problem. Instead she said only, "You came home early." It seemed to demand an explanation.

He smiled. "Come home late, it's taken for granted. Come home early, I have to explain."

"It's not just coming home early. Something happened to you today."

"Yes," he admitted. "Something happened." He told her about

Amy Bedford. "Maybe I did overpromise. But I felt I had to. Staring into her pleading blue eyes, so young, so terrified, I had to reassure her."

"What *are* her chances?"

"Good," he said, then moderated that to, "well, not exactly good. There's already an eighty-three-percent chance that the cancer could have spread into her bloodstream. But there's a possibility the chemo will counteract that."

"If it doesn't?" Emily asked.

He avoided that most distressing probability, saying, "It's silly to speculate. We'll know soon enough. Six weeks, eight. The tumor will recede or it won't. That'll dictate what we do next."

"So that's what brought you home early?" she remarked. "Simone was beside herself with excitement. She surely made the most of it."

"Wore herself out, it seems," Walt said, smiling. "She been going to bed early recently?"

"Come to think of it, she no longer pouts when I tell her not to watch television. Just goes right up to bed."

"Good."

"I guess she figures it doesn't do any good to stay up. Daddy won't be home in time anyhow." At once Emily apologized. "Sorry, darling, didn't mean to say that. I just couldn't help it."

"I try. Believe me, I try. It's just that something always comes up."

As he settled down to study some lab reports he had received that afternoon related to a case he was to operate on at seven in the morning, he considered: *Is Emily right? Is Simone's compliant attitude a silent form of protest against my frequent absences? Children are known to react in strange ways in response to secret hurts and rebuffs.*

In the morning he would get together with Dr. Rita Bristol, the oncologist, to establish a treatment plan for Amy Bedford's chemotherapy.

And, he remembered with some annoyance, all efforts to settle the malpractice suit against Peter Enright had failed. He would have to appear in court to testify when the case was scheduled to come to trial. Walt did not look forward to that chore with any sense of anticipation.

Everyone at University Medical Center considered Rita Bristol a very private person. Aside from her professional *curriculum vitae*, which included a Bachelor of Science degree from a university in the Southwest, a medical degree from a university in California and a record of excellent former service with two hospitals in the East, where she trained in her specialty, Oncology, no one at the hospital knew a great deal about her.

She was an attractive woman, tiny, dark haired. When dealing with patients, she was quite unemotional. What went on behind her quick and perceptive eyes few people could discern. But she was very open, direct and precise about the course of treatment she prescribed for patients who were referred to her.

She had no children, though she sometimes did allude to having been married. The way she spoke of it, it had been a long time ago and had ended unhappily.

What they did not know about her was that several times a year, when she could manage some days off, she flew East to Washington. There she went to visit the Vietnam Veterans Memorial in Washington, D.C., where she spent some hours. On her arrival and just before her departure she would run her fingers over one name on that cold monument, like a blind person reading Braille.

Then she would return to the hospital and quietly resume her duties.

Today, as she faced Amy Bedford and her mother, Dr. Bristol was her usual brisk, efficient self. She wore her black hair in a coronet that ringed her head and that seemed to have taken hours to fashion. But it served as an elegant frame for her precise features. She had obviously studied Amy's lab reports, physical findings, X rays, scans and pathology report, as well as Walter Duncan's report and his opinion.

Amy sat as still as she could manage at a time of such enormous tension and fear. Her mother sat beside her, trying desperately to exude an air of intelligent cooperation, devoid of emotion. If she could have controlled the nervous pulse in her throat, she might have succeeded.

Aware of all that, Dr. Bristol did her best to start the meeting on an optimistic note.

"Amy, I suppose you've heard horror stories of what happens when a person gets chemotherapy. Like ghost stories, they always tend to be exaggerated. That is not to say that it will be pleasant. Because there will be a war being fought in your body. The good guys are the chemical agents we give you. The bad guys are the maverick cells, the cancer cells. And, as in all wars, innocent civilians, patients, sometimes get hurt. So, yes, there will be times of discomfort. Nausea. Vomiting, even, for a time. But none of it as bad as you've heard. The important thing is, in my years of practice we've never lost a patient to the chemo.

"The main purpose you and I have is to shrink that tumor in your leg. If we can do that, then Dr. Duncan can do his operation, and you should have an excellent chance to beat this thing. So, every time you feel like quitting, every time you think to yourself, 'That bitch Bristol is trying to kill me,' just remember our aim. *To make that tumor in your leg shrink.* Okay?"

"Okay," Amy murmured, barely audible. Then she asked, "What happens if it doesn't?"

"Doesn't?" Dr. Bristol was taken by surprise.

"What happens if the tumor doesn't shrink?" Amy asked.

Unaware of what Walt Duncan might have said, Dr. Bristol decided that the truth was the safest answer.

"In that case there won't be any choice. Dr. Duncan would have to amputate."

A cold hand seemed to grip and twist Amy Bedford's stomach. The nipples of her young breasts became tight and hard. She turned to her mother. But Dr. Bristol intervened.

"Amy! I didn't say that will happen. I only said if you and I fail, it would happen. So it is most important that we each do our part. Every moment of the times when you're experiencing discomfort, nausea, every time you feel like your insides are being torn apart by the chemo, know that you are suffering for a good cause. Discomfort now, stress now, can mean that operation weeks from now. And then a whole new life. So instead of hating the treatment, think of it as a new chance. A chance that a girl like you would not have had too many years ago."

Amy faced Dr. Bristol, took comfort from the look of conviction in her deep, dark eyes.

"Now, Amy, this will be our routine for the next eight weeks. You will have to have nine doses of a chemical called methotrexate, administered intravenously. So you won't have any nasty-tasting stuff to swallow. But it can lead to vomiting."

"Will I have to be in the hospital?" Amy asked.

"Only three days at a time. One day to get the treatment. Two days so we can monitor the effects on your blood and urine, to see how well your body is tolerating the methotrexate."

"Miss three days of school at a time," Amy said.

"I'll talk to your school. We'll arrange things so you can go whenever you're able," Dr. Bristol said.

Amy nodded. But it was obvious she was not reassured.

Her mother reached out to pat her arm. "Remember, darling, Dr. Duncan said a year. What's one year, if it means being healthy for the rest of your life?"

Dr. Bristol was relieved not to have been the author of that extravagant promise. But she said nothing to detract from it.

"We'll work out something with the school, Amy. Home lessons. A special curriculum. And there will be some days when you can go to school if you wish. Now, I've arranged a room for you in the Pediatric Pavilion."

"I'm fifteen!" Amy protested.

Dr. Bristol smiled. "I'm afraid in medical circles we still consider that a proper age for the Pediatric Service. So, Monday morning. Eight o'clock!"

"Eight o'clock," Marion Bedford agreed. "Come, darling," she said. "We'll get you the things you'll need for Monday."

Rita Bristol watched them leave. She thought, *What a young, pretty girl she is. And to be faced with this.* With Dr. Bristol's knowledge of all the findings in the case, she felt inclined to be somewhat less than totally optimistic about the prognosis. She had seen similar cases go sour. Leading to amputation. And worse.

Even percentages and "cure rates" were no guarantee in any specific case. You followed those treatments that had proven successful in the past. Like the patient, you devoutly hoped for the desired outcome. The only difference between doctor and patient was, if things went sour, the doctor would suspect it first.

5

T HAT night Amy woke suddenly out of a dream from which she could only remember protesting, "I'm too young . . . too young . . ." She lay awake, exhausted, her bed damp with sweat. Her first conscious thought: *Once I protested to Dr. Bristol that I'm too old for the Pediatric Pavilion. Now I'm saying I'm too young, too young. . . .*

Vestiges of her dream began to come back to her. She had been protesting to a tall, shadowy person who hovered over her: "I'm too young to have this . . . too young to be so sick . . . too young for those words . . . whatever those words are that mean cancer . . . too young."

She breathed deeply, wiping the sweat from her young face with the palms of her hands. She felt as she sometimes did after a long, hard set of tennis against one of the boys on the team— an exercise that Swede Olafsen used to have her undergo often, to accustom her to more powerful strokes than she normally encountered in girls' competition.

Monday, she thought suddenly. *I will have to report on Monday for the first dose of that stuff that Dr. Bristol talked about. Methosomething. Which does all kinds of hateful things. Nausea. Vomiting.* She could almost taste the bitterness of it now. *What if it's all a waste? What if it's the result of one of those medical mistakes you read about in the papers all the time? Where the drug later turns out to harm the patient?*

She turned on her side. Became aware again of that slight but persistent pain in her leg. To her the enemy was the pain, not the disease. She could feel the pain. She had no proof of the disease.

Besides, she insisted, *a girl can't be training for the state finals one day and be threatened with death the next.*

Before she would submit herself to the horrors of chemotherapy she would do a little investigating of her own. She slipped out of bed. She went to her closet. She opened the door, on which her mother had installed a full-length mirror on her twelfth birthday. It was a sign that she was grown up enough to be concerned about the way she looked in dresses and designer tennis outfits. It was the age of becoming aware of boys.

She angled the door so that the mirror received the full glare of the overhead light. She stood before the mirror, put her right foot forward so that her naked leg was reflected. She turned it first one way, then another. She noticed no swelling. No change of shape, no deformity. She pressed it, she pinched it, she felt nothing different except for that annoying pain that stubbornly nagged at her day and night. But, she convinced herself, after strenuous training in preparation for the tournament, it was only natural that her leg might hurt. Sometimes it was her shoulder, from coming down too hard on her serve. Sometimes it was that burning sting in her arm called tennis elbow. Wherever it occurred, and however long it lasted, it was one of the expected wounds of the tennis wars.

She had played before despite pain. There was no reason why she could not do so again. She determined that she would.

She returned to bed. She fell asleep formulating the plan she would put into effect in the morning.

She woke earlier than usual. She pondered whether it was too early to make the call. She decided to risk it. Since her parents had refused her her own phone until her sixteenth birthday, she was forced to use the phone in the den or the one down in the kitchen. The den was safer. Her father, driven by his business, might be down in the kitchen at this early hour, making himself breakfast and getting ready to leave before Amy and her mother were even up.

She slipped down the stairs on bare feet. She noticed no light in the kitchen. That meant she had the whole ground floor to herself. She went into the den, sat at her father's desk, dialed his phone.

She was prepared with exactly what she would say if Brent Martin's mother answered. Fortunately it was Brent himself.

"Brent? Amy."

"Oh, hi!"

Though he tried to sound diffident, she could detect both the surprise and the delight in his voice. He had been trying to date her for the past year and had given up only when he realized that she did not feel the same way about him. So her call was a welcome surprise, to judge from his enthusiasm.

"Where've you been the last few days, Amy? I missed you at practice. Something wrong?"

"You know Swede. I had this pain in my leg, and he wouldn't let me work it out. I guess I'll have to do it on my own. So I wondered, this being Saturday, could you and I rally for an hour or two? Just to get my timing back?"

"If Swede said . . ."

"Not on the school courts. The public courts. In the park," Amy said. "Please, Brent?"

"For you, Amy, okay. What time?"

"Nine?"

"Nine. Want me to pick you up?"

Amy considered that for a moment before she said, "No. I'll . . . I'll meet you there. Get a court."

The grass was still dewy and moist when Amy Bedford appeared at the public courts. She looked well dressed in her navy-and-red warm-up suit. The colors contrasted with her blond hair

67

and her eyes. The trim cut hugged her young developing body in a most flattering way. She wore the warm-ups defiantly, as if to say to the world, "I am young, I am healthy; there is nothing wrong with me!"

She waited apprehensively for Brent Martin, afraid he might not show up. Perhaps discouraged at the last minute by Swede's order that Amy desist from all practice, he had reconsidered. But at nine, as promised, Brent Martin showed up, carrying his racket and a net bag bulging with used tennis balls that were still good enough for practice.

It was evident from the look in his eyes when he saw her that he wanted to kiss her. But the one time he had tried, she had resisted.

"Are you sure it's all right to practice?" he asked, as they both stripped off their warm-up suits.

"Of course it's okay. I feel great. I think the pain is almost all gone. Or it will be by tournament time." Amy assured him.

"Okay, then."

They started warming up from deep court. He hit long, easy strokes that bounded within two feet of the baseline every time. The sort of strokes Amy liked to return with equal length. Soon they widened the area of play, some of Brent's shots going wide of the center line and eventually into the corners of the court, making Amy move farther and faster than at the outset.

Brent hit with purpose and design, watching as she scampered after the ball, mostly making it in time to strike a good return. Sometimes, though she hustled after it, she could barely get a racket on the ball. Brent came to the net, ostensibly to put the ball away on a volley. But once there he tapped his racket on the tape and asked, "Amy?"

"Yeah?" she responded, breathless, her face glistening with perspiration.

"You're not getting to the ball like you usually do."

"I'm just warming up," she replied sharply, her impatience an outgrowth of guilt, not anger.

"You're already warmed up," the young man said. "Something's wrong."

"Nothing's wrong. Just get back there and feed me some short ones to bring me in to the net."

"Are you sure—" he started to say.

"God, you're worse than my mother when it comes to nagging. Now get back there!" Amy insisted.

"Okay. Sure."

He took up his place behind the baseline. He put the ball in play, a long stroke that Amy returned from her baseline. He followed with a return that bounced at the service line and made her race in for the return, then she continued three steps to the net. From there, she put away his return with a crisp volley that fell just inside the line but at an angle that he could not reach.

She started back to the baseline to repeat the pattern. As she walked away from him, Brent Martin noticed the same hitch that first had disturbed Swede Olafsen. Brent felt he should make her quit, but he knew how headstrong Amy was. If he didn't practice with her, there wasn't another boy on the team who would refuse. He decided to continue and to observe. At the first opportune moment he would insist they quit.

They followed through with set practice. After a time, she asked him to hit deep balls to her so that she could practice coming in to the net behind her own returns. She came in behind her forehand. Twice she even followed her backhand when she had hit it powerfully enough.

She was sweating, breathing hard, but feeling great. She had recaptured her old confidence. Pain or no, she felt in her mind and heart that she could beat any girl her age in the whole state. It was possible to believe that everything the doctors had said was wrong.

"Feed me some overheads!" she called to Brent.

He complied, sending high lobs that bounced just inside the court. Amy followed them, brought her racket up in anticipation, then came down with hard smashes, sending the ball into one corner or the other with such finality that Brent didn't even bother to pursue them.

Everything was working perfectly. The layoff hadn't done her game as much harm as she had feared. It was good again to feel warm and wet, with all her muscles responding so easily and so well.

"Let's play a few games," she called out.

"Sure," Brent responded. "Serve!"

Amy gathered up three practice balls, slipped one into the back pocket of her panties and started to serve. She didn't employ full strength on her first serve, deciding to ease into it. Brent returned it, a long, flat stroke that carried deep into the backcourt. Not too hard, but hard enough to demand a good return from Amy. She returned it. They exchanged strokes until, seeing an advantage, Amy came in to the net behind one of her own strong forehands. He hit the ball directly at her, but she was able to twist her body out of the way and execute a smart chop that dropped the ball just over the net and out of Brent's reach.

They played for about twenty minutes, accelerating their pace, increasing their strokes, testing Amy to her limit. But she stayed in the set, dogged and determined to prove to herself that she was as good as ever. Better, even.

She was back at her own baseline, waiting to receive Brent's serve. His first serve hit the top of the net for a let. He set up to deliver another first serve. This one came at her very hard, but fortunately was just beyond the service line, so she could sweep it aside and wait for his second serve. It was shorter and somewhat softer than his first, with a slight twist to it. She came in to meet it and sent it back deep to him. She raced in to reach the net, but her right foot went down under her. She fell forward, sprawling on the green concrete, scraping her knee. The pain was so sudden, so intense that despite herself she cried out. Brent raced toward her, vaulting the net to reach her.

He knelt beside her, saw the white skin where she had scraped it. Blood began to seep to the surface. Over her protests he lifted her in his arms and carried her to his car.

"Please don't drive me up to my door," she begged.

"I'm not going to let you walk," he said. "Not with that leg."

As they were rounding the corner of the street where she lived, she pleaded once more. But he remained adamant. As she feared, when they pulled up at her house, her mother was waiting at the front door.

"Please," Amy whispered, "please, Brent, don't make it any worse by trying to help me to the door."

"Okay," he said. "But tell her the truth. Don't hold anything back."

"We were practicing tennis. Why would I lie about that?"

"I don't know. But I have a feeling it was wrong," he said.

She opened the car door and slipped out. Fortunately her warm-up suit hid her scraped knee and leg from view. But she could not conceal her pain. The burning of her open wound made her injury quite obvious.

By the time Amy reached the door, her mother's face had changed from mere concern to a look of great distress. She assisted Amy into the house, led her to the kitchen, sat her down. Gently, she rolled up the leg of Amy's warm-up pants. She was appalled by the sight of torn skin and blood on the diseased leg.

After she had bathed it gently with warm water and mild soap, she covered the wound with Vaseline and placed a soft gauze pad over it. Then, without a word of recrimination, she went to the phone and placed a call to Dr. Corey.

"Call Dr. Duncan" was the pediatrician's advice. "I want him to see Amy at once! Do you understand? At once!"

"Well, well," Walter Duncan said as lightly as he could manage while he stared at Amy Bedford's right leg.

The young girl looked up at him from the examining table, trying to read the expression in his eyes. He did not seem as concerned as her mother had been, or as alarmed as Dr. Corey. In truth, he was far more agitated than both of them.

"Just tell me how it happened," Walt said, very tenderly palpating her leg, applying only the gentlest touch of his forefinger to the area of her wound.

She admitted practicing, stressed how good it felt. Yes, there was still a little pain, but it had seemed to grow less as practice progressed. In his own mind, Walter Duncan dismissed that as

71

an attempt to minimize her breach of his instructions. Finally she described the manner in which her fall occurred. She emphasized that it was in no wise due to the pain. She was not favoring her leg. She was not dragging it. It was just one of those accidents that will happen on a tennis court, as the doctor very well must know from his own tennis activity.

"So, Doctor, you can see that the pain had nothing to do with it."

Feeling exonerated, she lay back on the table, awaiting his response.

"Amy, it really doesn't matter how it happened," Walt Duncan said.

She felt enormously relieved. Evidently she had succeeded in avoiding his anger.

"Whether it was due to tripping on a step, getting out of a car, slipping on a damp floor, is not important. The only thing that does matter is that fortunately you didn't break your leg."

She felt even more relieved.

"Because if you had broken it, we would have had no choice. I would have had to amputate. Today!"

She stopped breathing. She could feel the skin on her arms and between her breasts pucker from fear. She had a moment of doubt, when she thought, *He's only saying that to scare me.* But when she looked into his eyes, she knew he was telling her the truth.

"Amy, right now, and we hope until we get your treatment under way, your danger is confined to this one area. From what we can determine now those cancer cells are all in here. Not yet in any other part of your leg. And we hope not floating free in your bloodstream. But should a fracture occur, then they'll break out and start rampaging through your leg and your body like armed terrorists seeking to destroy and kill.

"So in case of a fracture, the only safe course would be to remove the leg that contains the offending cells, and pray to God that we got most of them before they escaped."

Amy began to tremble. Duncan placed his warm hand on her shoulder.

72

"I said that would happen only if there had been a fracture. So, for the future, and especially while you're having chemo, I will have to insist that you wear a leg brace. We want to take no chances that you might suffer a fracture, even without strenuous activity."

"A brace? Like a cripple?" Amy asked.

Walter Duncan corrected her. "A brace, like a young woman with a dangerous condition that we want to cure."

"Would I have to wear it all the time?"

"Yes."

"You mean even those days when I can go to school?"

"Yes. At those times when you can go to school you will have to wear it."

"Then I won't go! I don't want them to see me like that!"

"Amy, I've already called Hans Metterling down in our Surgical Appliance Department. He's waiting to see you. And I've talked to Dr. Bristol. She said, instead of Monday your chemo will begin on Wednesday."

Hans Metterling's workplace in the basement of the hospital seemed to be a disorderly jumble of parts and pieces of a shiny metal called titanium. There were vises and clamps in which some of those pieces were in various states of preparation. Sketches lined the walls. Several fully completed prostheses which, but for their color and finely polished surfaces, could have been skeletal parts of human legs, were hung alongside the sketches on which they were based. In all this seeming disorder, an old man worked with perfect confidence, knowing where each and every tool and instrument was, and the state of each apparatus.

To Amy it seemed an overwhelming and haphazard sight. It made her fearful that the old man was not to be trusted with anything as vital as the brace on which Dr. Duncan had put so much importance.

Metterling gestured toward her to be seated. He did not attend to her at once, but concentrated on filing down to almost imperceptible fineness the metal part on which he had been working. He examined it closely, studied the sketch, applied three

73

more light touches of the microscopically fine-toothed file. He examined the object once more and seemed satisfied.

Finally he turned to Amy, who sat tensely awaiting his inspection. Instead of directing himself to her, he seemed to be disturbed by an afterthought, went back to the highly machined part and gave it two more gentle strokes with his file.

"Ah," he said, satisfied that it had been honed to the degree of perfection that he sought. "*Und* now"—he turned back to Amy—"Dr. Duncan has told me about you." His accented words seemed a rebuke. "A young girl, very pretty young girl, running around on a tennis court, trying like the devil to break her leg. Vell, ve are not going to let that happen. How do you like that, young lady?"

He peered at her over the high-intensity lenses he wore when he worked.

"Say, you really are beautiful, like Dr. Duncan said. Vell, for pretty girls old Hans makes a very pretty leg brace." He smiled. "If not exactly pretty, at least it vill be much nicer than we used to make. In the olden days—isn't that what you young ones call ten years ago?—in the olden days braces were made from heavy steel, leather. Nowadays, thanks for the space program, we have all new kinds of metals. Lighter. Better. Like this stuff here. See that?"

He lifted a long, slender metallic object built to replace the tibia of a patient. He brandished it to illustrate how light it was.

"Light as a feather," the old craftsman said. "The young man who gets this will never feel it any different from his own leg bone. He won't even know it's there. Marvelous how things progress in this world. Like you . . ." He looked at Amy. "We are going to make you a brace that will also be light as a feather. You like that, young lady?"

Amy tried to nod, but could not.

"I know, I know." He went on. "You are thinking, vat vill my friends say? A young girl like you, valking around with a leg brace. Vell, two things you can do. You can tell them you don't give a damn vat they think. Or else you can wear slacks and they

74

vill never know. Myself, I would wear the slacks. Now . . ."

He gently took her right foot, extended her leg and studied it. Then he began to mumble to himself, making what seemed hieroglyphic notes on an old pad on his worktable. Using a tape measure and calipers, he noted the circumference of her leg at various points, the length, the distance from knee to ankle, from knee to mid-thigh. It seemed to Amy that he had jotted down hundreds of figures, and all the while mumbling to himself in his own language, which was the German spoken in certain cantons of Switzerland.

As Amy became more tense, the old man said, "Ve come for a fitting in four days, no?"

"Yes, yes, of course," the young girl agreed.

"*Gut!*" he said, making one last note on his pad. He tugged on the untidy end of his white mustache as he studied his figures. While he did so, he took the moment to observe, "You know, young lady, I bet you think you are the only one. The only young girl or boy with your kind of trouble. Vell, if you look around here, you vill see all these . . . these parts which I have made . . . mostly for young people. Like you, fifteen, sixteen, some even younger and some older. Some much older. And I think to myself, between us, Dr. Duncan and me, ve give that old bastard cancer a good thumb in the eye. Ve say, ve are going to snatch avay from him people he used to take for granted. Duncan, he saves them, and old Hans, he makes them valk again. So don't you be afraid, little lady. That Valter Duncan, he does vonders. And I . . . I help out a little."

The old man smiled, staring at her over his glasses, to reveal the twinkle in his watery blue eyes.

"Ve come back in four days, no?"

"Yes, yes, Mr. Metterling."

"Hans . . ." He corrected. "Hans."

She left feeling greatly relieved and much encouraged.

6

AMY Bedford lay in her hospital bed. Her nervous fingers played with the hem of the sheet that covered her slender body. She stared at her mother, who stood at the foot of the bed, trying to smile encouragingly. Amy smiled back. For she felt that if she did not, her mother would soon begin to cry. Three times during the weekend Amy had discovered her mother in tears when she thought she was alone.

"You're going to be fine . . . fine," her mother kept repeating. "Before you know it, you'll be playing tennis again. Swede told me so. Said he'd talked with Dr. Duncan and Dr. Rosen, and they said you were going to be fine."

Amy kept nodding, though inside she was thinking, *Please, God, make her leave. Can't you see she can't take it? She doesn't know what to say. She keeps making up things. Swede never said that.*

To Amy's relief, Dr. Bristol entered, followed by a nurse who carried a tray of medications and hypodermics.

"Mrs. Bedford, please?" Dr. Bristol dismissed her.

Marion Bedford nodded, again trying to smile. "I'll be waiting outside, Amy, darling."

"There's no need," Dr. Bristol said. "She won't be wanting visitors for a while."

"I'll . . . I'll be in the waiting room down the hall. If she wants me at any time, just call me."

76

* * *

Dr. Bristol was filling the large hypodermic with a colorless fluid.

"Amy, this is the stuff. Methotrexate. Before we're through you'll hate that word. It will do some very distasteful things to you. Pain. Nausea. Vomiting. But remember, all the while that's going on this stuff is fighting those cancer cells. We have to shrink that tumor so that Dr. Duncan can save your leg. That's the important thing: *We are going to shrink that tumor!*"

She tightened a length of thin tan rubber tubing around Amy's bicep until a vein on the inner side of her arm stood out. She washed the area with an alcohol swab to sterilize it. She lifted the syringe, eased the needle into Amy's vein and felt the girl stiffen against the slight pain. Slowly she injected the powerful fluid into her.

"There we are. First treatment," Dr. Bristol said. "There'll be nurses available. . . . Just press that button. And don't hesitate to use it. We know what you'll be going through. So don't be ashamed to call for help. Meantime, you can read. Listen to the radio. Or some tapes. Even watch television."

"I brought some books," Amy said. "I don't want to fall too far behind on my schoolwork."

"Good idea, Amy. Anything I can do?"

Amy hesitated before saying, "Yes. Please, please send my mother home." Dr. Bristol's instinctive resistance made Amy explain: "I'd like to have her here. I'd rather not be alone. But it's too much for her. Too much."

"Amy, let her stay," Dr. Bristol suggested.

"She feels so helpless, she makes up things to say. Trying to give me courage. And it doesn't . . . it just doesn't."

"I can only suggest that she go. I can't force her," Dr. Bristol said.

"Then do that, please," Amy pleaded.

In the late afternoon, some hours after Amy had received a second injection of methotrexate, she began to feel the first waves of nausea. They started in her stomach and rose up until a fire was burning in her throat. She reached for the buzzer. But as she pressed it the feeling overcame her and the bitter greenish stuff began to pour from her mouth, flooding over the tidy white sheet and down her hospital gown.

She tried to stifle the rest of it but could not. She began to cry as she wiped her lips with her hands. A nurse came racing into the room.

"Nurse—nurse—" Amy began to say, but the words were drowned in another eruption of viscous, lumpy green ooze. The nurse held a stainless-steel basin to her lips, embracing the girl with her free arm.

"It's all right, Amy, all right," she murmured. "This is par for the course. So don't be afraid. And don't be embarrassed."

The first siege was over. Perspiring and breathless, Amy lay back in her soiled gown, pushing away from her the damp sheet and blanket.

"We'll get you into some clean things, and you'll feel better."

The nurse left quickly. Before she returned with fresh bed linens, Amy heard her door open quietly, almost apologetically.

"Amy," her mother ventured.

"Gee, Mom, not now . . . I'm a mess."

"I know. The nurse told me. Is there anything *I* can do? Darling?"

"The nurse is going to clean me up."

The nurse was back. "Out of bed, Amy," she said briskly, but there was no note of rebuke in her voice. Once the bed was free the woman quickly stripped it and remade it with fresh linen and a clean white blanket that had the honest smell of recent laundering about it. She shook out a fresh gown. "Out of that one, Amy." She sponged down the girl with a damp cloth, held out the gown and Amy slipped into it. "Now, back into bed."

The nurse placed another pillow behind her head and said, "There. Good as new, aren't we?"

"Until it happens again," Amy said.

"When it does, use this basin. And whatever you do, don't feel embarrassed. You're doing just fine." She turned to Marion Bedford, inviting her to leave. "Mrs. Bedford . . ."

"No, please," Amy interjected, "I . . . I want her to stay."

"Of course," the nurse said, surprised since she had been carrying out Dr. Bristol's orders.

The door hushed closed again. Marion Bedford stood at the foot of her daughter's bed, staring at her through blue eyes that betrayed what she had been doing in the hours she had sat out in the waiting room. She strained to observe her daughter, to see if she could detect and anticipate the next wave of nausea. At the same time she tried to appear diffident and unconcerned so as not to arouse her daughter's resentment.

In a while Amy began to feel that evil stirring in her stomach. The burning in her throat started. Her lips began to respond.

"Mama!" she cried.

Marion Bedford lunged for the steel basin, held it to her daughter's mouth and embraced her quivering body as the girl retched again. Amy was gasping and retching at the same time as her stomach felt it was being torn up by its roots.

The spasm gradually passed. She had sweat through her fresh gown. She was breathing hard. But for the present it was over. Her mother turned to set aside the basin.

"Mama?" the girl said softly.

"Yes, dear?"

"Hold me, Mama, hold me for a little while?"

"Of course, baby, of course."

There had been several changes of gowns, but no need to change bed linens. Between them, Amy and her mother had mastered the problem until it became a routine, an undesirable routine, but at least manageable. Between times, Amy was able to lapse into snatches of sleep. Her mother watched, occasionally wiping away the perspiration from her daughter's brow and cheeks.

When Amy woke the last time, it was dark out.

"Is it night? What are you still doing here, Mama?"

"It's only past six. And Dad's on his way. He's going to pick me up."

"Oh. Good!"

"You need to have your dinner."

"I don't feel like eating," Amy protested.

"Dr. Bristol was by when you were asleep. She said you should eat."

"It won't stay down," Amy argued.

"She said you'd say that. So she said to try anyhow. I'll buzz for Mrs. Sanchez."

"Is that the nurse's name?"

"Yes, Mrs. Sanchez. And did you know she has two daughters and a son? Her son is your age."

Mrs. Sanchez had placed the tray on the moving table, pushed it within Amy's reach and raised the upper section of the bed so Amy was in position to eat.

"Okay, now, go to it!" she ordered.

Amy surveyed the bland foods that had been ordered for her. A tiny salad. White meat of chicken. Baked potato. And melba toast.

"Yuck," she said.

"We called Burger King," Mrs. Sanchez said. "They were all out of Whoppers and double cheeseburgers." She smiled. "Give it a try, Amy. You need the nourishment. Please?" She turned to Mrs. Bedford. "Make sure she eats."

Amy had tried. The food was tasteless in her mouth. But she realized now why it was all so bland. Any spice at all would start the unhappy process all over again. She had eaten as much as she could, which was little enough. She was still staring at it when the door eased open. Her father peeked in, furtively, almost as if he expected to be ordered out.

"Daddy—" she said.

He embraced her with his right arm, for in his left arm he held a package. From its shape it contained a carton, its weight told her it was something substantial.

"I had my secretary scour the town for it, darling. Wait till you

80

see it." He started to unwrap it carefully. But when the procedure took too much time, he ripped open the carton impatiently. He produced a small black object, somewhat bigger than a portable radio. "How's that?" he asked.

"What is it?" Amy asked.

"Your own private television set. See the size of that small screen. You can watch television from any position you're in. You don't have to lie on your back and stare up at that set on the wall. You can lie on your side, face the wall, anything. And it gets great reception. Here, let me show you!"

He undid the tape that bound the cord and plugged the cord into the wall socket. He pressed the *on* button, waited for the screen to light up. Finally it did. He switched from channel to channel as a salesman would to demonstrate the quality of the reception. Unfortunately no one channel produced an acceptable picture. He was enormously disappointed.

"I'll . . . I'll take it down to the office. Fritch is great with anything mechanical. He keeps our computers functioning all the time. He'll figure out what's wrong."

Then he changed the subject. "Well, how did it go today, darlin'? Mom told me you had some rough moments. But you look fine . . . fine."

Amy tried to smile, thinking, *What if there were no such word as* fine*? Most people would be struck dumb. And you can always tell when they're not being truthful. They always say "fine." . . . Then, if they're really lying they add another "fine." But at least he's trying. He's had fifteen years to learn how to be a father. And he's still only trying.*

To ease his discomfort over the failure of his gift, she said, "It's not as bad as people said it would be. Is it, Mom?"

He noticed the dishes on the tray. "You didn't eat very much, darlin'." He examined the food. "Hospital food. No wonder. Listen, I'll order some decent food in for you. Name it and you got it."

The phrase was familiar to Amy. She had heard her father use it on the phone many times when customers he dealt with reached

81

him at home on some emergency. Whatever the customer wanted, Ed Bedford was quick to promise, "Name it and you got it." Then he usually had to hang up and ring his production foreman: "Get the hell down to the plant and start producing."

He was using the same words and the same reassuring air on her. *Poor Daddy, doesn't he know any other way to deal with people?*

To relieve him of his promise, Amy said, "It's really good food. Tastes better than it looks. I like it."

At the same time she kept praying silently, *Please, make him go before I have another attack of nausea. I don't know if he could stand it.*

Dr. Bristol came to her rescue when she entered briskly, dressed in street clothes, evidently on her way home.

"How did we do today, Amy?" she asked, then realized there was a fourth person in the room. "Mr. Bedford? Dr. Bristol."

"Howdy, Doctor," Bedford said. "How's it going with our little girl?"

"Based on what I saw and heard today, I'd say she is doing very nicely. Gets her medication when she should. Reacts when she should. And the way we expect. So we think if it continues this way, we are going to shrink that tumor down to size. Yes, I'd say our Amy is doing very well."

"Fine," Ed Bedford said. "Fine. . . ."

"Now, if I can suggest, I think she might want a little time to herself. Sort of get prepared for a night's sleep. What do you think, Amy?"

"Yes, yes, I'd like that."

Ed Bedford kissed his daughter, gathered up his gift, the papers and the carton it came in and started for the door. "I'll get this fixed for you, darlin'," he said.

Marion Bedford kissed her daughter and followed after him.

Once they were gone, Dr. Bristol said, "What was that?"

"My own private, personal television set."

"Does it get channels the others don't?"

"No. My father's not good at picking out gifts for girls. His secretary usually does it for him. She must have run out of ideas."

"Well, he tried. That's the important thing." Dr. Bristol consoled as she tidied up Amy's bed and pushed away the rolling tray.

"You didn't eat much," she said. "It's natural not to want food now. But make an effort. Whatever nourishment you can gain from it is worth it. You don't have much weight to give away. If you were soft and chubby instead of lean and athletic, you could afford it. So do try."

She started for the door, but Amy called to her, "Doctor—" Bristol turned back. "Yes, dear?"

Amy hesitated before asking. "When will we know whether . . . well, whether all this was worth . . . ?"

Before Dr. Bristol could answer, she felt the door open behind her. She half-turned to find Walter Duncan entering the room.

"How's our patient doing, Rita?"

"She's on target," Dr. Bristol assured him.

"Good."

"She was about to ask me something that you might be better qualified to answer," Dr. Bristol said. "Amy?"

The girl hesitated, then asked, "When will we know if, after all this . . . the chemo . . . the nausea, the barfing . . . when will we know if it was worth it?"

"You mean when will we know if it worked?" Walt asked, stating her fear more directly.

"Yes," she admitted.

"Six weeks, seven, eight at the most before we have a good indication if it's working. But don't worry about that now. Just follow the routine Dr. Bristol's laid out—"

Before he could finish, the girl burst out, "If it comes to a time when you have to . . . to take my leg . . . let me die!"

"Amy!" he rebuked, more strongly than he had intended.

"No, I mean it!" the girl insisted. "You see, I don't know what he'd do. I couldn't stand the look in his eyes."

"Whose eyes?" Walt asked.

"My . . . father's."

Walt glanced at Rita Bristol. Then moved closer to the bed.

"Amy, dear, listen to me. I'm a father, too. I have a little girl. Not as old as you. But I know how fathers feel. No matter what happens, he's always going to love you. And want you to live the best kind of life you can."

"You don't understand," the girl protested. "He has never got used to having a daughter. He wanted a son. He wanted someone to play football. And grow up to go to Harvard Business School. And take over his business one day."

Walt laughed. "Amy, women do that now. Go to business school. Take over businesses. Sometimes not even their father's businesses."

"He wanted a son," she insisted. "That's why I took up tennis. To make him proud. It got his attention," she confessed. "He just is not equipped to be the father of a girl."

"Every man wants daughters. They're the lovable, cuddly ones. The kind you can buy all sorts of fancy things for. Frilly dresses. Their first nightgowns once they get out of Doctor Dentons, and pajamas. I've never met a man who didn't want daughters."

"You have, you just didn't know it," Amy refuted. "Now, if something happens . . . and you know what that something is . . . he won't want a daughter, not a one-legged daughter."

"Amy . . . Amy, come now," Walter Duncan said.

But the girl turned away from him to hide her tears. Walt reached out to draw her to him, he embraced her, held her and soothed. "Amy, I gave you my word. One year of your life, and I'll cure you."

The Bedfords had left the hospital and were headed home. On most other nights Ed Bedford would not have been going home so early. For he always appreciated that hour or two of solitude after everyone else had left the office, when he could work without the interruptions that plagued his days. No phone calls. No executives knocking on his door or trapping him in the hallway to say, "Mr. Bedford, if you've got a minute, I have a problem."

His days were filled with such interruptions. It was only in the early morning, or after hours at night, that he was able to do the work, make the plans, decide on personnel choices, new products, new markets, that had built his business from a one-plant producer of machine tools to a company with plants in four states and customers in more than eighteen countries.

But tonight he had no tolerance for business problems. He drove himself and his wife home in his big costly Cadillac, the super-luxury model of which only a limited number were being produced this year. No foreign car for him. Support American industry was his creed. It had been his father's creed before him, when the old man was content to run his one factory without dreams of expanding into other states and other countries.

Ed Bedford had his own dreams and drives. Expand, expand, expand, both markets and production. But keep control. Always keep control. Never go public. Those of his contemporaries whose ambitions had been to build their businesses only large enough to go public with the stock had all been swallowed up by conglomerates and takeovers. They were now useless time-wasting has-beens with nothing to do but follow the sun and play golf. Nobody, nobody on earth would take over Ed Bedford and Bedford Industries. His stock was held by himself, his wife, Marion, who sat quietly beside him now, and the shares held in trust for Amy.

The one regret in his life was that he had no son to whom to pass on the business.

Of course, these days, women were taking a more important role in business life. In his business travels he was meeting more and more female executives. Ed was also receiving more employment applications from female graduates of business schools, the best business schools: Harvard, Wharton in Philadelphia, New York University. By the time Amy was ready, seven or eight years from now, a woman might be able to do it.

He had finally accepted that alternative. Out of necessity, not choice. Years before, the doctors had felt that, considering the complications she had experienced giving birth to Amy, Marion had better not risk another pregnancy. So a son, a son of his own, was out of the question. In the past they had discussed adopting a baby boy. But Ed Bedford knew that he would be satisfied with nothing less than his own. For a man who lived, worked and succeeded in the world of modern business, he still clung to certain archaic concepts.

Tonight, as he drove home from the hospital, he thought grimly, now even the alternative of Amy's taking over the business might be only a delusion.

Despite all the words of encouragement from those doctors, that older man—was Rosen his name?—and the younger one, Duncan, despite anything they said, Ed Bedford knew the score.

He had pursued the facts in every city he had visited since the day of Amy's original diagnosis. Between visiting his plants, or making calls on his more important customers, he personally covered a good part of the country, especially the big cities, where there were famous medical centers. Los Angeles, Pittsburgh, Chicago, New York, Cleveland. There the best of medicine, the finest of doctors and surgeons, the most modern medical equipment were to be found.

In each of those cities Ed Bedford would disappear for two or three hours to purchase the consultation time and the expertise of the best cancer specialists in the nation. He would ask questions, hard questions. He would get answers, hard answers, always cautiously circumscribed by the fact that those doctors had not examined the patient or seen her X rays and scans. What Ed Bedford insisted on knowing was, what were the best and most optimistic expectations in such cases, and the worst?

He had learned several things. First, that the plan of treatment designed by that younger doctor, Duncan, was approved by all the experts he had consulted. Several of them knew Duncan. Had shared platforms with him at medical seminars. So there was no denying Duncan's qualifications to care for Amy Bedford.

But Ed Bedford had also learned of the dangers. The realities. A leg fracture could prove fatal. Chemo might fail to produce the desired result. Surgery, even if successful, was not a cure.

Even amputation was not necessarily a cure. Amy's was an aggressive disease. Could travel to other parts of her body, not only to her lungs.

As with any problem or deal he faced, Ed Bedford insisted on knowing his potential losses as well as his possible gains. It was the only way a man could make intelligent decisions.

Except, he knew now, in this situation where his daughter's life was involved, no decision that he could make was important. It was all in the hands of the doctors. And factors over which none of them had any control.

They were approaching the house. Ed Bedford tried to rid himself of all his depressing thoughts. Much as he needed her comfort, he could not add to Marion's burdens by sharing them with her. She was taking this badly enough.

They ate dinner in silence. Several of Ed's attempts at conversation met with brief answers that discouraged him. He tried to catch furtive glimpses of Marion, who sat across the table from him, going through the motions of eating, but actually ingesting very little.

It stirred memories, unhappy memories, of the days after she had been apprised by her gynecologist that she must not entertain the idea of having a second child. She had lapsed into that same silent, detached attitude she was exhibiting now. She had resisted eating, had lost weight, and it had been necessary for her to seek psychiatric help to ward off a total breakdown.

God, he thought, *not again. Not now of all times. Amy needs her. I need her.*

With no appetite, no desire for food, he continued to eat, though chewing seemed difficult, almost impossible. Suddenly she broke the silence.

"It's our fault," she said.

"Our fault?" he asked, puzzled. "What?"

"Amy" was all she said.

"Amy? Amy . . . our fault?"

"We never should have encouraged her."

"What are you talking about?" he said, putting aside his fork and looking toward her. "Marion?"

"Tennis! Tennis!" She exploded intolerantly.

"What does tennis have to do with it?"

"We let her wear herself out. Too much practice. Too many matches. Just ran herself down, wore herself out."

"That has nothing to do with—" he started to say.

But she interrupted. "Yes, it does!"

He began to fear that she was farther along toward a breakdown than he had realized.

She continued. "I was reading in that magazine, *Women's* something or other. . . . It was in the bookshop in the mall. It said in there that nowadays doctors are coming to believe more and more that it happens when the immune system breaks down or gets too weak to fight back. And we let that happen. We let it happen. . . ."

Her voice trailed off as she began to weep. He went to her, lifted her out of her chair, embraced her. As he held her and felt her body spasms, he tried to soothe her.

"Mare, darling, please. . . . I've talked to the best specialists in the country. No one knows what causes it. They all agree with Dr. Duncan. He's doing the right thing. That means we're doing the right thing. So you must stop feeling guilty. We didn't cause it. We couldn't have prevented it. We are doing all we can. All we can."

Because he felt her body still trembling so pitifully in his embrace, he felt compelled to stretch the hard truth of his discoveries. "Some of those doctors I talked to . . . most of them . . . said she has a great chance to beat this thing. A great chance. I can't tell you all the cases they told me about where they got cures. One hundred percent cures. Without amputation, too. What we have to do now is give her all our support. If we believe, she'll believe. And if she believes, she'll make it. Those doctors told me so. All of them. Okay?"

She managed to nod.

"Then show me a smile."

He raised her face to his. She smiled through her tears.

"That's better. That's much better," he said. "Now I'll help you clear the table."

"No, don't bother. I can do it. And you're probably tired. Go on into the den. Read. Or watch television."

He was relieved to go. He went into the dark den. Did not trouble to turn on the light. But sat in his high-backed wing chair and started to weep. He felt alone. Very much alone. By lying to his wife about his discoveries he had cut himself off from the only ally on whom he could rely in this time of helpless despair. He would have to pretend not only before Amy, but now before his wife as well.

It was past midnight. Amy Bedford woke from one of the brief snatches of sleep she had been able to manage during a night of more nausea, more retching. She tried to console herself by believing that if the chemo was inflicting so much havoc on her, it must be doing equally terrible things to those damned cancer cells.

She pressed her leg to see if she could tell in some way whether that thing had started to shrink. Unable to use the proper designation, she referred to it as *that thing*. Her leg felt the same. Her pain was still there.

She prayed silently, *Get smaller. Shrink. Please, God, make it smaller so Dr. Duncan can operate, can take it out. Please!*

She lay awake a long time. Gently, she rubbed her leg. *Two whole months of this,* she thought. *Will I be able to stand two whole months . . . ?*

She realized, *I have to stand it. I must. Because if I can't, it will mean amputation. No more tennis. No more dating. What boy would want to go out with me after that? Not even Brent. And that means no marriage, no children. Nothing. I'd rather be dead. Dead!*

Eventually, she fell asleep once more.

When she woke again, it was dawn. The first day, the first night were over.

* * *

"Don't you X-ray me now?" Amy asked Dr. Duncan as he dropped by to see her before she left the hospital.

He smiled. "Amy, we're only at the beginning. The chemo needs time to work. We'll X-ray you in time. Meanwhile, we'll be checking your blood and urine. Every day. On days that you go to school, stop by here on your way."

"Why do you have to check that every day?" her mother asked, a new sense of apprehension in her voice.

"To make sure she's tolerating the chemo. Too high an acid content in her urine could lead to complications. Renal failure. We can do without that right now."

Mrs. Bedford nodded, but Walt could detect yet another sign of tension in the woman's eyes. *Damn it,* he thought, *hold on, woman. We're only at the start of this. Your daughter's going to need you, need you a lot, before this is over.*

"Now you just take Amy home. Let her rest for the next two days. This stuff knocks you out before you're used to it."

"But you said school. . . ." Amy protested.

"These first two days just stay home. Right now, you're probably a little weaker than you think. Know what I would do? Call my teachers, ask for the assignments, keep up. So when you go back, you won't be behind the others."

"I'll do that. . . ." Her mother volunteered eagerly.

"Amy?" Walt asked.

"I can do it, Mom," the girl said. She was brushing her long blond hair, which fell gracefully to her shoulders. If she were still playing tennis, she would have tied it back with a ribbon. Now she allowed it to hang loose.

She turned from the mirror, trying to smile. Walt knew the signs, the patient trying to appear stronger in the doctor's eyes as if to seduce him into believing she could be cured, would be cured.

"Mom?" she said, ready to go.

"Amy, before you go," Walt Duncan said, "a few reminders. By now you know about the stomach upsets. But there can be mouth sores. Inside your mouth. On your lips. Your tongue. They

90

may be painful. So you'll be tempted not to eat. Use a warm-water-and-baking-soda rinse to ease them. But do eat. I want a strong girl when I operate. Deal?"

"Deal," Amy said, holding out her hand.

She smiled at him again. He thought, *I hope ten months from now, a year from now, she'll still be smiling. Considering the possible complications, that she'll even be alive to smile.*

7

S EVEN weeks had gone by. Amy Bedford had appeared at the hospital periodically for her infusions of chemotherapy. The treatment had advanced beyond methotrexate. Dr. Bristol had put Amy on vincristine, a more powerful drug. Every step in her treatment was aimed at forcing that tumor to shrink, so that surgery was possible.

Amy had borne up well, enduring all the suffering inherent in the treatment, reporting to the hospital every day to have her blood and urine tested. She attended school only on those days she felt able, though both she and her teachers had resigned themselves to the fact that she could no longer keep up with her classmates. But she was determined not to fall too far behind.

Always, secretly, she counted the days. She marked them off on a calendar that she kept hidden in her desk drawer. If what the doctors had said was true, very soon they would take those crucial bone scans and X rays that would reveal whether or not the damned thing had shrunk.

Because if it hadn't—and the most recent scan did not indicate that it had—then . . . She could not bring herself to speak the word, or even acknowledge it silently.

Every day she would pose before the mirror, turn her leg this way and that to see if she could determine some change. It did look thinner. Perhaps that meant the thing was shrinking. But then, all of her was thinner. She had lost weight. In her legs, her arms, her face, her young breasts. She had never used the word *gaunt* in referring to anyone she knew. But she knew that she was now *gaunt*.

She no longer weighed herself on her mother's bathroom scale. It frightened her. Antinausea drugs had no salutory effect, so she suffered days when she was sure that five times more came up than she had eaten. With all that, losing weight was inevitable. Those sores that Dr. Bristol had warned about didn't make eating any easier. Some days she could barely abide the milk shakes her mother forced on her.

She had only one consolation: Soon it would be over. . . . Soon. . . . She dared not ask, then what? There were things worse than chemo. And no doctor had promised her that the chemo would stop if they did amputate.

The night before her crucial CAT scan, Amy slept even more restlessly than usual. She woke abruptly, distressed that the bitter burning warning of nausea was returning once more. She lay still. The feeling subsided. She had got so used to the constant repetition of nausea followed by retching that any hint of stomach uneasiness threatened to begin the tormenting cycle all over again.

She lay on her back, staring up at the ceiling of her room. The light and shadow of a streetlamp filtering through the birch trees outside her window played across the ceiling in response to the night breeze. It was a sight she had witnessed many times in her young life. Tonight it seemed quite different. Nothing else had changed, only herself. Yet nothing was the same anymore. Not eating, not sleeping, not going to school, not talking to her friends on the phone for hours on end.

Once you've heard that word *cancer*, that devastating word, nothing can ever be the same again. Yes, the doctors did say it could be cured. They had outlined a very complicated way of treating it. She was already into the first difficult part of it. But there were no guarantees. Not even that very gentle Dr. Duncan would give her any more than a promise to do his best. The most he said was that it could work. She could walk pain-free again. Might resume a normal life. But there was never an all-out promise. *Would, could, might, may* were the words.

Exhausted, sleepy yet sleepless, she turned on her side. The doctors had explained that, too. Chemo could knock you out, make you feel real spaced out for days after you had it. So sleep was important.

As she turned, she allowed her right arm to fall easily to the far side of her pillow. Her hand felt something that made her start. She reached across and turned on the light. She saw them, loose strands of her blond hair across the pink pillow. What she had been warned about had begun. A gush of tears came to her blue eyes. She hid her face in her hands.

After some minutes of weeping, she determined to face the worst of it. She threw back her blanket. She sat on the side of the bed before daring to rise to her feet and confront herself in the mirror. Finally, she was ready.

She stared into the mirror. It was not as bad as she had feared. Her blond hair, usually loose and flowing, seemed as thick and healthy as always. She felt relieved, for she had had quite frightening fantasies of what she would look like with sparse, straggling hair. Or no hair at all.

She was tempted to tug at some of the strands to see if they would come loose in her hand. She decided not to risk it. Instead, she picked up her hairbrush and started to give herself a vigorous brushing, intending to stimulate the blood supply, nourish her hair and overcome the effects of the chemo.

She continued until the brush felt strange in her hand. She put it down to flex her fingers. They felt tingly, then numb. She picked up the brush once more, exerting special effort, determined to use it with force. She raised it to her head. Suddenly her fingers failed to respond. She lost her grip. The brush dropped noisily to the dressing table, sliding off onto the carpet.

Terrified, she cried out, "Mom! Mom!" She ran from the room.

She burst into her parents' bedroom, crying, "Mommy, Mommy, I'm paralyzed. Paralyzed!"

Startled, Marion and Ed Bedford woke suddenly from exhausted, uneasy sleep. Marion bolted from the bed, embraced her sobbing daughter, trying to soothe her. "Baby, darling, now calm down. And tell me."

Her father stood off watching, so shocked and helpless that he could only stare at his weeping daughter.

"The brush . . . the hairbrush . . . I couldn't hold it, it just fell," Amy said through her sobs. "I can't hold anything now. I'm paralyzed."

"Amy! Let me see your hand!" her mother said.

Amy held out her right hand.

"Move your fingers."

The girl opened and closed her hand.

"There! See! You are not paralyzed," her mother said, trying to sound calm and convincing despite her own fears.

"But it tingles, and I can't hold anything."

Emboldened by his wife's demonstration, Ed Bedford picked up his own hairbrush and held it out. "Here, darling. Take this."

Amy stared at the brush, reached for it. When her fingers had enveloped it, Ed Bedford released it. For a moment his daughter held it, but then her numbed fingers lost their grip. The brush dropped to the floor.

"See, I told you. I told you!" she exclaimed, weeping once more.

"I'll call Dr. Duncan!" her father said.

"Ed! Ed! Not at this time of night," his wife forbade.

"If my daughter is in trouble, I don't give a damn what time of night it is. Besides, I'm paying him, ain't I?"

He reached for the bedside phone, dialed Information. Declaring it was a medical emergency, he was given the Duncans' private home number.

The phone alongside the Duncans' bed broke the night silence. Walter Duncan instinctively turned in its direction thinking Emergency Receiving or the Trauma Unit needed immediate expert advice or the intercession of a skilled surgeon.

He lifted the phone. "Duncan," he announced.

"Dr. Duncan"—Ed Bedford assailed him—"my daughter is in trouble. Big trouble."

"Who is this?"

"Bedford. Ed Bedford."

Walt Duncan sat up so suddenly that, though half-asleep, Emily turned to him. "Walt?"

"Shh . . ." He quieted her. "Now, Mr. Bedford, exactly what kind of trouble is Amy in?"

"Her hands. She can't hold anything. . . ." Bedford explained.

"Put her on the phone!" Walt ordered. He waited until he heard Amy sobbing. She was on the phone but could not talk. "Amy, Amy, can you hear me?"

"Uh-huh," she managed through her tears.

"Just listen to me, dear. And answer yes or no. Do you have any feeling in your fingertips?"

"Uh-huh."

"Is it a tingling?"

"Some."

"And do they feel numb other times?"

"Yes."

"Listen closely, Amy. You are having what we call neural toxicity. You may seem to lose function at times, but you are not paralyzed. There's no chance that you will be. The drug, vincristine, which Dr. Bristol had to give you, sometimes produces such aftereffects. But it's just a passing phase. Now, do something for me."

"Yes?"

"Are you standing up now?"

"No, Doctor," she said, no longer weeping.

"Stand up. Put down the phone. Walk back and forth across the room. Then come back," he ordered. He waited.

"I did it, Doctor."

"How did it feel? The same as always?"

96

"Not—not exactly."

"Then come in to see me tomorrow. Maybe we have to cut down on the dose or cut out the vincristine altogether. Now, you go back to sleep. Don't worry. You won't become paralyzed. The numbness will pass. I promise you."

"Yes, Doctor. I'm sorry we had to wake you, but I was so scared, so scared."

"That's all right, my dear. Anytime you're worried, or have any questions, you call."

"Thanks, Doctor, thanks."

She was about to hang up when her father took the phone from her hands.

"Doctor, you take good care of her, won't you? I mean, anything, anything in the world that would help her, you do it, and I'll pay for it."

"Yes, I understand, Mr. Bedford," Walter Duncan said, thinking, *Why do some people always assume that doctors have secret miracles for sale if the price is right?*

"Anything!" Bedford repeated emphatically.

"Of course," Walter said. "Now put your wife on the phone."

He heard her voice, straining to appear calm. "Yes, Doctor?"

"Mrs. Bedford, I can understand Amy's being extremely tense right now. Anything that happens is going to seem exaggerated in her eyes. After all, this is a crucial test she's facing in the morning. She may not even want to come to the hospital. Some patients refuse at the last moment. They'd rather not know the truth. So, no matter how she feels or what she says, you make sure she's at the Radiology Department in the morning at the appointed time. I want to see those X rays and scans at the end of the day. Make sure she's there!"

Walt sat on the edge of the bed, remembering, a bit late, to hang up the phone. He glanced at the electronic clock in the radio. Five fifty-three. Too early to get up, too late to go back to sleep. Besides, he had to leave for the hospital even earlier this morning. There were crucial matters to attend to. Four cases to be done, starting at six-thirty. Then a meeting of the Tumor Board to discuss the treatment of a number of cancer patients and institute treatment plans for several new cases.

Then, to complicate his life further, the Enright trial was finally in progress and the attorney, Silverstein, had notified Walt that he could be called to testify almost anytime now. And, finally, at the end of this day, Amy Bedford's scans and X rays, which would determine if the weeks of chemo had done what all that suffering was supposed to accomplish. Otherwise, that child's agony would all have been for naught. Having to tell her that she would have to undergo amputation would be even worse for him than actually performing the operation.

With all those thoughts roiling through his mind, he knew even brief sleep was out of the question. He would make up for it, a cold shower would do it.

During his shower he silently rebelled against testifying. It was the right thing to do, but inconvenient. He would never promise to do it again. Except that when the next case of medical injustice or quackery came along, he knew that he would. He could only hope that today the lawyers would not string things out so that he would have to appear again tomorrow.

He had dressed, quietly as possible, and without putting the light on so as not to disturb Emily. It was still dark out when he stopped by Simone's bedroom to kiss her good-bye. He bent close to her. As he was about to kiss her, she opened her sleep-shrouded eyes and because it was dark, she said, "Good night, Daddy," and slipped back into sleep.

He kissed her on the forehead, was about to rise when he sensed a touch of fever in her. He placed his hand lightly on her forehead. She was warm, in the way fever makes smooth youthful skin feel warm. Low fever, he diagnosed. Not alarming in a child. Yet it disturbed him. He must leave a note for Emily.

8

D R. Walter Duncan prepared to study the latest X rays of Patient Bedford, Amy. The room was dark. He slipped three sets of matching X rays into the wall-long viewing glass. He flipped on the light. First, he studied the set of X rays taken on Amy's initial examination.

He examined the second set, taken later but from exactly the same angles as the first set. Then he studied the third set.

He had no need to spend much time on her lung X rays. They were perfectly clear. No metastases evident in any of them. Encouraging sign.

He stared long and hard at the matching films of her leg and thigh. First at the initial set. Then at the second set. Finally the ones taken today.

If her lung X rays being identical was a good sign, the same did not hold true for her other X rays. Unfortunately they were alike, too alike. After two arduous series of treatments with methotrexate and vincristine, he had hoped there would be some clear sign of tumor shrinkage. Unless there was, his options would be nonexistent.

Poor child, he thought, *she's borne the whole difficult treatment with courage and good spirits. And now . . .*

His train of thought was interrupted when the door opened suddenly. Dr. Bristol was there.

"I heard Amy's new set of X rays are ready," the oncologist said.

"They are." Walt pointed to them with no enthusiasm.

Dr. Bristol gave her eyes a moment to adjust to the darkness. She compared the films, one by one, old sets, new sets, old sets, new sets. She did not say anything beyond making a slight discouraged sound.

"What do you think, Rita? Shall we give her another series?"

"It can't do any harm. We might be on the verge of shrinking the damned thing. Be a shame to quit now."

"Can she take it?" Walt asked.

"She's put up with the stomach upsets and the retching. Her mouth has been sore. Very sore. But I think she's still game. If you can delay amputation for three more weeks without endangering her life, I'd say let's go for it," the oncologist said.

"I'll go see her," Walt Duncan concluded.

Amy Bedford and her mother were waiting patiently in her room when Walt Duncan came in. The young girl sat up erect, trying to present an image of health and strength, hoping to discourage the doctor from any thoughts of amputation.

He was well aware of her attempt, even as he realized that this was not the same young patient he had first examined weeks ago. Her pretty face was thinner. There was an uneven red blotch alongside her thin cheek. Her blond hair still hung down freely but could not disguise the fact that it was much sparser than before, a few bald spots were evident on her pink scalp.

Still she stared up into his eyes, asking, begging for some good word, some report that would make all her suffering worthwhile.

"Hi, Amy," Walt said, trying to appear both casual and encouraging. "Dr. Bristol and I, we just had a go at those X rays of yours."

Before he could continue, both mother and daughter spoke at once. "What did you find? It is smaller, isn't it?"

"We . . . we think that we're on the verge," Walt said.

Verge was the only word Amy repeated, but it encompassed all

100

her disappointment, all her suffering, all her shattered hopes.

"We haven't given up, Amy. We'd like to try another series of chemo. Add still another chemical to the methotrexate."

"More chemo," Amy said, her eyes glistening with unshed tears.

"Amy, Amy," Walt Duncan said, taking her hand. "I know what you've been through. I know what another series can mean to you."

"You don't know anything!" The girl exploded in a mixture of anger and tears.

"Amy!" Her mother tried to silence her.

But weeks of suffering and hoping could not be stilled. "You don't know what it's like to look into the mirror in the morning and ask yourself, 'Is this me? Is this really me?' I don't know myself anymore. This isn't my face. This is the face of a patient with my name. But not me. I never looked like this before. I get up in the morning and find my hair on the pillow. Strands of it. Lots of it. I'll be bald soon. Completely bald!"

"Amy, please," her mother begged.

But Walter Duncan gestured her mother to silence.

Tears streaming down her face, the girl continued. "I won't go through any more. I can't. I can't face them. . . ."

"Can't face *who,* Amy?"

"Them. The others. The guys and girls in school," she confessed. "I can't let them see me this way. I can't." She lost control completely and wept freely, her thin body racked with sobbing. "Just let me die . . . just let me die. . . ."

"Amy!" her mother said in a hushed whisper.

Walt shook his head at her mother, indicating, "Let her cry, let her say anything she wants."

Soon, the girl was sobbing less and wiping away her tears with the handkerchief Walt had offered her.

Her first words were, "I bet I look even worse now. I'm a wreck. And it's all your fault!"

"You are not a wreck," Walt denied. "You are a young woman with red eyes, which will look perfectly natural, and their very pretty shade of blue, as soon as you get over this crying jag.

101

Now, what do you mean, you've stopped going to school? I said you could go. Dr. Bristol said you should go."

"Not the way I look!" The girl refused.

"Amy, when I said, 'Give me a year of your life, and I'll cure you,' I did not mean that was the only thing you could do. I meant that, as nearly as possible, you were to live your usual life, with some interruptions for treatment. You are going back to school!"

"Not looking like this I'm not!" she protested. She reached to her blond hair and came away with strands of it in her hand. "Look! There! See!"

"So that's it," Walt said, "that's really what's bugging you. Okay. Just wait here!"

While he was gone, her mother pleaded, "Amy, darling, he's doing his best for you. Please, please don't insult him. He's a very sensitive man. I can tell."

Walt Duncan was back, in his hand a bit of light green fabric which, when he opened it, became a surgeon's cap. He slipped it over Amy's blond hair, inviting her mother's opinion. "How's that? Or is this way better?" he asked, as he raked the cap to the side of her head. "I like that better, don't you, Mrs. Bedford?"

"It does have a flair that way."

He went to the medicine chest in the bathroom, opened the mirrored door so Amy could see herself. "Go on, take a look, Amy!"

The girl ventured toward the mirror, looked at herself and finally conceded, "It doesn't look too yuckie."

"It looks damned good!" Walt Duncan said. While she was staring at herself in the mirror, he continued, "Amy, what do you say? Are you game for another series of chemo? I believe it could do the trick."

She did not reply at once. She was reliving those days and nights in the grip of the medication, feeling her guts being torn out of her when she silently had pleaded, *Take my leg, take my life, only let this torment stop!*

"Amy . . ." Walt Duncan coaxed. "I believe we can still do it."

102

Finally she set her jaw and nodded.

"Good!" the surgeon said. He signaled Marion Bedford that he wanted to see her privately.

"Mrs. Bedford, I don't want your daughter to become a recluse. I do not want her to withdraw from life or become an emotional invalid. I want her back in school. I believe a patient's mental health is vital to her recovery. Now, does she have any special friends who might help?"

"There's one boy, she's not exactly going steady with him or anything, but they're both on the team. Brent Martin."

"Isn't that the young man she was rallying with when she took that bad fall?" Walt recalled.

"Yes, yes, that's the one."

"Ask him to call me," Walt said.

Near the end of the day, having returned from last rounds of his post-op patients and seen two others on whom he would operate in the morning, Walt Duncan pushed open the door to his office to find a stranger in the waiting room.

He was a young man, no more than seventeen. Blond, tall, thin, but with a frame that Walt knew would fill out as he matured.

"Your secretary had to leave. So she said to wait here," the young man explained.

"What's your problem, son? Who referred you?"

"You sent for me."

Puzzled, Walt started to say, "I sent for . . . Oh, you must be Brent Martin."

"That's right. I guess it's to do with Amy, since it was Mrs. Bedford who called me. Is there something you want to know? I mean, about that practice session when she fell? I tried to discourage her from working out. But she was so determined. If you know her at all, you know she's determined."

"Determined?" Walt said. "Come into my office, Brent."

Once the young man was seated alongside Walt's desk, Walt said, "Amy's overdetermined about some things. And not deter-

103

mined enough about others. She has refused to go back to school even on those days when she can."

"We thought she wasn't allowed to."

"She's not only allowed to, I want her to continue her normal life-style insofar as possible. We've got to keep her spirits up. I think you could help."

"Anything you say, Doctor."

"Talk to her. Get her to go back to school. Pick her up in the morning on your way. Anything that will make her feel she has to go to school."

"I could do that," the young man offered.

"It won't be easy on her. Because it, the treatment, isn't easy. There'll be days she'll refuse. Days she'll feel terrible. Weak. Sick to her stomach. She'll be self-conscious about losing her hair. Not looking as good as she did. It's your job to tell her that her hair will come back. Her weight will come back. She'll be a very pretty girl again. In a word, Brent, you have to be a cheerleader."

The young man nodded soberly. Then he asked, "It's the truth, isn't it? I mean about her hair, about her weight coming back?"

"As far as we know, it's the truth."

"Good. Because I wouldn't want to lie to her. Lie to her?" young Brent repeated. "I can't even get to talk to her. Since all this started, she's shut herself away from all her friends."

"Some people do," Walt conceded. "They feel cancer is something to be ashamed of. That they've done something wrong and are being punished. Is there any friend of hers who could change her mind?"

"Swede . . . I think Swede could do it, if anyone can."

"Okay, Brent. Your first assignment, talk to Swede. If you need reinforcement, I'll talk to Dr. Rosen. He and Swede are old tennis partners."

"I'll do my best," Brent promised.

He was headed for the door when Walt suddenly said, "Brent!" The young man turned to face him. Walt tossed a bit of green fabric to him. Brent caught it, opened it, examined it.

"What's this?"

"Surgeon's cap," Walt said, smiling.

"What do I do with it?"

"Convince Amy to go back to school, and I'll show you."

Swede Olafsen arrived at the Bedford home in late afternoon. He rang. Marion Bedford answered the door, her attitude protective, a woman on guard. As soon as she recognized Swede her eyes welled up.

"She won't see you. She won't see anyone," she warned.

"Tell her that I need her help," Swede said.

"Help?" The woman was puzzled, dubious.

"Just tell her Old Swede has a problem and he needs her help. Please? Go up and tell her?"

Mrs. Bedford hesitated, then started up the stairs. Swede waited. He waited a long time. Finally Mrs. Bedford came down.

"It's okay. But please don't stare at her. She's very self-conscious. Times I think she doesn't even want me to see her. She doesn't even like to go to the hospital. Whatever you do, don't ask about that cap she wears. She's losing her hair. Lost most of it, and she's very sensitive."

"Mrs. Bedford, I've been dealing with youngsters for thirty-six years now. I know how sensitive teenagers can be."

He identified Amy's bedroom by the partly opened door and the darkness. He knocked. After a moment came her soft, hesitant voice. "Come in."

He pushed the door open, stared in. In the unlit room with early evening lending more darkness, he made out her form. She was sitting in a chair in a corner of the room, huddled as if from the cold. She was not his girl, not his Amy Bedford, who had the drive and intensity to want to be a champion.

This damned disease has defeated her, he thought.

"Amy—" he began, "I know you're not feeling well. I've heard all about what those drugs do to a person. And I wouldn't bother you now, except I have a problem. With you out for this season, I've got to rely on Carole Wallace as my number one girls' player."

"Yes," Amy said, "I thought so."

"Well, you can tell a girl she's number one, but that's a long way from making her feel like she's number one. Nobody knows that better than you. Unless a girl feels she's the best, she won't play like the best."

"What can I do?" Amy asked.

"I think it would make a difference, a big difference . . . Well, Carole admires you, always has. If you could tell her how good she is, it would help."

"I'll call her if you want," Amy offered.

"You can't tell her how she's doing unless you watch her. You have to be there. You have to see her. Just calling won't do, Amy."

"That would mean I—" She could not bring herself to say it.

"That's right, Amy. To make it real, genuine, you would have to come back to school, wait till practice, spend the afternoon watching and then talk to her."

"Back to school . . . I can't do that."

"Why not?"

"Because," the girl said and seemed to draw back into the darkness even more. "I can't go back like this. I can't ever go back looking like this."

"If I didn't need your help, I wouldn't ask," Swede said. "You know what a state title means to me, to the school. And I've been thinking about retiring. After thirty-six years I feel entitled to it. But I sure would like that title, that trophy in the school gym, before I leave."

She did not respond.

"Amy?"

"I'll . . . I'll think it over" was all she would say.

As the tall white-haired coach turned to leave, Amy called to him, "Swede—"

"Yes, Amy?"

"I know what it means to you. So . . . okay, I'll do it."

Brent Martin waited down the block from the Bedford house. He had been waiting since quarter to seven in the morning. He saw Mr. Bedford's car pull out and start in the direction of the Interstate. Brent continued to wait. Finally he saw the front door open. Amy and her mother came out. There were some words between them. For an uneasy moment it seemed to him that Amy might change her mind and go back in. But finally she started down the walk. He waited until she was on her way in the direction of the school. He left his hiding place and hurried after her.

As he overtook her, he slowed down, trying to make his discovery appear accidental.

"Hi! Amy? That you?"

She half-turned to face him. He was pleased with the way she looked. With the way she wore that surgeon's cap. It sat perched on her head at a jaunty angle, fixed in place with bobby pins. She was thinner, but she was almost as pretty as ever.

"Hey, you look great, Amy!" Brent enthused.

"You think so?"

"I sure do. Love that hat, whatever you call it," he said. "Carry your books?"

"I can do that," she said, holding them tighter against her breasts.

"I only said that because I've read that in the olden days it was the way a young man showed his affection for a girl. By carrying her books to school. I think it's in Mark Twain somewhere. I know I read it. Or else I heard my grandma say that's the way Grandpa came on to her."

"Carry your books?" Amy repeated. "Is that the way they used to do it?"

"Yeah. I guess now it would be 'Carry your stereo?' or 'your portable computer.'" He laughed. She laughed, too. He felt encouraged. It was working. Or seemed to be. But the crucial test lay ahead. The moment when she would have to face them all.

They were a block away from the school. At the school doors Pam Sanford, who had been appointed the lookout, spied them. She entered the building, raced along the corridor, brushing by other students in her haste to get to her first-hour class. She said only, "Okay, guys. They're on the way!" At once everyone dropped into a seat, in anticipation of Amy's arrival. Not a word was said.

They waited what seemed an interminable time.

Amy and Brent entered the building, came down the corridor. The few students racing to beat the bell had little time to stop and stare as Amy passed by.

Finally, Brent and Amy were at the door to their first-hour room. He could sense her withdraw within herself. He reached out, gripped her arm. They both started into the room.

The sight that greeted Amy made tears of relief come to her eyes. Every girl in class was wearing a surgeon's cap, neatly held in place by bobby pins. And they were smiling. One girl cried out an enthusiastic welcome, "Amy!" She started toward Amy to embrace her, and soon all the girls crowded around her. Embracing, kissing, speaking words of welcome and delight at seeing her back among them once more.

As arranged, their teacher, Mr. Hitchins, entered the room late. Pretending his usual pedagogic severity, he said, "Well, now, shall we risk learning something about American history today?" Then he smiled and said, "Amy Bedford, to see if you've kept up with your home assignments, perhaps you would like to explain to us the effect of the Cuban missile crisis on American foreign policy."

Amy Bedford stood beside her desk and began, "Until the Cuban missile crisis, the Monroe Doctrine was the cornerstone of American foreign policy for the Western Hemisphere. . . ."

Hitchins leaned back in his desk chair. Class was under way, as usual. Amy Bedford was prepared, as usual. An important crisis had been met and overcome. The little conspiracy among Walter Duncan, Brent Martin, Swede Olafsen, and Alfred Hitchins had worked out very well. A small victory in a much larger and more desperate battle to save a young life.

It was twenty past four. Every tennis court behind the high school was in use. The members of the team were working hard. Routinely, Swede was pacing behind the backcourts watching, mentally criticizing, approving, encouraging. This time Amy Bedford paced with him. Aided by the brace on her right leg, discreetly concealed by her slacks, she kept pace with Swede, limping only slightly.

They drew close to the court on which Carole Wallace was working out against Ethel Lindquist, who had moved up to number two on the girls' squad once Amy had withdrawn. Amy watched both girls hit with good length and power. Swede always told her that in his youth young women didn't play tennis like that.

Amy concentrated on Carole Wallace's game. Carole was a tall girl, dark-haired, with powerful shoulders and arms that made her service her most deadly weapon. Unfortunately, once an opponent solved the pace of her serve, Carole was not as strong with her ground strokes. Amy could see what Swede was driving at.

Practice was over. The girls came off the court. They both greeted Amy with smiles and hugs.

"Good to see you back, Amy," Carole said. "But I'm afraid we're not up to your brand of tennis."

"You're not playing me, Carole. You're going to play number one against Eve Sampson, from Northside. And if you get by her, you'll play against Sue Axelrod of Wilson, and after Sue you have only Deedee Snider of Cleveland School."

"*Only?*" Carole echoed. "Deedee's tough. If I ever get that far."

"Carole," Amy said, drawing the taller girl closer to her, "I've played them all. And beaten them all, one time or another."

"Because you're you. But I'm me."

"I can tell you how to beat them. If you'll listen."

"Would you?" Carole asked anxiously.

"Every one of them has a weakness. Put *your* strength against *their* weakness and you can do it."

"You think so?"

"I know so," Amy said with conviction.

Swede stood off watching, catching a word or two of their conversation, enough to know that Amy had found a cause, a reason to come out of her self-imposed exile. He hoped it would help in her battle against the killer that was still in her.

109

* * *

When Walter Duncan returned to his office, he found a message on his desk. ED BEDFORD CALLED. WANTS YOU TO CALL BACK.

Walt glanced at his desk clock. Six forty-seven. If he had read Bedford correctly, the man was still in his office. He dialed the number. Bedford himself answered his private line.

"Mr. Bedford? Dr. Duncan. You called me. Is it about the latest course of chemo I've suggested? The first two haven't done what Dr. Bristol and I expected. So before I consider amputation, we want another shot at it."

"I know. My wife explained that. And I appreciate your not giving up without another chance. But what I was calling about is, my wife tells me that you and Coach Olafsen and that young Brent Marlow—"

"Martin," Walt corrected.

"Yeah. Right. Brent Martin," Bedford said. "You all got Amy to go back to school. That's terrific. I can't tell you how I felt every night, coming home to find her shut up in her room. Not wanting to come out, even to have dinner with us. You've all done a wonderful job with her. So I would like to do something to show my appreciation."

"Such as?" Walt asked.

"Is there something that young man would like, or something Olafsen would like, or the school would like? I understand those kids in Amy's class were terrific. So I'd like to do something. Maybe throw them a party. Or give the school something, some piece of equipment. Maybe a practice-ball machine."

"Mr. Bedford, if you want to know what I would suggest—"

"I'd welcome it," Bedford said.

"I would suggest that what they did—Brent, Swede, those young people in her class—can't be paid for by money or gifts or parties. I would suggest you spend more time with your daughter. And less time with your business."

"Doctor, you don't seem to realize that twelve hundred and seventeen people depend on me for their jobs. That's a big, big responsibility! If I let up, I let them down."

"Mr. Bedford, you have twelve hundred and seventeen employees. But only one daughter."

Walter Duncan hung up abruptly. He leafed through his other messages, found none that could not wait until morning.

He slipped out of his white lab coat and into his jacket and started home, late again, to see his own daughter.

9

MORE weeks went by; it was another day. Another early morning. Walter Duncan was standing at the kitchen table hastily downing some coffee from the automatic coffee maker, when, drawing her robe around her, Emily came in.

His hasty morning habit of drinking his coffee without even taking time to sit at the table always distressed her. But she knew he was operating especially early on those mornings, so she suppressed her impulse to mention it again. For he usually would joke, "I married you to get away from my mother. She used to nag me about that all the time."

As he turned to empty his cup into the stainless-steel sink, he became aware of her.

"Hi, hon, did I wake you when I got up?"

"No," Emily said. "I'd love to make you some breakfast. It won't take long."

"Thanks. Got to be in the OR before seven. Then have to spend half my day in court."

"That Enright thing?"

"Yes, that Enright 'thing,' " he replied. "Lawyers must get paid by the day to judge from the way they string out cases."

"I hope it doesn't get messy."

"Whenever a doctor botches a case it tends to get messy," Walt said. "Anyhow, my part of it should be over today." He kissed her, was on his way to the garage, when he suddenly remembered, "By the way, Simmie, she getting a cold?"

"Not getting, got," Emily corrected.

"She ought not to go to school for a day or two."

"But she loves school. And she's almost over the cold. She's surely not infectious."

"Take her temp. If she's got any, keep her home."

"She won't like it."

"Tell her Dr. Duncan insists."

He was pulling into the parking lot at the hospital, heading for his slot, when he suddenly braked. Fortunately there was no car behind him. He sat there a moment, itemizing in his mind the isolated symptoms he had noticed about his daughter during recent months.

Slight fever, paleness, unusually compliant attitude, those bruises, weakness. None extreme or crying out for attention, but all present nevertheless. Could a doctor become so immersed in his own specialty that he forgets all those other signs and symptoms he knew so well during his student days and his service as an intern?

No time for that now. He had to scrub and be ready to do an amputation on a sixty-two-year-old man with advanced diabetes.

He had finished his three cases for the morning, changed from OR greens back into his own clothes and gone down to his office.

As soon as he opened the door, Claudia greeted him. "Mr. Silverstein called again. I told him you'd be in court by the time the trial reconvened after lunch."

"And I will," Walt replied. He pretended to resent her reminder. It was a game they played. For without her quiet persistence he would have missed appointments, grand rounds and other duties he must perform in addition to surgery. "Claudia, how long will you be here?"

"Late as you want. Something up?" the young woman asked.

"Remind me."

"Of what?" she asked, puzzled.

"Just remind me. I'll know what," he said. "Oh, by the way, Amy Bedford. Her new X rays?"

"I checked. She's in Radiology right now."

"Good! I'll stop by and see her before I go to court. She's a terribly frightened child. And I don't blame her."

Once he left, Claudia printed in large letters on a sheet of plain paper: THIS IS TO REMIND YOU. Using his desk pen as a spindle, she mounted the sign prominently.

As Walter Duncan entered the courtroom he saw at once that Dr. Peter Enright was seated at the counsel's table alongside his lawyer. Walt realized he would have to confront his hostile former colleague throughout his testimony. That might make it uncomfortable, Walt realized, but it would change neither the facts and findings on which he would have to testify nor his medical opinion.

He was seated in the witness chair, had taken the oath, when Andrew Silverstein, counsel for the eighteen-year-old plaintiff, came forward to ask, "Doctor, will you tell the jury your background and credentials?"

Walt recited the details of his education, college degree with a major in biology, medical school, two years of internship, three years of residency, fourteen years as surgeon on staff at the University Medical Center.

"Are you certified by the National Board of Orthopedic Surgeons?"

"Yes."

"Doctor, how many papers have you submitted and had accepted by leading medical periodicals?"

"Twenty-three."

Silverstein then had Walter Duncan list the titles of those papers. After which he turned to the bench. "Your Honor, is there any objection to Dr. Duncan's being sufficiently qualified to give expert opinion on the matters involved in this case?"

The judge addressed opposing counsel. "Mr. Sullivan?"

"No objection," defense counsel Roger Sullivan replied as he seized his pencil and yellow pad, ready to frame the questions he would put to Walter Duncan on cross-examination.

"Doctor, have you made a study of the entire file in this case?" Silverstein asked.

"I have."

"And have you examined this young plaintiff seated at the table here?"

"I have," Walter replied.

"Will you tell the jury the condition in which you found this young man?"

"The general state of his health was good. But he suffered a noticeable dropped left foot."

"Did you attempt to determine the cause of that dropped foot condition?"

"I did."

"And what did you discover to be that cause?"

"In the course of removing a herniated disc, certain nerves were accidentally severed," Walter Duncan replied.

"In your opinion, Doctor, can those damaged nerves ever regain their function?"

"No, sir."

"Does that mean that this young man, eighteen years of age, will be plagued with that condition for the rest of his life?"

"Yes, it does," Walter said.

"Doctor, are you aware that this young plaintiff was an outstanding football player destined for an athletic scholarship to one of the best and most prominent universities—"

At that point, Sullivan rose to object. "Your Honor, however qualified the good doctor might be to testify to things orthopedic, I do not think his 'awareness' of things athletic is pertinent to this trial."

"Your Honor," Silverstein protested, "Dr. Duncan is a specialist in athletic medicine."

"Then confine his testimony to athletic medicine!" Sullivan shouted, growing red in the face.

Silverstein smiled and said, "Doctor, one last question. Based on your study of all the X rays, the electromyogram, the CAT scans, the details of the patient's history, including the diagnosis and the surgery performed, would you say that his treatment was in keeping with the current level of medicine and surgery as practiced at this time?"

Walter Duncan looked at Peter Enright, who stared back at him, half-defiant, half-fearful. Walt stated, "In my opinion, medicine and surgery practiced in this case was not up to that standard."

"Would you say then that the defendant in this case was guilty of malpractice?"

Walter Duncan nodded, then said, "Yes, yes, I think there was malpractice."

"Thank you, Dr. Duncan. Your witness, Mr. Sullivan."

At that point, the judge intervened. "Before the witness continues, I will take a ten-minute recess to accommodate another attorney with a case before me." He left the bench.

Silverstein said, "Doctor, you may leave the stand if you wish."

Walter Duncan stepped down. As he did, a man came forward to greet him.

"Dr. Duncan . . ." Walt studied him for a moment before identifying him as the man he had seen waiting outside James Rowe Russell's office the day of his meeting with that overbearing hospital trustee. The man introduced himself. "Tom Fraser. Worldwide Insurance."

"Yes?" Walter countered, curious as to Fraser's intent.

"We insure your hospital. Have for years. We also insure the hospital involved in this case. But the way things have been going lately, with jury verdicts running into the millions, we're thinking of getting out of medical coverage altogether. Or else raising our rates even higher."

"Fraser, you wouldn't be trying to influence my testimony, would you?" Walter Duncan asked.

116

"Only trying to acquaint you with the facts of life, Doctor. The facts of life in this year 1987," Fraser said.

"Thanks," Walt said crisply.

The judge returned. The trial resumed as Roger Sullivan approached the witness box.

"Doctor," Sullivan began, "are you aware of how the injury that called for corrective surgery was sustained in the first place?"

"The young man told me."

"And what did he say?"

"The injury was sustained during a football game. When he was tackled from behind, blindsided, and therefore defenseless."

"Therefore his original injury was not the fault of Dr. Enright, was it?"

"No, but—"

Sullivan interrupted. "Doctor, you answered the question when you said no. The fact is, the original injury was not the fault of Dr. Enright. Now, having established that, I ask you, if a young man suffering that same injury had been presented to you as a patient, what would you have done?"

"First, I would have taken his history. Determined the location of his pain, its possible origin. Then X-rayed him to see if I could determine the exact cause of that pain."

"Doctor, from your study of this patient's file, do you know if Dr. Enright followed the same procedure?"

"Yes, yes, he did," Walter Duncan admitted.

"So that, up to that point, there was no malpractice, was there?"

"No, sir. However—"

Sullivan interrupted once more. "Doctor, we'll get to the howevers in due time. Now, then, sir, if you *had* discovered that in this particular case there was intractable pain due to a herniated disc, what would you have prescribed?"

"Not immediate surgery," Walter replied.

"Doctor"—Sullivan rebuked him sharply—"I didn't ask you what you *wouldn't* have done. I asked you what you *would* have done!"

"I would have put the patient on a regimen of bed rest and

medication to give his body time to correct the condition. If that failed, I would have put him in traction for several weeks. But I would not have rushed—"

"Now, now, Doctor!" Sullivan interrupted. "Just tell the jury what you would have done."

"Sorry," Walter said, but he was annoyed by legal formality that prevented him from simply telling the jury exactly what he found and what he thought without so many interrupting questions.

"Now then, Doctor, let us suppose that after you had put the patient on medication, bed rest, and traction, the pain still persisted. What steps would you have taken then?"

"Then I would have considered surgery as the modality of last resort."

"So that the jury understands, are you saying you would then have performed a surgical procedure called a laminectomy on this patient's injured vertebrae?" Sullivan asked.

"Yes."

"Then there was no malpractice in deciding to perform a laminectomy, was there?"

"There was a rush to surgery which to my mind is extremely suspicious," Walter replied.

"A rush to surgery." Sullivan challenged. "What does that mean, Doctor? That Dr. Enright was bright enough to know what needed to be done? Or perhaps that you would have been too slow?" He turned to the jury, smiling, in an attempt to evoke their laughter. Some of the twelve complied.

Angered, Walter Duncan replied, "Surgery should be the last resort, not the first. Anytime it isn't, there is the suspicion—"

Sullivan interrupted, more loudly this time. "Your Honor, Your Honor—"

The judge banged his gavel, warning angrily, "Doctor, you will confine yourself to answering questions, not making speeches!"

Walter's first impulse was to ignore the judge and continue, but he controlled the urge and settled back in his witness chair.

Sullivan turned to the counsel table to pick up a sheaf of papers before he faced Walter Duncan once more.

"Dr. Duncan, am I correctly informed that at one time Dr. Enright was on staff at your own hospital?"

"Yes, sir."

"And did he attain that position after an examination of his credentials by your hospital?"

"Yes, he did attain his position after approval of his credentials by our recruitment committee," Walter was forced to grant.

"Doctor, tell me, is your hospital in the habit of welcoming on staff doctors who are accustomed to committing malpractice?"

"Of course not." Walter shot back.

"So can we assume that in all ways Dr. Enright met the high qualifications set by your own hospital?"

"You assume what you wish, and I will assume what I wish," Walter Duncan replied.

From his own counsel table attorney Silverstein tried to signal Walter to retain control and not allow Sullivan to goad him into unwise or damaging outbursts.

"Doctor," Sullivan continued, "I show you now a letter which I will introduce into evidence as soon as you identify it."

Silverstein rose in his place. "Your Honor, I insist on seeing the document before the witness does."

"Of course," Sullivan said, holding out the single sheet to him. He read it quickly, then returned it. "May I, Mr. Silverstein?"

Silverstein nodded. Sullivan turned back to Walter Duncan. "Now, Doctor, can you identify this letter for the jury?"

Walter scanned the document. It was a photocopy of a letter of recommendation, praising Enright most highly, the original of which rested in Enright's file in the hospital.

"Doctor?" Sullivan prodded.

"It is a letter from Inland State Hospital."

"Is that the same hospital in which Dr. Enright served for three years before joining your staff?"

"Yes, yes, it is," Walter admitted.

"So that Inland State was very well satisfied with Dr. Enright's work and professionalism."

119

"Not necessarily—" Walter began to say.

Sullivan cut him short. "Doctor, would you read to the jury the underlined portion of this letter?"

He handed the document back to Walter, who took it reluctantly. He glanced at the underlined sentences. His resistance registered in the angry surge of red that suddenly rose into his face.

"Doctor?" Sullivan urged smugly.

Walter glanced at Silverstein, who with a single controlled nod indicated Walter had no choice. He began to read: "The letter says, 'We have always found Dr. Peter Enright's ethics to be of the highest, and his practice of medicine and surgery to be in keeping with the best standards of the profession.' "

"And that is the statement from a hospital of good reputation and on which your hospital relied?" Sullivan asked. When the answer was not forthcoming at once, he pressed. "Dr. Duncan?"

"Yes, yes, it is." Walter Duncan reluctantly agreed. "However . . ."

"There you go again, Doctor," Sullivan said, smiling at the jury.

Walter Duncan turned to the judge. "Your Honor, unless I am permitted to tell the whole truth, as my oath stated, then we are going to give this jury a totally erroneous view of this case!"

"Now, Doctor"—the judge deferred indulgently—"just as you doctors have your own way of doing things, so do we in the legal system."

"Which may be why courts and lawsuits are in such disrepute with the people," Walter replied.

Silverstein was on his feet at once. "Your Honor, if I may. Dr. Duncan is a busy man, with many pressures on him. So that our methods may seem unnecessarily time-consuming and even wasteful as far as he is concerned. Hence his impatience and his outburst."

"This court will entertain an apology from the witness," the judge said gravely.

"This court will wait till hell freezes over before I apologize!" Walter Duncan said, rising up in the witness chair.

120

"Doctor . . . Doctor . . ." The judge reprimanded angrily.

"Now, do you want this jury to know what this case is really about or do you want to go on in your befuddling way to mystify and confuse them?" Walter demanded.

Even Silverstein intervened. "Dr. Duncan . . . Dr. Duncan, please—"

The judge banged his gavel. "Bailiff, remove the jury!"

Only after all spectators had been removed did the judge return to Walter Duncan. "Doctor, let me apprise you of your rights. It is within the power of this court—no, it is the *duty* of this court—to hold you in contempt if you persist in continuing this sort of conduct. Now, do we have your promise to continue with your testimony in accord with the rules of evidence and accepted courtroom behavior?"

Walter Duncan considered his answer for a long, silent moment. "Your Honor, a young man has been damaged for life. His athletic career cut short. The fault is the fault of this doctor. If I can tell the jury the truth about this case, I will continue your way. Otherwise I will have to do this in my own way."

"You realize, Doctor, that I can hold you in contempt?" the judge reminded.

"If telling the truth constitutes contempt of court, I guess you can," Walter Duncan said.

"Mr. Silverstein . . ." The judge resorted to the plaintiff's attorney.

"Your Honor, may I have a word with Dr. Duncan privately?"

"Yes, we will consider this case to be in recess for five minutes."

Silverstein led Walter to a corner of the courtroom.

"Duncan, our case depends on your testimony, so please, don't antagonize the judge. And don't battle Sullivan. Just answer his questions. And whatever else you want to say I will give you the chance on my re-direct examination."

"Will I have a chance to say everything I have to say?"

"Yes, everything," Silverstein promised.

"Okay, then," Walter Duncan finally agreed.

121

* * *

The jury was returned. Walter Duncan was on the stand once more. Attorney Sullivan resumed his questioning.

"To refresh your mind, Doctor, did this letter laud Peter Enright, describing his ethics to be of the highest and his practice of medicine and surgery to be in keeping with the best standards of the profession?"

Swallowing his anger, Walter Duncan was forced to admit, "Yes, the letter does say that."

"Thank you, Doctor. You could have saved us a great deal of time and trouble if you had admitted that in the first instance instead of deliberately trying to mislead and confuse this jury."

With an air of disdain Sullivan turned his back on Walter Duncan and started toward the counsel table.

Before Walter could explode in another angry outburst, Andrew Silverstein hurried forward to question him. A short man, so thin that he appeared frail, Silverstein broached his first question in a voice just a shade above a whisper.

The members of the jury leaned forward to hear his words. Which was what he intended them to do. For he was about to elicit the crux of his case.

"Doctor, if for the moment you can overlook the scurrilous attack on your motives and character—"

"Your Honor?" Sullivan rose to intercede.

"Yes, Mr. Sullivan?" the judge said, then turned to Silverstein. "Counselor, please, we can do without the prologues. Just ask your questions."

"Sorry, Your Honor," Silverstein said, satisfied that he had diminished Sullivan's attack. "Now, Doctor, in your opinion as an expert in the field, if a young man of seventeen who had been injured in a football game and suffered sciatic pain that extended down to his foot, and who showed signs of muscle weakness in that leg, came to you for treatment, what would you have done?"

"First an examination. A complete examination to determine the extent of the injury," Walt said.

"Dr. Enright did that, didn't he?" Silverstein said.

"Yes, he did," Walt conceded, wondering why Silverstein was reinforcing Sullivan's tactics.

"And would you also have taken X rays of the patient?"

"Of course."

"Well, didn't Dr. Enright do that?"

"Yes, he did," Walter said.

"Didn't he go even further and do a more revealing test, an electromyogram, to test nerve conductivity to the painful leg?"

"Yes, he did."

"And would you have done that?"

"Yes, I would," Walter Duncan replied, growing a little impatient with the attorney for whom he was testifying.

"Then, Doctor, in your expert opinion, where was the malpractice in this case?"

Walt realized now that Silverstein had cleared the way for him to testify at length and in detail, as he had wanted from the beginning. Much to Sullivan's frustration, Walt launched into his explanation, speaking now not to the lawyers, but to the jury.

"The X rays and the electromyogram could serve only one purpose. To reveal the source of the pain. Which in this case was a herniated disc. Now, faced with that finding, a careful doctor doesn't rush in and do surgery. You confine the patient to bed. To rest that area, reduce the inflammation of the nerve that is causing the pain. If that doesn't work, you put the patient into traction. Either at home or in the hospital. In other words, you give that young body a chance to heal itself. Three weeks, four, five, six if need be. One thing for sure, bed rest is not going to worsen the young man's condition. It can do no harm. That's important.

"The old Hippocratic oath, 'Do no harm to your patient.' Then, only if bed rest failed, if sedatives failed, if traction failed, would a good, careful surgeon consider invading the patient's body. Because every time you take that scalpel in your hand the patient is at risk. Under the best of conditions and with the surgeon exerting the utmost care, things can go wrong during surgery. The patient may respond unexpectedly to the anesthesia. Later, infections may set in. Surgery is the last thing you do, not the first."

Walter Duncan shifted in his chair to face the counsel table at which Peter Enright and his lawyer sat.

"And if you do surgery, damn it, you do it carefully! You don't leave a young man with a dropped foot and a leg brace for the rest of his life!"

Silverstein waited patiently until Walt Duncan had finished.

"Doctor, in your opinion, what was the cause of the damage to this plaintiff?"

"It is apparent from the later electromyogram that the L-five nerve in his spine was severed in a botched attempt to remove the herniated disc. When you sever the L-five, a dropped foot will result. And a permanent brace can be necessary."

"In your opinion, Doctor, is the severing of such a nerve during a laminectomy the result of faulty medical and surgical practice?"

"There is no doubt of it in my mind," Walter Duncan said firmly. "The surgery performed here was not in keeping with the standards of surgery practiced in this community."

"Thank you, Doctor."

Realizing the damage done to his case, attorney Sullivan came forward to remove from the jury's mind that last condemnatory barrage from Walter Duncan.

"Doctor, isn't it possible that two surgeons might differ on the course of treatment of the same case? Haven't you ever differed with your own colleagues?"

"Yes," Walt conceded.

"For example, haven't you ever been in a situation where one surgeon says, *operate?* And another says, *don't operate?*"

"Yes, yes, I have," Walt again conceded.

"Isn't that what happened in this case? Dr. Enright decided, operate. But later, a year after the fact, Dr. Duncan comes in and says, don't operate. What's the difference?"

"The rush to surgery, Mr. Sullivan, the rush to surgery," Walt

Duncan replied. "There are things in that patient's file that give us a hint as to why that happens."

"What things?" Sullivan asked. A moment later he would be very regretful that he had asked.

"Mr. Sullivan, the nonmedical facts. The notation of the fee paid by this young man's family. Four thousand dollars. For a young surgeon of thirty or thirty-one starting out, with a wife, a house and a mortgage, that could be a more powerful argument for operating than the patient's condition."

"Dr. Duncan, what would be *your* fee for similar surgery?" Sullivan pursued.

"Probably the same, depending on the patient. Some we do for free."

"Do you have a wife, a child, a house, a mortgage?"

"Yes, I do."

"Then couldn't we say that you, too, are influenced by the profit motive?"

"You could say it, but it wouldn't be true!" Walt shot back.

As he became aware of how profusely he was perspiring and how strongly his heart was pounding, in combined anger and stress, he realized that cardiologist Worthington had been right in prohibiting old Sy from being in this situation.

Having scored what he considered a crucial point, Sullivan proceeded to nail down his own defense.

"Tell me, Doctor, were you in the Operating Room with Dr. Enright when he performed the surgery on the plaintiff?"

"Of course not."

"Then you did not witness the situation that Dr. Enright found when he opened the plaintiff's spine, did you?"

"No, I did not."

"Then you don't know what you yourself might have done if confronted with that same situation, do you?"

"I know one thing. That young man sitting there at the counsel table is destined to have a dropped foot because someone severed his L-five nerve. Whoever did that was guilty of negligence. Gross negligence. There is no other conclusion we can reach, Mr. Sullivan."

125

"Are you saying that Dr. Enright is a negligent surgeon?"

"I am saying that in this case, yes, he was negligent," Walt Duncan replied firmly.

"Doctor, have you ever scrubbed with Dr. Enright?"

"No, I have not."

"Have you ever witnessed him perform surgery?"

"No," Walt conceded.

"Then you are basing your opinion of his work on this one case to which you were not a witness," Sullivan observed, an aside he made sure the jury heard.

Sullivan turned to the counsel table, seized the letter of recommendation he had referred to earlier and with a dramatic gesture thrust it toward the jury.

"Doctor, are you placing your judgment, your *biased* judgment, of this young doctor above that of the surgeons in a hospital at which Dr. Enright had worked for three years, doctors who observed his work, day in and day out, for three years?"

"I am judging only his work in this particular case," Walt insisted.

"Are you saying that all the surgeons whose names appear in this letter of recommendation were mistaken when they wrote, and I quote, 'We have always found Dr. Peter Enright's ethics to be of the highest and his practice of medicine and surgery to be in keeping with the best standards of the profession'? Unquote," Sullivan demanded in stentorian tones that reverberated through the courtroom. "Is that what you are saying, Dr. Duncan?"

In a voice just a shade above a whisper, Walter Duncan addressed the jury. "To someone who didn't know any better that letter would be very impressive—"

"Your Honor," Sullivan interrupted, "direct the witness to answer the question."

"Dr. Duncan"—the judge interceded—"I admit the question was framed a bit obliquely, but please do your best to answer it directly."

"I am doing that, Your Honor. But it is the kind of answer that requires a little background. So if I may—"

126

"Your Honor," Sullivan protested.

But the judge ruled. "The witness may lay a foundation for his answer."

"As I was saying"—Walter Duncan continued to the jury—"that letter would impress a layperson more than a physician. Because for a long time now we men and women in medicine have been burying more than our patients. We have been burying the sad fact that we have incompetent doctors and surgeons."

"Your Honor, the witness is rambling." Sullivan rose to protest.

"Counselor, suddenly I find his rambling very interesting," the judge said. "And since you have made so much of that letter of recommendation, I'm sure the jury would like to hear more about it. Doctor, continue!"

"These incompetent doctors, we know who they are. But we are powerless to do much about it. Because if we expose them, if we try to have their licenses to practice lifted, then we are in for very costly lawsuits. So, out of sheer practical necessity, what hospitals do is give these doctors extravagant letters of recommendation so that they will get other positions, in other hospitals, in other states and become some other community's problem."

He turned to confront Sullivan. "No, Counselor, to answer your question, no, I don't think the doctors whose names are on that letter were 'mistaken.' They were lying! Because they were trying to protect their own reputations, their own hospital, their own community from an incompetent doctor by dumping him on any unsuspecting hospital that would take him."

He faced the jury as he continued. "Someday we doctors are going to have the guts to discipline ourselves. Then we'll have far fewer malpractice suits and much, much lower insurance premiums. Patients will be better served, and letters of recommendation will have some value."

Silverstein rose to his feet. "Mr. Sullivan, I assume you have no further questions."

"No further questions," Sullivan said and sank back into his chair.

"Good," Silverstein said, "because the witness is a very busy man, and I would like to excuse him so he can return to the hospital."

Walter Duncan rose from his chair, shook Silverstein's hand and started toward the aisle to the door. But the judge called, "Dr. Duncan!"

"Yes, Your Honor?"

"Thank you for a most instructive afternoon. I am sure both the jury and this court will benefit from it."

Walt passed by Peter Enright on his way out of the courtroom. The younger surgeon glared at him. But Walt rushed by to get back to the hospital where two new patients awaited him, and there were his post-op rounds to make. The courthouse elevators being slow, he raced down the three flights of stairs to the street, where he slid into his car and started swiftly in the direction of the hospital.

Even as he drove, he felt himself in the grip of such an unusual compulsion that he had to force himself to slow down. At the stoplight he realized the source of his urgent need to hurry. He must conclude his day as quickly as possible and get home. Home. To Simone.

He had parked his car and was starting for the side entrance to the hospital when Alan Bridges emerged. A colleague on the orthopedic staff, Bridges's OR schedule was second only to that of Walt Duncan.

"Hi, Alan . . ." Walt greeted him perfunctorily as they passed.

"How did it go?" Bridges asked.

"Go? What?" Walt asked, confused for the moment.

" 'What'?" Bridges repeated angrily. "Is that all it meant to you? Something to do and then forget half an hour later?"

"What the hell are you talking about, Alan?" Walt demanded, anxious to get on with his tight schedule.

"I am talking about what you've just done to the reputation of every doctor who does orthopedic surgery!"

"Oh, you mean the case . . . testifying," Walt realized.

128

"Yes! That's what I mean. You and Sy may think that it's a highly ethical thing you two conspired to do. But I would like to remind you what this can mean to our malpractice-insurance premiums. Which are sky high already. Eighty thousand dollars a year! Whether I do one operation or a thousand. And with this case today, who knows how much higher they will go!"

"Al, before you go blowing off steam, did you examine the patient's file? Did you see the patient? An eighteen-year-old kid with a permanently dropped foot?"

"I didn't have to. I take it for granted that given a certain number of surgical procedures there is going to be an accident here and there, an unexpected outcome."

"This was no accident. It was lousy surgery!" Walt exploded.

"And if it was?" Bridges demanded.

"You can't just toss off a kid's lifetime defect with an 'if it was'!"

"To help one kid you decided to penalize thousands of orthopedic surgeons, innocent surgeons who had nothing to do with that kid. You and Sy made a very foolish choice when you decided to step into that case!"

"Sorry you feel that way," Walt Duncan said, pushing his way through the door.

"I'm not the only one who feels that way!" Bridges called after him.

It sounded like a threat. But Walt Duncan had no time to consider it. Rounds. New patients. Then home. Simone.

Yes, Simone.

10

H E stopped by his office briefly to see if Claudia had any emergencies to report. There were none. He was free to start his end-of-day rounds. Later than usual this day. He did not like to intrude on the nurses and orderlies while they were serving patients their early dinners. And he preferred that his patients enjoy as relaxed and peaceful a routine as possible.

His three patients who had had early-morning surgery were all awake. Despite some post-op pain and inconvenience, they were all doing well and not complaining. Even the old man on whom he had had to do the amputation was conscious and exhibiting a remarkably cheerful attitude. But Walt knew that the man's emotional trauma would come later, during his rehabilitation therapy.

He was chatting with Mrs. Colucci, who was recovering from a laminectomy and was relieved at last to be free of pain. She was expressing her enthusiasm about going home in a few days, when the beeper in the breast pocket of Walt's white lab coat summoned him to the phone. Its persistence announced its importance.

He picked up the phone on Mrs. Colucci's bedside table. "Duncan," he announced.

"Duncan? This is Rosen. Come down to my consultation room at once!"

The consultation room was dark except for the light from the shadow boxes. That light was screened through a number of X rays and scans that hung in pairs, side by side. As soon as Walt saw the dates on the X rays he knew who the patient was: *March 14, 1987. May 25, 1987.* Amy Bedford's first X rays and scans and now her latest, taken early in the day.

"Take a look, Walt, take a look!" Sy urged.

Walt studied the films, one set at a time, moving down the line from the left side of the wall of view boxes to the right side. Each set, before and after, X rays and scans, proved one thing: It had shrunk. Amy's invasive tumor had been, if not defeated, at least forced to retreat in face of those powerful chemicals.

"That's all we have to know," Walt said.

"Schedule her. Right away," Sy said.

"Right!"

Walt returned to his office. Though it was past seven o'clock he found Claudia still waiting.

"What are you doing here at this hour? Checking up on me? Between you and my wife I have no love life of my own," he joked.

"The way you asked me to remind you, I thought I'd stay on and remind you in person. Now, what can I do for you?"

"Get Amy Bedford on the phone. If her mother is there, have her pick up the extension phone."

He continued on into his office, saw Claudia's reminder spindled on his desk pen and wondered, if she had left such a conspicuous reminder, why had she lingered until he came back? In some way had he betrayed his personal urgency about being reminded?

The phone rang. "Doctor, Amy and her mother are both on the phone."

"Thanks, Claudia. Now go home!" He pressed the lit button

to pick up the line to the Bedford home. "Amy?"

"Yes, Doctor." He could sense the expectation as well as the fear in her young voice. She was trembling, and it was apparent.

"Amy Bedford, from now on I am going to hold you up as an example to all my patients who have to suffer the slings and arrows of outrageous chemotherapy."

"Doctor—" Amy started to ask but dared go no further.

"Yes, Amy. You did it! You did it! All that nausea, that retching, those mouth sores, those lost handfuls of golden hair? All worth it. Dr. Rosen and I just went over your X rays and scans. The tumor has shrunk enough for us to agree that surgery is now indicated."

"Oh, Doctor . . ." The young girl started to enthuse, but gave way to tears.

He never thought he could derive so much pleasure from hearing someone cry.

"Doctor," Marion Bedford interjected, "when do you want her there?"

"I'll arrange OR time and a room in the morning, and Mrs. Holcomb will let you know. It will surely be within the week. Possibly within two days. Meantime, let's all feel that we've won the first battle in a long war. Sleep well tonight, Amy, dear."

"Thank you, Doctor, thanks so much," the girl said.

He hung up. The signal light on his telephone complex no sooner went out than there was a knock on his door.

"Yes?" he called out.

The door opened. It was Claudia Holcomb again.

"I thought I told you to go home! Don't you have a husband and a son? Go home!"

"You sure you don't need me?" she asked.

"What makes you think I need you?" he countered.

"Just the way you asked to be reminded this morning," she said. "Is there trouble? Trouble I don't know about?"

"Claudia, please, just go home. I need the next hour to myself."

He had said it with such gravity that she did not reply but simply nodded and closed the door. She was tempted to remain

132

for, in the four years she had worked for him, she had never seen him quite like this. But, obeying his order, she took her coat and purse and slipped out quietly. She stopped at the hospital switchboard to instruct the operators: "No calls for Dr. Duncan. He does not wish to be disturbed."

Walter Duncan hesitated before he turned to the wall of bookshelves behind his desk chair. His eyes moved across the titles of the many medical textbooks, which embraced not only his own specialty but most of the others. He pulled down one large volume, bound in blue leather, a volume he had had no need to consult in years. He searched for the chapter describing signs and symptoms. He began to read:

> . . . *frequently presents as an apparent infectious process with an abrupt onset . . . and fever . . . patient may seem listless . . . compliant . . . joint pains may lead to a false diagnosis of acute rheumatic fever . . . petechiae, ecchymoses and other blemishes may appear. . . .*

He allowed the volume to drop to his desk. For the signs and symptoms he had just read related to a disease that, like osteogenic sarcoma, attacked the young in far greater numbers than the old.

Acute leukemia.

Like all parents confronted by such a terrifying possibility, his first reaction was to deny it. To argue it out of existence. There were differences between these signs and the ones Simone presented. The book said, *bleeding from the mouth and nose may present. . . .* Simone had none of that. *Enlargement of the liver and the lymph nodes. . . .* He must palpate her for that as soon as he returned home. Wake her, if necessary.

Besides, her skin blemishes, those black-and-blue spots, there was a good reason for those. Hockey. An accidental collision with an opponent. An unintended poke with a hockey stick. Banging into a school locker.

Yet some of those had appeared after she had been persuaded

133

to give up hockey for tennis lessons with Swede Olafsen.

He dabbed at the sweat on his face, felt suddenly that he dared not ignore any possibilities. What he must do now must be done in a way that would not unduly alarm Simone or Emily.

All the way home he considered ways in which to carry out his purpose without arousing unnecessary concern in his wife. By the time he turned into the driveway of their home he had decided.

He came in through the garage door, called, "Hi, hon! I'm home!" He realized he was making too great an effort to sound cheerful and hearty. Her call came back to him from upstairs.

She came down to greet him with a kiss. "Like a drink while I heat up your dinner?"

"Not tonight. Simmie still awake?" he asked, as casually as he could under the circumstances.

"We were just going over her book report for tomorrow. You know, she has a real . . . I hate to sound like a doting mother . . . but she has a real talent for using words. I wouldn't be surprised if someday she turns out to be a writer. Or else goes into some field that demands writing. Advertising maybe. Or television."

"I think I'll go up and say good night to our budding genius," he said.

"I didn't say she was a genius. But, as a pretty good editor, I know she does have some writing talent. Or, if you'd rather, an ability to use words. She's going to be something when she grows up. No matter what her father thinks."

She laughed. He laughed. With some effort. *I must go up now before Simmie falls asleep,* he thought.

As he reached the top of the stairs, he saw the beam of light at the base of her door go out. He had better get to her before she settled down for the night. He knocked.

"Simmie, Dad. Can I come in?"

"Of course, Daddy."

She did not turn on the light, expecting, as on most late nights, he would kiss her, snuggle with her a bit and then allow her to go to sleep.

He approached her bed, sat down on the edge, leaned over to her and kissed her. She put her arms around him and pulled him close. She breathed deeply, then said, "You didn't operate this afternoon, did you, Daddy?"

"How do you know?"

"You don't have that Operating Room smell."

"Impossible. I shower every time I finish up in the OR." He protested in mock indignation.

"The smell sticks to your hair. Like with people who smoke," she said. "I can always tell."

"Well, smell again and tell me where I was this afternoon."

She pulled him closer, pressed her face against his hair and inhaled deeply. Once. Then again.

"Give you a clue?" he teased.

"Please."

"Do I smell like a judge? Or two battling lawyers?"

"Court. Today was the day you went to court to testify!" she exclaimed. "Was it like television, Daddy? Did they swear you in, make you promise to tell the truth and all that?"

"All that. Now, baby, how are you feeling?"

"Fine!" she said.

"Any more of those black-and-blue marks?" he asked.

"No."

"I don't believe it." He pretended to protest.

"I'll show you," she said.

Eager to prove herself, she reached for the lamp on the night table and turned it on. *Good,* he thought, *far from being apprehensive, she is anxious to acquit herself. Anxious enough to solve my first problem, getting that light turned back on.*

She pulled up the top of her pajamas, exposing her back to him.

"Go ahead, Daddy, look!"

He made a close examination of her back and found no blemishes. He turned her slightly to examine her right side, then her

135

left. He detected nothing suspicious. He started to massage her back, asking, "There, how does that feel? Good?"

"Great," she said, enjoying the close physical contact with her father.

As he massaged he turned her gradually until she was lying on her back. He continued rubbing, eventually concentrating on her stomach, especially the area just below her ribs. There he pressed a bit more deeply and firmly until she squirmed in slight discomfort.

"Sorry, baby," he said. But his sensitive fingers told him that he had detected a slight enlargement of her liver. He gently reached the areas where he could palpate her lymph nodes, but he could detect nothing. Massaging his way back to the area of her stomach, he made one more effort to palpate her liver. He was less sure this time that there was any abnormal enlargement.

Further observation is demanded, Walt Duncan decided.

Emily came up the stairs to call, "Walt? Dinner's ready." She came bounding into the room, discovered them and asked, "Something wrong?"

"No," he said, "just giving a little relaxing massage. Now, baby, get to sleep."

"See you in the morning, Daddy?" she asked.

"No. I'll be leaving early."

"Again?" she asked, disappointed.

"Again. Oh, by the way, Simmie, you've heard me talk about that girl Amy Bedford?"

"Sure, Daddy, the good tennis player. Swede talks about her a lot."

"Well, she's making great progress. I'm going to be able to operate and possibly save her leg."

"Oh, Daddy, cool! Real cool! I bet Swede'll be happy to hear that."

"Then we'll tell him. Now get to sleep, darling."

While eating, he scanned the daily newspaper. His only chance to catch up on the national news. He had no time to listen to the radio or watch television news. Emily sat across the table, observing him until she could no longer control her curiosity.

"Simmie, she complain about something?" she asked.

"Simmie? No. Why?"

"I thought she complained about some pain or something."

"Has she been feeling any pain lately?" he asked, hiding behind the newspaper.

"No. She still has that fever. But no pain."

He felt relieved.

"I just wondered why you were massaging her."

"Well"—he improvised—"she was just about asleep when I went in. I felt guilty waking her. So I thought I'd soothe her back to sleep with a massage."

Emily must be content with his explanation, he thought. For she did not pursue it. In a while he asked, "*Has* she complained of anything lately?"

"No."

"Have *you* noticed anything?" he asked.

"No. Except that she does seem a bit tired. Probably that fever."

"Probably," he said, and pretended to continue to read his newspaper.

Closer examination was imperative. He must invent some nonalarming reason to have her checked over by their pediatrician. Or was he suffering the medical students' syndrome? Once they studied the signs of a disease they began to suffer the symptoms. They went through medical school, suffering one disease after another without having a sick day in all four years.

Observation, he decided, careful, prudent, nonalarming observation.

Attired in his white lab coat, Walter Duncan strode down the hall of the basement to the workshop of Hans Metterling. There he found the old technician whom he preferred to think of as an artist. Hans was studying a titanium appliance he had crafted to fit the exact and minute specifications determined with the aid of a highly ingenious computer. If all went as planned, this device Hans had executed should fit precisely into the space Walt Duncan would carve out of the bones in the right leg and thigh of Amy Bedford.

Hans demonstrated the slender but sturdy, shiny silver-colored device that would replace her diseased bones so efficiently that she probably would be able to enjoy an active life in the future. The apparatus was solid enough. It flexed easily at the knee joint, which was made of a strong, durable plastic that would last Amy for years, possibly for her lifetime.

Walt examined it carefully. Then asked, "How much leeway, Hans?"

The old Swiss craftsman proceeded to demonstrate how the prosthesis could be lengthened with a few exacting turns of the expanding rings at the end of both the leg and the thigh.

Amy Bedford's spine X rays indicated that she had some growth left in her. When that occurred, Walt could perform fairly simple surgery: lengthen the prosthesis so it kept up with the natural growth of her other leg. Thus both legs would remain the same length for the rest of her life. If all went according to plan, she never would be forced to hobble or suffer awkward walking or running.

If all went according to plan.

That reservation overshadowed all of Walt's thoughts. This kind of surgery was always a hazardous venture. How would the patient react during the surgery? What unexpected findings might confront the surgeon? Walt had seen the best of plans suddenly thwarted by a perverse nature.

Once Hans had demonstrated the prosthesis to Walt's satisfaction and the surgeon had handled it, made the lengthening adjustment to test it, then restored it to its precise original dimensions, he nodded and handed it back to the old technician. Hans wrapped it tenderly in its plastic covering, presented it to the surgeon and said a soft, very sincere, "Good luck, Valter, good luck. She is a nice girl."

Without dwelling on it, Hans had quietly acknowledged Walt's concern and reservations. Luck would play a part, a big part, in what would happen to Amy Bedford from now on.

With the device in his possession, Walt Duncan faced his last and usually most difficult presurgical obligation. He stopped by the office. Claudia had the long legal form waiting for him. He took it and started up to the second floor of the Pediatric Pavilion.

As he had requested, the Bedfords, Ed and Marion, were waiting at their daughter's bedside. Walt could tell at a glance that Marion Bedford had not slept the whole night. Her eyes betrayed it. Her nervous smile confirmed it. It flickered off and on, though she desperately tried to control it. Ed Bedford was by his daughter's side, seated on the arm of her chair, holding tightly to her hand.

For his daughter's reassurance or his own? Walt wondered. *But we had better begin and hope he possesses the strength that his wife does not. Before we are done this could be a harrowing experience for young Amy Bedford. First,* he thought, *for a lighter note.*

"Amy, I want you to meet something that is going to become a part of you. You might even want to give it a name. Like 'Hansi.' Why not? The Academy Awards are called Oscars. The TV awards are called Emmies. Well, this is a Hansi, in honor of Hans Metterling who designed it."

He carefully removed the plastic wrapping and presented the silver-colored device, holding it up, turning it one way and another, then flexing the knee joint.

"See how it moves, easily, naturally, like your own knee joint. It has a little locking device for stability. You'll learn how to control that in time. But this is it."

Amy held out her hand to touch the long, skeletonlike object of cold metal. But she dared not quite reach it. Her father reached for it. Walt passed it to him. He examined it closely. His knowledge, his experience of many years with machine tools of extremely exacting tolerance made him exclaim, "Man, this is a remarkable piece of work. What craftsmanship."

139

"That's our friend Hans. Amy and I both know him well by now, don't we?"

"Yes, we do," the girl responded. "A nice man. A very nice man."

"Well, Amy, this is yours. Yours alone. It wouldn't fit anyone else in this world. And tomorrow it will become a part of you for the rest of your life."

Walt retrieved the contrivance and was rewrapping it as he spoke, to be free for his next step. He felt the upper left-hand pocket of his lab coat to make sure the paper was there.

"Hansi wasn't the only reason I asked all of you to be here today. We have a formality to complete before surgery can be performed."

He presented the single printed sheet.

"This spells out the procedure I am going to perform, and that you agreed to. Amy, since you're still a minor legally it must be signed by your father or your mother. I want you to sign it, too."

The girl glanced up at him. She then looked to her father, who seemed as puzzled as she, and as tense. She turned back to Walt Duncan, waiting to hear.

"Amy, despite all the advanced tests, X rays, scans, CAT scans and biopsies, in a case like yours, when we go in surgically, we still can be confronted with findings we did not expect."

"What kind of findings?" her mother demanded immediately.

"Yes, what kind of findings?" Amy echoed, gripping her father's hand tighter.

"Amy, I want you to read the words on this line," Walt said, running his finger under the typed-in line in the form.

Before she could comply, her father intervened. "I'll see that first!"

Walt surrendered the form to him. Ed Bedford read the words. Slowly, he lowered the page. He stared at Walt Duncan. In a strained and barely controlled voice he said, "I thought this was being done to avoid anything like what's written here."

"It is," Walt said, "but, as I said, we can't be sure until we get in there."

140

"I want to see it," Amy demanded.

Walt took the paper from her father's hands and gave it to the girl. She took it, stared at it with unseeing eyes. Until Walt's finger underlined the words: *We understand and consent that, if in the surgeon's considered professional opinion, it is deemed medically indicated, for the patient's health and survival, he is authorized to perform an amputation of the area involved.*

"Amputation . . ." Amy was barely able to utter the word. "But you said, *'Give me a year . . .'* "

Her hand began to tremble so that the paper rattled. Her father had to remove it and hold it as still as he could. Behind the girl, her mother gave way to tears.

Walt leaned close to the girl, took her hand, spoke to her, eye to eye, in a soft but firm voice. "Amy, I said yes, 'give me a year and I will cure you.' And I will do my damnedest to accomplish that. Because you've been a terrific patient. But I have seen what can happen in the Operating Room. A surgeon goes in armed with all the tests, data and plans and knowledge, but he finds that nature has tricked him. What *seems* to be so *isn't* so. What seemed like healthy bone or tissue turns out not to be. An artery that looked clean, isn't. And without that particular artery the leg cannot remain vital. Then the surgeon has no choice. Save the patient's life. That's what this sentence means. It says, 'Doctor, do your best, but I trust you to save my life, above all.' "

"If you take off my leg, I don't want to live!" The girl exploded.

"Yes, Amy, you do want to live," Walter Duncan said. "You're too brave, too fine a person to want to give up your life. There's too much for you to do in life to quit now. Amy, sign this. Your signature may not have legal importance, but it's important to me. Because it is your expression of faith in your surgeon."

Amy stared at him, stared at the document and shook her head. "I can't, I can't," she protested. She turned to bury her face in her father's shoulder. He patted her gently on the cheek, stared across her at Walter Duncan.

"Doctor, do you need this in order to proceed?"

141

"We can't do surgery without an informed consent."

"You'll do your damnedest to save her leg?"

"You know I will."

"Okay," Ed Bedford said, more calmly than Walt Duncan had expected. "My daughter's life means everything to me." He took the pen out of his inner pocket and, holding the form against the wall, he wrote his name more shakily than he had ever done before.

Walter Duncan received the signed form, asked softly, "Amy?"

"I can't, I can't," she repeated without looking up at him.

11

I T was late the next afternoon. Marion Bedford sat in the leather lounge chair in the corner of the hospital room staring at her daughter, who lay atop her bed dressed more like a girl in a college dorm than a patient awaiting surgery on which the rest of her life depended.

What if the worst happens? Amy Bedford was thinking. *Would any man want to marry a girl with one leg? How could a man make love to a defective woman? Will I have to limp through life alone, a hobbled cripple? Oh, there are stories, I've read them in magazines, seen them on television, about people who overcome the worst disasters and triumph in the end.*

I would rather have my own two legs than have to be a hero. I would rather have my life as it used to be. With dreams of love and marriage and children. If I had known from the outset that all these weeks of chemo, with the nausea, vomiting, mouth sores, hair falling out, if all that might end up meaning nothing, I would have done something about it.

Something was a vague word. But she knew what it meant. *Suicide.*

How she would have done it she did not know. But if she had to, she would have found a way. Anything to avoid being crippled for life. Anything.

They had not spoken for more than an hour, mother and daughter. They had not even tried to console each other. They did not know how.

Marion Bedford had her own thoughts, none of which served to strengthen her own resolve. *I've failed,* she thought. *I'm supposed to be her tower of strength in times of trouble. Until now, I have been. I've seen her through all the ailments of childhood. But who could have expected this? And from a simple pain that when it first appeared she didn't even think to complain of it. And now, what Dr. Duncan said. What can I say to her? It's going to be all right? So what if they have to amputate, you'll be alive and well? Alive? Well? Who can call that being alive? Or well? From the time she was a pretty little blond child I used to think, She'll make such a beautiful bride. Now she may never be a bride. Beautiful, yes, but no bride. No bride.*

She became aware that Amy's breathing had settled down to a shallow, almost imperceptible degree. She had dozed off, finally, thankfully. Mrs. Bedford slipped out of the room to make some inquiries at the nurses' station.

Amy was still dozing when her door eased open. In contrast to the quiet that had prevailed in the room the sound, soft as it was, startled her. She turned toward the door, expecting the nurse, more medication, another test. She found a young man of twenty-four, tall, quite good-looking. At a less tense time she would have referred to him as a hunk. She assumed he was another young intern on the staff, though he did not wear a white lab coat.

"Amy Bedford?" he asked, pausing in the doorway.

"Yes."

"May I come in?"

"Yes."

He came to stand at the foot of her bed. "My name is Josh Tedrow. Dr. Duncan asked me to stop by."

"You a friend of his or an associate?"

"Both. In a manner of speaking," he said, smiling.

"A manner of speaking?" Amy asked, puzzled.

"We work together. Mind if I sit down?"

"No," she replied, still puzzled.

He crossed the room to settle into the lounge chair. He leaned back, causing the footrest of the lounge chair to thrust forward. He raised his long legs onto it and leaned back at his ease. "There. That's better."

"Mr. Tedrow, what are you doing in here?"

"Walt asked me to drop in. He said that with surgery approaching you might be feeling a little queasy."

"After all the chemo I've had, queasy is a very small word for what I feel," Amy said.

"Isn't it hell?" the young man remarked. He rose from the chair, approached Amy. He leaned against the foot of the bed. "I'll bet there were times when you said, 'If this is getting cured, I'd rather die.'"

"More than once."

"And times when you felt so lousy that you wanted to call Walt and curse him out?"

"More than twice," Amy said.

"Well, I actually did it," he said, moving to the chair alongside her bed. He sat down, crossed his legs. He leaned in her direction as if to impart a secret. "I got him on the phone one night. I told him to hell with his chemo and with him. I didn't want anything to do with his treatment or his surgery."

"You . . . you had surgery?" Amy asked, surprised.

"Yes. Same as you're going to have," he said.

"But, you . . ." She did not say it.

She did not have to. He said it for her. "I look all right. I feel great. I move well. Walking, sitting, crossing my legs, you never noticed." He patted his left leg. "This is the one. Now I do everything I want. Walk, run, swim, sail, golf. Only thing he asks me not to do is ski. I guess the risk of falls is what he's afraid of. But everything else is okay."

"He asked you to tell me this, didn't he?"

"Part of my deal with him. If he cured me, I promised I would do this every time he asks." Tedrow smiled. "It's the best deal I ever made. Because I know how it feels to be facing that thing tomorrow. Wondering how it will turn out. What you'll find when you wake up. Well, I'm a pretty good example of what you'll find. A great life ahead of you."

He uncrossed his legs, rose from the chair, took her hand. "Amy, I was just about your age. Just as scared. Just as debilitated from the chemo. Just as hopeless in some moments. Nights I'd wake up crying. Wondering why God picked me out to die so young. But then Walt would come in, with his big smile, his confidence, and I'd say, 'I'm going with him all the way. He's going to cure me. I'm reaching for life, and he's going to help me get it!' "

"You went through the same thing, all of it?" Amy asked.

"All of it. The chemo, the surgery, the chemo after. A whole year of it. And here I am six years later. You can do it, Amy. Just go into that room tomorrow morning saying that, believing that."

Tears came to her eyes. He leaned down and kissed her on the cheek. Very softly he repeated, "You can do it, too."

Her mother came into the room. Tedrow patted Amy on the cheek. He winked at her, turned and said, "Mrs. Bedford?"

"Yes."

"You've got a fine daughter. A very brave girl. She's going to be okay." He left.

Marion Bedford watched him leave. Once the door closed, she asked, "Who is he?"

"Josh Tedrow."

"Isn't he a little old to be a friend of yours?"

"Maybe. But he is. He is."

There was a soft, almost apologetic knock at the door. Mother and daughter both turned to see. Another nurse, no doubt, with another medication. That never stopped.

The door opened silently. A ruddy-faced, white-haired man peered in, smiling.

"Swede!" Amy cried out, her first impulse one of relief and

146

joy to see her old coach. Then she turned away in shame. Her illness seemed a betrayal of all the care, time and effort he had lavished on her.

"Amy? Amy, dear?" the coach said softly in rebuke. "We don't hide from each other. Not us."

She turned back. Her blue eyes filled with tears.

"I came to wish you luck tomorrow," Swede said. He smiled. "Like before a big match. You know, those nervous minutes before you go out onto the court. When everything feels tight. In your stomach there are butterflies. And your hands are cold. Let me have your hands."

She held out her hands to him. He took them in his own big, strong hands, browned from the sun and speckled with age. Her hands were indeed cold.

"Good," he said. "I like it when a player is nervous before a match. One should never be overconfident. That's when an opponent who is not nearly as good can take you by surprise."

He was rubbing her cold hands as he talked.

"Tomorrow, that's going to be like a match. So you be up for it. Say to yourself, 'No matter what I find when I wake up, I will face it. I will overcome it.' Remember the first time you went to the finals? You were only a freshman. Everybody said, 'We don't give that scrawny kid a chance against a senior who has already won the title once before.' You *were* a scrawny kid at the time. But I said to you, 'Play one point at a time. Don't look back at your errors. Don't look forward to the next game. Play this point.' You believed me. And you did win. A scrawny kid, and you went all the way. Because you knew that to lose a point, or even a game, is not to lose the whole match. Every time you come up to that service line, it's a new point. Well, tomorrow is like that, Amy, dear. If you lose a point or two, there's still the whole match left to play. And my girl, my Amy, is not going to let down. No matter what happens. Right?"

She stared into his delft-blue eyes, into his Norseman's face, lean and ruddy. "Did Dr. Duncan ask you to come here?"

"No," he said, quite simply and honestly.

"Someone did," she insisted.

"Yes. Your father," Swede admitted.

"My father?" She seemed surprised.

"He said he couldn't do it. He didn't know how. But he wanted someone to say to you, no matter what happens tomorrow there's a whole life before you. He wants you to go into that Operating Room with the same eagerness, the same fight as you go into a match. And come out the same way, no matter what happens."

"I may never be able to play again. Or run again. Or even walk straight again."

"Amy, my dear, is that what you think life is? All those things you said, they disappear anyhow. Slowly, perhaps. But the time comes when none of us can play anymore. Or run much anymore. But we live on. We find our place. We do the best we can with what we are. That's what life really is. Whether we are sixteen or sixty, we do the best we can. You've always done that. That's what made you a champion. Be my champion tomorrow, Amy. Promise?"

She stared at him, began to weep, but managed a smile and nodded.

"That's my girl," Swede said. He kissed her wet cheeks. "That's my girl," he whispered.

Before Walter Duncan left the hospital for the evening he reviewed all the X rays, scans and lab tests of Patient Bedford, Amy, in anticipation of tomorrow's surgery.

He dropped by her room to say good night. He found that her father had managed to convince her mother to go out and have her first meal of the day. Amy was alone.

"How do you feel, Amy? Ready?"

"Josh Tedrow was here today," she said.

"Nice young man, Josh."

"You cured him. And he said he made a deal with you. To come speak to any patient you asked him to."

"He's never turned me down. Never too busy. He's lived up

to his part of the bargain. And you will, too."

"Me?"

"Yes. That's the only thing I am ever going to ask of you. That when you're cured, you'll do the same. Come back to give some other kids the courage it takes, when they're coming up to the wire. So that they will know that others have gone through it and come out strong and healthy."

"I wouldn't know how to do that," Amy said.

"When the time comes, you'll know, Amy, you'll know," Walt Duncan said confidently. He patted her hand. "Ready, Amy?"

"I'm ready," she said with conviction.

"Good, good," he said, relieved that she was feeling much better than when he had seen her earlier in the day. He examined her chart. No signs of fever or other ailments. All lab reports indicated that she was in excellent condition for surgery. "See you in the morning."

She nodded. When he was at the door, she called out, "Doctor?"

"Yes, dear?"

"That form you wanted me to sign," she said. "If you still want me to, I'll sign it now."

He stared at her. She stared back. Smiling. The look in her clear blue eyes was strong and determined.

He started down to his office for one last check on his late calls. On the way he realized that his momentary satisfaction with Amy's signature on that consent form had turned to a disturbing sense of guilt.

By the time he reached his office and turned on the lights, he realized why. His emotional involvement in Amy's case had roots deeper than were first apparent to him. Amy had become like a second daughter to him. But he also had concerns, deep concerns, about his first daughter. His examination of Simmie had yielded no specific findings, but neither had it served to abate his anxieties.

149

He wondered, *Am I being a parent instead of a physician? As so many parents do when faced with life-threatening disease in their offspring, have I been practicing denial? I've observed it too many times in other patients. Can I be guilty of the same thing? And like those other loving parents, is my denial stronger because the disease is more threatening? From the moment I had even a suspicion of it, I should have turned Simmie over to another doctor. Well, I will. But first, one more test. Without alarming Simmie or Emily, I will do it. Tonight.*

On his way out he stopped in his treatment room, collected a sterile hypodermic, a specimen bottle and several needles. He wrapped them in a surgical towel, placed it carefully in his coat pocket, turned off all the lights and started out.

The corridor from the elevator to the parking lot had never seemed so long.

"I'm going to take a blood sample from Simmie," he said to Emily. When his wife reacted with surprised concern, he tried to minimize the danger by explaining, "I think that cold may have left her with a low-grade infection. I'd like to track it down so we can treat it."

"Good idea," Emily agreed. "Want me to help?"

"Would you?"

While Walt Duncan prepared the hypodermic, Emily broached the subject to Simone.

"Darling, Daddy wants to get only the littlest bit of blood from you. So he can take it to the hospital and have it analyzed. That way we can get rid of this fever."

"It won't hurt? Will it?" the child asked. Her soft brown eyes tried to conceal her fear.

"Would your dad hurt you?" Emily asked.

"No . . ." The child considered, then admitted, "No. Not much, that is."

Emily held Simmie in her arms, pressing the child's face against her own, while Walter deftly inserted the needle into the vein of

150

her thin arm. He drew up the plunger slowly, filling the glass tube with bright-red blood. He injected the blood into the small specimen vial and sealed it.

In the morning he would give it to Victor Ogura, the hematologist in the hospital, for whom he had the highest regard.

12

I N 1942, after the Japanese attack on Pearl Harbor, Victor
Ogura had been removed with his family from Tarzana, California, to a camp for enemy aliens in Montana. A mere
boy, no alien since he had been born in Tarzana, he came out of
that camp determined to put behind him the pain and insult involved in being treated as an enemy of his native country. He
resumed his education, went on to the University of California,
then to medical school at UCLA. Though his father had been a
gardener who spoke English with a marked Japanese accent, Victor Ogura lived out the traditional American pattern in which the
children of immigrants become Americans and are absorbed into
the society, bringing credit upon their parents, themselves and
their country.

A diligent man, tops in his profession, one could generally find
Victor Ogura bent over his microscope, intent on making diagnoses that could determine the life or death of patients unknown
to him. He did not prescribe, or perform surgery, but his opin-
ions were vital in the treatment of many life-threatening diseases.

Early this morning Walter Duncan stopped by at Ogura's
office.

"Hi, Vic."

"Walt . . ." was all the greeting the hematologist said, as he
turned from his microscope. "What's up?"

Walt handed him the vial with blood that had been kept under refrigeration since the night before.

"Oh, okay," Ogura said, as he usually did.

"Vic, as soon as you know, call me."

"Of course. What are we looking for, sarcoma cells?"

"Just tell me what you find. Okay?"

"Okay." Something about Walter Duncan's evasiveness made Ogura ask, "Who is it, Walt? Special patient?"

"No. Routine. Just tell me."

"I'll run it through right away."

"Thanks." Walt headed for the door, then stopped. "Oh, I'll be in the OR all morning."

"I'll leave the message with Claudia."

"No. I'll . . . I'll call you. Okay?"

"Sure, Walt, okay," Vic Ogura agreed. He was puzzled by Walter Duncan's strange conduct. But Ogura said nothing else. He turned back to the slide he had under his microscope.

In Room 205 of the Pediatric Pavilion, Amy Bedford had been awakened early. A hospital barber shaved her right leg very carefully. A nurse washed it from toe to hip with an antiseptic solution. Then she said, "Come, dear, take this." She held out a small paper cup with two little white pills.

"What is it?" Amy asked.

"It'll settle your nerves."

"My nerves are great. I'm real cool," the girl protested, thinking some show of courage was demanded of her now.

"Take them anyhow," the nurse coaxed, for during the washing she had detected Amy's rapid pulse.

Amy tried to appear diffident. "Sure, I'll take them. If nothing else, it'll settle *your* nerves."

"Good," the nurse said.

At that assent a white-clad orderly, a middle-aged black man, pushed a gurney into the room.

"Who's the little girl going for the buggy ride?" he asked. Then, pretending to catch sight of her, he said, "Prettiest patient I've had all day."

153

Amy laughed. "It's only six-thirty in the morning."

"Then the prettiest patient I *expect* to have all day," he said. His eyes gave a command to the nurse. She moved to the side of the bed. Together, they lifted Amy easily and swung her onto the gurney. The nurse covered her with a blanket.

"Good luck, sweetie," she said as Amy was wheeled out the door.

On the ride to the elevator, Amy kept thinking, *They must know how scared I am, else why all the smiles, all the jokes, none of them very funny.*

On the way down, the elevator stopped at every floor to admit hospital personnel, those coming on shift in uniform, the ones leaving in street clothes. Each new passenger glanced at her, then pretended not to have seen. One of them greeted the stretcher attendant.

"Howdy, Ralph. Still charging by the mile?"

They reached the OR level. Amy felt herself being wheeled down another corridor and into a room smaller than she had expected.

"Is this it?" she asked, disappointed.

"No, honey, this is what we call the holding room. You'll be in good hands from here on. Good luck!" Ralph said.

"Thanks."

The door facing her opened. The same anesthetist who had interviewed her the afternoon before came in, this time dressed in Operating Room greens.

"Amy. Good to see you again. Now, we're going to insert this IV into your arm so it's ready to receive the anesthesia. After the first sting, you won't feel a thing."

He tightened a rubber hose around her upper arm, gently pushed the needle of the IV into her arm, then untied the hose. As he did, Walter Duncan came through the same door.

"Amy, hi. How we doin'?" he asked, smiling. "Comfortable?"

"I . . . I think so."

"Butterflies?"

"Uhhh . . . maybe a little," she admitted.

154

"Well, that's nothing to worry about. Dr. Sy is in there. And Dr. Corey. And the most terrific OR team you'll ever see. Everything is under control. Everything."

"Doctor, what if . . . I mean if you have to do . . . if you have to amputate, how will I know?"

Walt Duncan took her hand. "Amy, when you come out of the anesthesia, we will count your toes. Together. You and I. Then you'll know. Ten toes. That's what we're shooting for. And we're going to make it. Y'hear?"

"Okay, Doctor, I hear."

"Good girl." He turned to the anesthetist. "Let's bring her in."

She was wheeled through the door into the large Operating Room, which seemed a maze of overhead lights and electronic instruments banked behind what she knew was the operating table. She felt herself being lifted off the stretcher and onto the table. She stared up at the lights. They blinded her for the moment. She stared about and saw no faces, only eyes and masks. From behind the mask came a familiar voice.

"Amy . . ."

It was Dr. Corey. The man standing beside him had warm, moist, compassionate eyes that she recognized.

"Dr. Sy?"

"Yes, Amy." He then proceeded to introduce every member of the masked team and identified his or her function during the surgery. "And this, Amy, is Miss Kimble, the anesthetist's assistant. She now will put some sensors on you, so we can monitor your condition during the operation."

Kimble was affixing the sensors to Amy's body, while the anesthetist himself affixed a blood-pressure cuff to her left bicep and hooked it up to an instrument that began to register her blood pressure on a green electronic screen.

Walter Duncan turned from the sink where he had just finished scrubbing. He held up his hands while a nurse pulled thin surgical gloves down over his outstretched fingers. Then she powdered his gloves with an antiseptic. He was prepared to approach the table.

"Ready, Amy?"

"Yes, Doctor," she said.

He gave the anesthetist a head gesture. The man proceeded to feed the barbiturates into the IV in her arm. While Walt waited for a signal from the anesthetist, he glanced at the wall clock. It felt almost as if he had another engagement to which he had to rush off. It was not his habit. Once in the OR he had no time frame, no schedule. Only the case under his hands mattered. If it took a half hour or six hours, performing the procedure with utmost care and skill was his only criterion. Yet today he was glancing at the clock.

Just before the anesthetist gave him the signal to begin, Walt realized he was wondering not about the operation but about how far along Victor Ogura was with that specimen of Simone's blood.

He could not afford to let his mind be diverted by anything during this intricate surgical procedure. There were too many critical decisions along the way to permit his mind to dwell on anything else. Still, there was Simmie . . . and those disturbing signs and symptoms . . . and that blood specimen . . . and Ogura. . . .

The anesthetist was signaling. The patient was under and ready. Time for the surgery to begin.

Walter Duncan did not respond by word or action.

"Walt . . ." The anesthetist prodded.

Even Sy Rosen noticed, for he bent closer to ask in a whisper, "Walt, you all right?"

"Of course I'm all right. Why?"

"I don't know, just . . . Well, I've never seen you hesitate like this. If you're not feeling right, let's not begin."

"I'm feeling fine. Fine!" he protested.

He held out his hand. His nurse, who had assisted him on hundreds of previous cases, stared at him before she slapped the scalpel into his hand. The doctor did seem a different man today. With some other surgeons she had assisted, she might have suspected a hangover. Possibly even the effects of drug use. But not Walt Duncan.

156

Scalpel in hand, Walt knew that from that moment on he must, insofar as humanly possible, forget about Ogura and Simmie and everything except Amy Bedford, whose future, in fact whose life, could depend on what happened in the next three or four hours. He alone would be responsible.

He would be battling nature, which could be tricky and cruel in such situations. No one, no doctor, no surgeon, no X ray or scan technician could predict with certainty what he would find once he made that first long incision. Any of a dozen times during the procedure if he found tissue, arteries, veins, nerves or edges of bone to be tainted by the cancer, he would have no choice but to amputate.

At such moments the surgeon's skill could not prevail. The patient's courage would not count. All the prayers in the world would not win absolution. If any of those findings appeared, he must amputate. If by chance he had been misled by the scans and he removed a fraction less of diseased bone than he should have, he would have to amputate. There must be clean, safe margins of tissue and bone on either end of the resected area; otherwise he had no choice. Amy's leg would have to come off.

With such fears and concerns in mind, Walt Duncan made the first long, frontal incision from Amy Bedford's mid-calf to halfway up her thigh. Clean. Straight. Bloodless for the first instant. Then the blood oozed forth. Walt signaled, and his assistant used the electric cautery to seal off the bleeding.

Carefully, he retracted the tissue to reach the major arteries, the femoral artery and then the vein. Walt teased them away from the area of the bone. He held each in his hand, peering closely as he examined them. He could breathe a bit easier. There was no sign of tumor attached to either long vessel. If there had been, it would be a sign that the tumor had escaped the bone. There would be no clean blood supply to the leg, thus no hope of keeping it alive.

That hurdle passed, he then eased away the sciatic nerve. Again, clean. Now, with the same exquisite care he teased the peroneal nerve away from the bone. Luck was with him. And with Amy Bedford. Clean.

157

He exchanged a look with Sy Rosen, whose watery eyes peered at him over his face mask and agreed: *So far, so good; let's push on.*

He was staring down at the exposed bone, from mid-calf to mid-thigh, the patella joining the two. Careful measurements, comparison of X rays, scans and computerized tomography CAT scans had delineated the area of cancerous bone. He had marked off the limits of diseased bone and the contiguous clean bone that should constitute a safe margin below the diseased bone in the tibia and above the diseased bone in the femur.

Now, he had only one shot at it. If he cut through the bone and the seemingly safe margin turned out to be infected with cancer cells, again he would have no choice. Amputation was the only course if the tumor had been invaded and opened to contaminate the rest of her body. Such was the aggressive, vicious nature of this particular form of cancer.

So, this next move, involving the use of the sterile stainless-steel electric saw, had to be perfect, both margins clean, otherwise there was no hope of saving Amy Bedford's leg.

He stared at the exposed bone, at the markings he had made. He glanced at Sy, whose eyes expressed his own fear and hope that these were the proper, safe, clean margins that would allow the original plan for surgery to proceed.

Finally Walt held out his hand. The chief nurse passed the high-speed electric saw to him. At the designated place on the tibia he applied the saw blade and started it. It cut cleanly and swiftly through the bone. Then he did the same to the upper end of the field of the operation. He cut through the femur. Again, swiftly, cleanly. He removed the patella and passed it to the nurse to be saved for later in the procedure.

Now came the real test. The ultimate and deciding test that would decide Amy Bedford's fate. For if the margins were not clean, not only her leg but her life was in danger. For if the disease had been set free into her body, she would not survive for very long. Months. Possibly.

He scooped out samples of bone above and below the excisions. He dispatched a nurse to the lab for an immediate frozen section to determine if the margins were healthy.

It would take minutes. But long minutes that would seem like hours, until the pathologist would phone back his report.

There was nothing to do but wait. Walt Duncan looked up at the wall clock. It had been more than an hour since the surgery was begun. During that time had Ogura examined Simmie's blood sample? If he had, had he reached any conclusion? Let it be benign. Let all those signs and symptoms turn out to be just that, signs and symptoms that did not add up to any dread diagnosis.

Sy Rosen detected his uneasiness. Unaware, since he knew nothing of Simmie's condition, Sy assumed Walt's concern was solely for Amy Bedford's condition.

"Don't worry, Walt. I think you got it all. You certainly left safe margins."

Walt Duncan did not appear to be encouraged, Sy noticed. *This is not the Walt I've known. What's wrong with him today? Does he feel he made too extravagant a promise to the girl? "Give me a year, and I will cure you." Those words had convinced the girl to make the choice she had. And now, it was possible, yes, possible that despite her choice she still might lose that leg. Not your fault, Walt. It's happened to all other surgeons in our field. Even to you. And to me. It is one of the risks of this particular specialty. You can't blame yourself.*

The phone rang. Every head in that Operating Room turned in its direction. The chief nurse answered it. She smiled; she looked to Walt Duncan. She nodded. He did not accept that as the final word. He approached the phone, took it.

"Peter. Walt. Let me have it."

"Clean," the voice came back. "All samples clean."

"No question?"

"Not in my mind. Of course we'll put it through the regular lab procedure. But I've never seen cleaner."

"Thanks, Pete," Walter Duncan said.

He returned to the table. He signaled his nurse. She passed him the titanium prosthesis, the shiny metal skeleton. He flexed it at the knee to reassure himself that it would work easily, com-

159

fortably. That done, he drilled an indentation in the top of Amy's tibia and packed it with surgical cement. While the cement was still fresh and soft he sank the pointed lower end of the prosthesis into it. Once he had safely anchored it there, he extended it until the fins in the upper end of the titanium reached and locked onto the lower end of Amy's femur. The metal skeleton was now firmly entrenched, replacing the diseased bone, which he had removed.

He signaled the nurse for the patella that he had removed earlier. Using small, strong stainless-steel screws, he affixed it to the plastic knee joint of the prosthesis. If Amy's healing proceeded without any reverses, the bone of the patella would grow into the ridges in the prosthesis.

The procedure was not yet completed. Since skin coming in direct contact with metal might cause infection, it was necessary for Walt to manipulate the muscles so they covered the titanium. He worked slowly, using pressure and only enough force necessary to gradually work the muscles of Amy's calf over the prosthesis. He was ready now to bring the skin over the muscles and close the surgical field.

Closing was only one step in the final procedure. Once he had sutured the wound, Walt held out his hand for a hypodermic. He injected the area with fluocinolone. When he had done that, the nurse signaled one of her assistants. The young woman turned off all the lights in the Operating Room. Walt turned on the Woods lamp over the operating table. An ultraviolet lamp, it cast its strange light over the long, freshly closed wound. If, aided by the fluocinolone, Amy's skin glowed yellow in that light, it meant that the sutured skin was live tissue. If it was not, Walt would have to go back in and reclose the wound.

Fortunately an unbroken yellow glow delineated the entire length of the sutured field.

All that was left for Walt to do now was insert some drains and apply a pressure dressing to assist in healing. Then he encased Amy's entire leg and thigh in a Jordan splint, a cast with Velcro closures, so that he could open it easily to observe how the wound was progressing.

Amy Bedford was finally ready to be removed to the Recovery Room.

Amy Bedford was lifted carefully and moved onto a gurney. As she was being wheeled out, Walt Duncan ripped off his surgical gloves.

"Excellent, Walt, first-rate surgery," Sy said.

Corey, Amy's pediatrician, patted him on the shoulder. "I don't witness much surgery. And rarely anything like this. But I know an artist at work when I see one. Shall we go up and see the Bedfords? They'll want to know. You know how parents are."

He wanted to reply, *Yes, yes, I know damn well how parents are. Today more than ever.* Instead, he said, "Of course. They'll want to know right away."

They found the Bedfords in Amy's room. It was obvious that Marion Bedford had been weeping. It was as obvious that Amy's father felt ill-equipped to deal with her tears. For she was sitting in the easy chair while he was looking aimlessly out the window. At the sound of the door opening they both turned at once, spoke at once, and with the same solitary word.

"Doctor?"

Walter Duncan entered the room with Dr. Corey just behind him.

"Mr. Bedford, Mrs. Bedford, everything went as well as could be expected. Of course we still have a few rivers to cross. But up to now it's been very successful."

"Successful?" Dr. Corey interpolated. "I'd say perfect! This man is a genius. An absolute genius! You made the right choice of surgeons, Ed. Amy couldn't be in better hands."

"Thank you, Doctor. Thank you," Bedford said, holding out his hand. As they shook hands, he said, "I won't forget what I said. See my little girl through this and I will fund any experiment you name."

"We'll do our best," Walt said, for there was another vital test ahead of him, perhaps a half hour from now, when Amy would come out of the anesthetic. Meantime, he asked, "Mind if I use the phone?"

161

He lifted the phone and dialed an intra-hospital number. He held for three rings before there was an answer. Finally he heard the fourth ring cut short.

"Vic? Walt. Any . . ."

A woman's voice answered. "Dr. Ogura is not here at the moment. Can I take a message?"

"Tell him . . . no, tell me, did he have a chance to examine that specimen I left with him early this morning?"

"Sorry. What specimen?"

"This is Dr. Duncan, Walt Duncan. Did Vic have a chance to examine that specimen?"

"If you asked him to, I'm sure that he did."

"Well, did he say anything?"

"Sorry, Doctor, not to me."

"Okay, okay. Tell him I called." He hung up.

Dr. Corey asked, "Something wrong, Walt?"

"No, no, everything's fine. Just fine. I'll get the results later. Now I'd better go see how Amy is coming out of it."

He went up to the Recovery Room to confirm, if possible, that his surgery had fully succeeded. For despite all his skill, there was still one test for Amy to pass. A simple one. But critical in her young life.

He could hear her slight moan as he approached the door of Recovery. *Good,* he thought, *she's come out of it.* As he stepped into the room, he found her trying to raise her head up from the pillow and stare at her leg. He knew what was going through her young mind.

Are they there, are they both still there? she was asking in great trepidation.

"Yes, Amy, they are both there."

She looked up at him. Her pale, damp face reflected her fear, her relief and her gratitude.

"Now, Amy, one more thing. Can you move your toes? Let me see!" he said.

He stared down at her right leg, waiting. Finally he saw her

162

toes, extending out of the lower end of the cast, begin to move. First they just moved, then she wiggled them playfully.

Good, he thought, *excellent. No residual nerve damage. She can make it. Can make it all the way. If we're lucky.*

Two hours later Amy Bedford was moved back to her room under the care of a nurse who had orders to administer medication to ease her pain or discomfort.

Her father greeted her with a kiss. "Dr. Duncan said it went excellently. Just perfect."

Her mother kept smiling and wiping away tears.

13

A dozen times Walter Duncan looked at the message he had found on his desk when he finally returned to his office.

DR. OGURA CALLED. CALL HIM. URGENT.

A dozen times Walt tried to interrupt the pressures of his own practice to make that call. Twice he did. Only to discover that once Ogura was sitting in on a meeting of the Tumor Board. The second time, Ogura was out of the hospital to deliver a lecture on his specialty at the medical school.

It was just past six o'clock in the evening before the two doctors could make contact.

"Vic? What did you find?"

"Walt, can you come down to my lab for a minute?"

"Of course. Right away."

He did not have the patience to wait for an elevator. He raced down four flights of stairs. He was breathless when he burst into Ogura's lab.

"Vic, what is it?" he demanded.

"Walt, I don't know what this patient is seeing you for, but I would consider this the more serious problem. What I suggest now depends in part on whatever it is you're treating him for. My first reaction was, we must take a bone marrow sample. But that—"

"Bone marrow, you said, a bone marrow sample . . ." Walt interrupted.

"Yes. Clearly indicated by the low hemoglobin, low level of white cells, abnormal growth of blasts. . . . Walt, what's the matter with you?"

"It . . . she . . ." Walter tried to say.

Aware that his colleague's face had gone pale and his lips were twitching, Ogura asked, "Walt? What's wrong? Here. Sit down."

Walter Duncan sank into the chair. His face was now not only pale but damp as well.

"Are you all right, Walt?"

Walter Duncan nodded. He breathed slowly, but shallowly, trying to regain control. Then he said in a soft hoarse voice, "Vic . . . the patient . . . is not a patient. . . . "

Confused, Ogura asked, "Then—who?"

"Simone," Walt said in a whisper.

"Oh, my God!" Ogura replied.

"Tell me," Walt insisted, "everything."

"Everything is unfortunately simple. Findings like these demand a bone marrow sample so we can make a definitive diagnosis."

"What's your educated guess?"

"Leukemia," Victor Ogura said. "I'm so sorry, Walt."

Walter Duncan nodded, turned away from his friend and colleague of many years.

"Have her come in. Let's take that marrow sample. Then we'll know a good deal more," Ogura said.

Walt nodded again, vaguely saying, "Sure, sure, we'll know a good deal more."

"Walt, these days the percentages are much better than they ever were. We're getting results now we wouldn't have dreamed of when I first started in—"

Walter Duncan interrupted, exploding, "Don't quote me percentages! I don't care what happens to other children. I don't want to hear about remissions and cures unless it is remission for *my* child. I am tired of the consoling things we tell other parents to allay their damn-well-justified fears. I am only interested in—"

He said no more and fled the lab. Victor Ogura debated what he should do now. Finally he lifted his phone and placed a call. It was a breach of usual confidentiality. But this was not a usual case.

He dialed a three-digit number he knew well. When he received an answer, he said, "Let me talk to Sy."

"Yeah, Vic? What is it?"

"Sy, can I come right up and see you?"

"Vic, what are you saying?" Simon Rosen asked, staring across the desk at the hematologist. "That's my goddaughter you're talking about!"

"That's why I called you. You're the only one who has any influence over Walt."

"Influence? Why?"

"I've never seen him like this before. In a single moment the doctor, the surgeon, the scientist disappeared. I was facing a father as emotional and shaken as any layperson to whom I've ever had to give such news."

"Why not? Are doctors not permitted to feel like parents? Act like parents? If this were your daughter, Natalie, would you feel any different, act any different?" Sy demanded. Then he sighed sadly. "Oh, God, Vic, what's going on? Why is it that the children of doctors seem to be the special victims of the worst diseases? It's as if disease knew its enemy and was striking back."

"What about Walt?" Ogura pointed out. "And Simone?"

"I'll talk to him," Sy said wearily. "After all, who else should do it?"

Sy found Walter Duncan in his office, staring out of the window at the evening darkness. He had not responded to the sound of the door being opened. Not by turning to see who it was nor by inquiring.

"Walt . . ." Sy began.

The younger surgeon did not answer.

"Victor just told me." Still no response from Walt. "Walt, I know, it's like a knife in the heart. And nothing I might say can change it. Someone has to tell Emily. Then Simone. And that someone should be you. Though I will tell them if you want me to."

Walt Duncan remained silent.

"Walt?"

Without turning to face him, Walt said, very softly, "I will tell Emily."

"When?" Sy persisted.

"Tonight."

"If I can help, if you want me to be there . . ."

"I will tell her," Walt agreed.

"And Simone? What will you tell her when you have to bring her in for the bone marrow biopsy?"

"As little as possible," Walt Duncan said. He turned to face Sy. "She won't know the truth until I can't keep it from her. And don't argue with me, Sy. I know what a fetish we doctors have made of telling patients brutal truths. But Simone is not a patient. She's my daughter! Can you understand that? No, I guess you can't understand that."

He was venting his frustration and anger at the science of medicine by attacking his friend and mentor, by pointing out Sy's life as an unmarried and childless man. He recanted at once. "I'm sorry, Sy. That was a terrible thing to say. Forgive me?"

"I forgave you even before you asked," Sy said. "Nor do I blame you. There is no torment worse than seeing one's loved ones facing death and being unable to prevent it."

Something in Sy's voice, a nuance he had never detected before, forced Walter Duncan to look into Sy's eyes as the old man continued.

"Yes, I know. I was already a young physician when we were taken away. My whole family. I had been expelled from the staff of the hospital in Breslau. So I went home to get my mother and my sisters out of the little town in which my father had served all his life as the village doctor. I had this perfect plan to get them across the border into Switzerland, where we would be safe. Unfortunately I was too late.

"We were held two long days and nights in the synagogue, which they had turned into a prison. Crowded in, packed like firewood. Two days standing, old women and men dying on their feet and unable to fall because there was no room. And always the fear that they would douse the place with gasoline and set it on fire. We had heard stories.

"After two days, they marched us to the railroad siding. And up the ramp into the cars, like so many cattle being taken off to the slaughterhouse. Another three days on the train. Cold. Without food. Without water. More people dying. By now, some of the young as well.

"We ended up in two camps. One for women, one for men. Which faced each other, separated only by a high fence of barbed wire. We could see each other. Could almost touch each other. I watched them always. My mother, my two sisters. I could also watch the smoke rising from the row of chimneys. And I knew that odor.

"Most of all I could see the look of fear on their faces. I was the man of the family. Their eyes beckoned, *Help me, save me.* Despite the fact that they knew that was impossible. Still they could not avoid staring at me. I could not avoid feeling guilty.

"They disappeared one by one. My mother first. One day she was no longer there to stare at me, to beg for help. That day I watched the smoke with special pain. Then one of my sisters. Esther, the older. She was gone suddenly one day. My little sister, Miriam, alone, facing the inevitable. She could not accept it. So this one day, when they came for her, she ran from them in a futile attempt to escape. She hurled herself against the barbed wire. Where they shot her. She hung there, dead, until slowly her body slid to the ground, the rusty barbs of the wire making bloody tracks on her young body.

"All I could do was watch. And you want to give me lessons in futility, in frustration, in hopelessness? In cursing fate?"

"Sy, you never told me. . . ."

168

"I had no reason to tell you—until now," the old man said. "My boy, if I may suggest, tell Emily. Tonight. Gently, if you can. I will arrange for Simone to have that bone marrow biopsy before the week is out. But first, Emily."

Dinner was interminable. He tried to smile and laugh during Simone's mimicking of one of her teachers. He watched every mouthful of food she ate, as if nourishment could influence the course of her condition. Until he noticed that Emily had begun to stare at him, her eyes fixed on him and questioning.

He could barely wait until it was time for Simone to go up to bed. He went with her, watched her get into her nightgown, kissed her, tucked her in. At the door he turned for one last glimpse. She peeked from beneath her coverlet to smile at him. He blew her a kiss.

He tried to console himself by attributing too much to her animated state this evening. Hardly what one could call a state of lassitude or unusual compliance. It could have been his presence at dinner. He had raced home to be in time. That could have stimulated her. But surely she did not exhibit the signs tonight. Perhaps it would all turn out to be a laboratory mistake. He realized he was thinking like a patient again, not like a surgeon. Victor Ogura did not make such mistakes.

Emily was waiting downstairs. He had better face her and tell her.

He waited until she had cleared the table, stowed the dishes in the dishwasher and joined him in the den. He had rehearsed several different ways he would introduce the subject. Emily circumvented all of them by asking, "All right, Walt, what is it?"

Taken by surprise he merely glanced at her.

"Walt, I am not a fool. Yesterday you took a blood sample from our daughter. Tonight you acted very strangely. All through dinner you laughed a little too often and too heartily. You couldn't take your eyes off Simone. You followed every mouthful of food she took. As if you wanted to chew it for her. Now, what is it?

169

Because, no matter what it is, it can't be half as bad as not knowing."

"Darling, sit down," he said simply.

Once she had slid into the chair opposite him, he began. "It *can* be half as bad. It can be even worse."

"Tell me!"

"There is a possibility—no, I won't lie to you. There is preliminary proof that Simone has leukemia."

Tears welled up in Emily's eyes, but she did not cry. She was determined not to.

"And?" was all she could say.

"I'll have to take her into the hospital so we can do a . . . a bone marrow biopsy on her."

"Will it hurt?" Emily asked.

"I'll make sure that it won't," he promised.

They were both silent for some minutes before he said, "These days, they can do miraculous things with chemo in juvenile leukemia."

"Children still die, though," she said simply.

"But the odds are in her favor. Seventy percent, eighty percent." He tried to encourage.

"Which means that one out of every five dies," Emily said, reducing his statistics to facts. "One out of five," she repeated.

"We'll make sure she isn't one of them," Walter said, as firmly as his surgeon's mind would permit.

He was relieved that she had not cried. For if she had, he knew he would have broken down, too. As it was, she seemed to accept it as well as one could have expected, or hoped. Slowly, silently, she went off to bed. Alone. He wanted to give her a chance to fall asleep before he got into bed. He knew he would be restless.

He woke. It was still dark out. He felt the bed. He was alone. He rose, went down the hall, whispering, "Emily? Honey?" There was no answer. He eased open the door to Simone's room. There was no sign of Emily. But the fact that Simone's coverlet was tidily in place indicated that Emily had been in.

He went down the carpeted steps on his bare feet. There were no lights on, save the outdoor lights that the timer turned on and off automatically to ward off prowlers. He went into the den. There, crouched into a ball, legs drawn up close to her body, nightgown pulled around her to ward off the cool night temperature, he found Emily.

He could not discern if she was asleep or awake, for her face was turned from him toward the leaded glass windows.

"Hon?" he whispered huskily.

She did not respond. He came to her, looked down at her. Her eyes were open. She was not asleep. But neither was she responsive to his presence.

"Been up long?" he asked.

She shrugged.

"You mustn't make it seem worse than it is. She's going to need you in the months to come. Need you a great deal. The chemo. And whatever else they have to do."

"Why?" Emily demanded.

"You're her mother, that's why."

"I mean, why did it happen? Why did it happen to her?"

"Nobody knows."

"X rays. I've read that sometimes X rays can cause cancer. Especially leukemia. Didn't that happen in Hiroshima? All that radiation from the bomb, didn't the leukemia rate go way, way up?"

"Up," he admitted, "but not so much as people believe. But what's that got to do with Simmie?"

"Her braces," Emily said.

Walt was confused. "Braces?"

"The braces on her teeth. Orthodontics calls for frequent X rays. To make sure how things are progressing."

"Emily, darling, please, let's not get hysterical. A child does not get enough X rays in the course of such treatment to affect anything," Walt said, at the same time trying to lift her out of the chair so he could embrace her and warm her, since she had

171

begun to tremble. But she would not yield to him.

"If it wasn't X rays, what was it?" She persisted.

"We don't know. We will never know. So there's no use pursuing that. We've got to look ahead. To the definitive diagnosis. To the treatment. To the results."

"Didn't you have an aunt who died of cancer?" Emily asked suddenly.

"You mean my Aunt Birdie?"

"You went back home to her funeral that time."

"Of course."

"Well, if she died of cancer, maybe it runs in your family. Maybe it's one of those genetic things."

"I told you, we don't know the cause. May never know."

"But your Aunt Birdie, she did have cancer," Emily insisted.

"Yes, she did. But she was my aunt only because she married my mother's brother, Arthur. So there can't be any genetic connection."

"If you went to her funeral . . ."

"Emily, I was the only adult male left in the family, that's why I went," Walt explained.

"But, if . . ." Emily started to say, then finally began to sob for the first time since he had told her.

Now she gave herself to his embrace. He held her, pressed his face against her head and spoke softly. "Darling, it wouldn't do any good now to discover what caused it. We have to face the fact that it's likely there. And the question is, what do we do about it? We see her through the biopsy. If the results are bad, we put our heads together and arrive at the best treatment. And we see her through that. But we must never forget that the odds are four to one in her favor. Never let go of that: four to one that she will go into remission and live for years. Years!" he added for special emphasis.

She nodded. But continued to weep.

"Now, come back to bed. From now on you'll need your sleep. You have to keep up your strength for her sake, as well as your own."

He led her up the stairs and past Simone's room to their bedroom. He made her take a pill that would allow her to get some sleep. Once the pill had had its effect, he slipped into Simone's room, quietly. Sat in her too-small white rocking chair and stared at his daughter. She slept peacefully, unaware of her parents' fears. Her young, innocent face lit only by the glow of the night-light.

14

"**Y**OU'LL be easy with her" was Walter Duncan's instruction to his colleague Herbert Coleman, who was scrubbing to go in and secure bone marrow samples for Simone's biopsy.

"Walt, Walt"—Sy Rosen intervened—"I'll be there. Emily will be there. We'll see that Simone is well cared for. That she feels secure and safe."

"I'd be there myself—" Walt started to say.

"Walt," Sy interrupted, "you have patients waiting."

Walt hesitated a moment, then realized that he had better leave. His presence might distract Coleman. Sy would see that his godchild was properly treated, protected from pain and made as comfortable as possible. Walt went off to make his rounds.

He peeked in to see if Amy Bedford was awake. She was. She lay on her back, staring up at the ceiling. A trace of wetness alongside her cheek indicated that she had been weeping. Despite his own concerns, this child needed cheering up.

"Well, Amy, good news!" he announced as he entered.

She turned to him, in need of good news.

"We got the lab reports back," he stated.

"I thought you got the lab reports during the operation," she said, alarmed at the thought that her condition might yet be reevaluated.

"Those reports were okay. But we don't stop there. We continue to do tests of the bone we removed. We take thirty samples of bone along the edges. And we submit each of them to examination to see if they are clean. And you passed! One hundred percent perfect. All thirty. Clean! How about that?"

She brightened considerably. But only for a moment. Then she asked, "What if they hadn't all been clean?"

"Well, we don't have to worry about that now," he said.

"You would have to go back in . . . isn't that what you surgeons say—*go back in*? And amputate?"

"Amy, I told you they were all clean. So we don't have to worry about that. Now let's have a look at that wound."

He opened the closures of the temporary cast in which he had encased her leg so that it was immobile while the wound healed and the muscles assumed their new responsibilities. Eventually she would require a long course of specialized physical therapy for her body to regain its strength and her muscles to accustom themselves to her altered condition. But there was time for that. First, the healing—uneventful healing, please, God.

He uncovered her leg and thigh and studied the long, red, angry scar. His keen eyes were searching for any sign of improper healing. In one case out of four that did occur. Then the surgeon was forced to reopen the wound, go in and close it again, hoping to stimulate clean, healthy healing.

Fortunately Amy Bedford's leg looked fine. Walt decided to remove the drains. He summoned a nurse, ordered a surgical tray and basin. Carefully he removed the drains, examined them. Clean. *So far, so good, Amy,* he thought. *Let's hope it continues that way. Let's hope . . . let's hope that what Coleman finds isn't the worst.*

He was closing Amy's temporary cast. "Now, that wasn't so bad, was it, Amy?"

"Doctor, are you all right?" she asked.

"Of course I'm all right. Why would you ask something like that?"

"I don't know, just today you seem different somehow," she said.

175

"Me? Different? Don't be silly. I'm fine. Great," he insisted, forcing a smile.

"When you first came in, and when you were examining my leg, I thought you found something wrong. Just the way you looked. The way you talked. I mean, it seemed that you were trying to sound optimistic because you didn't want to scare me."

"No such thing, Amy. Everything is fine. So far, you're having what we like to call an uneventful recovery. Boring almost." He laughed, hoping to entice her to laugh.

But she did not and kept staring at him until he withdrew from the room.

It shows, he thought, *my mind is not with my patients. It's up there with Simmie and Coleman and what he'll find. I should be able to control it better.*

Emily Duncan had surrendered her young daughter to Sy Rosen. He had led the child into the treatment room, held her in his arms to reassure her, while Dr. Coleman administered a local anesthetic to her arm. After the first needle sting, Simmie relaxed, for the pain was less than she feared.

Once the anesthetic took effect, Sy turned the child's face toward his own as Coleman picked up a long, sterile stainless-steel needle. Coleman inserted it into Simmie's young skin, pressed it gently through the periosteum, that sensitive layer of her arm where, if she were to feel pain, it would occur. The needle finally met the solid resistance of her young arm bone. Coleman pressed the needle harder until he could feel it pierce the bone and sink into the soft area of her marrow. Once that was achieved, he turned the needle to excise a few drops of marrow. He then reversed the process. He placed some drops of marrow on a glass slide and deposited the rest in a test tube along with a chemical called heparin to keep it from solidifying.

Four times Coleman repeated the process, entering different areas of her young bones each time. Abnormal cell growth can vary in different parts of the body.

The entire procedure was carried out without pain to the

little patient and with a minimum of fear. Sy returned her to her mother.

"Take her home—" he started to say.

"What did you find?" Emily interrupted quickly.

"Nothing, yet," Sy said. "Just take her home. You can even take her to school if you wish."

"I'll take her home," Emily said. She grasped little Simone's hand and started out, but stopped to look back at Sy with a plea in her eyes, *Don't find anything, don't find anything.*

Sy's eyes tried to reassure her, but he was thinking, *Even a doctor's wife cannot accept the futility of hoping against hope at a time like this.*

By the time Sy returned to the room, Coleman had studied the samples on the slides and was viewing them under the microscope.

"Well?" Sy asked.

"Take a look," Coleman urged.

Sy studied the slides carefully, one after another. When he raised his head from the microscope, he stared at Coleman. It was obvious they had both reached the same discouraging diagnosis.

"We . . . we can't be too hasty about this. Let's submit them to electromicroscopy," Sy said.

Coleman knew it would not reverse the diagnosis. However, sensitive to Sy's relationship to the young patient, he agreed. "Sure, Sy. Right away. I'll call you with the results."

Sy went back to his own office to attend his schedule of consultations.

But he was plagued by the possibilities. Trying to deny what his own eyes had told him, he argued, *All right, so it's definitely leukemia. But it could be the no-cell type. In which case the prognosis is not bad. Not bad at all. No-cell responds to chemo. Responds very well. Eighty percent remission. Five-year remissions. Cures. The odds are excellent. Well, if not excellent, then very good. At least pretty good.*

Of course, the diagnostician in him argued, *from what I saw, and*

*Coleman saw, even though he didn't say it, it could be, likely is T-cell
or B-cell. Not so good. T-cell still offers hope. It can be treated. That's
the important point. The odds are not great. But still, it is treatable
with a degree of hope.*

However, he had to admit it in his heart of hearts, *if it is B-cell,
then . . . then that is a whole different situation. With B-cell, the
prognosis is worst of all. Still, there are reported cases of intensive
chemo that have produced remissions. There have been cases . . .* He
tried to console himself.

He realized now that as long as they had had the child in the
treatment room they should have taken a sample of her cerebro-
spinal fluid. To discover if the killer cells had invaded her central
nervous system. If he had not been so emotionally startled by
their findings, he would have called Emily back and taken such a
specimen.

But then, he thought, *ah, the ironies, the bitter ironies these hateful diseases produce. The longer we are able to extend Simmie's life,
the more likely it is that those deadly cells will eventually invade her
nervous system. Producing the final irony. To protect the most vital
organ in the human body, the brain, nature has set up a defense
between body and brain. The blood-brain barrier to prevent foreign
substances in the blood from invading the brain.*

*Unfortunately that very protection also functions to block out the
healing chemotherapy. Thus denying the brain its curative power. The
barrier meant to protect the brain virtually dooms it.*

Wheels within wheels, Sy thought, *and right now, none of them
promising.*

*We must watch Simmie closely for any neurologic signs—headaches,
apathy, irritability—all indicia of leukemia infiltration of her central
nervous system.*

The old man was forced to banish all thoughts of his godchild
now, for he had a long list of patients who had been referred to
him for consultation.

Walt tried to continue with his rounds. But he could not. He
was approaching Mr. Considine, the patient in Room 517, on

whom he would have to do a leg amputation due to his worsening sclerotic condition, which had induced gangrene, when he suddenly turned back and started for the elevator. He rode down to the main floor, exited the elevator and started down the long corridor, which was flanked by doctors' offices.

He entered the office with the bronze plaque reading DR. SIMON ROSEN. Eight patients were waiting to see Sy.

"Is he free?" he asked Bridget Kruzsik, Sy's secretary.

She could tell by the look on his face that it would do no good to say that he wasn't. Walt continued on into Sy's private office. Sy was involved in studying the file of the next patient he would examine. Expecting the patient, he continued reading, while saying, "Sit down, please. I'll be with you as soon as I finish reading all about you."

"Sy?" Walt asked anxiously.

The old man looked up, dropped the file to his desk and knew that the moment had come to speak some distressing, perhaps shattering truths to a man on whom he looked as a son. He would have preferred another time, different circumstances. But, then, there was no good way, no good time to say what needed saying now.

"Walt, sit down."

It was hardly necessary for Sy to say anything else. Walt knew that the diagnosis was among the worst, and the prognosis could not be much better.

"Was it—" Walt started to ask.

"Walter, we have to await confirmation from the Path Lab. But if I had to render a curbstone opinion, I would say acute myelocytic leukemia."

Walter Duncan was aware of the sweat oozing from the pores of his brow, his cheeks and his neck. His hands, strong and skillful, went cold and felt useless.

"It's not the end of the world, Walt. Leukemias are amenable to treatment. Vincristine, asparaginase, prednisone in heavy doses. We can have that thing on the run in three or four weeks."

Walter Duncan nodded in a vague manner that was meant to

end all discussion. He rose. "I've got Mr. Considine waiting. I've got . . ." He left.

The next morning, while Sy Rosen was studying a set of X rays and bone scans in his darkened consultation room, his phone rang. It was unusual for Bridget to interrupt him while he was studying a case. She had developed great skill in fending off all but the most urgent calls while he was thus involved.

So he was resigned; this interruption, annoying as it was, must be important. He hoped it was not James Rowe Russell, calling to discuss the large verdict that the jury had returned in the Enright malpractice case, based on Walt Duncan's testimony. Why didn't they settle that damned case so doctors could get back to treating patients? Anticipating that it might be Russell, Sy answered with impatient gruffness.

"Yes, Bridget?"

"Sy . . . ?" the tentative voice of Emily Duncan asked.

"Emily?"

"Sy, I . . . I have to talk . . ." She could not finish, for she broke down and began to weep.

"Emily . . . Emily, dear, please . . ." The old man begged. He waited until she finally recovered. "Now, my dear, what can I do?"

"I have to see you. Alone. Away from the hospital."

"Of course." He agreed at once. "Let me take a look at my diary." His finger raced down the entries Bridget had made there. "This afternoon at two?" he suggested.

"At two . . ." Emily considered. "Yes, Simmie will still be in school then. Two."

"Wherever you say," Sy agreed.

"There's a little tea shop just outside the mall," Emily said.

"I know the place. The tea is too weak. But the pastries too rich. I'll be there," he promised.

Usually by two o'clock the Tea Shoppe was half empty. Those women who had interrupted shopping in the mall to have lunch had already departed. Those who usually dropped by for tea had not yet arrived. It was simple to find a table for two in a corner, away from eavesdroppers and inquisitive help. They ordered quickly to achieve some privacy. Emily kept herself in restraint until they were served and alone again. But Sy could detect every nervous mannerism. She seemed to have too many fingers to know what to do with. On her upper lip, just above her hastily applied lipstick, was a glisten of sweat. She tended to bite her lower lip without being aware of it. He knew if she did not begin to talk very soon, she might break down.

"Emily, dear, exactly what do you want to know?" he asked.

She appeared relieved not to have to initiate the conversation. But first, a confession.

"I . . . I went to the library yesterday," she began. "I may not be a doctor, but I am a college graduate and an editor. I know my way around libraries. Including medical libraries."

Sy became a bit more tense. A layperson loose in a medical library might come up with all kinds of shocking misinformation that could only add to Emily Duncan's legitimate fears and anxieties. Better to scotch those mistaken impressions at the outset.

"And what did you discover there?" Sy asked.

"First of all, there are two kinds of acute leukemia."

"True."

"And one is much worse than the other. The worst of the two is called acute myelocytic leukemia. AML, the books kept referring to it," Emily said.

"Right," Sy agreed, awaiting the next question with considerable trepidation.

"The kind that Simmie has . . . is it AML?"

Sy paused before answering. For if Emily was asking, there was every indication that to spare his wife the worst news at once, Walter had hedged on the specific diagnosis. Perhaps he intended to let her adjust to the bad news bit by bit instead of all at once. But if she was asking so direct a question, Sy was compelled to give her a direct answer.

"Yes, my dear, Simmie's *is* a case of AML," the old man said.

"I hope you can understand and forgive Walt for being considerate of your feelings. For giving you time to adjust."

She nodded. Tears began to seep from her eyes, but she wept silently. Embarrassed, she used her napkin as a handkerchief, while two streaks of black made their way down her cheeks.

"Tell me," she finally said, "tell me everything. Because I have to know how to behave toward my child. I'll lie if I have to. I'll console her. I'll promise her anything. But I myself have to know the truth, even to be able to lie intelligently."

"Emily," the old man said, reaching across the table for her hand. "Lying might not be the way."

"I don't want her to suffer emotionally as well as physically. I have to be able to tell her that treatment can help."

"You can tell her that, without lying. The treatment can help. May help. But we can't be sure. Therefore, if and until the treatment appears to fail, you can truthfully say it can help. As for the pain and discomfort of the treatment, there is no purpose to lying. You can't tell a child she is not suffering nausea or not vomiting, when she is. You can't tell her that her hair is not falling out, when she is holding handfuls of it. Lying and reassurance are not the same."

Emily had stopped weeping, but her eyes revealed her persistent doubts.

"Emily . . . Emily, my dear, don't you see how much better it would be for both you and Simmie if you told her all the difficulties she faced, and then said, 'But Mommy will be with you all the time. We'll see it through together.' Your reassurance will mean more, because she will know you have been truthful with her."

She nodded slightly, accepting the old doctor's counsel. Then she asked, "Sy, for myself, I want to know what it will be like. The good. And the bad. I have to prepare myself as well as my child."

"Everything?" he asked.

"Everything," she said so firmly that he knew he must tell her.

"I don't know if this is the place, so if it proves too much for you, tell me and we will go elsewhere. To the park, perhaps, where we can talk without restraint of people close by."

"I can take it. Here. Just tell me!" she insisted.

"As you wish," Sy Rosen said. "Years ago, twenty-five, thirty, a leukemic child like Simmie with AML would last, at best, three months. But in the years since then we have made great strides. Our chemical weapons have dramatically increased the number of children who overcome the disease. Complete remission for years, and even permanently, is now commonplace.

"However," he continued, "those optimistic statistics apply more to the other kind of childhood leukemia. Unfortunately the history of AML is not so encouraging. Yes, we can induce remission in about seventy percent of AML cases, wipe out leukemia cells, restore normal bone marrow function."

"Seventy percent." Emily seized on it. "That's good, better than I dared to hope for."

"Emily, Emily, you said you wanted it *all*. Then just listen. The difficulty in AML cases is that most patients with that form of the disease, after remission, eventually relapse."

"Most patients," she repeated breathlessly.

"We're trying, we keep trying, new forms of chemotherapy. And there is always the possibility of bone marrow transplants."

"If that's what it takes," Emily volunteered, "I can give her some of my bone marrow. We're the same blood type."

"It takes more than just matching blood types," Sy pointed out. "Besides, we are getting ahead of ourselves. Let's see how things develop. There's always time for alternative treatments later."

"Is there anything else I should know?" she asked.

"Yes. Percentages, remission rates, cure rates, mean nothing. What happens to your daughter is the only thing that counts. And that we have to discover, day by day."

She nodded thoughtfully. She wiped her eyes again with her napkin, noticed the black stains from her mascara. She tried to joke. "I must remember to use less and less of this stuff as time goes by."

183

"More important, remember to show her smiles, courage, love and above all hope. I have seen cases where the doctors have given up, but the patient has not, and the patient has outlived some of the doctors. Our science of medicine with all its percentages, graphs, charts and its case histories piled up to the sky is still an inexact science. Honest doctors can be wrong almost as often as they are right. We work with what knowledge we have and what instincts we were born with. And we hope for the best."

Emily looked at her watch. "I have to pick Simmie up at school," she said.

They rose from the table. He kissed her on the cheek. And he watched her leave.

She is prepared for the worst eventualities, he thought, *but I wonder if she realizes how trying those eventualities actually will be. The days and nights of torment. Times when she will hold her retching child and wish with all her heart that she could be suffering the pain instead of her daughter. The days of seeing her child grow thinner and paler almost by the hour. The times, near the end, when she will offer, "Take my blood, give her my bone marrow," but it will be futile. Yet, who knows, there could be a miracle.*

Emily Duncan settled into her car, thinking, *One thing about Sy, when you ask for the truth, you get it. What did he really say? That Simmie has the worst of the two kinds. But that does not necessarily mean it must be fatal. There is a chance. We have to work with that thought, there is a chance. Small as it is, there is a chance.*

By the time she had picked Simone up at school, Emily Duncan was willing to forgive her husband for not telling her the whole truth all at once.

184

15

THE meeting of the Tumor Board convened at ten o'clock, five days after Amy Bedford's surgery, two days after Simone Duncan's diagnosis.

This evaluation of Amy Bedford's condition and the planning of her future treatment depended on the pathological evaluation of the bones excised by Walt Duncan. His surgery, skillful as it was, might yet be defeated by stubborn tumor cells that could outwit them in the end.

So, after excision, the removed segments of bone were kept intact and remanded to the pathologist for study. He had made a detailed microscopic and electromyocroscopic study of it. He had also studied samples taken from the safe margins during surgery. He had studied the cancer cells to see what percentage of them had been killed by the chemotherapy.

The board, consisting of a hematologist, an oncologist, a radiologist and a surgeon, in addition to Sy Rosen and Walt Duncan, awaited the report of pathologist Irwin Steele.

Steele confirmed the original diagnosis. As to the effects of the chemotherapy, he stated, "On microscopic analysis I found that almost ninety percent of the tumor cells had been killed by the chemo."

He looked in Dr. Bristol's direction. She nodded, saying, "We'll continue with the same regimen. There's no call for change."

Sy Rosen interjected. "Irwin, how close was the tumor to the edge of the excised portion?"

"Not close enough to constitute a danger," Steele replied.

Walt Duncan received that report with considerable relief. For if the answer had been otherwise, he would have had to go back in and amputate. A careful, concerned surgeon took no chances with such an aggressive enemy as osteogenic sarcoma.

The next case to be put before the board was the case of Patient Duncan, Simone.

The results of hematologist Ogura's observations, the confirmation of the bone marrow biopsies, led the board to agree that the conventional approach to acute myelocytic leukemia was indicated.

Bristol suggested heavy dosages of vincristine, asparaginase and prednisone for a period of four weeks.

Usually this regimen would induce remission in most leukemia cases. To avoid a swift recurrence of the disease, Simmie would have to receive consolidation therapy to destroy those cancer cells that had survived the first phase. For this second phase, Bristol planned a different mix of chemicals, since leukemia cells have a devilish ability to develop resistance, and quietly, to their chemical enemies.

But the consolidation phase would have to await the results of and reactions to the first phase. Ironically, the dangers of the second phase could only follow success in the first phase.

After the case of Patient Duncan, Simone, several others were discussed. But since none involved orthopedic surgery, Walt Duncan excused himself from the meeting. He fled down the corridor. Moments later he heard his name being called.

"Walter, Walt . . ." It was Sy, who had left the meeting right after him.

The old man caught up with him. "Walt, you can't let it get to you now. We have to give the treatment a chance. It's the least you can do. Don't go acting like Amy's father did at the outset."

"Sy, the last few days I've discovered that I am like Amy's

father. I'm just a father. Except for one difference. I know all the things that can go wrong. All the percentages, which are against Simmie. So forgive me if I act like what I am. A worried father, a terrified father."

To establish a warm, friendly relationship between doctor and young patient, Walt Duncan brought Dr. Bristol to Simmie's room in the Pediatric Pavilion of the hospital. While Emily stood at the foot of Simmie's bed, Walt introduced.

"Simmie, darling, this is Dr. Bristol. She will be in charge of your case while you're here. She is a very nice woman. And a friend of mine. So you can consider her a friend of yours, too. You do what she tells you, and you're going to be fine. Just fine."

He tried to avoid Emily's eyes as she forced a smile.

"Now, I'll leave you two to get acquainted," Walt said. His eyes signaled Emily to join him in the corridor.

Once outside, he urged in a whisper, "Please, darling, don't try to smile all the time. She'll know it's false. She'll lose confidence in all of us. Comfort her. Talk to her. But don't keep smiling when you feel like crying."

"Sorry, Walt, sorry . . ."

He kissed her on the cheek and said softly, "She has a chance, a fighting chance. I've seen lots of cases like hers recover. Lots!"

"Walt," she said softly, "don't you keep smiling when you feel like crying, either."

He realized that his false enthusiasm had not convinced her. He nodded and started down the corridor.

Throughout the morning he adhered to his rigorous schedule—examinations, consultations, studying X rays, bone scans and CAT scans, rendering diagnoses, prescribing courses of treatment, arranging for surgery, seeing patients on follow-up, feeling gratified with good post-op results, frustrated and dismayed by cases that did not develop as they should, racking his brain for alternative treatments that might yet reverse the deterioration. In all, it was a routine day in the crowded professional life of Walter Duncan.

With one exception. Throughout the day he felt as if he was dragging with him an extra burden, an intolerable burden. When he was not conscious of it, it was a shadow, a presence that followed him, clouding his thoughts, a presence that seemed to be constantly at his side. Every time he turned to pick up an instrument, look at a film, write out a prescription, that presence seemed to be there, inhibiting him. When he was conscious of it, he knew it was his daughter, in Room 219 in Pediatric. With an intravenous drip in her young slender arm, infusing what he hoped would prove to be life-saving chemicals into her body.

Four times during the day he found reason to go to the Pediatric Pavilion, to drop in and see how Simmie was bearing up. All four times he found her in bed, intravenous in her arm, the inverted bottle feeding the chemo into her drop by drop. She seemed in excellent spirits.

Aware of his concern, Simmie tried to reassure him: "It doesn't hurt, Daddy. I hardly know it's there."

"Terrific. That's my girl," he said, kissing her and tousling her dark hair. At the same time, he was keeping track of the time, only three hours since the IV had started. Two more hours, three, and the aftereffects would commence. The nausea, the retching. How would her young body, already too slim, contend with it? She had little weight to give away.

He had completed his first three surgical cases. With a half hour before his next scheduled operation, he stripped off his OR uniform and hurried back to his daughter's room. He found her in the arms of her mother, retching into a stainless-steel basin that was already partly filled. He slipped into Emily's place, took his daugher's frail young body in his arms and whispered to her, "It'll be over soon, baby. Just a little more and it'll be over. And don't worry, Daddy's here. Everything is going to be all right. All right."

He glanced to Emily, his eyes asking, *Has it been this bad all afternoon?*

Her eyes answered, *Yes, yes, and worse.*

188

He held his daughter closer as if to impart his strength to her. Her retching began to recede. Her body seemed to relax, but only a little. She breathed more deeply.

"Better, baby? Better?" he asked softly.

She tried to nod, but suddenly another wave of nausea welled up in her. He could feel her entire body tense into one large knot of pain as she began to retch again. The phone rang. Angrily, he half-turned to his wife.

"Don't answer the damned thing!" he said hoarsely.

It continued to ring. Without his permission, Emily lifted the phone. "Yes. Yes, he's here. I'll tell him." She hung up. "That was surgery. Your next patient is ready. You have to scrub."

Reluctantly, he surrendered his child to her mother. He kissed Simmie on the cheek. "Mommy will be with you, so don't worry, baby, don't worry. You're going to be fine."

By the time he was through scrubbing and had slipped into the sterile gown and gloves the OR nurses held out to him, he was in control again. Once more the efficient, capable, skillful surgeon who was equipped to deal with all the ills that afflicted the human skeletal structure.

Walt Duncan stood at his daughter's bedside, staring down at the sleeping child. Emily stood at the foot of the bed.

"Will it happen again?" she asked in a whisper.

"Not till they give her another dose of vincristine," he whispered back. "Poor kid, exhausted. But at least she can sleep now. You ought to go home and get some sleep yourself, hon."

"I'd feel better staying here, in case she wakes."

"The nurses will give her all the care she needs," he said, for he was concerned that Emily might run herself down and become unable to withstand the difficult times that lay ahead.

"When she wakes up she looks for me. It's that look in her eyes that says, *Don't leave me alone. I'm afraid.* I'd better be here."

"Then I'll have the nurse find you an empty room where you can take a nap," he said.

189

He came out of the room and exhaled wearily, exhausted from the strain of keeping from his wife his direst fears. His colleagues, including old Sy, had been very solicitous of his feelings when discussing Simmie's case, though out of respect they did not express any false optimism. But they had held back from Emily, to allow her to present a hopeful face to Simmie.

He arranged a place for Emily to catch some sleep. Then he started on his rounds. This was a big day for one of his patients: Amy Bedford. Amy would be getting out of bed today. On her feet. Both of them. Something he could not have promised a week before.

So far, so good for Amy Bedford, whose prognosis was better than little Simone Duncan's. Not that it was clear sailing for Amy. Far from it. Walt would have to impress on her the present and future danger to prepare her for her new regimen. It would begin with crutches.

He entered Amy Bedford's room, calling as cheerfully as he could, "Okay, lazybones! Today's the day you have to get out of bed."

"Can I?" Amy asked, starting to move.

"Not so fast, my dear. First, a little lecture. I wouldn't be Dr. Duncan if I didn't precede everything with a lecture, would I?"

He tried to laugh, but Amy noticed that he could not. She wondered, *Is there more bad news? Did they find something on my X rays? Why is he acting this way?* But she decided to play the game, whatever that game was.

"No, you wouldn't. What is it this time, Dr. Walt? A lecture about how to walk on crutches? I already know."

"Oh, do you?" He challenged, smiling.

"Sure. When I was eleven one summer at camp I broke my leg. My left one. I spent the whole summer hobbling around on crutches. So I'm an expert."

"Well, this time it may be a little different," Walt said. He presented the crutches. "These are the old-fashioned kind, that fit under your armpits. The reason for that is you are to walk without putting any weight on your right leg. Any weight at all.

So let's get these adjusted to the right height for you. Sit up, Amy."

She moved slowly, carefully, to a sitting position. Then, bringing her legs to the side of the bed, she sat up.

"Easy now, my dear," he coached.

She started to rise as he slipped one crutch under her left arm, then under the right. The crutches were a bit too high. He knelt beside her, loosened the screws of the adjustable slides and set them at the proper height.

"Now, Amy."

She let her body rest on the rubber tops of the crutches. He observed her carefully. She was able to stand without exerting any weight or strain on her right leg.

"Good, very good. Later today Hans is going to send up a leg brace for you. Once you have that, you can feel free to move about a little. Even go out of this room, which you must be getting sick of."

"I would like to take a little walk," she admitted. "Lying here, listening. People are just voices. I'd like to see what some of them look like."

"Soon as you get that brace," he promised.

Now for the lecture, he thought.

"Amy, we should review your new regimen. I did mention it before. But I'm sure you were so worried about the surgery that you didn't pay much attention. So let's go over it carefully again."

The look of cheer on her bright young face turned to one of sober concentration.

"Amy, what we did with the surgery was remove the origin of your cancer."

"You said you got it all," the girl said, a trace of fear in her eyes as she prepared herself to hear bad news, dangerous news.

"And we did. All, that is, that we could find. But cancer is a treacherous disease. We can cut it out, and there can still be cancer cells floating through your bloodstream or in other parts of your body that haven't surfaced yet. So we have to track them, like the police would hunt an evasive killer. Track them, hunt them down, wipe them out."

"How do we do that?" Amy asked.

"Chemotherapy."

"More chemo?" she asked. She could almost taste the bitter effects of the treatment.

"Yes, Amy, More chemo. Not for at least three weeks. Because chemo right now would interfere with your leg's healing. But after that, every two or three weeks."

"Every two or three weeks!" she echoed, her concern growing.

"Yes, Amy. For at least eight months," he said. "Remember, I said this would take a year. The next eight months are part of it," Walt Duncan said.

"I was planning on going back to school full time," Amy said.

"Not this year, Amy. Go when you can, try to keep up. But don't be disappointed if you don't pass all your exams. You shouldn't even try to take them. You're not ready yet."

She nodded, but her eyes became moist.

"Eight months more" was all she said.

"I'll want you X-rayed every month. Lung X rays."

"Why?"

"If those damned cells are at work in your body, that's the most likely place for them to show up." He informed her.

"And if they do?" She hesitated to ask.

"If they do, Amy, we cut them out."

"That's all, just cut them out?" she asked, suspecting she was not being told everything.

"Yes, Amy, we cut them out," he assured. "And we continue with the chemo."

"If I'm still alive, that is." She stared at him directly, asking to be contradicted.

"Amy, you've come this far in good style. Don't start feeling sorry for yourself. Not now. Believe me, compared to some cases I know, you're doing well. Extremely well," he said.

"Doctor . . ." she said, then hesitated, wondering if she would be considered impertinent for asking. She decided to risk it. "Doctor, are you all right today?"

"Of course I am. Why do you ask?"

"I don't know. The way you came in. So bright. Too bright. I thought you were covering up some bad news for me."

"I did mention about more chemo," he protested.

"But this was more," Amy pointed out. "Then when you just said, 'compared to some cases I know,' somehow it seemed strange, the way you said it. Why?"

He realized that this young girl was a great deal more perceptive than he had realized. Or else he was a great deal more transparent.

"Yes, Amy. You're right. One 'case' I know . . . she's my own daughter."

"Oh?" Then Amy dared to ask, "Is she very bad off?"

"She could be," he admitted.

"Is she here in the hospital?"

"On this floor."

"Would you mind . . . I mean, is she allowed to have visitors?"

"I think she might welcome that, Amy."

"If it's not too far, that'll be my first walk," Amy said.

"That would be very nice. But don't overtax yourself. Your muscles aren't going to be as strong as you think. It'll take time. So don't overdo."

"I won't, Doctor, I won't."

Once left alone, Amy Bedford reached for the crutches that leaned against the side of her bed. She slipped them in place, thinking, *I'll have my walk before Mom arrives. Then when I do it for her, she'll be surprised. And it's time she had a happy surprise. She's been crying too much, too much. Not when I'm looking. But I can tell. Why do parents think they can kid their kids?*

She rose to her one good foot, rested her full weight on it, made sure her right foot did not touch the ground. Several times she had dared to look when Dr. Walt had opened her cast to observe the wound and see how it was healing. The long red line of the incision, crossed by the sutures, was enough to make her know that she must treat this leg very, very carefully lest she undo all the work and skill that had gone into it.

She hobbled toward the door and realized that whatever she could recall from her life on crutches in summer camp did not avail her much. It was a process new and unaccustomed now, and she had better be very careful. She had not anticipated the weakness in her right leg, even without weight being applied to it.

After just enough steps to take her to the door, she decided not to venture down the hall to visit Dr. Walt's little girl. She was relieved to return to her bed, a bit breathy, far more tired then she had expected.

Where, she thought, *where is all the energy, all the strength I used to have? When I could go that fifth set, that sixth set, when I wanted to? Gone. Gone with my hair. Will it, like my hair, come back one day?*

Chastened, a bit frightened, she lay in bed wondering, *Is this the way it feels to grow old?*

It was early evening. In keeping with hospital regimen, Amy Bedford already had had dinner. She had tried to interest herself in a copy of *Seventeen,* but her ability to concentrate seemed to have failed her, too. She had turned off the television once she found that she was looking at the picture without watching, listening to the dialogue without hearing. One time she deliberately turned off the sound so she could speculate on what the characters were saying to each other. But their gestures and grimaces only appeared ridiculous.

It was almost dark outside, one of those late-spring evenings when dusk seemed soft and benign. The automobile traffic sounded far away. The human traffic in the hall was at a lull, just before the invasion of nighttime visitors, parents, relatives, friends who had been at their jobs all day or at school and were now free to come and stare, to smile and make endless conversation, as if silence, not illness, were the patient's enemy.

In all her days there in the hospital, Amy had become very skilled at reading the sound of footsteps. The nurses, with their small, swift scurrying footfalls on their way to some emergency.

The doctors, heavier, more measured, striding in the hall, stopping at one room or another. The visitors, each with individual treads and paces.

Then, her own visitors. Brent. She could recognize his footfalls, soft in his running shoes, but quite distinct. Several of her girl friends from school, the clipclop of their heeled shoes, their muffled conversations betraying they were in awe of a hospital. Their laughter just before they entered her room to disguise their own fears and mislead Amy into thinking they were carefree and happy to be there.

Finally her parents' footfalls. Her mother's, which she was used to, because Mom was there every morning like clockwork. Spaced just right, after the nurses had finished their morning routine and before it was time for Dr. Walt to make his rounds. Her father's footfalls, swift, sharp. All her life she had thought of him as a man in a hurry. Whatever he did—arrive home for dinner, leave in the morning, answer telephone calls, bark orders, take them out to dinner, examine her report cards, go to church, entertain company, talk to her, rebuke her, give her gifts, attend a rare school function—he did it all in a hurry.

Even the time her mother had forced him to take them on a vacation—a trip across the country to see this nation's rich and overwhelming natural beauties—he had cut it short by four days. He had had to get back to the business.

His sharp, staccato footsteps along the hospital floors reflected his attitude toward life. Do it. Do it at once. Get it done. Try though he might, once he was in her room, he could not conceal or restrain that same habit. Until Amy would wish, silently, *Why does he keep pretending he wants to be here? I know he loves me, he just hasn't got the time to show it. Go, Daddy, for God's sake, just go!*

She could hear his rapid steps approaching now. And hurrying alongside, her mother's steps. Amy raised herself, shinnied toward the edge of the bed, sat up, reached for her crutches, fixed them firmly in place under her arms and rose. She was determined that when they came in she would be facing them.

As usual, her father preceded her mother into the room, any room. His prepared smile gave way to a look of genuine surprise and delight.

"Amy! My God, Amy, you're standing. Marion, look, my daughter's on her feet! Isn't that terrific?"

He reached his daughter, carefully embraced her and kissed her on the cheek. He pulled back suddenly. "I'm sorry, darling, I didn't hurt you, did I? I mean, I didn't do anything to that leg, did I?"

"No, Daddy. I'm fine. Just great. And Dr. Walt said I could walk down the corridor whenever I felt up to it."

"Maybe we ought to get you a private nurse, to go along, make sure you don't hurt yourself," her father suggested. "It's no problem."

"Dad, I think Dr. Walt wants me to do things on my own. It's part of getting my strength back. Building up my muscles again."

"Whatever he says. He's the boss. That man is a miracle worker," her father enthused.

She dampened his enthusiasm considerably when she said, "He also said I'll have to go back on chemo."

"Chemo? Again?" her father asked.

"Every two or three weeks. For eight months." Amy informed him.

"That long? That often?" her father asked, his disappointment obvious.

"Ed"—his wife intervened—"he explained it all that day you couldn't make it. You were out of town on business."

"You never told me."

"I started to. Several times. You kept getting business calls. Besides, there was nothing you could do about it. It's something that has to happen. Part of that one year he talked about the very first time."

"Sure. Of course. I remember. Well, if my little girl has to do it, she will," he said. "That's what makes her a champion. Right?"

"Right, Dad!" Amy responded as heartily as was expected of her. But she was aware that she had disappointed him again. He

196

was hoping, expecting, to be relieved of hospital visits, and the concerns that went with them. As long as his daughter was confined to the hospital, her danger seemed worse. Once home there was the inherent promise that she was recovering, would recover. But weeks, then months of chemo, in hospital for a few days at a time, but in hospital nevertheless, the disease seemed closer again, more threatening again.

16

"OKAY, Amy, let's see how you can walk today," Walt Duncan said.

Amy started toward him on her crutches. He watched, trying to detect if, even by inadvertence, she was putting any weight on her right leg. No, that foot cleared the floor with every step she took.

"Perfect, Amy. Now we are going to put on that walking leg brace Hans has designed for you. You'll wear that until I evaluate you again to see if you're ready to put some weight on that leg—say, about twenty-five percent of your normal weight. But that'll be when I reevaluate you next, five weeks from now."

"Are you telling me I can go home now?" Amy asked.

"Yes!" Walt Duncan said. "But you have to remember, two things we're going to be watching for. Healing. And mainly any sign of infection. That's why we don't want any pressure on that leg. And why that leg brace. We want your leg muscles and tissue to heal cleanly around the implant. We don't want to risk any infection."

"Why do you keep harping on infection?" Amy asked. "I won't do anything dangerous."

"Amy, you'll be getting chemo every few weeks. While the

chemo is chasing those damned cancer cells, it is also weakening your immune system. That's why I keep harping on infection," he explained.

She nodded soberly.

"We will also X-ray your lungs every month."

"Still afraid of the thing moving into my lungs," she said grimly.

"For a whole year we have to be worried about that," he said. "Now, I've called your mother. She'll be coming for you this afternoon."

"Then I'd better see Simmie before Mom gets here."

"She told me you were in to see her. Several times. She likes you."

"I like her, too," Amy said. "She's very pretty, and bright. She sounds like a lot more than eleven."

"Sickness has a way of aging people faster than their time," Walt said.

"What's wrong with her?" Amy asked. "No one would tell me. Except I can tell by their attitude it's serious."

"It is," he admitted, "but we're doing everything we can."

"That means it's very serious. Doesn't it?" the girl asked.

"Amy, it's leukemia, of the most dangerous type," Walt said softly.

Amy Bedford made her way down the corridor on her crutches, which she now handled with a degree of confidence, if not ease. She was reaching the open door of Simone Duncan's room when she heard, "Mommy, why don't you go down and get some lunch for yourself? I'm fine. I'm feeling great." But Simmie's thin, reedy voice belied her determination.

"I won't leave you alone," her mother was saying as Amy entered the room.

"You won't have to, Mrs. Duncan. I'll stay with Simmie while you're gone."

"See, Mommy, you can go now." The child encouraged her.

"Okay," Emily Duncan said, proceeding to give Amy a list of instructions. "If Simmie gets one of those waves of nausea, just hold this pan up for her. And call the nurse. If a nurse doesn't come at once, keep ringing. And . . ."

"Mrs. Duncan, I know what to do. I've been through it myself," Amy pointed out.

"Of course. I'm sorry. I'll be back as soon as I can, darling."

As she bent to kiss Simmie, the child said, "Mommy, you don't have to hurry. Amy and I, we get along just fine."

The two young people waited until Emily Duncan was gone.

"I'm glad you're here," Simmie whispered. "I need someone to talk to. Do you mind?"

"No. Go ahead. Talk!"

"I don't think they're telling me the truth," Simmie confided.

"Of course they are. Your daddy has told me the truth. He's very up-front about everything. Good and bad."

"Then maybe your bad isn't as bad as my bad," Simmie said.

"What do you mean?"

"They tell me things. Like what kind of chemo I'm getting. And what to expect it's going to do *to* me. And *for* me. But there's one thing they don't tell me."

"What's that?" Amy asked.

"Am I going to die?" Simmie said. "They don't say anything about *that*. So I keep wondering. Did you wonder about that, too?"

"That. And worse. Like losing my leg," Amy admitted.

"Is that worse than dying?"

"I used to think so," Amy said.

"Of course, in my case, I don't have any choice," Simmie said.

"What do you mean?"

"Well, I can't say, 'Am I going to die or am I going to lose my leg?' I can only say, 'Am I going to die or not?' So you see, we're not the same."

"I know how you feel. I went through all that," Amy said. "Worrying. At night. When you're alone. No matter how much they visit, and talk, and smile, comes nighttime you're alone. You think of all those things they try so hard not to let you think about. Even after the doctors tell you everything there are still questions you forgot to ask, or were afraid to ask, or got only half answers to. So you worry about them."

"You, too?" Simmie asked.

"I guess every kid does."

"I know I do," Simmie said. "I never tell my Mom how I feel about dying. She's cried enough as it is. If I told her, she'd just about come apart. So I can't tell anyone."

"Not even your dad?"

"Especially not even my dad," Simmie said.

"But he's a doctor," Amy pointed out.

"So he knows how bad it is. And I don't think he's telling Mom everything. I know by what he says when he's in here. And then what she says. It isn't always the same. And she wouldn't lie to me. She might not tell me the whole truth. But she wouldn't lie. So if they're both not saying the same thing, it must mean Daddy isn't telling her the whole truth either. It all comes down to one thing. Whatever it is, it's too terrible to tell me," Simmie said.

"Don't worry. Simmie, your father won't let anything bad happen to you. Look what he did for me," Amy said by way of assurance. "I can walk on crutches now. Weeks from now I'll be able to put my weight down on this leg. And I don't have the cancer anymore. Your dad just cut it out. Cut it right out!"

Simmie looked at Amy in a way that forced Amy to ask, "Simmie, what's wrong?"

"Now you're starting to sound like them. All of them. Dad, Mom, Uncle Sy. They are so anxious to cheer me up that they think I'm an idiot. That I don't understand. Or that I can't feel what's happening to me."

She turned away from Amy's sympathetic gaze. Amy felt that she had failed.

There was a knock on the door. Both girls turned to see who it was.

Simmie called out, "Mommy?"

It was the nurse with the IV that would begin the next phase of Simmie's chemotherapy. To both patients that equipment was distressingly familiar. Amy leaned close to Simmie.

"Don't worry. I know it's awful when it's going on, but just remember it's always over. Always." On impulse she embraced the younger child. "Your dad's a wonderful man. He wouldn't let anything bad happen to you."

She hobbled out of the room on her crutches, knowing that within two weeks she would again be undergoing the same thing herself.

While Marion Bedford gathered up her daughter's belongings and packed them neatly in the small suitcase, Walt Duncan was issuing instructions.

"You return in fourteen days to undergo one day of chemo. Then two days at home to overcome the effects. You will do that every three weeks, depending on Dr. Bristol's observations. Concurrent with your first course of chemo we will X-ray you. At your fourth course of chemo we will do a complete bone scan."

"You still think it's there, don't you, Doctor?" Marion asked.

"We take no chances, do we, Amy?"

"No, Dr. Walt."

"Now, Amy, one thing more. Don't push things. Healing is a slow process. Keep that brace on. Walk carefully. Tripping or falling at this stage of things can ruin everything. Later, when everything is fixed in place and we're sure there is no danger, we'll start giving you physical therapy so that your leg and thigh muscles get used to their new duties. Being an athlete, you'll probably enjoy that a lot more than chemo, X rays and scans."

Mrs. Bedford had closed the suitcase. It was time to go.

"Amy, right now you have a great chance at a healthy, normal life. Don't jeopardize it."

"I won't, Doctor. And thanks, thanks a million."

Impulsively, she kissed him on the cheek, but in so doing lost control of one crutch and fell against him. He caught her, held her. "Amy, that's what I mean. Don't make any sudden moves. Slow. And sure. That's your prescription for now."

"I know. I'm sorry. I just had to thank you."

There was a knock on the open door. They turned. Brent Martin was standing in the doorway, asking, "Can't I help in some way? Carry your bags or your flowers?"

"Brent, shouldn't you be in school now?" Mrs. Bedford asked.

"I got permission. We thought you'd need a hand."

"Well, this bag is heavier than I thought," Mrs. Bedford said, surrendering it.

As he took the suitcase, Brent said, "Doctor, I want you to know, all of us thank you for what you've done for Amy."

"I've never had a more willing and cooperative patient. I'm proud of her. But I want you guys to remember, we haven't won this war yet. So save your thanks."

"Doctor, I hope Simmie is all right. She's a darling child. And bright. Even brighter than you know," Amy said. "Give her my love."

"I will, and thanks, Amy," he said. "See you in a few weeks when you come back for your chemo."

He watched with considerable satisfaction as Amy hobbled out on her own power, while Brent and her mother followed. None of them was as aware as he how much a part sheer luck had played in bringing Amy Bedford this far. Only he knew how many times along the way her treatment, his surgery, could have been frustrated by an unwelcome development that could have meant amputation or death.

Both those devastating possibilities must still be reckoned with, he knew.

That thought made him delay his next patient visit and go down the corridor to Room 219.

He found Simmie lying in bed, the IV taped to her arm, the needle inserted in her vein. She was listening to a cassette through her headphones. Emily was seated in the chair opposite the bed, smiling at her daughter, trying to give her courage.

"How's my girl doing?" Walt asked, trying to sound breezy and cheerful.

Simmie smiled at him, and though she had not heard him, she said, "Terrific. Mommy brought me a new cassette. The Outrageous."

Walt's puzzled look made her explain. "It's a new group, Daddy. Don't you ever listen to the radio? They're in the Top Forty every week."

"Oh, sure. The Outrageous. Great! I listen to them on my way to the hospital. Sometimes I sing along with them. When I can understand the lyrics."

Simmie laughed. "You do not," she said.

Even such a momentary fragment of laughter warmed his heart. But when he glanced at Emily he could see, behind her smile, her fear of what would be happening in a few hours, when the chemicals in Simmie's body would bring on the inevitable torment.

He kissed his daughter, patted her on the cheek. He kissed his wife, felt how rigid and tense her body was, but forced himself to leave to resume his professional duties. At times like this he felt totally inept, for his science had become so specialized that he was of little more help to his ailing child than a layperson.

There seemed to be more than the usual weekday number of cars parked along the tree-lined street on which the Bedfords lived. As Mrs. Bedford drove up, Amy observed, "Lot of cars, especially for a Tuesday."

"Mrs. Snedeker across the street. Probably having one of her bridge luncheons today," Marion Bedford said.

She turned her silver top-of-the-line Cadillac Seville into the driveway and up near the front door. Brent was close behind on his motorbike. So when Amy opened the door on her side, he was there to take her crutches, assist her to her one good foot and shepherd her along the brick walk to the front of the house. He hovered alongside every step of the way, calling to her mother, "Don't bother with that suitcase; I'll get it in a minute."

Amy made her way to the red brick three-step elevation in front of their big white front door. Brent had to restrain himself from helping her as she climbed one step at a time, crutches first, then left foot up, crutches first, then left foot up, crutches first, then left foot up. At the door, she was breathless from exertion. Brent reached for the shiny Colonial brass doorknob. He pressed down and the latch gave way easily. He pushed the door open for her and stepped back. Amy hobbled in.

She had managed only four labored steps into the foyer when she was surrounded by the excited voices of her classmates. "Welcome home, Amy!" From the living room on her right, from the dining room on her left, and from the landing on the second floor they rushed out to greet her.

Not only Amy but her mother was taken aback. After the first moment of surprise, they looked at each other and began to laugh and cry. Surrounded as they were by exuberant young men and women, they were quite aware that none of them had tried to embrace Amy for fear of threatening her precarious balance.

"This is just wonderful," Marion Bedford called out to them. "But shouldn't you all be in school?"

"We are," one of the girls said. "It's all been arranged. This is a class in social studies. On how to be a good neighbor and friend."

"Are you sure your teacher approved of this?" Marion Bedford asked.

"Call him, if you like," Brent said.

"Well, in that case, I'd better order in some food, lots of food, to judge from the size of this group."

"Too late," another girl called out.

"It won't take long."

"She means it's already been done," Brent explained. "We had to get your husband's permission to get in. When he found out why, he just took care of everything. He's quite a guy, when you get to know him."

"I guess he is quite a guy. When you get to know him," Amy said.

Sy Rosen stopped by Simmie's room late in the afternoon. The child was suffering even more wrenching aftereffects of the chemo. She was in Emily's arms, bent over the stainless-steel basin.

A look passed between Sy and Emily. He was asking, *Do you*

want me to relieve you? And she was responding, *No, Sy, I'm the only one who can do this.*

Quietly Sy slipped out the door. He felt guilty. Not because of the child's discomfort and suffering. It was the price patients with cancer had to pay to buy back their health.

But, based on Dr. Bristol's findings, he had to believe that thus far Simmie's suffering had not produced any encouraging results. Soon, if things did not improve, they would have to resort to other, more drastic chemicals to fight off her disease. And if those failed . . . Well, there was always the final and ultimate therapy. Which was as dangerous as it was promising.

He stopped by Bristol's office. She knew his question without his asking.

"No, Sy, no improvement."

"Should we change her chemo?" he asked.

"Not yet. Let's give it time," Bristol said.

"Oh, yes. Time," the old consultant said. "It's been weeks, months. How much time and how much endurance do you think a child that age has?"

"We do the best we can," Dr. Bristol said. "The best we can."

If he had not know her better, he would have silently called her by the name pinned on her by many patients who were sometimes unsettled by her cool, deliberate, scientific approach to all cases: *The Iceberg.*

But Sy knew it was Rita Bristol's facade, adopted by an extremely sensitive woman whose professional fate it was to deal only with the very sick and dying.

So he would be guided by her judgment. When it came time to change chemicals, she would do it. If more extreme measures were indicated, she would prescribe them, too.

As he went on toward his own office, he kept saying softly, "Oh, Simmie, Simmie. Simmie, if it would help, I'd offer my blood."

He could not erase from his memory the sight of his young sister's blood dripping from the barbs of that rusting wire as she slowly slid to the earth.

17

TWO more months passed. Simmie had had her fourth series of chemo. She was back in the hospital for what had become routine tests. The results were not encouraging. Oncologist Bristol decided that more potent chemicals must be administered.

When she announced her decision, Walt Duncan detected that she was being slightly less than totally frank about her fears. It was his job now to play the same sad game with Emily. He must broach the idea without alarming her.

Simmie had been put to bed. Emily and Walt were in the den when he said, "I had another talk with Bristol today."

"What did The Iceberg have to say?" Emily asked, anticipating bad news.

Walt tried to laugh. "I thought only patients called her that."

"She's a machine. A computer. Such and such results from the lab, white count, red count, and she grinds out dosages of chemicals like a coin machine dispensing cans of soda."

"Emily, that woman deals with the worst illnesses there are. If she became emotionally involved in each case, she'd go completely to pieces."

"Don't you ever get to be like that," Emily warned.

"I won't. No credit to me. It's difficult to become emotional about lower back pain. So lay off the poor woman."

"Okay, okay," Emily said. "You're so defensive about her, if I didn't know you better, I'd think you two were having an affair."

"Oh, come on, Em," he said. "Don't be ridiculous."

"What's ridiculous about it?" she countered, more serious than he had at first detected. "With what's happened to our lives in the last few months . . ." She turned away.

He went to her, gently took her by the shoulders, turned her about. Her eyes were wet. She averted her head. He made her look up at him.

"I've never said anything like that before," she admitted. "Never thought anything like that."

"The other woman is Simmie. Aside from my work, there doesn't seem to be room in my life for anything else," he confessed.

He held her close, kissed her. It was a tender but passionless kiss. She knew that.

While still in his embrace, she asked, "What about Bristol?"

"I told you that was ridiculous . . ." he started to say, but then remembered what he had originally started out to tell her. "She wants Simmie back in the hospital."

"I've had her there every morning to be checked up."

"She wants her there to stay."

"Stay?" Emily asked, becoming rigid in his arms. "What for?"

"A new kind of chemo. So she'd like her to stay."

"What kind of chemo?" Emily demanded.

"A new one. Experimental. Much stronger. Bristol thinks it might do the job this time."

"She wants Simmie in the hospital to stay? She used those words, 'to stay'?" Emily asked.

"I don't remember her exact words. But she did convey to me that she thinks Simmie should remain in the hospital during this entire course of chemo. It's a protective measure. Em, darling. What's got into you?"

"I don't know," she admitted, breaking free of him so she could wipe back her tears. "Just those words, 'to stay,' made it seem as if she was never coming home again."

"Dr. Bristol's doing all she can. We're all doing all we can. But there are no guarantees," he said.

She nodded, kept wiping her tears back with her fingers. Finally, resigned, she asked, "When does she want her there?'

"Tomorrow."

The next morning Emily Duncan brought her daughter back to the Pediatric Pavilion. She carried a small suitcase with Simmie's nightclothes, robe and bed slippers. And Matilda, her favorite doll.

As they stepped into the elevator, they discovered Mrs. Amiel, a young woman, blond, rather pretty. Her son had occupied a room adjacent to Simmie's during her previous hospitalization.

"Oh, good morning," Emily said. "And how's David doing?"

Inhibited by Simmie's presence, Mrs. Amiel said, "Oh, fine. He's getting along just . . . fine."

"I'm glad," Emily said.

But over Simmie's head the two mothers exchanged glances that revealed more of the truth than had been spoken. Mrs. Amiel's eyes betrayed her hopelessness. But still she tried to smile. Emily thought, *She was so pretty two months ago. Now she's aged not months but years, years. Am I looking at myself a few months from now?*

"If David can have visitors, I'm sure Simmie would like to drop in. Wouldn't you, dear?"

"Of course. If they let me out of bed," Simmie said.

"David would love it," Mrs. Amiel said.

The elevator door opened. They parted quickly, Mrs. Amiel hurrying down the corridor to see her young son.

"He's very sick, isn't he, Mom?" Simmie asked.

"Yes, dear."

"Then why did she say he was doing fine, when he isn't?"

"Just . . . just trying to keep up her own hopes, I guess. Poor woman."

209

They were passing an open door when they heard a familiar voice: "Simmie, that you?"

Simmie went to the open door, peered in to discover Amy Bedford in bed, an IV stand alongside, with the needle fixed in her arm.

"Amy . . ." Simmie was delighted to see her.

"Yes. I'm back for mine. You, too?"

"I guess so," Simmie said.

"Well, I've got only four months to go," Amy said.

"Amy," Emily asked, "did they do your X rays yet?"

"Yep. Clean, they said. I get a complete bone scan tomorrow. And if that's clean, I get to go home for another three weeks."

"You will. Walt said he's very satisfied with your progress so far," Emily said.

"Did he? I mean, sometimes when the doctors say that, I wonder what they're really feeling. Are they just encouraging me, keeping up my spirits? Or do they really mean it?"

"When my husband says that, he means it." Emily assured her.

"I've learned one thing," Amy said, seeking to encourage Simmie. "I find the more chemo I get, the better I tolerate it. So, Simmie, you've got something to look forward to. It's going to get easier."

"That'll be something," Simmie said.

"Look, when they get this IV out of me, I'll come visit. Okay?"

"Oh, sure!" Simmie said. "Please!"

Amy Bedford had had her dose of sensitizing material in preparation for her bone scan. She lay on the flat couch that would soon slide her under the huge, round all-seeing eye of the scanning apparatus. She felt herself being moved back until she was surrounded by the metal mechanism. She kept two fingers of her right hand crossed in superstitious tribute to the goddess Luck.

Please, please, don't let them find anything. Please.

There was a sense of being alone, cut off from the rest of the world. No one else could influence her fate now. Not her mother. Not her father. Nor his money. Nothing mattered now but the verdict this machine would finally render. She could feel her heart pounding. She wondered if that, too, could register on a scan. Nothing seemed to operate in the instrument. It made no sound, seemed to have no moving parts. It was silent, like a conscience, but it could hand down verdicts of life or death. *Let it be life,* she pleaded fervently. *Let it be life.*

In her office in the Oncology Wing, Dr. Bristol once more studied the lab reports of Patient Duncan, Simone. White cell count. Red count. Blood platelets. No single number was extremely distressing, but taken together the figures were not encouraging, either. The patient's condition was slowly deteriorating despite all the chemo she had absorbed.

Adriamycin, Dr. Bristol decided. A little extreme and not without risk. But the time to try such medications was while the patient was still strong enough to tolerate the effects.

Starting tomorrow, she would put little Simmie Duncan on adriamycin.

Amy Bedford had been returned to her room. Despite the reaction to the chemo she had had earlier in the day, she was free to leave her room, go to the solarium, sit and catch up on school assignments or visit. She chose to visit.

The little Amiel boy was still there. She always looked in on him when she came back for chemo. He was a pleasant little boy who looked paler and thinner each time. His mother always seemed so delighted to have visitors. It relieved her of the burden of smiling and reassuring her little son. Yes, Amy would visit him.

But when Amy reached his door, it was closed, and there was a sign: NO VISITORS. She hesitated, then turned and started down the hall on her cane. Her progress in that regard had pleased Dr. Duncan. She had gone from depending on her crutches to keep all weight off her right leg to permitting 25 percent of her weight to rest on it, to wearing a brace and using her crutches, to her present state, a brace to protect her leg and a cane to support her. She felt satisfied that it was not only an achievement, but it bore out precisely the timetable Dr. Duncan had promised.

She made her way down the corridor with great care. One risk she was determined not to run, falling and damaging that skillfully fashioned instrument of titanium and plastic that took the place of her diseased bones. Concerned as Dr. Duncan had been about the way she healed, she did not want to risk his having to go in again and replace that prosthesis, even though there was a spare resting safely in Hans's machine shop.

He had shown it to her the day before she left the hospital the first time. She had gone down to thank him for his skillful work, and he had proudly displayed the spare for her, saying, "Ve are alvays ready. In case you need it. But take care, little Amy, take care."

She reached Simmie's room. The door was open. Amy looked in. Simmie was in bed, her doll embraced in her right arm. Amy watched for a moment, realized that the younger child was asleep. She was about to turn away, but decided to go in and study her very closely, which she could not do when the child was awake.

She stood at the foot of the bed, leaning forward to get a closer look at little Simmie. She was a pretty child. With small, exact features like her mother's. When she grew up, she would be like her mother. Pretty, dark-haired and petite. Amy had admired Emily Duncan from the first time she had seen her. She had thought, *A man as nice as Dr. Duncan deserves a beautiful wife.* Yes, if she grew up, Simmie would be like her mother. *If?*

Amy wondered, *Why am I thinking something like that suddenly? Is it because of the way she looks, so thin, so pale? And her cheeks so sunk in. She wasn't like that the first time I saw her. But then neither was I before they started me on the chemo. She'll get over it. As I did. And maybe they'll get her a wig, like I have. Do they have wigs for kids so young?*

The nurse wheeled some equipment into the room. She was surprised but not distressed to discover Amy there. She smiled at her and was about to speak, but Amy signaled her to be quiet and pointed to Simmie, who was still asleep.

Amy turned on her cane and started out of the room, glancing

212

at the medical equipment and observing, *I never need anything like that when I'm getting chemo. I wonder what's wrong?*

Emily Duncan had dressed hurriedly and was on her way to the garage when the phone rang. *Not another friendly inquiry,* she hoped. Much as she appreciated the concern of their friends, she was tired of giving the same vague reports to as many as eight or ten friends every day. She thanked them for their offers to relieve her of the burdens of everyday householding, shopping or other chores. But she would rather not have to keep explaining. Especially to the mothers of children who were in Simmie's class at school. Lately, Emily Duncan had become aware of her resentment, her definite resentment of mothers with healthy children.

For an instant she considered refusing to answer the phone. But it might be the hospital. She had to answer.

"Hello . . ."

"Emily, dear . . ."

She recognized her own mother's voice.

"Yes, Mother?"

"Emmie, Dad and I have been talking it over, and we feel we should be there—" her mother began.

"Mother, please, don't go to all that trouble."

"It's no trouble. No trouble at all. And we feel—"

"Mother, I don't think it's wise. Walt doesn't think so either. Not with Dad's heart condition. So you just stay out there in Arizona until we send for you."

"And when will that be?" her mother asked. "When it's too late?"

"Don't say that!" Emily rebuked her mother.

"What are we to think? The only reports you give us are so vague. And there's no real sign she's getting better. Is there? Emily, is there?"

"Mother, please. I'm late to the hospital now."

Her mother was determined. "I was talking to a neighbor here in the condo. They went through the same thing. Not exactly

213

leukemia. But some other terrible disease. Their grandchild passed away before they ever got to say good-bye."

"Mother, I don't want to hear about other children and what happened to them!"

"We still think we should come!" her mother insisted.

"No!" Emily said bluntly. "I have to spend all my time with Simmie. So, much as I love you, I cannot be bothered running a household for you and Dad. I have time for only one thing now, my daughter!"

"Are you *forbidding* us to come?" her mother asked, her hurt most obvious in her strained voice.

"If you want to put it that way, Mother, yes, I am forbidding you. Now, I have to go to the hospital. I'll call you later."

"Yes, later, always later," her mother said. She hung up without saying good-bye.

The conversation with her mother had unnerved her. On her way to the hospital she had to make an exceptional effort to drive carefully. By the time she arrived, she felt under control. Sufficiently so to acknowledge that her mother's love for Simmie, her dad's love for his granddaughter were no less than her own. Their need to be with her at this time was as strong as hers. She must call them back tonight and be a great deal more pleasant and understanding.

Her sense of total control was severely shaken by what confronted her as she entered Simmie's room. The child lay on her back, an IV in her arm. Fixed to her chest the familiar sensors, which Emily identified immediately as necessary for an ongoing electrocardiogram. Their cables led to the machine and the oscilloscope.

Good God, Emily feared. *Has the toll of the chemo been so severe that her heart has finally given out? We must stop torturing her. We must!*

Whatever self-control she had been able to muster deserted her now. The sound of her weeping caused Dr. Sy Rosen to turn from Simmie's bed.

214

"Sy?" Emily asked through her tears.

He gestured her away from the door and out into the corridor. Once the door was closed, she asked, "What happened?"

"Nothing. That equipment is to prevent anything *from* happening," he explained.

"They're doing an electrocardiogram. That means a heart attack."

"Emily, please, before you start imagining the worst, let me explain. Dr. Bristol is now using a more powerful drug on Simmie. Adriamycin. Which sometimes produces side effects. Tachycardia. Very rapid pulse. Premature ventricular contractions. Skipped beats. And other heart complications. So while they administer the drug they also monitor her heart to make sure none of those occur."

"And if they do occur?" Emily demanded.

"She stops the treatment at once. And everything will be restored to normal," the old surgeon said. When Emily did not respond, he said, "Emily, you believe me, don't you?"

She finally nodded.

"I have told you, my dear, I will never lie to you."

"I'm sorry, Sy. But I just had a run-in with my mother on the phone and I guess it undid me."

"She wants to come, eh?"

"Yes. What do you think?"

"I'm the wrong one to ask. Frankly, if you and Walt had moved out to California when he had that offer from UCLA and Simmie was this sick, I'd come. Whether you said to or not. So I know how grandparents feel." He smiled. "Not much help, am I?"

She kissed him on his wrinkled cheek. "I'll call Mother and tell her to come."

"Good. After all, your daughter needs you now. But you are also a daughter. So there's no shame in needing your mother."

18

AMY Bedford had returned to the hospital for her next series of chemo. Her next X ray. This time, however, no scan. For it had been only two months since her last scan. She knew the routine too well by now. Chemo every three weeks. X ray of lungs every month. Complete scan every three months. She was now five X rays, two scans and twenty-one series of chemo into the treatment. She could begin counting from the other end now. Only four X rays to go, two more scans, and eight more series of chemo.

The course of her treatments resembled one of those pursuit mysteries of which she had read more than a few during her long days in bed. The doctors kept pursuing those killer cells as if they were enemy submarines. Hoping to track them down, wipe them out. And all the while they kept taking soundings, trying to find out if the enemy was still there. Except they didn't call them soundings but X rays and scans.

A year before she had been a healthy, strong young woman whose sole aim in life was winning the state tennis championship for herself and the team championship for Swede Olafsen. Now, as she stared at her face in the hand mirror she always brought with her, she found an emaciated, almost bald young woman who was lucky just to be alive.

But, damn it all, she was alive. And determined to stay that way. Not only for herself but for her mother, who was so devoted, and especially for her father. He had revealed depths of feeling that she had never suspected.

On the mornings she had to return to the hospital for chemo or testing, her father would linger over breakfast with her. Now he ignored the phone that would ring almost without stopping, when once he used to seize it eagerly. He never failed to call her at the hospital at least four times every day that she was there. When he visited at the end of the day, he never came empty-handed.

He will surely be doing the same today, Amy thought as she made her way down the corridor to the room assigned to her. She still depended on her cane. But only until she had progressed sufficiently in her physical therapy program to build up those hip and leg muscles to assume the functions her now missing knee muscles once had performed.

It was early. Very early. The carts were still in the corridor, ready to receive empty breakfast trays. Amy looked for the room assigned to her, noticed that she had just passed a door with the card in the slot reading DUNCAN, SIMONE. *So little Simmie is still here.* Strange. The last time she had asked Dr. Walt about his daughter he had said, "Oh, she's coming along. Coming along," then applied himself more intently to studying Amy's healing leg, making her walk up and back without any assists from the crutches or cane.

Amy wondered, *Was he avoiding talking about Simmie to ease his own pain or because he did not wish to discourage me? I must stop in and see Simmie when she's awake.*

Behind her closed door, Simmie Duncan was awake. She lay in bed clutching her doll, Matilda, waiting for her mother to arrive. The nurse had been in to take her breakfast tray and remind her cheerfully, "No chemo today, sweetheart. Isn't that good news?" Simmie had tried to laugh, but the muscles of her tender stomach ached too much from three days of nausea and throwing up with wrenching strain.

Inside her mouth, her upper palate and the edges of her tongue bore open lesions, which were very painful even though the nurses had swabbed them with soothing medication.

Simmie held Matilda tightly, trying to derive some comfort from her nearness and familiarity.

Some day soon, Simmie thought, *I'll be going home, and then all this will stop. The needles. And the doctors. So many doctors. And the way they smile at me, they must think I'm a dummy. That I'm not afraid. They don't have to keep trying so hard to make it seem like it's nothing. Uncle Sy. Even when he smiles, his eyes tell me how serious it is. He was the one bought me Matilda when I was only eight.*

She hugged the doll more tightly. She began to sing to it, very softly, a melody her mother used to sing when she was much younger. By the time she was three, they were singing it together. In more recent years, once she started putting herself to bed after doing her homework, they no longer sang together.

Outside the door she could now hear the usual morning noises. The wheeled carrier that held the breakfast trays as it rolled softly from door to door collecting the empty trays. The scurrying footsteps of rubber-soled white shoes as nurses went by her door on their ways to carry out their early-morning duties. She could hear morning greetings as nurses passed one another for the first time of the day.

Suddenly she heard the sounds change. Footsteps seemed to stop, then they all moved rapidly and at once in the same direction. There was tense whispering, which made Simmie sit up in bed. She could not make out the words clearly enough to understand what was happening. She settled back in bed, but could not rest. She no longer hugged Matilda, but leaned in the direction of the door and strained to listen.

There were other sounds now. She recognized one voice. Mrs. Hutchinson's. She was floor supervisor and had made it a point to drop by at least once a day and inquire, "And how is Dr. Duncan's little girl?" At first, Simmie had welcomed that distinction. But as the days wore on, and she felt not better but worse, she had begun to resent Mrs. Hutchinson's attention. What did she say to other children when she looked in on them? Or didn't she bother to look in on children whose fathers were not important doctors?

Mrs. Hutchinson's voice sounded quite concerned and extremely professional as she said, "We'll get the certificate filled out later. Meantime, move him off this floor."

Curious, and free of a confining IV, Simmie Duncan slipped out of bed. She went to the door, pulled it open just enough to peer out into the corridor. She heard sounds once more. Voices. Footsteps. The hushed sound of rolling rubber wheels.

Furtively, Simmie strained to see. First, Mrs. Hutchinson, in her usual white uniform, a blue sweater thrown over her shoulders. She looked back at something. The something came into Simmie's view. It was a rubber-wheeled stretcher pushed by a young student nurse. On the stretcher, completely covered by a white sheet, was a form that could not be concealed or misidentified. It was the body of a child. A boy, Simmie knew. Else why would Mrs. Hutchinson have said, "Move *him* off this floor"?

Through wide, frightened eyes Simmie watched until the small procession passed out of sight. She felt suddenly cold. She began to tremble. She turned back to her bed. She crept in between the warm sheets, reached for Matilda, who felt warmer than herself. She held the doll close, lay stiff and still until she pulled the covers up over her head.

When Emily Duncan came in for her usual morning visit, she found her daughter hiding that way.

"Honey, what are you doing?"

"Just . . . just playing games with Matilda," Simmie replied.

"Come out. Let me see how you look this morning." Simmie wriggled up out of her hiding place and smiled at her mother.

"That's my baby," Emily said, but she could read fear in her child's eyes. "Honey, what it is? Something wrong? Are you in pain?"

"No, I'm fine, Mommy. Honest. Just . . . just . . ."

"Just what, darling?"

"Can I go home?" Simmie blurted out.

"Home?" Emily repeated. The question had caught her by sur-

219

prise. "There are still things the doctors have to do. When you go home depends on what Dr. Bristol says."

"What if she *never* says I can go home?" Simmie asked.

"Why would she say that?"

"Because maybe they'll always find new things to do to me."

Emily sat on the side of the bed, took her child in her arms, brushed back her thinning dark-brown hair and stroked her pale, cool skin. She held Simmie's face to hers and spoke into her ear softly. "Simmie, darling, the doctors are trying new things because that's the way they'll discover the right thing that will cure you."

"They don't cure everybody," Simmie said.

Despite her effort not to let that happen, Emily felt her own body stiffen.

"No, darling, the doctors can't cure everybody. But when they find the right thing, they will cure you."

Simmie tried to look up into Emily's eyes, but she was held so tight that she could not. She shuddered.

"I'd better get you back into bed and cover you up."

"All the way up?" the child asked.

Emily did not understand the significance of her question. She eased her child back onto the bed and brought the covers up around her, fitting them close to her frail body.

"There, isn't that better? Warmer? Sweetheart?"

"Yes, Mommy," the child finally answered.

Just after lunch, once Simmie had fallen asleep, Emily took the opportunity to go out to the nurses' station to make some urgent phone calls. It was there she discovered that, early that morning, young David Amiel had died of his lung disease. That sweet, gentle little boy, not yet nine years old. She had spent much time with his mother out in the visitors' lounge. Nice woman. Terribly frightened. Now her worst fears had come to be.

Emily thought, *I must write a note. Or send flowers. Something.*

Of one thing she was sure. When Simmie woke, she would have to talk to her about it. She would not allow her to go on concealing her fears.

* * *

Simmie moved in her sleep, letting Matilda drop from her embrace and fall to the floor. Emily bent to pick up the doll. When she placed it on the bed, Simmie opened her eyes.

"Mommy?" she asked, to make sure.

"Yes, baby, I'm here."

Simmie smiled, reached for Matilda.

"Would you like a drink? Something cold?"

"Uh-uh." The child declined.

"Anything at all?"

"Nope."

The child lay still, then started humming to her doll.

"Simmie, did something unusual happen early this morning?"

"Early this morning . . . something . . . Oh. Oh, yes. Someone. Some child must have died."

"How do you know?"

"I . . . I heard sounds. So I got out of bed. But don't worry, nobody knew. I went to the door. I peeked out. And I saw this stretcher. There was a . . . there was something covered by a sheet. It was a person. A little person. A boy."

"You know Mrs. Amiel? She's come in a few times to visit."

"Oh, yes. She's a very nice woman. Was it—?"

"Yes, Simmie. It was her son."

Simmie thought a moment. A look of fear slowly darkened her pale thin face. But she said nothing.

"Simmie . . . when you saw that, did it frighten you?"

"Uh-huh," she said very softly.

"Is that why you were hiding?" Emily asked.

"I wasn't hiding," Simmie said.

"You were under the covers," Emily pointed out.

"I was—I was trying to see how it felt."

"How what felt, darling?"

"How it felt to be lying there on that stretcher all covered up. Dead."

Emily fought hard to control her impulse to embrace the child. But she knew that any overemotional reaction from her would serve only to frighten her child even more.

221

"Mommy, how *does* it feel?"

"I don't know exactly how it feels. But I know one thing. There is no pain."

"No pain at all?" the child asked.

"No pain." Emily reassured her.

The child thought a moment, then nodded slightly. Seemed satisfied.

"It's nothing to be afraid of, Simmie. Because it is something that is going to happen to all of us one day. It's as much a part of living as being born."

"Do babies feel any pain when they're being born?"

"I don't think so. Or else the doctors wouldn't have to slap them on the bottom to make them give that first cry."

"Is that what they did to me?" Simmie asked.

"No. You'd just been born and the doctor handed you to the nurse and you gave a cry by yourself. And the doctor . . . that was Dr. Breland . . . he said, 'Emily, you've got yourself a real healthy one here. Good heart. Good, sound lungs.' "

"He said that?"

"He surely did."

"What did Dad say?"

"Dad?" Emily echoed, puzzled.

"He was there, wasn't he?" Simmie persisted.

"Well, actually—"

"I know. He was at the hospital operating. Wasn't he?"

Emily smiled. "Simmie, darling, we were at the hospital, too. We were in Maternity. But Daddy was up in the OR in the Orthopedics Pavilion. Operating. But I said, 'You call Dr. Duncan and tell him he is the father of a baby girl.' They did. They got a message into the Operating Room."

"And what did he say?"

"Uncle Sy told me. You see, Daddy was assisting him at the time. Uncle Sy says your daddy said, 'Sy, we're naming the first one for you.' "

"Was that true, Mommy?"

"Yes, we'd talked it all out before you were born. Uncle Sy's been like a father to Daddy. So we agreed, Simon if it was a boy, Simone if it was a girl. Uncle Sy held you when you were christened. He gave you that gold bracelet that we're keeping for when you grow up. When he brought it to the house, he said to me, 'Em, I won't be there by the time Simmie gets married. But I would like for her to wear this on her wedding day.'"

"We'd surely invite him to the wedding, wouldn't we, Mommy?"

"What he meant was that everyone dies at some time. He thought his time would come before you were old enough to get married. And he wanted to be remembered."

"I wouldn't forget him. Even without that bracelet." Simone said.

"He wanted to be near you. That was his way."

"Was he . . . when he said that, when he was thinking about dying, was he afraid?"

"No. He wasn't afraid. He seemed like a man who had completed his life's work and was content to die," Emily explained.

"Was he tired and did he want to rest?"

"Yes, that's one way of saying it, darling. In fact, not long after that he retired from surgery and became a consultant. But he's lived a long time since."

19

DR. Bristol laid out the data on Sy Rosen's desk.

The old man tugged at his small tight beard, reluctant to examine the material. He had a strong, distressing hunch about what had forced Dr. Bristol to ask for this meeting. Finally, he picked up the lab results, shifted his position so that the glare of his desk lamp fell on the pages with the intensity of a spotlight. He studied the data. The results were even worse than he had feared.

Damn, he thought, *Simmie, that innocent, bright child to be faced with a white count so low. And her platelet count even lower. Both counts severely diminished by the chemo. Inviting the possibilities of not only infection but of hemorrhage. Yet the diseased cells have not been wiped out. That's the trouble with chemo. It attacks healthy cells as well as the cancer. The very white cells and platelets relied on to fight disease become victims of the chemo.*

Sy tossed the reports onto the desk, looked up at Dr. Bristol and asked, "All right, Rita, what are you suggesting?"

"Of course I'll take this to the Tumor Board. But first someone should discuss this with Walt Duncan."

"I'll do it. But we have to suggest a plan of treatment. What will you propose?" Sy asked.

Rita Bristol looked down at the old man, at his watery eyes

224

that made no secret of his torment. *Why is he asking me? He knows what is the last remaining resort in a case as intractable as Simmie's. But if for his own emotional needs he requires me to say it, I will.*

"Extreme cases demand extreme measures. Superlethal doses of chemoradiotherapy to wipe out all of the malignant cells, and also her own bone marrow. Then infuse healthy donor marrow to reconstitute her body's immunologic systems."

"Total body irradiation," Sy commented, indicating his reluctance.

"In this case, yes."

"Including cranial radiation," Sy said, nodding sadly. For the treatment was not without substantial and potentially undesirable aftereffects.

"I'll prescribe prednisone, of course, to counteract any swelling of her brain," Dr. Bristol said.

"You realize, Rita, that Simmie has no siblings."

Dr. Bristol nodded.

"Then you also realize the risks," Sy said.

"I never said she was an ideal candidate for a bone marrow transplant. But I know what her chances are now. None. That's why I wanted to talk to you. You know the family well. Are there any donor candidates that I don't know about?"

"No," Sy said.

"Then I would like to do histocompatability tests of Walt and his wife to determine their blood and tissue types. And use the marrow from whomever is the closest match to Simmie."

"That's extremely risky procedure, *Doctor.*"

"Can you suggest an alternative, *Doctor?*" Dr. Bristol demanded.

"I will talk to Walt at once," Sy said. "Yes, I'll talk to him."

Dr. Bristol started to gather up her lab reports, but the old man brought his hand down on hers. Looking up at her, he said, "You know how bad the odds are."

"In this case there is no treatment of choice."

He nodded. Dr. Bristol took her reports and started out of the room. At the door she stopped to remind Sy, "Of course, once the superlethal doses of radiation and chemo start, I'll have to confine Simmie to reverse isolation."

"Of course."

Walter Duncan took the news with no show of emotion. Old Sy almost wished his protégé would break down, cry, curse or explode in fury at the fates that so often befell physicians and their offspring. But Walter Duncan had listened emotionless, as if receiving reports concerning a patient who was a stranger to him. Before Sy had even finished, Walter Duncan relieved him of the chore.

"Yes, yes, Sy, of course. Bone marrow transplant. The problem of donors . . . I suppose you and Dr. Bristol have considered that. Did she say when she wants us to give her marrow samples?"

"She didn't say, but from what I saw there's not a day to lose," Sy said.

"I will talk to Emily as soon as I get home." He started for the door.

Sy could not contain himself. He called out, "For God's sake, Walter, act like a father, not a doctor!"

Walter Duncan turned slowly to face his mentor, and Sy could see the glisten of tears on the younger man's cheeks.

"I've got to tell Emily. And she is no fool. She will know how desperate we are. Only one step away from giving up altogether. This news might just be the thing that will force her to crack up."

"Walt, would it help if I told her?" Sy asked.

"This is something she deserves to hear from me," he said. "Now, I've got my rounds before I can meet Emily."

He had completed his rounds of patients, those he was preparing for surgery, those on whom he had already operated, including Amy Bedford, who was back in the hospital for her triweekly chemo treatment. Which coincided with his six-week checkup of

226

her healing leg. He stopped by her room, examined her leg and was satisfied with her progress.

"We have to get you started on physical therapy and get you off that cane," he remarked. "How's the chemo going? Still as bad?"

"I must be getting used to it," she said. "It feels so natural now to have nausea that I can't remember when it wasn't so. On good days I wake and ask myself, what's missing?"

Because of his unusually grim attitude, she had tried to make a joke. She realized she had failed.

"Doctor?"

"Yes?" He responded briskly, expecting a question related to her future progress.

"Is Simmie really that bad off?"

He glanced at her, a look that resented her intrusion into his private sorrow.

"Every time I come back for my day of chemo I visit her. She never complains. I know how I felt when I was getting the worst of my chemo. I used to bitch and complain."

"You did not!" he contradicted.

"Oh, yes I did. Not to you. Sometimes not even to my folks. But I was furious. Inside. I kept rebelling. 'Why me? What did I ever do to anyone?' Simmie isn't like that. She's just as sweet and—" She had intended to say "resigned," but at the last instant realized it was the wrong word for the situation. "She is very sick now, isn't she? I mean, really very sick."

He nodded gravely.

"Nobody ever said it. But I can tell from the look in your wife's eyes. There's a way mothers have of smiling when their fear is worst. I've seen it in my own mother's eyes. Your wife has that look. I'm sorry, Doctor, very sorry."

"Thank you, Amy, I appreciate that."

"Am I butting in when I go in and talk to her? I like to think it encourages her to see a patient who's also young and getting better. That's what we all need, to know it's possible to get better."

227

"Of course. Feel free to go in. At least today. After today that may not be possible."

"Oh? Why not?"

"Something we call reverse isolation" was all Walt said. "Now, I'll talk to Brud Simpson about setting up a program of physical therapy for you. He'll see you before you leave tomorrow."

He had visited all his patients, returned all his calls, left instructions for his morning surgery. He found two messages from James Rowe Russell, chairman of the trustees and dominant non-professional power in the hospital. Obviously Russell assumed that Walt was avoiding him. For his second message read: I WILL WAIT IN MY OFFICE UNTIL I HEAR FROM YOU.

That made it an obligatory call, the kind that old Sy used to call First Commandment calls. For in the Decalogue where it said, "Thou shalt have no other gods before me," Sy had amended, "except for hospital trustees."

Walt called Russell's office. The man was as good as his word. He answered the phone himself, meaning that by this hour even his secretary had gone home.

"Oh, Duncan," Russell greeted, barely able to conceal his hostile attitude, "what can I do for you?"

"Since you called me, sir, what can I do for you?"

"For one thing you can listen to a letter I just received from the hospital's attorneys. 'We have just been informed by the law secretary to one of the appellate judges that the verdict of two million five hundred thousand dollars against Dr. Peter Enright has been upheld. Less than an hour ago we were notified by the insurance company that for the forthcoming year malpractice premiums for all hospitals in this district will be increased one hundred and fifty percent.' "

Russell repeated, "One hundred and fifty percent, Duncan. Do you know how much that means?"

"One million plus?" Walt ventured.

"Two million four," Russell corrected. "Next time you feel the urge to place your 'ethical duty' above common sense, think about this experience. Think twice."

228

"Sir, are you threatening me?" Walter Duncan asked.

"*Advising,* Duncan, *advising,*" the man said coldly.

Before Walt could react, Russell hung up on him. There was nothing to do now but go to Room 219, pick up Emily, take her home.

And tell her. About Simmie. And bone marrow transplants.

He embraced his daughter, felt the frailness of her body in his arms. She seemed half the size she had been only months before. The disease had inflicted its devastating effect on her, chemo and its consequences had done the rest. He sat alongside her bed, held her tenderly in his arms, told her all the things he had done today, would do tomorrow. Told her all his plans of things to do with her just as soon as she was released from the hospital. All she had to do was get better.

"Will I, Daddy? Get better?" she asked, her face pressed against his chest.

"Of course. After all, would Uncle Sy let anything happen to his favorite niece?" Walt said, patting her head and finding strands of her dark hair coming off in his fingers.

They were halfway home. Nothing had been said. There was nothing to say. Except, perhaps, that Simmie looked even paler, thinner. There was no need to say that.

Walt and Emily had stopped for the traffic light at the corner of Main and Chestnut, at the edge of the shopping center.

"Do we need to pick up anything?" he asked.

Emily did not answer.

"Milk? Oranges? Anything?" he asked again.

Again, she did not answer.

"Em? Darling?" He turned to her to find her weeping silently. "Em, Em . . . please . . ."

She shook her head, continued to weep, powerless to hold back the tears. He turned to embrace her, but the light changed to green. Some impatient driver behind him was leaning on the horn. Walt started his car forward with a jolt. He regained control and continued along Main to the turnoff at Sycamore, a quiet street leading to their own neighborhood. He reached out to draw her close. His arm around her, to comfort her, he drove slowly.

"Em, you mustn't give up. There are still things we can do," he assured her. He glanced down at her. She was staring straight ahead, her eyes still moist, tears threading their way down her cheeks.

"In fact, I was going to tell you. We both have to be tested. Tomorrow, if possible. They have to find out which one of us is most histocompatible with Simmie."

He had expected her to ask why, but she remained silent, resting against him, barely breathing.

"You see, there's a procedure called a bone marrow transplant. It's really miraculous, the way it works. In leukemia the body's own immune system doesn't produce the proper number of healthy disease-fighting white cells. The fault is in the bone marrow. So what we can do now is eliminate completely Simmie's faulty bone marrow, using heavy concentrations of chemo and radiology. Just wipe it out. Then take bone marrow from a compatible healthy donor, like you or me, and inject it into her intravenously. Eventually the healthy bone marrow transplant stimulates the growth and development of new, healthy bone marrow in the patient. That way our healthy cells teach Simmie's system to start breeding its own healthy cells."

He awaited Emily's reaction to his reassuring explanation. There was none. He felt compelled to continue.

"Of course, during the treatment there are some difficulties. Inconveniences, really. You see, Em, when they wipe out Simmie's bone marrow with chemo and radiation, they also wipe out completely her body's resistance to disease. All disease. Colds. Infection. Pneumonia. So, during that time, the patient has to be in what we call reverse isolation. Simmie will be moved to another room. A small suite, actually. With a little anteroom separating her from the outside.

"There'll be facilities for visitors to wash. And sterile gowns to wear. Of course, anybody with a cold or other infectious disease won't be allowed in. But otherwise you can spend just as much time with her as you do now. We just have to be more careful, that's all."

He felt he had made the least painful explanation of the treatment of last resort.

They had arrived at the house. The automatic timer had turned on the lights in the living room and the kitchen, so the place did not seem so deserted. They entered the kitchen from the garage.

"Hungry?" was all Emily asked.

"No. A drink maybe, but no food," he said. "You?"

"Nothing. Not now."

"You should eat something," he said. "I heard you have only coffee at the hospital. And then, only when the nurses bring you some."

"Later," she said.

He was tempted to insist, but he was relieved that she was no longer weeping. He went into the den, was mixing himself a light whiskey and soda when he heard her steps move from the foyer carpet onto the polished inlaid-wood floor behind him.

"Drink?" he asked.

"Walter," she said, "what does GVHD mean?"

He had to grip the whiskey bottle firmly so as not to drop it. *Where had she come upon that term? Why? If she had discovered that bit of medical knowledge, enough to ask what it meant, she must know a good deal more about bone marrow transplants than she let on.*

"GVHD," he began. "Well, that's . . . that's graft-versus-host disease. For shorthand we simply call it GVHD."

"What does it *mean?*" she insisted.

"Well, it means . . . what I just told you," he avoided.

"Walter!" she demanded very firmly, in a way that allowed for no further equivocation or evasion.

"What it means . . . Well, there are transplant cases where, instead of achieving the desired result, the graft starts to attack the host, the patient, that is."

"So that a bone marrow transplant could actually do Simmie more harm than good," she said.

"Now, honey, you know that any treatment, even the surgery

231

I do, can sometimes backfire. Infection. Pneumonia. Lots of complications are possible. We do the best we can with what we have."

"The best we can with what we have," she repeated in bitter sarcasm. "And when the best is no better than the worst?" she demanded. "What about those times?"

He knew now that he had to address her fears directly. "Em, how did you run across GVHD?"

She stared at him, angrily at first, then gradually her anger gave way to tears. "I'll have that drink now." She went to the nearest easy chair and sank into it. Walt mixed her drink, brought it to her, placed it in her hand. Gently he brushed her straggling dark hair away from her face.

He sat down opposite her. "Em?"

She sipped her drink. Two tiny sips. She stared off and away from him.

"This afternoon . . ." she said. She seemed reluctant to continue. He did not prod, but waited. She began again. "This afternoon, after I fed Simmie what little she could eat, I was coming out of her room to get rid of her tray. As I reached the door I heard a familiar voice. Dr. Bristol's. She was asking, 'Did you tell him yet?' I heard another voice, Sy's, and he said, 'He's been in surgery all day. I'll tell him as soon as he's free.' But that wasn't all Sy said."

"What else?" Walter asked.

"He said . . . he said, 'Rita, do you think a bone marrow transplant will do any good?' She said, 'Sy, you know the odds in bone marrow transplants.' And Sy said, 'Yes, unfortunately I do.' "

"Em, I never promised you it was foolproof." Walter Duncan defended.

"I'm not done yet!" Emily responded sharply. "After I heard that and once Simmie fell asleep, I went down to the hospital library. And I asked that woman there—"

"Mrs. Robinson, the librarian?"

"She was most helpful. I asked her for the latest published information on bone marrow transplants. She hunted down several medical papers for me. Like the ones you read late at night after you come home."

"Em, those papers are meant to be read by doctors, not lay-people!" he protested.

"Walter, I am not illiterate. I have a B.A. in English lit. I have been an editor and, on occasion, still am. I can understand what I read. There were things in those papers that I was able to understand. Such as graphs, charts, figures."

"Figures?"

"Percentages. Odds. Cure rates," she said, her voice rising in anger now.

"Em, Em, please—" He tried to interrupt.

She would not permit him. "There are all kinds of bone marrow transplants, I discovered. Bone marrow transplants from the patient's own marrow when she is in remission. Then marrow from an identical twin. Then bone marrow from a partially matched or unrelated donor. Is that right?"

"Yes, yes, that's right."

"The worst odds, the lowest cure rate, is when they transplant bone marrow from a partially matched donor."

"It's true that the ideal match would be from an identical twin. But Simmie has no twin," Walt said. "She doesn't even have a sibling. There's only the two of us who are related to her genetically. Who have a chance of being histocompatible. We're doing the best we can."

"Not exactly, my darling," Emily said.

"There isn't anything else left to try!" he protested.

"That's precisely what I mean, Walter. We're at a time when little lies won't do any longer. When being 'considerate' of my feelings won't wash. I don't want to be told half-truths. I don't want to watch you demean yourself by trying to tell me things tonight that I discovered this afternoon are not so. From now until the end of this, I want to know how bad it is. I want to be able to be honest with my daughter. She is very intelligent, very sensitive. She is much sharper than you think. I can tell by the look in her eyes that she knows. So I can't go on playing games with her. Only the other day—"

The glass dropped from her hand. That it fell to the carpet prevented it from shattering.

"Em . . ."

"Only the other day my daughter, your daughter, asked me, 'Mommy, how does it feel to die?' "

"Em! Emily!"

He went to her, pulled her up from the chair and held her tightly as her body shook from sobbing.

"Emily, darling, please . . ."

Through her sobs she was able to say, "From now on I've got to know the truth, the whole truth . . . from now on."

"Of course, darling. The truth. Everything. But just hold fast to the thought that it isn't hopeless yet. Difficult. Against the odds. But not hopeless. Remember that."

"Will you tell me when it is?" She challenged.

He hesitated only briefly. "Yes, yes, I'll tell you."

20

EMILY and Walter Duncan had both given samples of their blood, had had their bones pierced under local anesthetic so that their bone marrows could be extracted in sufficient quantities to allow the laboratory to compare them with samples of Simmie's blood and marrow. Once the many factors and characteristics were compared, it became clear that Emily's genetic characteristics matched Simmie's more closely than Walter's. Though Victor Ogura did say to Sy Rosen and to Rita Bristol, "I've seen closer matches."

Sy started to reply. "Vic, if we had any alternative . . ."

Ogura nodded with sad understanding. "If only there were a sibling."

Once the decision was made to attempt the bone marrow transplant, Simmie Duncan had to be prepared for the process. It was a debilitating procedure, commencing with intravenous doses of the chemical cyclophosphamide for two consecutive days.

Being a more powerful drug, cyclophosphamide had the unfortunate and more taxing aftereffects of such drugs. Simmie was racked with nausea and vomiting. More than once Emily held her in her arms, while the child felt torn apart by the rebellion of her body against the treatment.

There were many moments when Emily desperately needed to cry but did not dare. Moments when she asked herself, *Is my child's suffering worth it? Why not let her die?* But as long as there was even a faint, dim chance she steeled herself to her young daughter's agony and carried on.

She made promises to Simmie, trying to instill hope, kept soothing, "Darling, it may hurt now, but once you're better you'll forget all about this."

After those two days of agony were over, there remained six days of additional treatment. Six days of superlethal radiation. For the transplanted marrow to have an opportunity to succeed, the patient's body must be almost completely clean of all cancer cells. Since there are areas of the body where the most powerful chemotherapy cannot penetrate or be effective, such as the central nervous system, radiation is relied on to accomplish that end. Total body irradiation. TBI. If the immediate side effects were not as apparent as those of chemotherapy, TBI was not without serious consequences.

One thousand rads a day, for six consecutive days, an extremely high dose of radiation. Not only intended to wipe out all cancer cells, but all of Simmie's marrow function as well.

Frail little Simone Duncan had had the last of her six days of radiation. The following day, Emily Duncan would subject herself to becoming a donor to replace her daughter's diseased bone marrow.

Because she was being prepared for a surgical procedure, minor though it might be, Emily could not be at Simmie's bedside. Walt Duncan canceled his surgery for the morning, postponing his most emergent cases to the afternoon and his others to the end of the week.

He entered the small reverse-isolation suite in which his daughter had to be quartered. Since her own defenses had been wiped out and it would take her body three to four weeks to fight off disease and infection, every visitor had to be as aseptic as possible.

Walter paused at the stainless-steel sink to wash his hands thoroughly. As he did, he looked through the glass into the room at his daughter, who lay in bed, motionless, her face turned to the window, and the world outside, as flowers and plants turn toward the sun.

Dispassionately as he was able, he tried to assess her condition. She looked even paler than before, much thinner, too. *And why not*, he thought defensively, *after what she's been through these past ten days? Weeks of chemo, followed by cyclophosphamide, then total irradiation. She seems to have lost half her pitifully low weight.*

He slipped into a sterile gown and put on a surgical mask before he approached the inner door. She heard his hand on the knob. Without turning, she asked in a small, thin voice, "Mommy?"

"This time it's Daddy," he said.

She turned in alarm. "Where's Mommy? Something's happened to Mommy."

"No, no, no, darling, nothing's happened to Mommy."

The child seemed only slightly reassured. "I don't want to be alone," she said. The significance of that did not fully register on her father.

"We'll all be in from time to time. Mommy. Daddy. Uncle Sy. And that nice girl, that patient of mine, Amy Bedford. You always like to see her."

Simmie nodded. Her pale, sunken face had begun to remind him of photographs he had seen of concentration camp children.

This is devilish medicine we practice, he thought. *We fight the disease by methods that attack the patient's ability to resist. It's almost as bad as exorcism.*

She moved and could not resist giving a little cry of pain.

"Does it hurt, baby? Where? Tell Daddy."

She seemed apologetic as she moved aside the light coverlet. He saw an area of her side and her leg that was covered with tiny blisters. Despite all the precautions doctors and nurses invoked, radiation burns were inevitable from doses so massive. He reached for a tube of petroleum jelly and lightly smeared some on the affected places.

"Better?"

"Uh-huh," she whispered, as if it hurt even to talk.

"It'll go away, darling, it will. And you'll feel better."

"When?" she asked, with childlike directness.

"Soon." He evaded.

"Very soon?"

"Very soon," he replied.

She seemed to take comfort in that. She held his hand close to her emaciated face until, reassured, she drifted off to sleep.

At the same time, in another wing of the hospital, another part of her treatment was beginning to take place.

In a small operating room, hardly large enough to accommodate the anesthetist and his equipment, an assisting nurse and the operating table, Emily Duncan lay on her back, a surgical drape covering her body. The anesthetist had decided to put her under completely, as much to combat her emotional state as to render her impervious to any pain that might be involved in the procedure.

Once Dr. Bristol had received the signal that the patient was under, she reached for the sharp-pointed sterile stainless-steel instrument that resembled a long hypodermic needle with a flat cap at the top. But it was much stronger than the usual hypodermic, for it would have to withstand being pushed through the skin, the tissue, and then with considerable force deep into the donor's bone.

One would not have suspected that a person as petite as Dr. Bristol had the required physical strength for the job. However, once the nurse had turned Emily Duncan on her side, giving Dr. Bristol access to her exposed lower back, the doctor started to push the sharp hollow instrument into the bone of her pelvic girdle, the area most productive of bone marrow. The pointed end passed easily through the skin and soft tissue until it struck hard, unyielding bone. Dr. Bristol pressed with considerable force until she felt the bone give way and knew that she was now into the softer, inner marrow-rich area of the bone.

Having achieved that, Bristol removed the flat cap from the needle, signaled the nurse for the glass syringe. She screwed it into the top of the inserted needle. Slowly, she pulled up the plunger. Soon she had accumulated a hypodermic full of a mix of bloody serumlike marrow. She emptied it into a sterile test tube and sealed it.

She repeated the same procedure three times. When she was done, she sent the nurse off with the test tubes and with instructions to have the lab process the marrow to screen out any large particles.

When Emily Duncan was conscious, she found herself in a small private room in the hospital. She was alone. The procedure had not been sufficiently critical or discomforting to call for the presence of a nurse. She lay awake, momentarily unaware of the reason for her presence in this place, or for the dull pain in her lower back. She was reaching for the buzzer to summon a nurse when she heard the door ease open slightly. She turned to look.

Dr. Simon Rosen peered in.

"Emily, dear, how are you? Feeling a little pain, perhaps?" the old man asked.

"How did it go? Were they able to get enough out of me?" she asked.

"They got plenty." Sy assured her. "I just came up from the lab. Everything is okay."

"Have they given it to her yet?"

"Not yet. Later this afternoon," he said.

"Later? The sooner she gets it, the sooner it can start to work," Emily protested.

"She'll have it soon enough. Right now, hours aren't important. It will take weeks for her body to use your healthy marrow and begin manufacturing its own."

"Sy . . . will it work?" Emily asked.

"Emily, that's why we're doing it. To find out if it will work. Up to now, everything is exactly as it should be. Exactly."

"Can I see her?"

"For now and through tomorrow you're to rest in bed as much as possible."

"I would like to see her. Now!"

The old surgeon hesitated. Then he relented. "Of course, why not? But you will have to scrub and wear a gown and mask."

"I know."

Several hours later, Dr. Bristol infused the marrow intravenously into the arm of Simone Duncan. If nature and luck were with them, Emily's marrow cells would circulate through Simone's bloodstream, eventually to home in the narrow cavities of the sick child's bones.

After that, it remained to be seen whether her immune system would begin to produce healthy marrow on its own.

Whatever the doctors' plans, hopes and fears, nature alone would determine that.

21

EMILY'S parents, Charles and Madeline Ingraham, arrived on the Monday afternoon following the infusion of healthy bone marrow into the frail body of Simone Duncan. Since Emily insisted on remaining at her child's bedside, the Ingrahams took a taxi from the airport. Instead of going to the house, they went directly to the hospital.

Without warning or preparation, Emily found herself confronted by her mother and father, who stared at her through the glass of the small anteroom. It was obvious that they were startled to find their granddaughter in such total isolation. Before they could express their concern, Emily came out to greet them.

As always, her father moved to embrace her. She moved back.

"Please, Dad, this gown has to remain sterile."

"Yes, sure," he said. But it was painfully clear that he felt rejected.

Her mother had always been the more forthright. "Em, why sterile gowns? What's going on here? And why weren't we told?"

"Mother, please! I can't take time to explain now. But if you want to see Simmie and spend time with her, you'll have to do the same. Wash your hands thoroughly. Put on one of these gowns. And a mask."

"I would still like to know why my granddaughter . . ."

"Mother, either you wash and put on a gown or else I will have to ask you to get out," Emily said.

"Maddy, do what she says," her father suggested firmly.

They washed with deliberate and meticulous care, then slipped into sterile green gowns. They waited in the doorway until Emily said, "Simmie, darling, guess who came all the way from Arizona to see you?"

"Grandma, Grandpa . . ." the child said weakly.

"Right, Simmie," her grandmother said, drawing close to the bed. She half-turned to Emily, asking permission to embrace her grandchild. Emily nodded. She gathered the child up in her arms and pressed her face against her. "Oh, Simmie, how good it is to see you again. Oh, child, child . . ."

Her reserve deserted her. Shocked by the sight of her grand-daughter, the poor woman broke into a flood of tears. Emily was sympathetic, but to protect her child she ordered, "Dad, take her out of here!"

"Maddy, come!" He put his arm around his wife and guided her out of the room.

Emily kneeled at the bedside. "Grandmother's so glad to see you that she just broke down and cried. But just think, they came more than a thousand miles to see you."

The child stared at her through eyes now sunk deep into her painfully thin face. "Do I really look so bad?"

"Of course not, baby." Emily was quick to reassure. "It's just that the last treatment hasn't had time to take effect yet. You have to understand how Grandma feels. Being so far away and worrying about you, it was such a relief to see you that she just broke down. She used to do the same with me when I'd come back from college after being away for a few months. She was always a good crier, your grandma," Emily said, smiling. Finally the child smiled, too.

"She'll come back, won't she?"

"Of course. Just give her time to gather herself together," Emily said.

"And Grandpa, too," the child said.

"Both of them," Emily promised.

* * *

She found them in the visitors' lounge. In one corner, Charles Ingraham hovered over his wife, who sat facing away from the other visitors, hiding her tears in her handkerchief.

"Maddy . . . Maddy . . ." he pleaded.

"I can't help it . . . I can't." She continued shaking her head and crying.

Emily drew close to them. Her father looked to her, giving that shrug of helplessness she had seen from him many times before. He had never been able to manage his wife when she was in one of her more emotional states. Emily indicated that he release her. She placed her hands on her mother's shoulders and turned her about. She took the shapeless damp handkerchief from her hands. Her mother tried to avoid her.

"Mother! Mother! Listen to me!" Her mother finally stared up into her eyes. "You are going back in there. You will smile. And you will talk to Simone of pleasant things. I don't want her to see in your eyes how startled and frightened you are. Walt and I don't do that. And we won't let you do it."

"But the way she looks . . . it's plain to see . . ."

"Plain to see *what?*" Emily demanded angrily.

Madeline Ingraham glanced at her husband, then turned back to her daughter. "She's going to die."

"This last treatment hasn't had time to work yet," Emily insisted, possibly more for her own morale than her mother's. "It'll take weeks, several more weeks, before we know."

"Emily, listen to me. The real reason we came—"

"Maddy! Don't say it!" her husband intervened.

"This whole big hospital, her father, who's supposed to be such an important surgeon, haven't been able to help her. You can see it in that child's pinched face. Why, she weighed more four years ago when she came to stay with us than she does now."

"Maddy, I said no!" Charles Ingraham insisted in a low voice, but firm enough to cause other visitors to turn and stare at them.

"At least I have to tell her," his wife replied, with equal determination. Ignoring her husband, she seized Emily by the arms and pulled her close. "Now, we have this on the best authority.

243

There is this family in Sunburst, which is only a few miles from our town. They have this little boy. He's about nine, maybe ten. He, too, has some kind of terrible cancer. They had tried everything. The hospital in Phoenix couldn't do a thing for him. They even sent him to Chicago. No help. Then they took him across the border into Mexico. There's a doctor there people say all kinds of wonderful things about . . ."

"I am not taking Simmie to Mexico!" Emily protested.

"I'm not saying take her to Mexico."

"Then what are you saying?"

"Maddy—Maddy, please, no," her husband begged.

"Charles! Stay out of this! It's clear to me they've exhausted all their treatments. This can't do any harm."

"Mother, what is it?" Emily asked.

"Emily, the real reason we came here, in addition to seeing Simmie, is so I can tell you face to face about that little boy. When the doctors, all of them, even the one in Mexico, had given up on him, there was this preacher . . . this group called Messengers of God. He came to Sunburst and he put his hands on that boy. From that moment on he started to improve. It was like a miracle."

Emily stared at her mother, then at her father, who shrugged to indicate that he did not subscribe to his wife's convictions.

"We've come here to take Simmie back with us. To see that man of God," her mother said with a degree of religious conviction Emily had never seen in her before.

"Mother, we can't take Simmie out of that isolation room, no less let her travel a thousand miles."

"It's the only way. The child is dying."

"Mother, stop saying that!"

"You have to try everything now!"

"We are trying everything. Everything medicine knows about her disease," Emily said.

"And what's the result? The child has death in her eyes."

"Maddy!" Ingraham tried to restrain her with his embrace.

She thrust his arms aside. "No, Charles. Now, Emily, if you don't want that child's life on your conscience, you'll either let me take her or else you'll let us bring that man here!"

For an instant, only an instant, Emily Duncan wavered. If her mother had spoken any single truth, it was that all that medicine had offered till now had failed. She herself had had the same feeling of despair, the same realization that her child's battle, her torment, her pain, all had been in vain. Indeed, if Emily's bone marrow did not succeed, even the doctors were prepared to admit final defeat.

Then, her sober intelligence prevailed. She was able once again to distinguish between desperation and reality.

"No, Mother. She remains here. And in the care of her doctors."

"Em . . ." her mother persisted.

Her husband interrupted more firmly than before. "Maddy, you said what you came to say. And our daughter said no. Now, this is what you will do. You will go into that room. You will wash all signs of crying from your face. You will put on one of those gowns and you will go back in that room. You will smile at our grandchild. You will talk to her. You will sing to her, like you used to when she was only a little tot. But you will not let her see fear."

The woman appeared to resist, but then, as she usually did, she finally yielded to her husband's judgment. Once she started from the room, Emily whispered to her father, "Dad, that boy she spoke about, did he actually recover?"

"We don't know. We never knew the boy. Or his family. We just heard. He may just have been in spontaneous remission for a while."

His use of a phrase that she would not expect from a layperson made Emily glance at him quizzically.

Almost with embarrassment he admitted, "I didn't want to bother you or Walt too much. Not the way things are. So I've been talking to our own doctor. And to a Dr. Bernhardt. He's a cancer specialist in our local hospital."

He took his daughter by the hand; he lifted her chin so he could look into her eyes.

"Now, you tell me, Em, is it as bad as it looks?"

She tried to nod.

"Is it true that this last treatment hasn't started to work yet, isn't expected to work yet?"

"It'll take a few more weeks before we know."

"Then I tell you what I am going to do. I'm going to take your mother home. Back to Arizona. You've got a tough enough job as it is. You don't need to keep pretending for our sakes as well."

"Thanks, Dad. For understanding," she said.

"Look, darlin', about your ma. You know she's not the kind of woman to take up with faith healing. But she's been so worried, so desperate, she'd do anything to save that child. Don't forget, Simmie's as much part of us as you are. It made us feel young again to have her come along. We could relive all the things we used to do with you when you were her age. Who'd ever have thought that I'd be out there playing on the lawn with a four-year-old? But there I was, rolling around on the grass with Simmie. Going to the zoo. The amusement park. Things I hadn't done in years, not since you were a kid. Yes, she's meant a lot. To your mother, too. Who else in this world can give a cook greater satisfaction than a child who dotes on her baking and cookies? Why, when Simmie was coming to visit, your mom would plan for weeks ahead, every meal, every cake, every cookie, every brownie she was going to make for her.

"Then, a few days before, we'd go shopping. She'd fill two big shopping carts full of stuff to feed her. Why, there isn't a child in this world could eat all the things your mom bought for Simmie. In a way, I think that all the love your mother didn't have a chance to lavish on you once you went off to college she saved up for Simmie. It was that saved-up love that made her start thinking about things like faith healing. She's desperate, Em. We're both desperate. I'll do my best to keep her in hand. But don't think I feel any different than she does."

Emily reached up, drew his face down to hers, kissed him. "I know, Dad. I know. We each have to see this through in our own way."

"Do you want me to take your mom home?" he asked.

246

"In a day or two," Emily said.

"Okay, baby. You can depend on me."

"Thanks, Dad."

Three weeks had passed since the injection of Emily's transplanted bone marrow into little Simone Duncan.

Each day Emily had appeared at the hospital early in the morning, scrubbed, slipped into a sterile green gown and spent the day with her ailing child. Each day she fed her. Each day she watched, expecting some change, some miraculous change. She found none.

Most days she held her retching child while she suffered reactions to the methotrexate that Simone had to endure to help her body deal with the foreign bone marrow. At the same time, Emily, along with Walter and old Sy, kept searching for some warnings of the dread graft-versus-host disease, in which the treatment itself becomes the patient's enemy.

Despite the known and discouraging statistics, which Walter no longer attempted to keep from her, Emily kept hoping, seeking signs of improvement. Even during the first two weeks, when she had been told there could be no visible or actual change, she had insisted she detected signs of recovery.

Several times each day, at every opportunity he could manage, Walter Duncan rushed in, scrubbed, gowned himself and visited with his daughter. He embraced her, talked to her about pleasures past and promised those yet to come. He told her funny stories about his own childhood and made her laugh. About her paternal grandfather, whom she had never seen because he had died before she was born. When he had to, he held her as she retched from the methotrexate. All the while he would feel her body growing lighter, thinner, her pale skin barely covering her fragile skeletal structure.

Each time, Emily's eyes searched his, pleading, *Tell me that you detect some improvement, tell me the transplant is working.* He had seen that look in the eyes of other mothers and fathers. He never had expected to see it in his own wife.

Sy Rosen came by several times a day to smile at his namesake and encourage her. To nod reassuringly to Emily. But he saved all his observations and suggestions for Dr. Bristol. Each day he cornered her in her office.

"Well, Rita, what?" he asked simply.

"We don't know yet," she would say.

"Don't know or don't want to say?" Sy retorted. "White cells. Lymphocytes. Platelets. Is her system beginning to respond, to produce healthy cells?"

"The signs are not encouraging, Sy," Dr. Bristol admitted.

"And GVHD? Any indication?" Sy asked.

"Not yet."

"Not yet? Does that mean you're sure it will occur? Why not switch from methotrexate to cyclosporine? Or prednisone?" Sy urged. "They're both effective in preventing GVHD."

"*Sometimes* effective," Dr. Bristol corrected.

Sy nodded, accepting her modest rebuke. For in his anxiety over Simmie he had not only invaded his colleague's specialty but he was trying to shape the established facts of her science in his patient's favor.

"Rita, let me know. Keep me informed. If there's anything I can do . . . we can do . . ." The old man had run out of words. Nothing he could say would influence the outcome.

Even in cases where the match was from an identical sibling and the chances were better, the odds were very bad indeed. Forty to 50 percent of such cases developed GVHD. Once established, GVHD was virtually resistant to any treatment. Soon it might attack Simmie's liver or her skin or her stomach, or all of them. In the final phases, it would predispose her body to any chance infection. The end would become inevitable.

22

AT the end of the twenty-sixth day after Simone Duncan had received Emily's BMT, bone marrow transplant, Corinne Scammon, the nurse assigned to caring for Simone, took her temperature during the usual morning routine. Since the child had exhibited no signs of an elevated temperature in many days, Scammon glanced at the reading and was about to shake down the slender instrument when she stopped suddenly.

She held the instrument up to the light. Her eyes followed the silver line past the red digit to 101.2 Fahrenheit. Emily stood at the foot of her daughter's bed, so Scammon said nothing, shook down the thermometer and placed it back in the alcohol.

She went directly to the floor phone and paged Dr. Bristol. The doctor did not answer at once. But within the hour Dr. Bristol came up to the Pediatric floor to search out Scammon, who was engaged in inserting a chemo IV into the arm of Amy Bedford. Amy was back for her routine chemo treatment and her monthly lung X ray.

"Dr. Duncan left orders, soon as I get all this cytotoxin into you I'm to take you down to Radiology."

"I know," Amy said. "One day soon I expect to light up and glow in the dark."

They were both laughing when Dr. Bristol came into the room. Conversation was brief.

"You called me, Scammon?"

"The patient in two-twelve."

"Yes?" Dr. Bristol asked urgently.

"One-oh-one point two," Scammon said.

"Thanks, Scammon. I'll have a look." Dr. Bristol hurried away.

"Miss Scammon," Amy said. "The patient in two-twelve, isn't that Dr. Duncan's little girl, Simmie?"

"Yes."

"Maybe I'll drop in later, if I'm able. She's a nice kid."

"I wouldn't drop in. Not today," Scammon said.

"Oh, I know all about scrubbing and wearing a gown—"

Scammon interrupted. "I wouldn't. Not today."

Amy Bedford did not insist.

"Good morning, Doctor." Emily Duncan greeted Rita Bristol as she came into the room. It was a cheerful greeting, as if to seek favor with the doctor and thereby encourage an optimistic verdict.

"Good morning," Dr. Bristol called back, smiling. She went to Simmie's side, took her hand to find her pulse. But it was a ruse to cover her closer observation of the child's eyes. In a moment, she reached to feel Simmie's brow. Hot, dry. She reached for the thermometer. She took the child's temperature. Trying to maintain the pretense of casual interest, Dr. Bristol held the delicate glass tube up to the light. Scammon was right. Except that now the temperature read 101.3.

"Let's have a look," Dr. Bristol said pleasantly. She pulled back the light blanket and the sheet. She raised Simmie's hospital gown and made an examination of her body, front and then back. Her eyes detected the first signs of a rash, not yet angrily red but threatening to become so.

She turned the child on her back, pressed lightly on her stomach. The child withdrew in some pain.

"Easy now, Simmie, we won't do that again. Relax."

Dr. Bristol drew down the child's gown, covered her again. In so doing she found herself confronted by Emily's inquiring stare from across the bed. Dr. Bristol smiled encouragingly.

"See you later, darlin'," Dr. Bristol said cheerily as she left.

She went directly to the nurses' station. She picked out the chart of Patient Duncan, Simone. She studied it for certain significant entries. Scammon's entry of her temp was there. Followed by an entry of slight loss of weight from the day before. No entry indicating signs of bowel obstruction known as ileus. But enough signs, in combination, to make Rita Bristol lift the phone and ask for Dr. Sy Rosen's office.

Sy Rosen was returning to his office after assisting at a hip replacement on an old friend of his. Routinely, he held out his hand as he passed Bridget's desk. His secretary of many years just as routinely handed him his batch of accumulated messages. She had placed Dr. Bristol's message on top. Sy barely glanced at it, kept going toward his private office. But the instant his hand touched the knob, he realized suddenly what that message said.

He stopped, stared down at it through the lower half of his bifocals.

DR. BRISTOL WOULD LIKE TO SEE YOU AT YOUR FIRST FREE MOMENT.

He dreaded making the call, but instructed: "Bridget, get her!"

Sy Rosen sat back in his creaky old desk chair. He tugged at his thin beard as he stared across the desk, hesitant to ask, "Okay, Rita. What?"

"She has a temperature of one-oh-one point three."

"Any other signs?"

"Indications of exfoliative dermatitis have broken out on her back, slight abdominal distention with sensitivity."

"Any signs of hepatitis?" Sy asked.

"Not yet," Bristol said, with a significance that did not escape the older doctor. "But there is further if slight detectable weight loss."

Sy Rosen nodded sadly. "The classic signs. GVHD."

"Most BMT patients get it," Dr. Bristol reminded.

"And despite incubating Emily's marrow before you transplanted it. Damn it, one day we have to find a way—" He brushed aside vain hopes and expectations to ask, "Shall we increase the methotrexate?"

"I'm giving her all she can tolerate now."

He nodded, accepting her appraisal of the situation. "It's some science we practice, Rita, if the disease doesn't kill, the treatment does."

"We knew the risks. But we had no choice."

"Rita . . . if you had to say, what would you estimate are the chances of reversing GVHD in Simmie's case?"

"Sy, like you, I've seen some rare cases that beat the odds. So it's tough to say. Unfair really. Misleading."

"Based on your experience, your knowledge, what would *you* estimate her chances to be?" he asked.

"Between very bad and none at all."

"Then you consider her terminal?" Sy asked.

"The slightest infection, interstitial pneumonitis due to the effects on her lungs of the chemo, or a hemorrhage, anything could do it. Anything."

"Would you do something for me, Rita?"

"What more can I do?"

"I haven't the heart to tell Emily. Or even Walter."

"It's my case," Dr. Bristol said, accepting the obligation to inform the parents.

She started for the door. Sy stopped her. "Rita. Wait. I'm not that much of a coward. They have a right to hear it from me."

He put in a call to Walter Duncan. Bridget reported that Dr. Duncan was in consultation and had left orders not to be interrupted.

Later, Sy thought, *with what I have to say, later will be good enough. Soon enough.*

Walter Duncan had been summoned down to Radiology by Dr. Wiswell, who had been in charge of Amy Bedford since her earliest X rays and scans. For comparative purposes, Wiswell had mounted on the wall of glass all the sets of Amy's X rays. When Walt entered the room, one glance alerted him to serious trouble.

"Walt, take a look" was all Wiswell said.

Wiswell turned off the overhead lights, flipped on the back lights. Walt Duncan started at the far left end of the wall of glass. Lit from behind, the films presented their shadows and shapes, light and dark. Both doctors moved slowly down the line.

Clean, clean, clean, Walter noted silently. Until he came to Amy's final set of X rays. There Wiswell had circled in soft red crayon a shadow that did not appear on any previous films.

Walt looked to Wiswell.

"When this showed up on this morning's films, I jumped the gun on her scans and did them. You can see it more clearly on the scans. Very defined hot spot."

"Damn it!" Walt said. "She was doing so well . . . so well."

"Fortunately it's encapsulated. It should be excisable."

" 'Fortunately,' " Walter Duncan shot back angrily. "What's so fortunate about having a metastasis? I thought we had this damned thing beaten! But it never ends, does it? It's like a guerrilla war. Those cells just keep hiding in secret parts of the patient's body. Hiding in the bloodstream. Just waiting for the surgeon and the oncologist to feel the least bit confident. Then the enemy bursts forth again. Clowns! Charlatans! Making our reassurances to the patient sound like so many deliberate lies. Well, maybe they are. Or maybe we are so vulnerable on our poor record of cures that we lie without even meaning to. To cover all our failures."

Walt realized that Wiswell was staring at him. He became self-conscious.

"Sorry. I guess it's all the pressures. They build up until a man can't take them anymore. But she'd been doing so well I was not expecting this. I'll talk to Levin in Thoracic Surgery. And, of course, to Amy and her folks. Damn!" he repeated, but almost as a whisper this time.

* * *

253

Ed and Marion Bedford both had arrived at the hospital within a half hour after Walter Duncan's call, she from home, he from an important executive staff meeting at his main office.

They waited anxiously in Amy's room for Walt's arrival.

"Has Dr. Duncan said anything to you, honey?" Ed asked his daughter.

"Only that he wants to speak to us all together," Amy said.

"Probably some new kind of treatment," her father said. "I told him, anything new that'll help my little girl, I want it. And I don't care what it costs. So it must be something new. Maybe to help you with your physical therapy."

He smiled confidently. Nevertheless, he kept mopping his face with a handkerchief that was already limp.

"Hey, I know. He's ready to discharge you ahead of time. I told him, soon as you're able, I'd like for all three of us to go on a trip. A cruise, maybe. Would you like that, darlin', a cruise? This time of year they say it's great up in the Scandinavian countries. The fjords, the mountains and things."

Marion Bedford could contain herself no longer. "Ed, please let's just wait and hear what the doctor has to say."

He fell silent. The air in the room grew dense with unspoken fears.

Walter Duncan entered. "Sorry to keep you waiting. But I had . . . had things to do down the corridor."

"Doctor—" Ed Bedford started to say, but his wife's sharp glance interdicted him.

"Mr. Bedford, Mrs. Bedford, Amy, what I have to say will sound discouraging at first . . ."

"Doctor, what is it?" Amy asked anxiously.

"Amy, before you think the worst, listen to everything I have to say. We have discovered something in your last X rays. And the scans confirm it. A spot. Metastasis."

"You're saying she still has the cancer?" Ed Bedford accused, as if surgery and medicine had both betrayed him.

"Mr. Bedford, I am saying that, as in many other cases of this kind, the cancer has spread to her lungs. That is not so serious as it sounds. Because this particular kind of cancer when it hits the lungs is encapsulated. It is in small, tight areas that we can just cut out, leaving the lung intact."

"What if the disease is still there—" Ed Bedford started to say.

"That's why we do chemo for a whole year," Walt explained. "To chase down those cells and wipe them out."

"But you didn't!" Bedford shouted. "After putting my daughter through hell, all those terrible seizures of nausea, vomiting, why she's half the size she was when all this started. Look at her! Look at what the treatment's done to her. Why only two nights ago I couldn't sleep. So I went down to the rumpus room where Marion keeps all our photographs of Amy. I looked through some of those shots I took of her last year, before this whole thing started. I tell you, I couldn't recognize her. She's not the same person anymore. I said to myself, 'She will be; she will be. She's getting along so well; she's beaten this thing. A year from now she'll be like in those pictures again.' Now, today, you tell me . . ." He shook his head in dismay and started to mop his face again. "I guess you don't know how it feels to be the father of a sick child. Helpless, that's what it feels like. Helpless."

"I think I know the feeling, Mr. Bedford. Now that you've got everything off your chest, let me continue."

He turned to Amy. "Amy, we are going to have to operate again. This time, since it's your lungs, I'm asking Dr. Levin to do it. He's an excellent surgeon. He's done many cases like this. I will scrub with him and I will be there all the time. Watching over you, making sure you're doing okay. The main thing, Amy, don't think that this is an unusual development. We hope against it. But we do anticipate it. And the odds are in your favor. Very much in your favor."

"How much in her favor?" Marion Bedford demanded.

Walt ignored both the older Bedfords and took Amy's hand. "Amy, you've been a real trooper through all of this. You're one of the most willing and cooperative patients I've ever had. So I want you to know the truth. Patients with one metastasis in the lung, and no other involvement, have a seventy percent chance of surviving. Living five years and beyond for a totally normal life. Seventy percent. Those are damned good odds."

Amy nodded soberly.

"So you have to go with us the rest of the way. Surgery. Chemo. We're going to have to change that to a new one we call cisplatin. It's a little rougher than what you've had. But with your courage and determination, you can make it."

Amy stared into his eyes and nodded. "Okay, Dr. Walt, okay."

"Good. Because Dr. Levin has an opening in his schedule tomorrow morning. We should do this at once."

She nodded again. He patted her on the cheek. He started for the door when Bedford called to him, "This Levin, he's the best?"

Damn it, Walter Duncan thought, *why does every relative want to know if the doctor is "the best" or "the greatest"?*

He turned back to Bedford. "If my child could be helped by lung surgery, I'd pick Levin. Does that answer your question, Mr. Bedford?"

They were silent after Walt Duncan had left. Until Marion Bedford said, "Ed, go back to the office. I'll stay with Amy for the rest of the day."

"Yeah . . . yeah . . ." he said vaguely. Instead of leaving, he went to the night table and picked up the phone. He dialed a number. "Cathy, it's me. Tell them I will not be coming back to the office today. Or tomorrow. Yes, yes, I know. So I won't preside at the national sales conference. Tell Burke and Chambliss they'll have to carry on without me. I don't pay them six-figure salaries for nothing."

He hung up the phone. He turned back to his daughter.

"Dad, you really don't have to stay. I'll be okay."

"Baby, I'm not staying because I *have* to. I'm staying because I *want* to."

Within hours after Walt Duncan's visit, the preparations for Amy Bedford's impending second surgery were under way. The technician was in to take blood samples. An anesthetist came by to take all her statistics and her medical history. In late afternoon, after his morning surgery, Dr. Alvin Levin came by.

When Dr. Levin introduced himself, Ed Bedford stared at him before shaking his hand. "You're . . . you're pretty young."

"Beats being just pretty," Dr. Levin said, smiling. "Don't worry, Mr. Bedford, I've been briefed on Amy's case. I know what to do. And I do it very, very well. By this time tomorrow it will be over. Amy will be in Intensive Care and we can all breathe a whole lot easier."

He approached the bed. "Amy, I've had a chance to study your X rays. Based on those, we go in, retract your ribs, reach that sucker and remove it easier than coring an apple. It comes out clean. There's nothing much to it. Of course, your parents will have to sign the usual informed consent."

"Will it say anything about . . . about amputation?" she asked.

"No. This time there's absolutely no possibility of that," Levin promised. "See you in the morning, Amy."

23

OLD Sy knew the Duncan family routine these days, knew it only too well. At the end of a long day, once Walter had finished his busy day of surgery, consultations, examinations, rounds and preparations for the next day's surgery, he arrived at Simmie's room, exhausted but determined to greet his young daughter with a smiling, optimistic look on his lean, lined face.

By that time Emily would have fed Simmie what little the child could eat, tucked her in tenderly, sung to her, kissed her and waited until the child drifted off to the sleep she needed so desperately. She would sit by the child's bed, holding her cold, wasting hand, observing the slight rise and fall of the blanket as it followed her shallow breathing.

Walter would arrive, wash carefully, slip into a sterile gown and enter the room silently. He would look to his wife, who, most times, would signal him not to talk. His daughter had not been asleep so long that she was deeply under. He would watch her closely, as if he could determine her condition by mere observation. He was trying to delude himself into believing he could see signs of improvement that did not exist.

As the dread illness was sucking the life out of his daughter, so were the demands on his wife endangering her, not only physically, but emotionally as well. Loss of sleep, loss of weight were factors that, in combination, could bring on nervous exhaustion, even a total breakdown.

She would not have eaten during the day, using as her excuse that it was too much trouble to leave, go down to the hospital cafeteria, then have to scrub again, slip on a fresh sterile gown and mask to be admitted to her daughter's room once more. It seemed easier to forego eating. He insisted on sending up food from the hospital kitchen. It did not seem to improve matters. Emily ate nothing by day. At night, whether they ate at home or went out, every meal ended precipitously with the tears she had held back all day.

Knowing the Duncans could be found in Simmie's room, Sy called the nurses' station on the second floor and left a message. When the nurse went down the corridor to Room 212, she found Emily holding tightly to her daughter's hand, reluctant to leave, though the child was finally in a deep sleep.

The nurse came in to say softly, "Dr. Rosen asked if you would stop by before you left. Both of you."

"Em," Walter urged, "Sy wants to see us. Please? Come?"

She nodded vaguely, leaned over to kiss her child on the forehead.

"Fever," she said. "Her fever is worse."

They arrived at Sy's office. The old man had spread out before him the reports from Dr. Bristol and the lab. He motioned the couple to take seats. Emily sank into a chair. Walter remained standing. He peered past the glow of the desk lamp at his old colleague, whose face reflected the grim news he was about to impart.

"Em, Walt, I have conferred with Dr. Bristol. There is no doubt that Simmie is experiencing GVHD reaction. The bone marrow transplant we hoped would start her on the road to recovery has begun to attack her body. Dr. Bristol has already put her on cyclosporine. But—" He paused. Sighed. Then said simply, "She has virtually no chance at all. No chance."

"I failed her," Emily said softly, as if to herself.

"Em, no!" Sy refuted.

"I failed her. Whatever it was she needed from my bone marrow, I didn't have it to give."

"Em," Walter said, "we told you it was a long shot. It was something to try when there was nothing else."

"I failed her," Emily continued to repeat, "I failed her. . . ."

Walter looked to Sy Rosen, who could not conceal his shock at Emily's reaction. Walter put his arms around her, lifted her and held her in a tight embrace.

"Em," he said softly, "Em, you didn't fail. Medicine failed. We don't yet know enough to defeat this terrible disease. If anyone's to blame, we doctors are."

He shepherded her out of the office. Sy watched them leave, shaking his head with grim concern. For what lay ahead, Emily Duncan was ill-prepared.

They were in the hospital parking lot. Walter was unlocking the car door when Emily suddenly said, "I'm not leaving."

"Em, you've got to get some sleep," he insisted.

"I'll sleep in a chair in her room," she said, starting swiftly back toward the Pediatric Pavilion.

He raced after her, caught up, seized her, made her face him. "Em, you can't. You'll disturb her. She needs her sleep, too."

"She needs her mother. When doctors fail, when all medications fail, a child needs her mother more than ever."

Violently, she broke free and ran toward the entrance. He caught up with her at the door. She struggled with him, summoning strength he did not know she possessed. If she were that determined, he knew he had better acquiesce.

"I'll get a cot set up for you," he finally said.

A night maintenance man found a cot. To prevent his breaking the isolation so vital to Simmie's chances of survival, Walter himself set up the cot alongside the child's bed. He exercised great care to be as quiet as possible. But Simmie stirred several times,

260

opening her eyes just long enough to ask, "Daddy? That you?"

"Yes, baby, now go back to sleep."

Once Emily was bedded down, Walter Duncan started for home. He got as far as the front door of the hospital, but decided to remain. He found one of the small rooms where residents on overnight duty usually slept between calls. He removed his shoes, lay down on a bed uncomfortable for his long form, placed his hands behind his head and stared up at the ceiling.

God, he thought, *after all these years, here I am again, sleeping on a hospital bed in the residents' quarters. Back then we were called interns. Back then I used to think ahead, to the future. We'd get married. Em and I. Have children. Have a house. A modest one to start. Then a child or two, or even three. I'd get going in practice. Sy's assistant. Then take over when Sy was ready to retire. I had it made.*

"Had it made." That terribly misleading, self-deluding phrase that's become a part of our language and our lives. Security. We all pursue it. We deceive ourselves into thinking that we've achieved it. That finally we have it made.

Until, suddenly, fate or nature or God Himself intervenes and you discover there is no such thing. You plan and work, scheme and dream, but in the end you have control of very little, if anything.

Simmie, oh, Simmie, what a life I had planned for you. Did you know that I have a college fund set up for you? Some kind of bonds my broker talked about that would provide you with all the money you could possibly need for college and beyond. Before that, trips, to some of the most beautiful parts of this country. Then to Europe, to the Middle East, to see the historic places, the great monuments of bygone ages. I'd take time off; we'd go together.

All the things I never had, you were going to have, Simmie. Everything.

Yet here I am, afraid to go home to an empty house. Afraid that, as always, my first instinct when I get home, no matter the hour, I'd race up the stairs to your room to kiss you good night. But you won't be there. I'd go into the den to have my predinner drink with your mother. And she won't be there. Then I would realize that if the two of you aren't there, I don't belong there either.

So I am hiding out in this little room. Half my life gone, and I'm back where I was so many years ago. Walter Duncan, who had it made.

He had fallen asleep finally, a restless, tormented sleep. He woke not slowly, but startled. It took a moment for him to realize where he was. An instant later, he realized why. He also recalled that he was due up in the OR to scrub and assist at Amy Bedford's lung surgery to remove that malignant node. He must shower, have several cups of coffee and get to surgery.

First, he would stop by Simmie's room and see how she was, and Emily.

He entered the anteroom of the isolation suite, prepared to scrub and slip into a sterile gown, but what he heard from inside the room made him pause and listen very carefully.

"Simmie, darling, if you could have anything in the world, what would you want?" Emily asked.

"Home, Mommy. I want to go home."

"Home?" Emily equivocated.

"I want my own room again. My own things again. My dolls. My toys. My books. My stereo." As if confiding a secret, she added, "I don't like this place, Mommy. I'd rather be home."

"All right, baby. If that's what you want, Mommy will take you home."

Walter's impulse was to blurt out, "No, Emily! You can't do that!" Instead, he forced himself to remain silent. No purpose in upsetting the child. He would discuss this with Emily later. Instead, he slipped into a gown, forced a hearty smile and entered the room.

"Good morning, sweetheart." He greeted his daughter.

"Daddy! Daddy, guess what? I'm going home. Mommy's taking me home. Won't that be terrific!" She smiled, actually a bare flicker of a smile.

"Yes, yes, that's fine," he agreed. "Of course, we have to talk to Uncle Sy about it first, though."

"Do we?" Emily challenged.

"Yes, Em," he said. Then with equal emphasis on every word he added, "We have to talk to Sy first "

"Oh, he'll say yes," Simmie interjected confidently. "He never says no to me about anything."

"We'll see, baby. We'll see," Walter said.

The nurse came in with Simmie's breakfast. It gave Walter a chance to gesture Emily outside the room. Once out of Simmie's hearing, he asked, "Em, how could you promise that? We can't take her home now."

"Why not?" she asked sharply.

"Now more than ever she needs all the medical care we can give her."

"Why?" Emily demanded.

"Em, for God's sake—" He started to protest.

"Yes! Tell me why. What can they do for her now? Nothing. Sy as much as said that last evening. There is nothing left to do now but watch my transplanted marrow slowly kill her. Well, she is going to be home. Where she wants to be. With the things she loves. Where she has lived all her life. Home, Walter, home! To you it's the last place you go. To her it's the first place! It's everything. I am taking her home!"

"Em—" He started to plead.

"She is going home. Today!" Emily declared with finality.

He could not stop to argue. He was overdue in Surgery. He said only, "Don't do anything until I get back. Promise?"

"I can wait that long," Emily said. But she was more determined than he had ever seen her before.

Amy Bedford was sedated but still conscious when Walter Duncan entered the Operating Room in gown, cap and mask. He leaned over her.

"Amy . . ."

She looked up and into his eyes. "Hi, Dr. Walt. Last night, before I fell asleep, I was thinking—"

"Yes, Amy?"

263

"Simmie, how is she? I haven't been allowed in to see her the last two days, so I wondered."

"She's getting along, Amy, getting along," he replied.

The anesthetist spared Walt the obligation of enlarging on the lie when she said, "Doctor, I need access to the patient now."

Walt patted Amy on the cheek. "You're going to be okay, Amy. When you wake up, that thing will be gone and you'll be good as new. Good as new."

During the surgery, Walt assisted by retracting and by applying the electric cautery device to seal off any bleeders. He admired Levin's skill. The young chest surgeon handled tissue carefully, yet worked with great efficiency and speed. He removed the cancerous lesion from the lung, dropped it into the kidney-shaped stainless-steel basin and had it rushed off to the lab for a preliminary biopsy to make sure it was not a fresh carcinoma but a metastasis from the original sarcoma. The fact that a patient had one form of cancer did not preclude her having another. Surgery could not be completed without knowing.

Ten minutes later the word came over the OR phone. Yes, metastatic osteogenic sarcoma. That meant it was safe for Levin to close.

They had wheeled Amy Bedford out of the OR and into the Recovery Room. Walt and Dr. Levin were stripping their gloves, taking off their masks and caps, when the younger man observed, "You get very restless don't you? Unless you're the one doing the surgery, Walt."

"Why? What makes you say that?" Walt demanded.

"You get antsy. Time there I thought you were going to grab the scalpel out of my hand and excise that thing yourself. As if I was too slow. Something wrong today?"

"Wrong? No. Nothing wrong," Walt said. "Except I have to get hold of Sy." That statement seemed to require an explanation. "There's a case we're both interested in that we've got to discuss."

"Of course. Sure," Dr. Levin said. "Nice of you to assist. It sure set Amy's mind at ease."

Levin watched him leave the OR. He thought, *What's come over Walt? This isn't the first time we've scrubbed together, but he's never been like this before. It can't be Amy Bedford. I know how he feels about his young patients, but a single metastasis to the lung isn't all that threatening. If that's all she gets, she's going to make it.*

Suddenly he realized, *Oh, my God, how stupid can I be? Simmie. I forgot about Simmie. We surgeons are so involved in our own cases we have no time for the simplest human concerns of others.*

"Walt!" Dr. Levin called. "Walt! I meant to ask—"

But Walt Duncan was already gone.

I will have to send the child a gift. Flowers, maybe. Or a doll. Or a book. Something, Levin thought.

"Sy, it's up to you to talk Emily out of it," Walt insisted. "She promised she wouldn't do anything until I get back. So she's waiting. Talk to her, Sy. She'll listen to you."

"What should I tell her?"

"Tell her she absolutely cannot take Simmie home!"

The old man rubbed the backs of his fingers against his thinning beard, then asked, "Why must *I* tell her?"

"What do you mean?" Walt demanded. "We have no facilities at home. Even with twenty-four-hour nursing, we can't do anything for her there."

"Walt," the old man said softly, "we can't do anything for her here."

That simply stated truth made Walter Duncan slump down into the nearest chair.

Whatever one's own private thoughts and fears, they never sound as final or real as when someone else pronounces them.

24

SIMONE Duncan was home once more, in her own bed, under a bright coverlet of red-and-white floral design. She looked about her and inhaled.

"It smells so sweet here, Mommy," she said.

Her mother nodded, smiling, holding back tears.

"It's good to be home." Then she added, "They won't be giving me any more of that chemo here, will they?"

"No, darling. Now would you like something to eat? Some cereal, perhaps?"

"No. Some . . . some pancakes? No sausage, just pancakes, with lots of syrup."

"Of course, darling. I'll go down and make them right away," Emily promised. She started for the door.

"Mommy?"

"Yes, dear?"

"Cindy . . ." She pointed to the top shelf of the bookcase opposite her bed. Emily was puzzled. The child pointed to the doll on the top shelf. "Cindy—you remember, Daddy brought her home for me that time he went to the seminar in California."

"Of course," Emily said. She reached for the brightly dressed doll with flaxen nylon braids.

Simmie cradled the doll in her arms, straightening its braids.

"Hi, Cindy. Did you miss me?" she asked. "Well, I'll be here from now on." She patted the doll on its cloth cheek.

Emily turned once more to start down to prepare an early lunch. She had not taken two steps out of the room when what she heard arrested her sharply.

"Cindy, would you like to belong to Kimmie, or maybe Lynne? I think you'd like Kimmie better. But you can choose."

Emily drew against the wall and out of sight. She listened closely, unable to breathe.

"Or should I let Kimmie choose? She's my best friend. Oh, I like Lynne, too. But Kimmie is my best. We went to day camp together. We were on the same basketball team. You'll like her. Maybe what I'll do is give you to Kimmie. And give Oscar the Clown to Lynne. He's the one we got when we went to the circus that time with Uncle Sy. Remember? Then there's my ice skates. Who'll I give those to?"

Emily was tempted to rush into the room and protest, "No, no, you mustn't!" Instead she leaned against the wall and wept silently as she heard her daughter softly dispose of what she considered her most precious worldly goods.

Simmie was dozing when Emily entered her room carrying a tray with hot fresh pancakes, butter, a decanter of golden syrup and a full glass of cold milk.

"Simmie?" Emily said gently to wake her. "Simmie, lunch."

The child turned slightly to face her, opened her eyes, then closed them again.

"Simmie? Pancakes! The way I make them on Sunday mornings. Don't they smell great?"

The child ignored her invitation and said, "Mommy, how does it feel when you die?"

"Who said anything about dying?"

"Does it hurt?" The child persisted.

Emily realized that she could no longer evade the issue. For her child's peace of mind, the time for pretense was over. She set the tray aside on Simmie's desk. She took the child in her arms, embracing her as Simmie had embraced her flaxen haired doll.

"No, darling, it doesn't hurt. In fact, when it happens, there's no pain at all. All the pain is over."

"Before—is there pain before?"

"If there is, we'll get Dr. Bristol or Uncle Sy to give you something and you won't hurt anymore."

"Or feel sick in my stomach?"

"No. There'll be no more of that either, sweetheart."

The child lay still, absorbing what her mother had said. "How does it happen, Mommy?"

Emily found herself unable to answer.

"Will anyone be with me?" the child asked, explaining her question to Emily's relief.

"Of course, darling. I'll be here. Daddy. Maybe Uncle Sy. One thing for sure, you won't be alone."

"And after? What happens after?"

Emily could not control her tears. Without sobbing, she let them roll slowly down her cheeks as she talked. "After . . . we'll still be here. You won't be alone."

"Will I ever see you again, Mommy?"

"Sometime, somewhere we will meet again," Emily said.

"It will be so sad, to be away from you for a long time," the child said. "So sad." She became aware of Emily's tears on her own cheek. "You crying, Mommy?"

"Uh-huh," Emily admitted.

"Is it all right? To cry, I mean?"

"If you feel like it, darling, it's all right to cry."

The child turned to her mother, buried her face between Emily's breasts. Soon Emily felt the warm moist tears of her young child seep through her dress.

After a time, Simmie asked. "Mommy, can Kimmie come to visit? And Lynne? And Stephanie? What I have, it isn't catching, is it?"

"I think it'll be all right, but I'll check with Dr. Bristol."

"I'd like to give them their things," Simmie said.

"I'll ask Dr. Bristol soon as I can get her on the phone," Emily promised.

The child seemed reassured. Suddenly she asked, "You're sure I won't be alone, will I, Mommy?"

"No, darling, when it happens, you won't be alone."

From that night on, Emily slept alongside her daughter. By the fourth day, once Simmie had been stabilized back at home, she was allowed to have visitors. At first Dr. Bristol had demurred, not wishing to expose the debilitated, immunologically defenseless child to the possible diseases of her young friends. Then, realizing it could make no difference now that the transplant had failed, the doctor had given her permission.

For a brief time, encouraged by the presence of her three friends, Simmie became animated. She told them of her adventures in the hospital. The treatments. The nurses. The awful nausea and retching. Some of the funny things that happened. And that nice girl, real grown up, who had become her friend, Amy Bedford.

"Did you know she was the tennis champion of the high school? She could even beat some of the guys on the team. She came to see me lots of times. We had fun together. She even got me a cap to wear when my hair started falling out. That's what happens, your hair starts falling out."

Emily listened, encouraged by her daughter's sudden spurt of energy. Perhaps in her own environment, surrounded by her own friends, she would thrive.

To prevent Simmie's exhausting herself, Emily announced, "Girls, time for cookies and ice cream!"

None of them appeared to have the usual eagerness for ice cream or cookies. Not even Stephanie, who was somewhat plump and known to be a lover of all things sweet. Somehow they sensed that this might be the last time they would see their friend. Before they departed, Simone disposed of her possessions as she had planned. Kimmie and Lynne refused the dolls Simone had planned for them until Emily insisted, "Simmie wants you to have them."

To Stephanie, Simmie gave her ball-point pen, which Ste-

269

phanie had once admired in class. Gifts in hand, the three started to leave.

"Don't go. It isn't catching," Simmie pleaded. "Is it, Mommy? Tell them that what I have isn't catching."

"Of course it isn't catching. But you need to rest now. It's been quite an afternoon, and you need your nap."

Simone waved to them as they slipped through the door, waving back.

They were gone. While Simmie talked on, Emily straightened the cover about her pale and wasting daughter.

"They liked their gifts, didn't they, Mommy?"

"Yes, darling. They loved them. It was very sweet and thoughtful of you to do that."

"After I'm gone, will they remember? I mean, every time they look at their presents, will they remember me?"

"With gifts or without, they'll remember you. We'll all remember you. You will never be forgotten, or alone. You'll be with us always. In our minds. In our hearts."

Reassured, the child closed her eyes and drifted off to sleep.

In the days after his daughter was taken home, Walter Duncan went about his duties at the hospital like an automaton.

Fortunately the years of study, accumulated knowledge and experience, which had made him such an excellent surgeon, served him well. He worked diligently and skillfully in the Operating Room, though his thoughts and fears were all with his daughter.

Whether he was consulting about a laminectomy to cure a painful spine, performing a resection to excise a cancerous segment of bone, repairing a shattered bone due to an accident or advising against surgery that would prove useless, a part of him was always with Simmie.

Every usual function had become so routine that once he found himself scrubbing for an operation until Sy reminded him that he had already scrubbed. Every ring of his telephone, every beep of the electronic gadget in the pocket of his lab coat became an alarm. Even his colleagues' friendly and best intended inquiries about Simmie were a source of torment.

His child was with him more in illness than she ever had been in health.

Despite a new work schedule, shortened to allow him more time at home with little Simmie, he always felt that he was depriving her. His urge to race home was so overpowering that each day, as he drove out of the hospital parking lot, he had to caution himself to drive carefully. For he was always tormented by the gnawing fear that this time, this day, he would arrive too late.

But when he reached home, Simmie was still there. In her bed. In the room she loved. She always brightened on seeing him. Weak and enervated as she had become, she tried to smile and even laugh at his little jokes. But the effort proved too much, and eventually, responding to a look from Emily, he would cease trying to amuse her. He would lie down beside her and hold her until she lapsed into sleep.

Below, in the den, things were always the same. Walt made them each a drink. Emily never finished hers, and by the time he finished his, the ice had turned to water. They talked. But only to break the silence.

Once Emily asked, "Shall I send for my folks?"

"Not yet," he said. He had no need to elaborate. For neither of them could face up to how her parents would react if they saw Simmie in her present wasted condition.

Their time in the den always ended with the same caution, Emily saying, "Walt, you really should eat something."

At the table, he toyed with his food, moving it about to make it appear used, but never touching it. Coffee. He did drink lots of coffee. It seemed to keep him going.

After dinner, he went back into the den, again by habit. He dug out of his briefcase the latest medical papers that Claudia had collected for him. He began to read. But after three or four pages, realizing that he had not absorbed a single thought, he tossed them aside.

He looked across the room at Emily, who sat at her own small desk, writing.

271

"What do you keep writing?" he asked.

"Thank-you notes. To people who sent Simmie things while she was in the hospital," Emily said. "Do you know some of your old patients who heard sent gifts? Flowers mostly. I want them to know we appreciate it."

"Yes, yes, we do appreciate it," he said vaguely.

Then, as had become his practice since they brought Simmie home, he went upstairs, listened at her door. Hearing nothing, he became fearful. He eased the door open, listened more closely and was relieved to hear her faint breathing.

Amy Bedford came back to see him for her routine six-week checkup. With her new X rays before him, her scans in hand, Walt Duncan was able to reassure her that there were no new metastases apparent.

"Still have that seventy percent chance?" she asked.

"I'd say it's even better than seventy percent by now. Just keep coming up with X rays like this and your year will be over before you know it," he said. "Now get up on this table and let me have a look at that leg."

He palpated her leg and her thigh. His fingers probed the muscles that now embraced the titanium prosthesis he had inserted. She was healing well, on schedule. But she needed a more exacting and strenuous physical routine.

"Okay, Amy. Everything is fine," Walt Duncan said. "Let's get up to Physical Therapy. Some things I want to see."

Brud Simpson, in charge of the Physical Therapy Department, had Amy get up on the treadmill. He affixed the halter around her body so that she would not fall if she overdid and lost her balance. Walt and Brud stood at a distance, not to be overheard.

"Okay, Amy, let's go!" Walt commanded.

Amy started walking on the inclined treadmill. It was difficult, trying to motivate that leg that still had not attained the peak of muscle strength and coordination. She was beginning to perspire freely. Too freely to suit Walter Duncan's professional tastes.

"Put her on the balloon," he said.

Simpson wheeled the Beckman cart close, so that Amy could breathe into the balloon as she walked. Walt watched the register on the computerized device. As he had suspected, she was exerting too much energy, using up too much oxygen for the effort required. She was driving herself too hard and uneconomically.

"We have to build up her aerobic capacity. The less oxygen she has to use, the better."

"We're working on it, Doctor," Simpson said.

"Let's see her on the bicycle."

"Okay."

Walt watched as Amy tried to make her right leg function smoothly during the rotating motion required to make the pedals revolve. She gave up in despair, seeming about to cry. He went to her side.

"Amy, Amy, remember, you are learning to use that leg with a new set of muscles. You have to get used to the fact that there is an artificial knee behind that kneecap."

"But I'm trying, I'm trying . . ." She broke down and started to weep.

He put his arms around her. "Amy, if you believe anything I ever told you, believe this: The time will come, not too long from now, when you will be doing this easily, without even a thought. But we have to work hard to get there. Okay?"

She looked up at him, smiled through her tears and said, "Okay, Dr. Walt. Whatever you say."

"Now, get on the cross-country ski simulator. Nothing will build up your muscles better than that sliding motion."

"Will do," Amy said.

As he turned to leave, she caught his arm. "Dr. Walt, how is *she* doing?"

"I wish she were doing as well as you," he said.

"Would it be all right . . . I mean, I don't want to intrude or anything, but would it be all right if I went to see her even though she's home?"

"She'd love it. She talks about you very often."

273

He left Amy in Simpson's charge, with one final word: "Keep her active. But don't let her overdo. She's the kind who might. She's still got that championship drive in her."

He started out of Physical Therapy, thinking, *Why don't I feel more satisfaction in a case like Amy Bedford's? It wasn't too many years ago that a child like her would be doomed. Yet here she is, alive, vital, and my biggest fear is that she'll overdo.*

If only he could have done as much for Simmie. . . . If only some doctor could have done as much for her.

As Simmie's condition continued to deteriorate, Walter Duncan came home from the hospital earlier each day. Sy covered for him in consultations and in Tumor Board meetings. Twice when there were unusual cases to present at the regular Monday grand rounds, Sy made the presentations, using Walt's files and his slides. On many cases Sy did Walt's post-op rounds, since he also had been present at the surgery. Anything to ease Walt's burdens during this difficult time and allow him to spend more precious time with his daughter.

Every moment he was home and Simmie was awake Walt spent in her room. He regaled her with stories of his youth, his schooldays. He told her tales, not always totally truthful, about his father, whom Simmie had never met. And about his mother, whom she had known only briefly before she died.

He told Simmie of the day his dad had brought home their first color television set. What excitement there was.

"Daddy, you mean there was another kind of television?" the child asked.

"Oh, yes. There was black and white. In fact, there was a time we didn't have any television set at all."

"But every house has a television set!" the child protested. "We have three. Stephanie's house has four."

"Well, darling, when I was just a little boy, there were lots of people who didn't have even one television set."

"Gee . . ." the child replied, saddened to learn of girls and boys were were so deprived.

Emily watched as she listened to her husband try to keep up a running recounting of his youth, which Simmie always called "the olden days."

I almost wish he would stop, Emily thought. *It's painful to see him try so hard to pretend. Some moments I detect that he almost believes he can make a difference, can reverse the inevitable.*

Under the pretext that Simmie needed her rest, Emily was able to shoo Walter from the room and back to their own bed for the sleep he so desperately needed.

On the sixth day of the third week after Simmie's return home, early in the morning, while it was still dark out, Emily was wakened by her daughter's voice.

"Mommy . . ."

Emily responded sleepily. "Yes, darling? What would you like? Some water? Fruit juice?"

"Mommy . . . I'm so warm, so wet . . ." Simmie's voice seemed suddenly muffled. "And I'm so . . . so tired . . ."

Emily came alert. With a startled move she reached behind her, groping for the switch on the bedside lamp. She flicked on the light. Then she saw it.

Blood was seeping from her daughter's mouth, tracing down her chin and onto her nightgown.

"Simmie!" Emily cried out, taking the child in her arms and rocking her. "Walter! Walt! Walt!" she called desperately. For she knew. She had read enough, been warned enough, to know this was one way it could end. A massive hemorrhage. She began to weep.

"Don't worry, Mommy. I'm all right. It doesn't hurt. It's like you said, it doesn't hurt. . . ."

Roused from sleep, Walter Duncan came rushing into the room, hardly able to face the light without blinking. He saw what was happening. He raced to the bedside, tried to take the child from her mother's arms. But Emily resisted.

"No . . . no . . . I promised her. I promised . . ." She kept protesting and weeping.

Firmly, yet careful not to inflict pain on either his wife or his child, Walter Duncan separated the two. With the child in his arms, he realized what had happened. What had threatened for so long had finally happened. He held Simmie, rubbed his large strong hand across her soft thin cheek.

The struggle was over. The pain. The agony of the treatments. The battle within her wasted body. It was all over. His child was finally at peace.

25

THE funeral of Simone Duncan, aged eleven, was held on Saturday morning. Several of Simmie's friends and classmates attended in the company of their parents. Kimmie brought the flaxen-haired doll Simmie had given her.

Emily's mother and father were there, having flown in from Tucson. When they arrived at the house, the first thing her mother said was, "As I expected, too late." Which caused Walt to intervene on Emily's behalf.

"It wouldn't have mattered if you were here or not. Emily's been wonderful throughout it all. Brave and wonderful."

Emily's father gripped her mother's arm to warn her against replying.

The ceremony in the church was brief and tasteful. The choral group of her grade in school sang two songs. The minister spoke well of Simmie, recounting the high points of her too-short life.

Emily and Walt followed the casket up the aisle of the church toward the bright sunny day outside. Behind them came Sy and other colleagues and employees from the hospital.

As they reached the last row of pews, Walter noticed that at the first seat on the aisle stood Amy Bedford, leaning on her cane. Alongside her, Brent Martin, who had driven her there. Amy made a slight, bashful, almost indiscernible gesture with her hand to greet Walt and make her sympathy clear to him. He nodded in appreciation.

At the cemetery there were only Walt, Emily, her parents and Sy. Emily had not wanted any intrusions on this most private and final moment in the brief life of her daughter. The minister spoke a simple prayer consigning little Simone Duncan to eternity and the mercy of God. He turned to Walt, signaled one of the attendants to hand him the first symbolic spade of earth. Walt could not bring himself to take it. Again the minister urged it on him. Walt stared down into the grave but did not move.

Sy stepped forward, took the shovel into his own hands and sprayed the fresh brown earth over the casket. Emily's father took the shovel from Sy's hands and did the same. Still Walter Duncan did not move.

The ride back from the cemetery was accomplished in silence. Emily, her father and mother, sat in the backseat of the limousine. Walt and Sy sat on the set-up seats. No one spoke. What was there left to say, except to complain against the injustice of it all?

Sy had thoughts of his own. He was disturbed that at the final moment Walter Duncan had not been able to perform that single last duty for his daughter. It was not like Walt, not the Walter Duncan he had known from the time he was a young, bright, eager and meticulous surgeon. Sy had stood at Walter's side when an aged patient expired on the operating table. Walt had been as careful and professional in closing that patient as he would have been if the patient were still alive.

Yes, it disturbed Sy Rosen.

Several of the neighbors were waiting for them when they arrived home. Despite Walt's orders, they had prepared a hearty meal for the mourners, few as they were.

Lunch was eaten in silence. There were no attempts at amusing stories and remembrances that are usually told about the de-

278

ceased to brighten such mournful times. Walt ate little. Excused himself early and drove off.

"Probably gone to the hospital," Sy said. "Maybe it's the best thing for him now."

Later, out back in Emily's flower garden, her father, seeking some common ground to converse with Sy, said, "Dr. Rosen, was there anything in the world that could have been—"

Sy interrupted. "We did everything. Everything. Maybe too much."

"Too much?" Emily's father asked, puzzled.

"We should have let her go sooner. Poor child," Sy said.

After some minutes of silence, Ingraham said, "I . . . I'll have to change my will now."

"Me, too," Sy said. Then he asked, "What college did you pick out for her?"

"I was thinking maybe she would have liked Arizona State. Someplace where we could have seen her often. You know, one damn trouble with these wonderful retirement colonies, they separate families. Never get to see your own grandchildren. Arizona State would have been wonderful. Or even UCLA. That's not much more than an hour's flight from Tucson."

They were silent for a long moment before Ingraham asked, "You?"

"I picked out the University of Chicago. For the same reason. It's only an hour's flight from here. And it's a fine school." Then Sy added, "I hope you don't mind. My thinking I was her grandfather."

"From what Emily's told me, you deserve the privilege. 'Sides, every child is entitled to two grandfathers."

"I'd better go," Sy said. "To do what I can to relieve Walt of his obligations, today of all days." He started away, turned back. "She loved the circus, did you know?"

"Yes, I know."

"I took her twice. We had a wonderful time," Sy said.

"She was a child who loved to laugh," Ingraham said.

"And the look of wonder in her eyes when they did some

279

fantastic stunt, like shooting the man out of the cannon, or the high-wire artists. God, she had the biggest, brightest, darkest eyes."

"Are you sure there was nothing more—" Ingraham started to ask, then apologized. "No, if there were, you would have done it."

Sy was on his way to his car when Walt pulled up in the drive-way. Sy approached him to say one last word of sympathy. But he noticed that Walter was taking out of the rear seat of his car files, books, several framed diplomas.

"Walter, what's the meaning of this?"

"I don't think I'll be going back there. Emily needs me now. I can't treat her like I treated Simmie. She's going to get all my time now. She's been through hell. I've got to make up for it."

"Walter, listen to me—" Sy started to say.

"Sorry, Sy. I've made up my mind. I left instructions about my cases that are still due for surgery. Pendleton will take care of those."

"Walt, wait a minute! You can't just walk out."

"I already have. Emily needs me."

"Walt, I know how you feel," Sy said. "But—"

Sharply, Walt interrupted. "You can do one thing for me. Amy Bedford. She's been so determined, so faithful to the treatment, with all its penalties, that I would like you to take on her case yourself."

"Of course. But Walt, that does not address the real issue. You. You have to come back!"

"Why?"

"You owe it to the profession. To your patients, present and future. And, in the end, to yourself."

"I owe? I? I owe no one anything!" Walt exploded. "Simmie! Yes. I owed her. I owed her a hell of a lot more than coming home late when she was already asleep. I owed her a lot more than kisses she never knew I gave her. Times when she had done something to be proud of, and I was not there to see it. Other fathers were there. Other fathers applauded, laughed, shared experiences with their daughters. But not Walter Duncan. Oh, no! He was off 'serving humanity.' Humanity? Faces that come and go and most I'll never see again. But the one person who was part of my life, who was my life, I didn't have time for. Well, I have nothing left now except Emily. I owe her all my time, all my love. She needs it. You can see that for yourself."

The ready answer was on Sy's tongue, but he knew it would make no impression on a grieving man as guilt-laden and tormented as Walter Duncan was at the moment.

So Sy limited himself to a hand on Walt's shoulder and a soft, "Walt, we Jews have a mourning ritual called *shivah*. During that week a man does not leave his home. Does not wear shoes, but slippers. Does not sit on a usual chair but on a low box or stool. In the biblical tradition, he makes a symbolical cut in his coat, as in the ancient rending of one's garments. And one of the main foods that is served is the egg, because it represents the continuity of life. However, after seven days a man puts aside his mourning and returns to life. He does not forget the dead, whom he remembers and prays for every day for a whole year. Then every year thereafter. But he resumes his life and the life around him. I will not mention this again to you for the next seven days. But after that I must."

"It won't change my mind," Walt insisted.

"I will be back in a week, Walter," Sy said.

Before the week was over, Sy called Emily to ask, "Is there anything I can do for you? Is there something you need?"

Nothing. The neighbors had been very kind, bringing in food, helping with visitors, and always at Emily's beck and call to perform any errand or duty.

"And Walt?" Sy asked.

He heard Emily pause. Then she confessed, in a furtive voice, fearing that Walt might overhear, "The first two days he greeted visitors. But by the third day, when a group of her schoolmates came to say how they felt about Simmie, he suddenly exploded at them. He told them to get out. That nothing they had to say would matter. Nothing could be changed. Simmie was dead. Gone. And would never come back."

"Oh, no!" Sy said, agonized.

"Since then he's been spending his time in Simmie's room. When I ask him to come down, he refuses. When I insist, he says, 'I'm making up for the time I should have spent here.' Sy, Sy, I don't know what to do . . . I just don't know."

He could hear her gasp and begin to cry.

"Emily . . . Em . . . I'll come by and talk to him," Sy promised.

Sy Rosen knocked gently on the closed door to Simmie Duncan's room. There was no response.

"Walt? Walt!"

Still no reply. Sy turned the knob and pushed the door open. The room was in darkness. The blinds were down and shut against the daylight. He discovered Walt lying atop Simmie's bed, his huge frame almost grotesque on a bed so short and small.

"Walt?" Sy challenged.

"Your week isn't over yet" was Walt's response, angry, hurt, as unrelenting as before.

"I can't wait," Sy said. "We are having problems at the hospital. Patients on whom we need your advice. Patients in mid-treatment. Patients who are asking for you, because they have confidence in you only."

"I'm sorry. Dr. Walter Duncan is no longer available. His time is now his own. His troubles are just as important as anyone else's. His family, what is left of it, is as important as any other family. Tell them!"

"You have to go back to practice sometime. Why not now?" Sy demanded.

"If I go back . . . and I say *if* . . . I will not go back to that hospital. Never. I will never step foot in that place again. I'll take Emily away somewhere where she can forget all this. It's the least I owe her!"

"You owe it to her, do you?" Sy argued. "Well, my dear Dr.

282

Duncan, you may feed yourself such noble-sounding fairy tales. So you are going to sacrifice your career, your tenure at the hospital, for Emily's sake? That is a lie. I'll tell you what you are really doing. You are indulging in a selfish act of retribution.

"Yes, retribution! This science, to which you have devoted your life, has disappointed you. Deserted you. At the time when you would have given anything in your possession to save the one you loved most dearly, your own science failed. After devoting your life to it, saving patients for whom other physicians held out little or no hope, it let you down. Our hospital let you down. You are an angry man, Walter Duncan. A vengeful man. 'If medicine failed me, I will fail it.' That's what you're saying.

"Walt, you know as well as anyone, there are no guarantees. You've lost your share of patients. We all have. We are not perfect. We will never be perfect. Our enemy prevents it. We conquer one disease, another appears. When we conquer that, there will be others. You want perfection? There is none."

"I didn't ask for perfection!" Walter Duncan exploded. "I just wanted one little girl to be saved. To survive. One little girl. My own daughter!"

"Walt—" Sy sought to continue.

But his protégé shut him off. "No, Sy. No more. No more do I put aside my needs, my wife's needs, for the sake of others. No more!"

No matter how long delayed, the moment had to come. The mourners were gone. The condolence calls and cards had ceased. Emily's mother and father had left to return to Arizona. Sy had to be at the hospital full time to carry on with his own and Walt's duties.

For the first time the house was empty. And silent. For want of anything else to say, from sheer habit, Emily asked, "Would you like some coffee? I'll put on some fresh."

"No thanks," Walt said without looking in her direction. He stared off through the den window at the garden beyond and saw none of it

283

"Is there anything I can get you?" she asked.

"Yes. I'd like my daughter back," he said.

"No, Walter, oh, no, you won't do that to me!" she exploded suddenly.

"Do? To you? What have I ever done to you? Except maybe deprived you of a husband. Stolen from you and Simmie the time that was due you," he said bitterly.

"I wasn't referring to that," Emily said.

"Then what were you referring to?" he demanded.

"You want to place the blame on me, don't you?"

"I said nothing like that, nothing!" he protested.

"Of course not," she replied, tears forming in her eyes. "It's not something you'd come right out and say. You are too kind, too considerate! The hell you are! You want me to say it. So later I can't accuse you. Okay! I'll say it. What do you think's kept me awake all these nights? Ever since it was clear that she was going to die? From the moment Dr. Bristol said, remember her words, 'By this time we should be seeing some results.' But there were none. And then it began. What you noble and wise scientists call GVHD. When the transplanted substance that is supposed to cure turns on the patient and begins to kill.

"I lay awake nights, sat up with her in the hospital, watching her as the marrow from *my* bones destroyed my daughter. *I* killed her."

"Em, no! They told you at the outset it wasn't a perfect match. But it was her only chance, a desperate chance. We all knew that."

"You don't understand!" she shouted at him. "A desperate chance could have failed. But this was different. My marrow didn't just fail Simmie. It attacked her. It killed her. I killed her. There, I've said it! Now, are you satisfied?"

She started to cry, her whole body convulsed in spasms. He tried to embrace her. She shook him off violently.

"Killed her . . . killed her . . ." She kept moaning.

"No, Em, no. You did all you could. All you could," he protested. "Me, I'm the one. My fault. Yes, my fault. If only I hadn't been so busy taking care of other people's children, worrying about their illnesses. I should have known. I should have recognized Simmie's symptoms. The signs she exhibited. Looking back on it, they were so clear. Those discolorations on her skin. Her tiredness. Remember how pale she seemed? How tired, so amenable to any suggestions? She was practically begging for me to recognize her illness. And I was just too damned busy with other people, other illnesses. All her life I was too busy, too busy. She lived and died without ever having had a full-time father. The fault was mine, all mine!"

He turned from her and slumped into the nearest chair.

"Quality time," he said vaguely. "Did you ever say anything about quality time? I never had *any* time with Simmie, not really. Surely not enough time to give her a chance at life. I should have spotted those symptoms earlier. I should have . . ."

"That's not what Sy said." Emily contradicted him.

"What? What did Sy say?"

"I asked him if we'd discovered it earlier, would Simmie have had a chance? He said no. Once it was there, the odds were against her. Time would have made no difference. We know now nothing would have made any difference."

They were silent for a time.

"Those last nights," he confessed, "I was half out of my mind. Delusional. I was actually conversing with Disease. With Death. I tried to strike a deal. Give me my daughter's life and I will give up the practice of surgery. And I meant it."

It was night. He had not turned on any lights. He had not answered the telephone. He sat in the den feeling neither hunger nor thirst. Feeling only the stillness in the house. He rose from the chair, went up to find his wife. He passed Simmie's door, which was open. He came to their bedroom. That door was closed. His first reaction was one of panic. Had Emily, in her guilt, done something rash to herself?

He pushed open the door. He found Emily holding a hanger of clothes. On the luggage rack an open suitcase.

285

"Em?"

"I think maybe I want to go away from this place."

"Where?"

"I don't know. My mother's maybe. Someplace."

"And leave me alone? With all this emptiness?" he asked.

"Every time I pass her room I'll be thinking, 'Part of me attacked her, killed her.'"

He took the hanger out of her hands, tossed it aside, enfolded her in his arms.

"Em . . . Em . . . We've got only each other now. And I need you. I need you very much. Because I, too, am going to start a new life. If there's going to be any going away, let's go away together. There's nothing to keep us here anymore. I'm not going back to the hospital. I told Sy. I may not ever practice surgery again. Or medicine. I owe them nothing! Nothing!"

He raised her face and kissed her on the lips. He pressed his face against hers.

"Do you forgive me for what I did to Simmie?" she whispered.

"I forgive you for all sins, real and imagined. I forgive you for being too kind and understanding. For living with the urgencies, emergencies and deprivations that are part of the life of every woman married to a doctor, I forgive you."

He kissed her again. This time she responded. He could feel stirring within him longings he thought had died with his daughter. He had never needed to be closer to Emily, to be part of her, than he did now. He carried her to their bed. He lay down beside her and slowly began to undress her.

"At a time like this . . ." She protested in a whisper.

"We will never need each other more. Or need to love each other more," he said.

It was so late that they could hear the sound of the bells from the church, which was some streets distant from their home. It was a sound they heard only when all other neighborhood sounds ceased.

She lay in the crook of his arm, her head resting on his chest, her hand on his cheek.

"Did you mean what you said about not going back to the hospital?"

"I meant it."

26

D R. Simon Rosen had just completed his checkup of Amy Bedford. Her X rays were clean once more. The surgery on her lung had accomplished its purpose, and healing was excellent. And she had had no further recurrences of metastases. The year almost over, things augured well for her future.

While Amy and her mother waited in his examining room, Sy went out to his desk. He asked his secretary to place a call to Simpson in Physical Therapy.

"Brud, Dr. Rosen. I have here Dr. Duncan's patient Amy Bedford."

"Oh, yes, great girl. Only one fault, she works too hard. But her progress is remarkable."

"That's what I wanted to ask you about. She's still on a cane. But it seems to me she's strong enough to get rid of it. What do you think?"

"Okay with me. But I'd still like her to finish her therapy here."

"Of course. I'll stress that. Thanks."

Sy was about to hang up when Simpson said, "Doctor, what about Duncan? Is he sick? Why isn't he back?"

Sy thought a small lie was appropriate. "He's having some family trouble."

"Of course. I understand. His wife must still be badly shook up."

Sy did not respond.

"All right now, Amy, let's see you walk the length of this room, back and forth. Without your cane."

Amy looked at Sy, then at her mother. She rested her cane on the examining table. She started away from them toward the far wall of the long narrow examining room. One foot before another, always hesitating the barest instant before putting down her right foot. Then pushing it down in the way that caused the prosthesis within her leg to lock, hold firm and support her full weight.

She was not as smooth as she would be one day, as her recovery continued. But she was on her own. She could manage without any assists. Aside from the chemotherapy, which would continue for one more month, she could resume a normal life.

"Amy, you're on the last lap. The final set of the championship match. A little more chemo. Another X ray, another scan, and your year will be up."

"My year?" she said. "There were days—and nights—when it seemed like a hundred years!"

"I know, child, I know," Sy said. "But it was worth it. Right, Mrs. Bedford?"

"Very much so," Mrs. Bedford said, beaming. "Believe me, eleven months ago, and many times during those eleven months, I never thought I'd see her live to walk like this."

"Well, you have, and she will get better and better."

"Dr. Rosen, something I was going to ask Dr. Walt, if he was here—"

"Yes?" Sy invited Amy's question.

"Can I play tennis again?"

Sy smiled. "Amy, my dear, 'can you?' Yes, in time, I suppose so. Should you? Not if I were you. And I am a tennis player from way, way back. Swede can tell you. But I would not risk it. Sure, we have a replacement for that prosthesis. It's resting in

289

Hans's shop right this minute. Have we replaced your kind of prosthesis before? Of course. Do we like to? We always like to avoid unnecessary surgery. You are now fifteen—"

"Sixteen," Amy corrected. "And I had chemo on my birthday."

"Okay. Sixteen. You have to pick up your life again. Think about college and a career. Think about dating, and courting and marrying. And having children. Not spending more time in hospitals. So I would pass up tennis."

Amy nodded solemnly as she considered Sy's advice. Then she brightened. "Doctor, all during the long months I've had one ambition: to show Dr. Walt the day when I could walk on my own."

"He would have been delighted." Sy assured her.

"Can I show him?" Amy asked.

Sy's look of puzzlement made her explain.

"If I went by his house, do you think he would see me? I'd like to walk up to his door without crutches or a walker or a cane."

Sy nodded. "Yes, I think that would be a good idea. A very good idea. But call him first. Let him know you're coming."

"Okay. Sure." Amy agreed.

While Amy was in the dressing room slipping out of the white patient's gown and into her own clothes, Sy said softly to her mother, "Mrs. Bedford, does your husband play golf?"

"When he finds the time. Why?" the puzzled woman asked.

"A girl like Amy, so well coordinated, and with such an urge to excel in athletics, needs something to take the place of tennis. Tennis, for her, can conceivably be a dangerous sport. The sudden starts and stops. The possibility of falling on the court. Golf could serve a double purpose. It would channel her drive, talent and desire into a safer sport. And it would bring father and daughter closer together."

Mrs. Bedford nodded, smiling. "Dr. Rosen, I can confess now that ever since Amy showed signs of getting well I've been afraid he'd go back to his old ways. Golf together could be a very good idea."

"Suggest it. Subtly," Sy said. "As we Jews are wont to say, 'Harm it couldn't do.' "

"Walt, there's a call for you," Emily said as she leaned into Simmie's room, where her husband spent most of his time now.

"I don't want to talk to anyone," he said.

"It's a patient."

"Sy takes care of my patients now."

"It's Amy Bedford. She wants to talk to you."

"Amy . . . Amy Bedford. Okay. But she's the only patient I'll talk to."

He went down to the den to take the call. He listened while Amy explained the purpose of her call. Walt refused to see her. After she pleaded, he finally acquiesced.

Once he had, Emily said, "You really ought to shave and get into some more respectable clothes."

He nodded, grimly. But went back to Simmie's room.

"Brent, you have to drive me, you just have to," Amy Bedford said over the phone.

"I'd love to, Amy. But I don't have wheels. My car's in the shop. And my mom is at the same charity lunch as your mom. So there's no car here."

"I could take a cab," Amy said, "but I wanted you to be there when I show him. After all, you're part of this, you know."

"Hey, I've got an idea. Why don't we go by motorbike? That's the way I get to school until my wheels come out of the shop."

"Motorbike? I haven't been on that since before all this started. It'll be like old times. Pick me up in half an hour."

"Oh, one thing. You have to wear a helmet."

"Of course," Amy said. "Now I better get dressed."

Brent Martin was extremely careful, making sure Amy was properly and comfortably in place on the rear seat of his motorbike. He waited until she strapped her helmet in place. He started up the noisy engine. They took off for the suburb where the Duncans lived.

The trip was uneventful until within a few blocks of the Duncan house. A large transcontinental moving van came up on their left side. Brent slowed down to allow it to pass. Once it went by he resumed his speed.

Then, without a signal, the truck turned right into Brent's path. He jammed on his brakes, but the momentum was too powerful to stop in time.

Brent's motorbike crashed into the side of the turning truck.

The woman who lived in the corner house heard the scream of brakes and the crash that followed. One glance from her window and she seized her phone and dialed 911 to report the accident.

"And from what I can see you better send an ambulance!" she said. "Maybe two!"

With sirens blaring, red and white lights revolving, three squad cars converged on the scene of the accident. They formed a barrier to block all other vehicles. Moments later, an Emergency Medical Services ambulance pulled up. The technician in charge leapt out of the back of the wagon, while the driver hauled out a stretcher.

"What have we got here?" the technician asked the policeman in charge.

"Two kids," the officer replied. "Lucky they had helmets on. But the boy seems hurt real bad."

The technician knelt over Brent Martin, who was just returning to consciousness. The technician asked, "Feel any pain, son?"

Brent was able to mumble, "Yes, sir . . ."

The technician made a swift appraisal of the boy's condition, paying special attention to the area of his neck. He called out to the driver, "Bring the spine board!"

Very carefully, with the technician supporting Brent's head, they lifted the boy onto the rigid spine board and carried him to the ambulance. The technician fixed Brent's head firmly in place with the straps that were part of the spine board.

The technician now had time to examine Amy Bedford. He found her pulse, took her blood pressure, examined her for any gross injuries. He concluded that apart from shock she had come through the experience with no discernible physical injury. But he insisted that she come with them to the hospital, where there would be a follow-up diagnosis and assessment of any covert injuries.

As soon as Brent Martin was carried into the Emergency Room at University Medical Center, the resident's first look made the next step automatic. An immediate single lateral cervical X ray was called for. While the X ray was being processed, the resident asked Brent, "Feel any pain, son?"

"Yes," Brent whispered.

"Let me see you move your legs. The right one first."

Brent's response was barely discernible.

"The left one now," the resident ordered.

Brent tried, but could not move it.

"Now your arms, right one first."

Brent responded with great effort.

"Now the left," the resident said, though he had already formed his diagnosis and was calling to the nurse, "Get Dr. Pendleton down here. If he's busy, find me someone in Orthopedics or Neurosurgery. Stat! We've got a hot one here."

From the examining table on which she lay, Amy Bedford called, "Get Dr. Rosen! Please!"

"Rosen?" the young physician asked. "Simon Rosen? You know him?"

"I'm under his care now."

"Why didn't you say so? Nurse, find Sy Rosen. No matter where he is."

Minutes later Sy Rosen came racing into Emergency, asking breathlessly, "A patient of mine? Where? Who?" Before they could tell him, he spied Amy Bedford, whose superficial face wound was being debrided and washed clean of blood by one of the nurses. Sy approached her table.

The young doctor tried to get his attention. "Dr. Rosen, this other patient—"

But Sy brushed by him to reach Amy. He performed a careful examination of her right leg. Pressing, probing, his experienced, sensitive fingers finally reassured him. Her right leg seemed intact and uninjured.

"Amy! Stand up!" he ordered.

"Dr. Rosen." The younger man tried to intrude.

"Amy! On your feet! Let me see you walk."

The legs of her slacks ripped and slightly bloody, her sweater torn from the impact with the ground, her face displaying a small open wound, Amy Bedford proceeded to walk up and back, up and back. Relieved, Sy Rosen said, "Good, Amy! We'll X-ray you. But that leg seems okay now. Okay."

He turned to the younger physician. "Now, Doctor, what's on your mind?"

"This patient here."

"Let's have a look."

Very carefully, Sy Rosen examined Brent Martin. He did not need much time to confirm the young doctor's apprehension.

"He probably needs surgery. And right away," Sy said. "Get me Pendleton, or if he's busy, Harvey or Bridges. One of them must be free. Meantime, call upstairs and reserve an operating room. Also get hold of Braham in Neurology. We'll need a neurosurgeon to assist."

27

MINUTES later, Dr. Alan Bridges, one of the experienced orthopedic surgeons in Sy Rosen's department, came racing into Emergency.

"You sent for me, Sy?"

"Alan, have a look at this young man. But very carefully."

Sy and Amy both stood alongside Alan Bridges as he made his assessment of Brent Martin's condition. Amy was in tears. Sy tried to comfort her, putting his arm around her.

She kept crying and saying, "My fault, it's all my fault. I asked him to take me to see Dr. Walt. Otherwise this wouldn't have happened. Will he die? Please, Dr. Rosen, tell me the truth."

"Amy, we don't know yet. But there are other things to worry about. Like what happens if he lives."

"What do you mean?"

Before Sy could answer, Bridges turned from the table. His glance to Sy indicated he would rather not discuss the patient's condition in the presence of the young woman. With a head gesture, Sy led Bridges to a corner of the room.

"We've got to do a total spine X ray—" Bridges began.

"Of course!" Sy interrupted impatiently. "What else? Dislocation of the spine. Possible spinal cord injury. Loss of movement in the legs."

"Partial. But clearly discernible. But you already know that, why did you send for me?" Bridges asked.

"We have to do surgery on him at once!" Sy said.

"Surgery? In a case like this? Not me!"

"What do you mean, not— Bridges, are you telling me that you *refuse* to do surgery? I'm ordering you to!"

"Dr. Rosen," Bridges replied very formally, "need I remind you that you are no longer Chief of Orthopedic Surgery? And that professor emeritus is merely an honorary title?"

Furious, Sy Rosen seized Bridges by the lapels of his lab coat. "Bridges, as one doctor to another, I am asking you to do surgery to reduce the injury to that boy's spinal cord."

Purposefully choosing his words, Bridges said, "Dr. Rosen, in my professional opinion, the chances of the patient's recovering from the surgery indicated in this case are so slight that I do not think the risk to the patient is justified."

"You don't think the risk to the patient is justified? Or you don't think the *doctor* wishes to risk it?" Sy asked, his face flushing in anger.

"I do not think the risk to the *patient* justifies it," Bridges corrected.

Without another word, Sy went to the wall phone. He barked an order at the operator. "Get me Walt Duncan. At home! And insist he come to the phone."

He held on, glaring across the room at Dr. Bridges. Meantime, Amy stood at the side of the examining table, desperately holding Brent's hand. He had lapsed into unconsciousness, and she was trying to wake him, to bring him back. For she had the terrible fear that if he did not wake soon, he would never wake.

Sy spoke into the phone. "Hello, Walter. Oh, Emily. I want to talk to him. Won't come to the phone? Damn it, you tell him that I want to talk to him! There's no time now for mourning. I must talk to him!"

No one in Emergency dared to move. Even the nurse who had fixed the IV into Brent Martin's arm hesitated before turning it on. All was quiet and very, very still.

Finally, Sy Rosen said, "Walt? That you? I want you down here at once. An emergency. The kind in which minutes can count. We've got a trauma case that demands decompression of the spinal cord by open reduction. It's an impact trauma case. And from what I can see there is constrictive bony tissue that could leave this young man a quadriplegic."

"Sy, I told you—" Walter started to say.

"Wait, it's a young man you know. The young man who helped you with Amy Bedford's case when she was going through hell. Now he needs your help!"

"That young man? Martin . . . something?"

"That's his last name. Brent is his first name. Walt, you know what can happen to nerves under pressure for any length of time. Come down here! Stat!"

Walt had never been able to refuse Sy Rosen. Finally, this time proved no exception.

"All right, Sy, I'll be there."

"Good. And Walt—"

"Yes?"

"Let Emily drive you down. Just to make sure."

Walt Duncan hesitated. "Okay, Sy, okay."

In twelve minutes Emily Duncan's car pulled alongside the ambulance dock. Walt Duncan, with a full growth of beard, dressed in old corduroy pants and wearing an unpressed navy blue wool shirt, stepped out of the car and started up the concrete steps to the level of the Emergency Room.

With Emily trailing behind him, he entered. Sy pointed him to the examining table. Walt approached it, stared down at the unconscious young man. He was about to examine him when Sy reminded, "Doctor, don't you think you ought to wash first?"

While he was washing, he became aware of Amy's presence. "Sy, was she involved? Was she hurt? What about that leg?"

"The leg seems fine on palpation, but we'll put her through a course of X rays. It's the young man I'm worried about."

Walt Duncan returned to the examining table. Carefully, applying only the lightest, most delicate touch, he proceeded to evaluate the condition of young Brent Martin.

He turned to Sy and to Alan Bridges, who stood just behind the old man. "You've got to go in and decompress him. There's no other chance."

"Then do it," Dr. Bridges said.

"Not me. For God's sake, Alan, after what I've been through these last days, I wouldn't trust my own hands. You have to do it."

"Do I? Would you like me to cite for you the statistics in cases like this when surgery is done perfectly? The mortality rate? The rate among patients who survive but lose motor ability in their legs or their hands or all four limbs? Would you like to hear those statistics?"

"Alan, he's a young man of seventeen. He's got his whole life ahead of him. Would you doom him to spending it in a wheel-chair?" Sy said.

"I won't stop anyone else from operating, but not me. Oh, no! And if you don't mind, excuse me from assisting, too."

"Alan, look at my hands," Walt Duncan pleaded, holding out his large hands, once powerful, now trembling slightly. "I can hardly keep them steady. Alan?"

Sy Rosen intervened. Grimly, with great sadness, he said, "No, Walt. It's no use. You are looking at a new breed of doctor, who, between taking a risk to give the patient a chance at a full life and choosing to save his own hide, chooses the coward's way out."

"Don't you call me a coward," Alan Bridges shot back. "I didn't create this system. You know damn well that if I was to operate and this boy died, or was left paralyzed, there could possibly be one hell of a malpractice suit against me. Everything I worked for, security for my wife, education for my kids, would go down the drain. This patient is a seventeen-year-old boy with years to live. If he survives as a paralytic, what size malpractice judgment would be staring me in the face? Five million? Ten million? Who knows what a jury will award? But if I don't operate, where's the malpractice? Just a doctor's opinion that in this particular case surgery was too great a risk to the patient's life."

Walt Duncan turned on Alan Bridges.

"What the hell are you, Bridges? A businessman or a doctor? What are you doing in this profession anyhow? Passing through to earn a few bucks so you can retire at an early age?"

Dr. Bridges answered in carefully selected words: "I do not think this patient presents a justifiable risk for decompression surgery. Especially when some self-righteous, self-anointed 'saint' like you might go into court and testify against me. As you did against Enright."

"Some of you will never forget that, or forgive me for telling the truth, will you?" Walt demanded.

"Gentlemen, I have given you my considered professional opinion. I advise against open reduction in this case."

Dr. Bridges left the room, glaring at the two nurses and the young Emergency Room doctor, who were shocked at his conduct.

"Walt?" Sy asked.

He had no need to ask anything more. Walter Duncan knew what that meant. If surgery was to be done, it had to be done at once. He felt his hands at his side, still trembling. Whether in anger or nervous exhaustion, he did not know. But he could not move to accept Sy's challenge.

Sy looked to Emily, who had stayed out of range of the hostile confrontation among the doctors. Sy's eyes beckoned her to intervene. Slowly she came toward her husband. She put her hands on his shoulders.

"Walt, he's a young man, a kid really. He's got a whole life ahead of him. You have to do it."

"I—I no longer 'have' to do anything," he said. "Besides, I don't think I can. Not anymore."

"All the skill you had, did that disappear in just days? What you were able to do ten days ago you can do now. Walt?"

He did not reply, but neither did he give any sign of assent.

"Walter," she said, "what if surgery could have saved Simmie and a doctor had refused to do it?"

His eyes welled up with tears. He asked softly, "Did anyone get in touch with Brent's folks?"

"I did," Amy said.

"Then they should be here any moment," Walt said, as he turned to Sy. "I'll start scrubbing. You get the informed consent from his folks when they get here. Meet me up in the OR."

He started out of the door. Sy went to Emily's side. "Thanks, my dear. You said all that he needed to hear."

Open reduction. The phrase went through Walt Duncan's mind as he scrubbed diligently to attempt his first surgery since his daughter had died. It was a small two-word phrase. Almost innocuous in its sound. But it meant the delicate surgical procedure of removing pressure on the nervous system of a trauma victim. It was very difficult, very sensitive work, calling for the utmost care on the part of the surgeon. Bits of sharp, jagged spinal bone must be carefully separated from the spinal cord, while the surgeon tries at all times not to damage the nerves themselves. He or she must try to preserve what mobility still remained in the patient's arms and legs, hoping to enhance that and eventually restore the patient to full use of his limbs.

Open reduction. What an innocuous-sounding phrase to cover all the dangerous possibilities inherent in this surgical procedure.

All through surgery Walt would be aware that in a case like this the odds were always against the surgeon. Walt had had his share of such cases. His results were better than average, but he had also suffered his losses. Still, it was a risk he had to take to give the young man a chance at a useful life.

Sy came alongside him to scrub at the adjacent sink. "Clemmons in Neurosurgery has agreed to assist. He'll be right up."

"Good man, Clemmons, good man," Walt said. He was just rinsing his hands and arms for the last time when he said, "About Alan Bridges, it's really not his fault. It's what the system's done to many doctors and surgeons. Good people, capable people, are being frightened away from the best practice to the safest practice."

Once Walt had thrust his hands into the rubber gloves the nurse held for him, he began to feel more at ease. This was what

300

he was used to. Despite the surprises that might confront him when he got inside the patient, he felt equipped to deal with them. Far better equipped than he was to deal with the sorrows of his own personal life.

With Clemmons at his side, and Sy across the table from him, Walt proceeded with considerable delicacy and caution to reach the site of the trauma. He laid back flap after flap of skin, tissue, and the *dura mater* that protected the spinal cord.

He had reached the area of the damage. It was evident to the naked eye that bone splinters from crushed vertebrae were pressing on the spinal cord. Allowed to remain even for a few hours, they would result in irreversible paralysis. Yet, removing those tiny fragments would not necessarily assure total recovery. And the attempt to remove them might inflict even further injury.

Bridges was absolutely right, Walter Duncan thought. *At this point in the procedure, the surgeon can do everything correctly and still the odds are against the patient's recovery.*

He consulted Clemmons with a look. Clemmons nodded. Walter Duncan began the delicate task of extracting the tiny bone splinters from Brent Martin's spinal cord. That done, he proceeded to perform the fusion that would prevent any future damage. The nerve had been decompressed. What happened thereafter was in nature's hands.

Walt gave specific orders. The patient's head was to be immobilized with skull tongs to avoid movement and further risk, and to encourage uneventful healing. Clemmons would follow up the neurological aspects of the case. If all went well, the boy could have a promising future. It would mean weeks or even months of healing. But at least he had a chance now, a fair chance. They wheeled him out to Recovery.

Walt Duncan was tearing off his rubber gloves. He tossed them at the waste container and missed. As he untied his surgical mask, he became aware that Sy was staring at him from across the table, his face still masked, only his watery blue eyes exposed.

"Good work, Walt," Sy said.

"Beautiful work," Clemmons said. "That's a very lucky boy. I hope he appreciates it." He held out his hand. "Walt, it's a pleasure to scrub with you. It's like going to watch your old college team play, when you're sure they're going to win. Makes a man feel relaxed and confident."

Clemmons left the OR. Sy was stripping off his gloves and mask. "Walt," he said, "as long as you're here, I wonder if you would do me a favor?"

"What, Sy?"

"I've got a little boy in two-twenty-nine Pediatric. Take a look at him?"

"What do *you* suspect?" Walt asked.

"I don't want to influence your judgment. Just take a look, okay?"

Walter Duncan pondered the request a moment, then relented. "Okay. Just this one."

"That's all I ask," Sy said. "But as long as you're going to do it, shave first. And comb your hair. You look like a rock star, not a surgeon."

28

WALTER Duncan's careful examination of the slight ten-year-old patient was not nearly so revealing as was the boy's case history. Once Walt had studied that, he gestured Sy to join him outside the room.

"Sy, you didn't need my opinion. His X rays and scans tell the whole story. Osteogenic sarcoma."

"What do you suggest?"

"Chemo, of course. Right away."

"I've had him on chemo. Eight weeks now," Sy said. When Walt looked at him dubiously, the old man explained, "I didn't want to bother you. Not with what was going on in your life these last eight weeks."

Walt nodded, a single brisk nod that indicated his appreciation. Then he asked the crucial question: "Did the thing shrink?"

"Noticeably," Sy said.

"Then it's obvious: Go in and do a resection," Walt said. "Get the damned thing out. Of course, at his young age, with all the growth he's got left in him, he'll need another prosthesis in a few years. But that's no big deal."

"Of course, Walt, that's what we ought to do, but there's a problem," Sy said.

"What?"

"When you looked at his file, did you catch the name?"

"Does it matter?"

"It was on his chart."

"I know. Mangan. Or something like that."

"Did you also notice his address?"

"What difference could that make?" Walt responded.

"St. Mary's Foundling Home."

"An orphan?"

"Not that lucky," Sy said. When Walt looked confused, Sy explained. "An abused kid. The court took him away from his parents. That's also why the doctors were so late in detecting his sarcoma. When he complained of pain, they assumed it was a residual of the abuse he'd suffered."

"Natural mistake," Walt said. "But it's not too late."

"Fortunately. However, my problem is, this is a charity case. Who can I ask to operate without a fee? One of our eminent surgeons who drive sixty-five-thousand-dollar Mercedes? You know the excuses I'll get. So, Walt, just this one last case is all I ask. . . . Do it for me? And for that kid? He's a nice kid, you have to admit."

"Yes. He's a nice kid all right," Walt said. "But we're determined, Em and I, to go away. Somewhere. To forget this place. And everything that happened here."

"Are you going to leave your memories here, too? Going to forget Simmie, too? What happened to my family was more than forty years ago. Do you think I ever forget?"

Walt evaded replying by saying, "I'll do the little boy's case for you. After that, I want to be free. Free!"

They stood alongside each other, at stainless-steel sinks, scrubbing with antiseptic green soap, using stiff nailbrushes. Walter Duncan and Simon Rosen.

"Quite a kid, isn't he?" Sy said.

Walt seemed taken by surprise, lost for the moment in the details of the surgery he was about to perform, his concerns about what he might find and his hopes for what he might accomplish.

Sy continued. "The boy. The kid you're going to operate on.

304

Considering what he's been through, he has terrific spirit. Great will to survive.

"You see a kid like that, makes you wonder. Don't his parents realize what a gift they've been given? What a precious gift? How could anyone abuse a child like that?"

They were in the operating theater, where a group of medical students was assembled to watch Walt perform the resection on the young boy. Not only would they be present at the surgery, but for their education a large closed-circuit television screen would permit them to peer directly over Walt's shoulder as he worked.

Sy and Walt were making one last study of the scans and X rays on the wall of the operating theater when Walt asked suddenly, "What's going to happen to him?"

"I'm depending on you to determine that, Walt."

"I mean, after we do the surgery. Let's assume that he makes a good recovery. What happens to him?"

"I don't know. I guess that's for the courts to decide. Or some social service agency," Sy said. "After all, I'm no lawyer."

"I hope they don't give him back to those parents," Walt said. "Just look at these healed fractures on his X rays. He must have been abused since infancy. How the hell are things like this allowed to continue?"

"Walt, we're only responsible for his medical welfare. We can't go around correcting all the evils of society," Sy said.

"I'll never forget the look on his face, the eagerness in his eyes, first time I examined him," Walt said. "They were pleading, *Like me, love me, accept me.* How could anyone raise a hand against a kid like that? You've got to follow up on this case, and not just medically."

"I agree," Sy said, glancing furtively at Walt and thinking, *He said, "You've got to follow up." I wish he had said, "I will." But he will have to arrive at his own salvation.*

The surgery was long and intense, but it went well. Walt's skill was matched by a cooperative nature that allowed him to perform a very clean resection, remove the diseased bone and allow for safe margins that would give the young patient every chance of recovery. The titanium implant that Hans had designed and constructed fit perfectly. That it would need replacement some years from now was a minor consideration.

Walt had the satisfaction of knowing that the boy they wheeled out of the OR after five and a half hours of surgery had the odds in his favor. With a good response to chemotherapy, he could enjoy an active and long life.

As he was stripping off his surgical gloves, Sy said, "Walt, long as you're here, take a look at Brent Martin."

"You said he was recovering nicely," Walt countered.

"He asks for you. He wants to see you. And after all, you owe it to him. Remember what he did for you in Amy Bedford's case."

"He was a big help," Walt conceded. "I'll drop by."

Brent Martin was lying in bed, his neck fixed into rigid position to avoid risk to his spinal cord. When he heard his door swing open, his eyes strained to see who it might be. Another nurse with another hypo? Or his mother? Or one of his friends, of whom he was allowed to see only one at a time. He was delighted to discover that it was Dr. Walter Duncan.

"What's up, Doc?" Brent tried to joke.

"That's what I came to find out," Walt said. "How do you feel?"

"Considering I am in this twentieth-century torture chamber, not bad."

Walt drew back the covers. "Let's see you move your toes." When Brent had complied by moving his toes, Walt palpated Brent's legs, pinching gently to induce automatic responses. "Good." He grasped Brent's right hand. "Press. Good. Harder. Very good." He repeated the same procedure with Brent's left hand. "You're doing great, kid, real great."

"Doctor, I've been hearing things. . . . I mean, people who work in hospitals—nurses, residents, staff people—they think that patients are out of it. So they talk about us like we weren't here. Or didn't understand."

"We do get careless sometimes," Walt conceded.

"From what I heard, if you hadn't volunteered to operate on me, I might be completely paralyzed by now. Is that true?"

"Any halfway good surgeon could have done it, Brent."

"I understand at least one 'halfway good surgeon' refused," Brent said.

"There was some . . . some disagreement on what should be done," Walt admitted, continuing his examination.

"When I think I might have had to spend my life in a wheel-chair . . . You know, nights I wake up, and even though I know now it won't happen, I . . . I cry," the young man confessed. "Just the thought that it might have happened terrifies me. I get cold sweats."

"Well, it's not going to happen, son. You're going to be okay," Walt said.

The door opened suddenly. He could hear a familiar voice calling out, "Brent, I just— Dr. Walt, sorry. I didn't know you were in here."

"Amy! You're not using your cane," Walt said, smiling.

"No. And look," she said proudly as she walked the length of the room and then returned to face him. "How's that?"

"Wonderful. Wonderful! Just great, Amy."

"Remember, you said, 'Give me a year of your life'? Well, we did it in only eleven months!" she boasted.

"We sure did. From now on, nothing to do but build up that leg with exercise, get a checkup every three months and a bone scan every six months."

"And no more chemo!" Amy exulted.

"You're a free woman, Amy. You can take up your life again. School. Dancing. Swimming. Bicycling. Even tennis, if you're very careful," Walt said.

"I've been thinking about that. I've decided in favor of golf."

"Good idea."

"Dad thinks so, too. He says it'll give us a chance to spend time together." Her eyes misted up as she admitted, "One thing that made all this worthwhile—he's really my dad now. And he's really a terrific guy when you get to know him."

"There is one other thing, Amy," Walt said. "An obligation *you* have."

"Oh? What?"

"Remember I said you'd have to talk to other patients?"

"Yes."

"Well, come with me. You'll excuse us, Brent, if I borrow Amy for a little while?"

"Just make sure to send her back."

As they walked down the corridor, Walt said, "Amy, there is a boy in Room Two-twenty-nine. He's just had your kind of surgery. He's only ten. And very scared, because he doesn't have a family. Not anymore. So he needs all the courage you can give him. Okay?"

"Depend on me, Dr. Walt."

Walt pushed open the door to discover a nurse feeding the boy cold fruit juice through a glass straw.

"Did you want to examine him, Doctor? I'll get the surgical tray . . ." the nurse offered.

"No. We're just in for a little talk," Walt said.

The nurse left the room.

"Thomas Mangan, I want you to meet another patient of mine, Amy Bedford."

"Hi, Tommy."

"Amy, walk up and down for Tommy. Let him see what he's going to be like a year from now."

Amy walked up and back before the boy's bed, holding herself as erect as a fashion model and moving almost flawlessly.

The boy raised his head off his pillow to watch, his blue eyes wide with wonder. "You had the same thing—" he started to ask.

"Even worse, Tommy," Walt said. "And look at her now. Well, I'll leave the two of you to get acquainted."

As he closed the door behind him, he heard Amy saying, "You are the luckiest kid in the world to have Dr. Walt as your doctor."

* * *

He had returned to his old office to get his coat and leave. There was an urgent message from Sy Rosen. CALL AT ONCE!!! Three exclamation points.

So that's his game, Walt thought, *to snow me under with so many new cases that I'll abandon my plan.*

He lifted the phone, dialed Sy's private number and when he answered, Walt said, "Listen, you old faker. I know exactly what you're up to. And it won't work. Emily and I are going away. Far away! And we are not coming back! Got it?"

"Not even for the ceremony?" Sy asked.

"Ceremony? What ceremony?" Walt asked.

"Well, I hold here in my hand an announcement from James Rowe Russell himself. Which I need not tell you is the same as getting it right from God."

"Sy, I am no longer interested in anything that the august James Rowe Russell has to say. He can run this hospital any damn way he pleases!" Walt said.

"You could at least pay me the courtesy of listening to what the announcement says," Sy said.

"Russell, no. You, yes. Shoot!"

"I quote: 'On Friday afternoon next we will hold a special ceremony in the main auditorium of this hospital to celebrate receiving a gift of two hundred and fifty thousand dollars for the Walter R. Duncan Research Fund. This grant to be devoted to such orthopedic research projects as the honoree deems beneficial.' How's that for a quote?" Sy asked. "Walt? Are you still there?"

"Still here. And speechless. Who in the world would do something like that?"

"More quote: 'The monies to fund this project come to us through the kindness of Bedford Industries, and Mr. Edward Bedford, father of one of Dr. Duncan's patients.' Unquote. Walt, how would it look if you weren't there?"

"Well . . . I . . . I guess you're right, Sy. Okay. I'll be there. but I'm not making promises beyond that."

"I didn't ask you to, did I?" Sy replied. He hung up the phone, smiling.

309

* * *

Walter Duncan hung up his phone, too. He hesitated only a moment before dialing.

"Em? Darling? After all you've been through, I hate to ask this of you. But we're going to have to put off our trip for a little while."

"Walt, I know. Sy called me first, to ask if it was all right."

"And—"

"If I hadn't said yes, he wouldn't have asked you," she said. "He is a very kind and considerate man, your old friend."

"Em . . . you know what I thought? If it's all right with you . . . I thought I would ask them to change it to the Simone Duncan Research Fund. Em?"

"I . . . I think that would be very nice. I want people to know that there was such a person as Simone. And to remember her always." He could detect a slight hint of tears in her voice.

"Em, why don't you get into your car, drive down here and we'll go out to dinner together? We haven't been out in so long."

"I'd love to, darling."

"And while you're here, there's someone I want you to meet. He's ten years old. And he's got big problems. Medical problems. But other problems, even bigger. He's staring at a long recovery period. And he's practically alone. They had to take him away from his parents."

"Take him away . . . ?" Emily questioned.

"The court has forbidden his parents to have any contact with him. He was abused. Badly abused."

"Oh, no!" Emily sympathized.

"So he's alone. Except for Amy, who'll be dropping by for patient-to-patient therapy. But what he needs as much as therapy, perhaps more, is to know he's not alone. He needs someone to visit him. Spend time with him. Bring him a gift every so often. To let him know that there are kind and loving people in this world. Mostly that he is worthy of being loved. I've never seen a kid who needed it more. Em?"

"Of course, darling. I'll be there as soon as I can."

310

* * *

The second floor of the Pediatric Pavilion had settled down for the night. All visitors had departed. The nurses were preparing their patients for what they hoped would be a restful, uneventful night.

Walt Duncan and his wife, Emily, arrived at Room 229. Walt knocked softly. He eased the door open. "Tommy? Still awake?"

"Yes, Dr. Duncan."

The boy tried to edge up in bed despite the confining burden of the Jordan splint on his left leg.

"Tommy, I want you to meet my wife, Emily."

The boy stared at her through his blue eyes, barely nodding in acknowledgment.

"I hope the two of you get to be good friends in the next weeks. Very good friends," Walter Duncan said.